BURNING BRIGHT IN THE BLACK

IRON DOGZ MC

RENÉ VAN DALEN

BURNING BRIGHT IN THE BLACK

Iron Dogz MC Book One

Copyright © 2019 René Van Dalen

E-book ISBN 978-0-620-83999-0

Paperback ISBN 979-8-851-41655-2

Cover Design and Art - Danielle Burrows Art

facebook.com/danielleburrowsart/

Cover Copyright © 2019 Danielle Burrows

Cover Photograph Unsplash.com /Angelos Michalopoulos

Editor - Marianna Couper

All rights reserved. In accordance with the U S Copyright Act of 1976, the scanning, uploading and electronic sharing of any part of this book without permission of the publisher is unlawful piracy and theft of the author's intellectual property. Thank you for your support of the author's rights.

This book is a work of fiction. Names, characters, places and incidents are a product of the author's imagination or used fictitiously. Any resemblance to actual events, locales or persons living or dead is coincidental.

Warning: This book contains graphic language and sexual content. Intended for mature audiences, 18 years and older.

DEDICATION

13 1 13

For the ones who hold my heart
You make every small step
Feel like I'm wearing thousand-mile boots.

†††

That which we are, we are
One equal temper of heroic hearts,
Made weak by time and fate, but strong in will
To strive, to seek, to find, and not to yield.

Ulysses
Alfred, Lord Tennyson

AUTHOR'S NOTE

When I published this book I was an absolute newcomer and made some mistakes. Mistakes I wanted to correct but never got to do. Deciding to publish in print gave me the opportunity to fix a few things.

The book has been revised and re-edited but the story hasn't changed. I'm hoping it makes for a more enjoyable reading experience.

It has been an amazing experience sharing the men and women who make up the Iron Dogz MC with you.

Thank you for enjoying and loving them as much as I do.

Trigger warnings: This book contains graphic language, sex, violence, abuse and violent situations.

Important note: My books are set in South Africa and written in **South African English**.

I use Afrikaans and Zulu words in my writing. I've translated those as the story unfolds. Please check the glossary at the back of the book if you find one that slipped through the cracks.

As with all my books I take walks on the dark side.

Come and walk along with me.

ONE

Iron Dogz MC - Johannesburg

Hawk

Rage surged through Hawk as he inspected the broken seals and locks on the shipping container.

A totally empty container.

Everything gone.

They had guaranteed safe transport and delivery of the sealed container and now this cluster-fuck. How the hell did the bastards get past the security they had in place? A better question would be how they had known which container to target. There were twenty containers awaiting transport in the yard and only this one had been touched.

None of the others had so much as a scratch on them.

Someone had talked.

They had a goddamned rat in their house.

Kicking the side of the container viciously Hawk fought to control his rage. He needed to hit something or someone.

Kicking the container again he listened to the empty gong as his boot connected with the steel.

Fucking hell.

This was going to cost a shit-load of money to fix. Not to mention how pissed-off the client's going to be that his goods had been stolen while in their supposedly safe hands. The bastard will take his business elsewhere if they weren't seen to fix this and fix it fast.

"What do we know?" Hawk snarled still staring into the empty container.

Jagger, the Iron Dogz Security Officer, stepped up next to him. Anger spiking through his voice as he gave his report.

"We had unexpected loadshedding (scheduled power outages) last night. The generators kicked in, but not immediately, the power was off long enough for the bastards to fuck with our security. They knew exactly how long it would take for the gennies to kick in."

He gestured towards the cameras and fences. "They looped the cameras, re-routed the fence alarm, cut the fence, and took their time taking what they wanted. By the time the patrol came back around and picked up that the fence had been breached they were long gone."

"What about our back-up measures?"

"By some strange fucking coincidence, they went down as well, and we both know what that means." Jagger bit out.

"What I would like to know, is how they knew there would be loadshedding (scheduled power outage) in the first place? This area wasn't scheduled, at all," Kid snapped while looking at the silent men, waiting for someone to answer him.

"The bastards most probably bribed someone to fuck with the transformers," Ice growled angrily.

"This is bullshit. Why weren't we ready to deal with a black out?" Kid, his Sergeant-At-Arms, was furious and looking for someone to take it out on.

As much as Hawk wanted Kid to start breaking heads to get at the truth, now was not the time. They had to play this one close to the vest.

They had a rat. And the fucking bastard was someone in his inner circle, had to be. They were the only ones who knew about the back-up security systems, the hidden cameras, and alarms.

He knew without a doubt the rat wasn't one of his officers, he trusted them implicitly. They'd been his friends for years before stepping up to take his back when he took over the club after his dad's untimely death. His friends had backed him against the elders when he started pulling the Iron Dogz MC out of the deep dark shit they'd been buried in.

By no means was the club squeaky clean but they weren't filthy either. He had pulled them out of running drugs and guns and the club had been able to concentrate on their legitimate businesses. No longer looking over their shoulders all the time, until now.

Having a traitorous rat in his club fucking sucked.

It was time to get rid of the pest, to become the exterminator.

"Jagger, you and Beast work this together, find the fucker," Hawk ordered; his voice quiet.

"We're on it."

They inclined their heads slightly as he turned his back on the empty container, walked to his bike, climbed on and rode out of the yard with Kid and Ice following. They've had too many little things going wrong lately, now this. Someone was targeting the club and when he found out who it was, they were going to regret fucking with his club.

They were going to regret fucking with him.

He had worked too damned hard to lead his club towards a cleaner future to have a rat fuck it up. His club would never be a shining example of how to play nice with society. They would always have one foot in the dark. But it was up to him to keep the dark from swallowing his brothers as it had swallowed his dad and granddad. He would go down before he allowed it to happen. And he would take whoever was fucking with them down with him.

He needed to ride, to get himself under control before he faced his brothers.

Pointing his bike towards the Magaliesberg he breathed a little easier as he rode down the winding road. A long ride was what he needed right now. The sun beat down as they rode, and the scent of his bike, hot tar, green veldt grass and thorn trees filled his lungs, calming the rage. Riding with his best friends, his brothers, did the rest.

TWO

Road Warriors MC - Johannesburg South
DC

The tattoo was almost complete.

It was an amazing piece if I had to say so myself.

Colin "Raj" Chetty had asked for a metal dragon and that's exactly what I gave him. It was made up of overlapping metal plates with screws, rivets, and springs. A mechanical dragon. It was going to cause a riot on our website. And not all of the uproar was going to be about the dragon. Raj was seriously gorgeous. Dark golden skin, long black hair, very handsome with exotic green eyes, and he was seriously ripped.

Raj was a member of the Road Warriors MC, my dad's club, and an ex. Our split had been inevitable, he wanted more than I could give. Plus, he's a touch too controlling.

Today was our last session, mainly shading and touch ups. His skin was great to work on and I was honoured he had chosen my ink to decorate his body. But I couldn't wait to finish.

It wasn't that I didn't want to work on my ex's skin. It wasn't that at all. We were still friends, our relationship ending hadn't changed that at all.

The reason was Deena, my horribly spoilt little sister.

The little bitch had totally played me.

She was supposed to be spending part of her school holidays with her two best friends. However, with their help, she'd run off with some guy. A guy she'd picked up in a club. A club she wasn't legally allowed to enter because she was sixteen and underage. I'd no idea she'd run off until I tried to call her last night and got her voicemail. She knew that was a total no-no. Calls from family were not allowed to go to voicemail, *ever*. It was one of my dad's unbreakable rules.

I would've been freaking clueless had I not found her dismal report card stuffed under the couch cushions.

When she didn't pick up my call, I called her friends. They tried to evade my questions but I've been in the secrets business far too long to fall for their bullshit. After I involved the mums her two partners in crime revealed Deena's gushing texts. Apparently, she'd found the love of her life and asked them to cover for her until Sunday. When she'd dash home, before her daddy got back from his business trip.

Doc on a business trip? What the hell was she telling her friends about our family?

Unfortunately, she hadn't told her friends where she was.

The mums and I got the story of their night out from her two accomplices in dribs and drabs.

BURNING BRIGHT IN THE BLACK

On Wednesday night the three of them sneaked out and took an Uber to a club in Fourways; Deena supplied the fake IDs to get them into the club.

Trust me, whoever made and sold those ID's were in deep shit when I found them. I had the two girls' fake ID's and will definitely sniff out the origin. Once I had the little bitch safely back home.

According to the girls Deena met some guy at the club and left with him. The little bitches didn't get a name, or if they did, they'd forgotten it. All they could remember was it started with a D, he wore a leather waistcoat thingy, and he had a big bike.

Bloody hell.

Hopefully, the bastard had been out looking for fresh pussy and not for a way to get to Doc.

I knew Doc was going to blame me for her disappearance. He was going to rain hellfire down on my head. And when he finds out she'd run off with a biker, blood was going to flow, and I would not be exempt from the bloodletting.

She went missing on Wednesday night, today was Friday. I had to find her before Doc gets home on Sunday afternoon.

Good freaking luck to me.

My dad, Mark "Doc" Michaels, was on a run visiting some of their club's chapters. Doc was the president of the Johannesburg chapter of the Road Warriors MC.

He also had a seat on the National Council, the ruling body of the Road Warriors MC.

Worrying about my dad wasn't important right now. What was important was finding the little bitch. I had called in back up. I had Rico and Skinny, two club brothers I trusted, checking camera footage at the club in Fourways while I finished Raj's tattoo.

On Thursday evening I had called our half-brother, Derrick Townsend. When the bastard answered his phone, he was knee-deep in vagina and blew me off with "I'm busy, I'll call you back later," before I could explain. Hours later and... still waiting on a call.

So typical of the men in our family. After all these years why the hell did it still surprise me?

"DC!"

I heard my name over the music pumping through the speakers. Glancing over the half-wall around my station I saw Rico and Skinny walking up. I watched them with narrowed eyes.

Shit.

My insides clenched at the look in their eyes. I wasn't going to like what they had found.

"Give me a minute, Raj. I just have to take care of this quickly."

I turned off my machine, ripped my gloves off and dumped them in the hazards container. I inclined my head telling the brothers to follow me to my office. I parked my ass on the edge of the desk as Rico closed the door and leaned back against it.

"You found her."

"Yes."

Nothing more, just yes. They were pissed off though.

"Where?"

Then Rico gave me information I did not want to hear.

"Iron Dogz compound, she's found herself an outlaw biker, DC."

"Fuuuck!"

I slid my hands over my face into my hair, clamping the strands in my fingers.

This shit was going from bad to worse. Doc was going to have a fucking heart attack and then he was going to kill me.

"What the hell is this guy thinking? She's only sixteen."

"You know she doesn't look like a sixteen-year old, DC. I'll put money on it the poor bastard doesn't know she's jailbait or that she's Doc's little princess." Skinny snorted angrily.

Skinny was right. My little sister looked years older than what she was. Model beautiful, tall, and slender with long blonde hair and clear blue eyes. She easily passed for twenty when she tarted up, and she did that shit regularly.

"Okay. Let me finish up with Raj, then we'll go fetch her and bring her home."

Skinny and Rico both shook their heads rejecting my plan.

"This is going to cause shit, DC. We can't just walk in and drag her out. You have to call Doc," Skinny said in an angry growl.

"He finds out about this after we clean it up, he's going to fucking kill us and then take our patches."

"Let's at least call Tiny and Skel, we need their help to get it done without getting beat to shit in the process," Rico tried.

I shook my head.

"None of them can find out about this. Deena is Doc's perfect little princess; they will storm the Dogz clubhouse and that will drag us into a war. We really don't need that shit. Let's try and fix this with as little blow-back as possible. I promise I'll tell Doc as soon as we have her back and locked up in a freaking nunnery."

Gods, deep down in my gut I knew it wasn't going to be that easy. Nothing with Deena was ever easy.

Skinny and Rico looked at each other, sighed heavily and shrugged. I let out a small sigh of relief. If they had insisted on calling Tiny, their VP, my plan would've been toast. The only reason they agreed to help me was because we worked together on club shit all the time and they trusted me.

My gut churned as I returned to my workstation. I avoided Raj's too interested eyes. I couldn't tell him about the shit going down with Deena. He would definitely call Tiny and Skel. I couldn't allow that to happen. This was another Deena mess I had to clean up. Like I've been doing for bloody years.

I have been taking care of my little sister ever since the day her mother dumped her at the front gates of the compound and disappeared. She was a pretty four-month old baby and I was thirteen, almost fourteen. I might have been only thirteen but by that stage I had seen a lot and I wasn't a naïve little girl – at all.

My dad travelled constantly for the club and it was left to me and two of the old ladies, Liddy, and Zelda, to raise my little sister. Over the years I gave up a lot for her. My dream of going to University to study fine art crashed and burned. The dream of becoming an artist became just that, a dream. I changed, I hardened and slowly became part of the life.

The biker life.

I only slipped Doc's leash once, but it didn't last long enough.

As soon as I had finished high school I signed up as an apprentice tattoo artist with Pixie Maingarde of Mainline Ink in Cape Town. Doc exploded. He wanted me home, looking after Deena. I tried to explain but he refused to hear me. Our arguments where loud and fierce and shook the compound. I refused to budge. It was Tiny and Liddy, his old lady, who convinced Doc eventually to let me go. I moved to Cape Town for two years learning my craft.

The move didn't take me away from the club though. It just transferred me to the Cape Town chapter where I became Freeze's responsibility. He and his brothers took me in and were good to me while down there. Being away from my dad and his overprotective brothers allowed me a freedom I never had before. I experienced quite a few firsts while in Cape Town; Rooster being the man who delivered many of those firsts. We didn't last and our breakup wasn't nasty. The relationship had just run its natural course. And he became one of my best friends.

At the end of my apprenticeship, I returned to Jozi to work at Mainline Ink II, Pixie's second studio. And, surprise, I picked up right where I had left off. Taking care of Deena.

I'd been doing it for too many years and I was tired of it. So damned tired. Don't get me wrong, I love my sister and would do anything for her. But I'd reached the end of the line. I was tired, just so sick and tired of my life not going anywhere.

Pissed that I had to raise a child while I was still a child myself. Sick of always being the bad guy when Deena pulled one of her stunts. Something she did on a regular basis. Deena's latest escapade made me realise just how fed up I was of being the responsible adult. I've never had a chance to be irresponsible, to act out and do stupid shit like the other club kids. None of the men who showed an interest in me stuck around when they realised Deena was part of the deal. And I really couldn't blame them.

I was tired and done. So totally done.

It was time for Doc to step up and take responsibility. He got away with being the fun guy for way too damned long. He gave Deena anything she wanted, sometimes even before she asked. When I said no, he said yes. When I insisted on good grades and an education, he laughed it off, saying she would never need it. Her husband would take care of her. Deena sucked it all up, believing it was her destiny to be pampered and taken care of by a man.

I never believed in that crap. Growing up in a MC will do it to you. Deena and I had lived at the clubhouse until shortly after my fourteenth birthday when things suddenly changed.

My half-brother Derrick, who I never knew existed, came looking for his father. Finding us living in the clubhouse he insisted that we moved out and into a real home. I went from being an only child to having two siblings – one a little baby, the other an angry young man.

Derrick's mum had raised her son away from the club's influence, but it was obvious from the start he was a force to be reckoned with, just like our dad. Intense, focused and very determined to get his sisters away from the club and into a house.

I hated him for interfering. I loved living at the clubhouse where I had a lot of friends who helped with Deena. The house my dad moved us to wasn't far from the clubhouse but I was left alone with a surly housekeeper-nanny and a screaming, demanding baby. After ruining my life Derrick disappeared again only visiting sporadically over the years.

Doc had been a loving but mostly absentee dad. He was too busy with his club, his brothers, and his women to pay much attention to me. Liddy and Zelda, Tiny and Stoney's old ladies, raised me while Doc flew in and out of my life. Living in the clubhouse I saw a lot of shit a little girl should never have seen.

Spoilt by the brothers and running wild in the clubhouse I turned into a little hellion.

I learned damned quick that for most of the brothers a bitch had only one value. Pussy. Bitches were not important, they were interchangeable and disposable. So, I set out to prove I wasn't a girl, something that got me into a lot of shit.

I got into scrapes, fought, and rode bikes with my best friend, Jake Stoddard, Tiny and Liddy's eldest son.

I wore little biker boots, jeans, and club t-shirts same as Jake and refused point blank to wear dresses. Doc had to find a school that allowed pants and not the obligatory little skirt. That's the reason why I ended up in a school with no uniforms and art as a major subject.

The only concession I made to being a girl was keeping my hair long, and I only did that because Stoney's hair was long. He became my mentor and surrogate dad, a man I loved and looked up to.

While we were kids Jake and I were inseparable but he stopped hanging out with me around his fifteenth birthday when he discovered his power over girls. I was pissed at him but it did have one good side effect, I turned to art as an outlet and found a whole new world.

I was firmly in the friend zone and with my focus on art was totally okay with it. When we were both older and Jake became "Skelly", a patched member of the club, we reconnected and picked right up where we'd left off. He is one of my best friends and my only confidant.

Derrick kept in contact, not constantly but he tried to help with Deena. Just not this time. And right now, I really needed him. Deena had been acting out the last few weeks.

But this was way over the line of teenage rebellion. Unfortunately, I knew why she was going off the rails.

Misty, her bitch of a mother, had suddenly reappeared and tried to see Deena on several occasions. According to Misty she wanted to give Deena a better life and save her from becoming a biker bitch.

Her little girl had a great future ahead of her as a model and a movie star, just like her mother. It was damned laughable. The bitch used to be a stripper and porn star, many, many years ago, before her lifestyle and age took care of her looks. Now she was a used up, saggy-bottomed, bleached blonde, drug addict, trying to get her claws into a meal ticket. My baby sister.

The crazy bitch wasn't going to get anywhere near Deena.

Was. Not. Going. To. Happen.

I would end her before I'd let her get her claws into my sister. I already had her under surveillance. It was only a matter of time before she made the wrong move. Only a matter of time.

I hated that my entire day had been taken up by reliving the past.

The past was just that, the past. It was done and couldn't be undone, however much we might wish it could be undone.

I shut it all down as I closed up shop.

Taking in a deep breath I walked over to where Skinny and Rico were standing next to my shiny black F250 double cab.

My beast.

I loved the damn thing even though it was a giant petrol guzzler. It was big, heavy, and strong enough to pull a fully loaded bike trailer and high enough to go *bundu bashing* (off roading).

Perfection.

THREE

Hawk

Riding down the narrow road with his brothers Hawk's mind wasn't on the road. He kept going over the break-in at the yard, and the small shit hitting some of their strip clubs, and he kept coming back to the same conclusion. They were being targeted. He needed to find out by whom and why. The shit that had gone down at their yard could not be glossed over. They had to make an example of someone and fast.

Which was why he was on his way to talk to the man who usually heard all there was to hear.

The ride to Kosmos helped to clear his head and by the time they pulled into Zeffers he was as calm as he was going to get under the circumstances.

Zeffers was a biker pub and grill. Wimpie Malan, the owner, made sure his pub stayed firmly in the neutral zone. Everyone was welcome, no matter which club you rode with.

Looking up at the fancy sign outside the building Hawk grinned.

BURNING BRIGHT IN THE BLACK

When he first opened, Wimpie had had other "fancy" ideas for his establishment. From the name, Zephyr Restaurant, it's very apparent what those were. He hadn't a hope in hell to get those off the ground once bikers discovered it and changed the name from Zephyr Restaurant to Zeffers. The name stuck, no matter how much Wimpie complained. On Saturdays and Sundays, it was packed with citizen bikers rubbing shoulders with club brothers. The food was legendary, drinks well-priced, and Wimpie's place was a favourite haunt and a neutral zone for several clubs.

Wimpie heard a lot of shit he passed along very judiciously. Hawk didn't delude himself that he was the only one on the receiving end of information. Wimpie was an equal opportunity snitch. Only he didn't see it as snitching, he claimed he kept the biker world on an even keel. Spreading information where it was needed and keeping his brothers breathing. He considered everyone who rode a bike his brother. Whether you rode a road bike, a sport bike, a scrambler or even a fucking scooter. You were part of his brotherhood. Weird, but it worked for him.

Hawk walked through the restaurant to his favourite table against the far wall, next to the large open windows overlooking Hartebeespoort dam.

Giving chin lifts to brothers from other clubs relaxing with their beers as he made his way past them.

From his table he had an uninterrupted view over the water, peaceful and glittering in the afternoon sun. No boats dragging skiers all over and no ferries either. It would change later in the afternoon when the weekenders started arriving.

He sat with his back to the wall and Kid and Ice dragged their chairs so they had clear views, inside and outside. Setting his helmet on the extra wide windowsill Hawk acknowledged Sarie, one of the waitresses, with a slight nod when she waved at them.

She was a pretty blonde with a great body she showed off in a tight-fitting tank and short shorts. She walked over with a wide welcoming smile on her pretty face and hips swaying seductively.

He fucked her about two weeks ago and it was obvious she was expecting another ride on his cock.

"Hi Hawk, hey guys, good to see you again. What can I get you?" She stood with one hip cocked, her arms crossed under her big tits, pushing them up and almost out of her top.

Ice and Kid grinned as they looked at the tits on offer. Hawk looked and felt…nothing. Not a thing. Just the usual disinterest after he had taken what he wanted.

"Three drafts, and tell Wimpie I'd like to talk to him." Hawk worked hard to sound even a little bit friendly, but judging by the look on her face it hadn't worked.

"Okay, he's busy in the back but I'll let him know you're here." She walked away, her ass cheeks on show, hips swaying.

And he still felt nothing.

Zero. Zip. Not even a tiny twitch of interest from his cock. He was definitely not going back there.

She was bending deep over their table, setting their drafts down when Wimpie appeared. He was a short, round, happy man. He had a round face, a round body and a large belly that overhung his baggy jeans. He had a deep jovial laugh and always had a smile on his ruddy face. He was bald on top but had grown the hair he still had and wore it pulled back in a skinny grey tail down his back.

Right now, though, the man was pissed, seriously pissed.

"*Sarie. Wat het ek vir jou gesê?*"

(Sarie. What did I tell you?)

"*Ek weet. Ek weet. Ek het ander customers buite.*"

(I know. I know. I've got other customers outside.)

Wimpie sighed, his anger falling away as he watched her stalking angrily out the open doors onto the veranda to attend to her other customers.

"Do me a favour, Hawk. Please don't fuck my staff again. She's a good waitress but now she's dreaming of leaving here on the back of your bike. We both know it's never going to happen."

"Don't know why she would think that, it was just a fuck. A one-and-done and I made sure she knew it. We didn't even leave the parking lot, for fuck's sake. And not fucking liking your warning at all," Hawk growled.

Wimpie grinned. "Not a warning, more like me begging you not to fuck them. It's hard enough getting them to move here in the first place. Now the bitches all think if they fuck a biker, they're going to get his patch and live happily ever after in badass biker land."

Ice and Kid burst out laughing. Shaking his head Hawk joined in the laughter. Wimpie's huge overhanging belly jiggled as he laughed while mopping his sweaty face with a big khaki handkerchief.

Leaning his elbows on the table Wimpie was suddenly very serious. And as usual he passed on the information as if he were in fucking Game of Thrones.

"I've heard some troubling tales lately, Hawk. There are whispers about a viper hiding in plain sight, slithering around your castle, preparing to take your crown. If I were you, I would call in my knights, check on the loyalty of my nobles and serfs. The strike is set to come from within. Trust no one. Male or female, my liege, no one is to be trusted."

"Fuck, Wimpie. Do you have to always sound like you're in Game of Thrones or something?" Kid complained.

"Best fucking show ever," Wimpie shrugged.

Hawk ignored them as he mulled over the information and warning. He let out a hard breath as he made a decision.

"If I'm to win this war I'm going to need your ears, your loyalty. You call me, day or night, if you hear anything about my kingdom, anything at all."

"You've got it my liege." Wimpie nodded enthusiastically.

Picking up his draft Hawk drank deep, wiped the foam from his moustache, set the beer down and relaxed against the back of his chair. He was so fucking tired of all the shit he had to deal with and just sitting here having a beer with friends and looking out at the water calmed him. He knew when he got back to the clubhouse he would be back in the thick of things. Taking some time now would make it a bit easier to deal with the shit waiting for him.

The sun was setting when they left Zeffers and the road was busy. They had to take it easy all the way home and it was full dark when they pulled up outside the clubhouse. The usual Friday night party was in full swing and Hawk's belly growled when the smell of meat on the *braai* (barbeque) hit him. He hoped like hell they had enough meat because he was suddenly ravenous.

As he took off his helmet and set it down on his seat a big black SUV raced into the parking area and came to a rocking stop.

What the fuck?

The door was kicked open violently It was Rick Townsend, a friend of the club, and the man was pissed. Eyes burning, mouth clamped in a thin line kind of pissed.

"Rick, what the hell…"

It was as far as he got. The music cut off suddenly and loud angry voices spilled from his damned clubhouse. His easy afternoon evaporated like mist before the sun. He was seething as he stalked up the steps into the clubhouse. Someone was going to be wearing his fucking size fourteens up their ass.

He couldn't believe his eyes when he shoved the onlookers out of his way.

A bitch he had never seen before had Dollar's latest blonde by the hair and was snarling down at her. The bitch was short, looked a bit chunky with caramel skin and dark hair scraped back into a tight braid.

Dollar's blonde bitch was clearly terrified of her.

Not in his fucking house. Not fucking happening.

The dark bitch was about to learn a hard lesson. Bitches did not fight in his clubhouse, not ever.

And he was the one who was going to teach her that lesson, right the hell now.

FOUR

DC

The Iron Dogz MC owned a 20-acre plot of land on the R562. At the front of the property, closest to the road was the head office from where they ran their various companies. The club compound was further back on the property and was a fortress when they wanted it to be. The only access was through heavily guarded gates.

Luckily, it was Friday. Like most other MC's they partied on Friday nights, and the gates were opened for bitches who wanted a walk on the wild side.

And that was how I was going to get inside.

The guys would have to pretend to be hang-arounds. Shit could get nasty if they were recognised so their kuttes were in a locked box behind the back seat. They weren't allowed to wear their kuttes in a cage anyway. That's what they called cars, cages.

I parked with the rest of the vehicles and as close to the front door as I could then turned to look at the two very pissed off men.

"You let me do the talking, and keep your heads down. Hopefully, I can get her out without causing major shit with the Dogz. I hope like hell no one recognises us."

"We should have waited for Rick, DC. He wanted to go in with us," Rico growled.

I shook my head; I was still angry with my brother.

"I don't give a damn, Rico. When I called him about this shit, he was too busy getting laid to talk to me, now when I'm almost inside he's all over it and he wants me to wait. There's no time, we need to get her out of here. We all know the poor bastard has banged her already. Plus, we know how rough it gets in a clubhouse on party nights. If Doc finds out about this, he's going to lose his freaking mind and go to war with the Dogz." I sighed and shook my head. "Actually, it's not if he finds out, it's when he finds out."

They both groaned and nodded. They didn't say another word because they knew me, knew I could handle myself and would handle whatever we found. Getting out we walked past the line of bikes pulled up at the front of the clubhouse.

Quite a few of the Dogz were already in the clubhouse, and they were starting the party early. I didn't know their president's bike but there was a very obvious gap at the head of the line of bikes. I kept my fingers crossed he wasn't around. I wanted to be in and out before he got involved.

Hell, when the Dogz found out Deena was Doc's underage little girl there was going to be a shit storm. A huge freaking shit storm.

Two large bastards were slouched in chairs on the wide veranda watching us as we walked up.

"You lost?" The bald and heavily tattooed one barked while his disinterested eyes slid over me. Covering up and dressing down had worked.

"I'm here to pick up my sister. Young, tall, blonde, classy, looks like a model. She inside?" I kept it casual and non-threatening.

They both laughed before the dark haired one answered. "Yes, babe. She's inside. Dollar's not going to be pleased if you pull her out of here now. He's getting some classy-girl head right about now."

I tensed when I heard Rico swear low and ugly. I threw him a look and walked up the steps and into the gloomy interior. The assholes behind us laughed uproariously. Anger at Deena's stupidity rolled through me. She knew enough about the life to know this was a fucking disaster waiting for one little spark to start a war. It was a death sentence for the poor bastard whose life she had ruined with her spoilt brat stupidity.

I stepped into the smoky semi-dark interior. The very familiar smells of cigarette smoke, weed and alcohol assailed my nose. There was a certain part of those smells I really didn't want to think about. Not with my little sister somewhere in here. Narrowing my eyes I scanned the room, and there she was. My sixteen-year old little sister, on her knees with her head in some fucker's crotch while several others watched avidly.

Rage unlike anything I had ever felt took me under.

I didn't think I just reacted.

Stalking over I grabbed her long blonde hair and jerked her head off the bastards' dick. I snatched her back hard enough that she fell on her barely covered ass. I had my hand twisted in her long hair. She screamed in pain but I held on and lifted her ass off the floor, glaring down into her heavily made-up face and swollen lipped red mouth. The crotch sprang up off the couch, dick sticking out of his unzipped pants, glistening and angry looking. He reached for Deena but backed off when I snarled at him like some kind of wild animal. His buddies backed off as well but quickly formed a ring around us.

"DC!" I heard Rico voice but ignored it until he stepped up behind me and put his hand on my shoulder.

"I got this, Rico." I hissed looking at the girl I'd given up so much for.

She was wearing teeny-tiny glittering silver hooker shorts and a barely-there white tank top, no bra. My little sister was dressed and acting like a club slut. On her knees servicing a fucking biker bastard.

"Please, DC. Please, please, please don't hurt me." She pleaded tearfully.

"You like where you are now, bitch?"

I viciously snarled at her in the sudden quiet that had fallen in the Iron Dogz clubhouse.

Someone had turned off the music.

I was so far out of line I was on another damned continent. It was going to cause shit but I didn't give a damn.

My beautiful baby sister, a sister I had raised to know better, was looking and acting like a club slut. A dirty club whore just like her bloody mother.

I was done with the little bitch's shit. It was time she learnt there were consequences to her actions.

"Please, DC. Please." She whimpered.

"I asked you a question." I snapped and jerked her hair. "Do you like where you are now? Is sucking biker cock what you want from life, bitch?"

"Please, DC." She tried again.

"Not going to ask again, bitch. Answer my questions."

"Please, I don't know what you mean." She whispered.

There was rustling in the big room but I ignored it. I was too deep into my rage to give it a second thought. From the corner of my eye I saw Derrick stepping up. I ignored him, he should've talked to me when I called.

"Do you want to be on your knees sucking biker cock, taking it in every goddamned hole they want to give it to you? You want to be a club whore like your mother? That's the question, bitch. Answer. Now."

She collapsed in on herself, going back down on her knees and I held on to her hair, stretching her neck out and back, making her meet my eyes.

"No, DC! No! I like Dollar, only him. Not anyone else. Please, DC!"

The rustling became a bellow.

"What the fuck is going on here! Who the hell is this bitch and why the fuck is she causing shit in my house?"

I looked up and met a pair of very angry amber-yellow eyes.

Well hell.

This must be the president of the Iron Dogz himself.

A shiver ran down my spine as I stared up into his angry eyes.

A shiver that settled low in my belly, warming parts it shouldn't have warmed.

He was damned tall with a wide chest, narrow hips, and long legs. I could see he had tattoos on both arms but it was too gloomy to see whether they were any good. His dark blonde hair was shaved short at the sides with the top and back left long and braided

Like a damned Viking.

His beard was a darker blonde than his hair and wasn't overly long. It was trimmed around his mouth and along the line of his jaw but left longer at his chin with his neck shaved clean. He was imposing and impossibly sexy and gorgeous.

Catnip for pussies.

Before I could say a word, the crotch, apparently named Dollar, stepped up. Thank the Pope he had his cock back in his pants and zipped up.

Not something I wanted to look at ever again.

"Don't know who she is, Prez, but that's my girl she's got on her knees there. My girl's not club pussy, she's a nice girl."

I didn't give his boss a chance to say a word.

I just let the crotch have it.

"Girl is the operative word here; you cradle robbing asshole. She's freaking sixteen years old!" I shouted as I pulled Deena off the floor and shoved her at a very angry Derrick.

Shock flitted over Dollar's pretty boy face.

"What? I didn't know. I met her at a club on Wednesday night. She told me she was nineteen, almost twenty."

He looked at Deena.

"Fuck, baby. What are you trying to do to me?"

Deena sobbed. "I just wanted to be with you, Dollar. I knew you wouldn't give me a chance if you knew how old I really was."

Typical of the spoilt bitch.

"Bloody hell. Always wanting what you can't have and taking it, no matter who you run over in the process. This is so damned typical of you, Deena. Did you even think what would happen to him when dad gets home?" I snarled not letting her answer as I rubbed my hands over my tired eyes and face.

I looked at the young biker.

"I'm taking her home. You want to see her again you stay away until she's at least eighteen. You have a year and seven months to make your case to her daddy. As far as I'm concerned, I'm washing my hands of the little bitch. I'm freaking done with you and your shit, Deena. Done. So completely and utterly done. Whatever happens to you from this point onwards is up to dad."

A deep, husky rumble of a voice stopped me in my tracks as I started turning away.

"Rick, who the fuck is this bitch and what is she doing causing shit in my club?"

I so wanted to kick his male ass and opened my mouth to give him a piece of my mind but "Rick" got there first.

"She's DC Michaels and the kid is Deena Michaels, Doc's girls, and my sisters. DC came to drag Deena home before Doc gets back from his run. She's actually trying to save Dollar's ass."

Derrick explained quietly and groans erupted around us and some very proficient swearing by the president of the Iron Dogz.

"My fucking office. Right now," He snapped as he stalked out of the room followed by the two men with him.

"Dollar, get your fucking ass in here!" He shouted over his shoulder as he headed out.

Derrick shook his head as Skinny and Rico started to follow. I nodded when they looked at me for confirmation. I handed Skinny my keys.

"Wait for me outside." I said softly before I followed the men.

Derrick held Deena's hand and led us down a darkened corridor. I listened to her crying. For once it did nothing, nothing at all. No sympathy or compassion, just nothing. Something inside me had finally snapped where Deena was concerned. I was empty, so damned empty and tired. Tired of dealing with the drama that surrounded the shit she pulled on a regular basis. This time she was going to have to take responsibility for her actions. I was done taking Doc's anger to save his little princess.

The president of the Iron Dogz' office wasn't anything like Doc's. My dad's office was a total shithole, this was not.

It was neat with great furniture. A massive desk sat at one end with a throne-like leather chair behind it and two smaller chairs in front. A large leather couch was pushed up against one wall; the painting above it came as a total surprise. It was of a group of bikes parked on a sun-drenched street with bikers lounging on their rides and sidewalk.

It was one of my early works done before I got pulled so deep into club business it darkened my work. Now everything I did was dark, very, very dark.

Like this life.

"Oh my God, DC, that's one of ..." Deena started to gush, I glared at her and she immediately shut up. I did not want to talk to her right now.

No one would know it was one of my paintings because I had only signed the initials DJM in the lower left-hand corner. The D was for my club name, Demon Child, the J for my real name, Jasmine, which I hated, the M for Michaels. The club and my friends called me DC, the shortened version of Demon Child.

It was my dad who started calling me his Demon Child, his little hellion of a baby girl. I think it was Tiny who turned it into DC, which stuck.

I look nothing like my dad or siblings. They are all tall, blonde, blue eyed and beautiful. I'm short, dark, and when compared to them, rather plain. Dark hair, dark eyes, and golden caramel skin that gave away my bi-racial parentage.

My dad's Demon Child or DC.

But I had another name in our club, a dark and hidden persona. I was the Crow, who did dark deeds when required, lived in the dark and thrived there.

The big man behind the desk lifted a hand pointing at the chairs. Derrick pushed me down in one, settled Deena on the couch then sat down next to me.

"How the fuck do I keep Doc from coming for my brother, Rick? He didn't know she was fucking underage. What are our options?"

Derrick looked at me with a raised eyebrow. I shrugged angrily. He wanted to handle it so let him freaking handle it.

"He's not going to know about this if you shut it down on this side. I don't have his ear but DC does. She'll handle it."

The big ass and his men sniggered derisively.

"She's a bitch, Rick. Never heard of her until today. Being Doc's daughter doesn't give her any power." Cole "Hawk" Walker threw at Derrick while slanting a derisive glance my way.

Derrick looked at me, a question in his eyes and I knew what he was asking. Was he freaking kidding? He had only been told because Doc needed him on a job. Now he wanted to bring the freaking Dogz in on it. He stared at me and nodded but I shook my head.

No, hell no. This was club business and not my place to share.

"Club. Business. Rick." I snarled. Biting off each word.

"I know but it's the only way, DC. We have to explain and they won't talk, I give you my word."

Really? His word?

Shit. Shit. Shit.

I knew I had no other option. I shuddered internally, gave him a chin lift in permission. This was becoming a bigger damned disaster than what I had expected. Doc was going to kill me. He was definitely going to kill me.

"What I'm about to tell you stays in this office. I need your word on it."

Derrick, now Rick to me, stared at Hawk until he nodded.

"You have it."

My brother looked back at me, I huffed out a breath angrily, crossed my arms over my chest and shrugged. I was so totally going to get my ass kicked when Doc got home.

Rick looked at Deena and Dollar then back at Hawk. "This is not for their ears. Send them out while we talk."

Hawk nodded at Dollar and we waited until they were out of the office. And then my brother revealed shit that was going to dump me into deep shit with the club. They were going to skin me alive for revealing our secrets.

"She's not just any bitch, Hawk. She has power, fuckloads of power. She's Doc's Crow."

Shocked silence reigned for a minute.

"Bullshit!"

The man on his right burst out, Kid Warne, their Sergeant-at-Arms. A dangerous man with whom I had done a job a few months ago. Doc had me do a favour for the Dogz and Kid had been their point man.

At least he hadn't seen me working, just saw the results.

"The Crow is a man. I've seen him, worked on some heavy shit with him five months ago."

"You ever get anywhere near him when it went down? There were three Warriors between you and Crow at all times. He is completely covered, never a hint of skin. Small man speaks in a low hiss with eyes that shine like black glass from behind his mask. Any of that at all familiar to you?" Rick asked.

Hawk's sudden chuckle in the heavy silence was a shock and my eyes locked with his.

"Interesting." He said softly, his amber-yellow eyes never leaving mine.

I saw the quickly hidden flash of anger in those eyes.

"You came into my house, little bird, and you caused one hell of a scene, now we need to make it go away. You disrespected my club; my territory and I can't have that. And I can't have Doc at my throat either. Those fuckers out there gossip worse than the bitches. You know you have to pay. I can't let you walk away from this." He gave a knowing little smirk.

I so badly wanted to wipe the smirk right off his face. And what was this shit calling me little bird? I know I should have handled the situation differently but seeing Deena on her knees sucking biker cock just made me see red.

I *cocked up* her extraction and now I will have to pay the price.

Rick was about to say something but I tapped his arm and shook my head. This was going to suck big time. I didn't want to dip into my savings to pay off these assholes.

I had plans for the money. Big plans.

"How much?"

The smirking bastard watched me intently as I waited for his answer.

What he wanted made me want to rearrange his handsome smirking face.

FIVE

Hawk

Hawk relaxed in his chair and stared at the small dark woman sitting opposite him. Fiercely intelligent, very dark, almost black eyes stared right into his and he smiled, she didn't.

The girl who had been sitting on the couch was an ice cool beauty. But this one, this one was all dark fire and passion. She wasn't tall or as conventionally beautiful as the blonde. She was short, dark, and exotic. He had no idea what her body looked like under the bulky leather coat that hid her entirely. Her black hair was pulled back in a tight braid and her face was clean of any make-up. Her skin was golden caramel, what he could see of the little that was visible.

It was her big almond shaped eyes with the mile-long lashes that caught his attention. They snapped and smouldered with fire and anger that fascinated him.

Something inside him wanted to tame her, make her submit to him, make her give him everything.

What the fuck?

This was going south pretty damned fast. She was not his type. Definitely not his type. He would not be going there even if his cock wanted her. He needed her for something totally different.

"You misunderstand, little bird. It's not how much I want. It's what I want."

Hawk watched as something flashed in her eyes. Rick sat forward and swore softly. He ignored him, for now at least. This was the way things were done in their world. Rick was a brother, he would understand, eventually.

"Name your price, Hawk."

He smiled again as she snapped at him with irritation in that smoky, sexy voice.

"My price is you, little bird."

She frowned in confusion. "What do you mean? I'm not sure I fully understand what it is you want from me. Why don't you spell it out for me."

She just couldn't help herself, this little bird. So very snappy. He was going to enjoy this.

"My price, little bird, is you. You, in my club, for six months, doing what you do but you will be doing it for us."

He saw the instant fury flashed in those dark eyes. They all tensed as she slowly leaned forward. Rick snapped a hand onto her shoulder and gripped tightly but she ignored her brother as she glared at him. As he watched her eyes turned from dark fury into ice.

The cold emotionless words coming from her mouth shocked and left him speechless.

"Cole "Hawk" Walker. Thirty-eight. President of the Iron Dogz MC for the last seven years. You were voted in after the sudden death of your father Gage "Bounty" Walker in a car accident at the age of 52. Mother, Erin Mallory Walker, died of breast cancer 13 years ago at age 43. Married Candice "Candy" Collins at 24 after getting her pregnant, lost the child, divorced at 26, a year after your mother's death.

"Iron Dogz Trucking became very successful under your rule. Your club has connections to several persons of interest to the SAPS and Interpol. No arrests, but several times noted as a person of interest and pulled in for questioning.

"You live in the family home on the Iron Dogz property with your paternal aunt, Beryl Davids. You have three regular women, Laney Wills, Jane Warne, and Lizzy Hamilton. Wills has terminated two pregnancies, Warne one. They terminated because the kids weren't yours. So far Hamilton hasn't conceived but she's been trying, so I'd watch my sperm if I were you."

She raised an eyebrow as she continued.

"Your best friends are your cousin and Vice President, Gray "Ice" Walker, thirty-seven, and Sergeant-At-Arms, Nate "Kid" Warne, thirty-eight, brother to Jane Warne. The Iron Dogz has a long-standing truce with the Road Warriors and is allied to the Sinner's Sons as is the Warriors. You have history with and are bitter enemies of the Evil Disciples and, lately the ED's have started pushing into Iron Dogz territory. Soon there will be more than just pushing."

Hawk sat silent as those detached icy dark eyes ripped into him and started a fire in his gut. They had a mole, as Wimpie had warned him, and fucking leaks to see to, soon. But first he had to force her to his hand. This angry little bird who, if she were who they said she was, would find him his mole.

"The Crow is all about information and retribution. I acquire it any way I have to, and it's a known fact that I pay very well for any and all information I don't have to extract. Your club's been leaking information like a sieve for a few months now. Your club pussy and private pussy leak information. Your hangarounds leak information without even realising they're doing it. Some brothers talk when they're pissed and banging club pussy. I collect it all for when I might need it, like right now."

She pushed out a hard breath and sat back, resting her small hands on the arms of the chair.

"I live quietly and do my job. I'm off the grid as far as possible. I'll give you three months with no visible interaction. Linking myself to you and your club is not going to happen. It would destroy everything I've built over the last ten years."

"Ten years? Impossible! You don't look a day over twenty-two. How fucking old are you?" Ice grated out.

"She's thirty-one." Derrick answered. "Today actually."

Hawk grinned and winked at the little bird.

"You going to have a party, little bird? If not, feel free to hang with us tonight, we'll make sure you have one hell of a birthday."

He watched her as he threw out the invitation. She didn't blink, didn't react at all, her face cold and impassive, but those exotic dark eyes burned with icy fire.

"Thanks for the invitation Hawk, but I'm taking my sister out for dinner tonight." Rick growled and gave him angry eyes.

"Maybe next time then, little bird." He grinned and winked, ignoring Rick's angry eyes.

The woman sitting in front of him like a cold statue raised an eyebrow and said not one word. She was locked down tight. As far as he could see everything in her life has been about her family, her club. A family, it seemed, who used her, like Dollar's spoilt little bitch. Maybe not Rick, he saw the pure rage in his eyes and gave a slight dip of his head. He would take care of the little bird while she worked for him.

"I need your expertise, DC, and I'm not budging on the six months. We're being pushed, you're right about that, but we aren't the only ones. We've had complaints from some of our other chapters and from a few of our support clubs. But now is not the time to talk about this."

He pushed himself up out of his chair and moved around his desk until he stood next to Rick.

The little bird was up and out of the chair standing silently next to her brother.

"I have some shit to sort out over the next couple of days. Let's meet back here next Friday night around eight."

She opened her mouth to shoot him down but Rick got in before her and those dark eyes flashed in pissed-off annoyance.

"I'm in the middle of something and have to get back to it, can't be here. She'll be here but with protection. Try and keep it as low profile as possible."

Hawk almost smiled.

"I can live with that. Just make sure whoever comes with her knows what's going down. I don't want some asshole causing shit when things get a little bit hot around here."

Rick smiled, it wasn't a nice smile at all, and he wondered what the hell that was about.

"Oh yes, they will know what's going down. She'll have two in her close protection detail, they go where she goes."

Hawk nodded, agreeing. But there was more to get done tonight.

"Let's get those two back in here and sort this shit out."

Kid left and came back with the two trailing behind him. The little bitch immediately looked at her sister for help. That shit will have to stop while the little bird worked for him.

"You into Doc's little ice princess, Dollar?"

He asked his eyes meeting those of the angry little bird before he looked at Dollar.

The little princess's breathing sped up audibly. Fuck, she was clueless. She wouldn't last long if she didn't learn some control.

"Yes, Boss. I'll wait out the time but after I'll be there to see where this goes," he immediately answered.

"Fuck. Okay, but if this causes problems with Doc, it's your hide, not mine."

Once again, his eyes captured the dark little bird's. She stared right back, not blinking, not looking away.

Fuck. He wanted her.

Leading the way out of his office Hawk moved to the side and watched as Derrick "Rick" Townsend hurried his sisters out of the club.

He had always known Rick's father was Doc Michaels; President of the Johannesburg chapter of the Road Warriors MC. Rick never hid it from him.

What he hadn't known was that Rick had a close relationship with his sisters. Rick kept his personal life very personal because of his job. It was glaringly obvious he was very protective of them. It was going to be a problem. He had uses for DC Michaels that might not sit right with his friend. His world wasn't as black and white as Rick's.

Then there was his other problem. A sudden and very personal problem.

Hawk wanted the dark little bird, badly.

He was going to have to explain it to his bitches, and they're not going to be happy. He didn't give a shit though; he wanted the little bird and he was going to have her. Tame, in his hand until he's had his fill.

Only then would he let her fly away. Or maybe not, only time would tell.

He felt sorry for Dollar. The look Rick threw him as he walked out said he was going to call Dollar into the ring and beat the shit out of him. He wasn't worried as Dollar could take care of himself. If he wanted the ice princess for more than just pussy, he'll have to prove that to Rick, and ultimately Doc Michaels.

Leaning back against the bar he watched as Rick and Dollar escorted the girls out. His eyes narrowed, as he took in the controlled way DC moved, she was a fighter, he was sure of it.

"Why are you allowing the whore to walk out of here after the shit she just pulled?" Jane snapped angrily while rubbing her tits up against him.

It was the last straw after an extremely shitty day.

"Who the fuck do you think you are questioning my decisions? Get the fuck away from me."

He grabbed his beer and stalked away from the bar, snagging Lizzy's hand, and pulling her up the stairs. Tonight, he needed soft not Laney's bitching or Jane's anger.

Fucking Lizzy didn't go as planned.

The little bird's warning kept hissing in the back of his mind. He just couldn't get into it and gave up trying, settling for making her come with his fingers then sending her away.

He felt sure once he fucked the dark little bird he would be back to normal.

Back to fucking all night long. Back to having a bed full of pussy whenever he wanted it.

He had to get her out of his system.

And she would be once he fucked her.

He hoped.

SIX

DC

I came clean to Doc on Sunday night.

Today was Tuesday, and only now could he talk to me without losing his shit.

Telling him about Deena and the deal I had struck with the Iron Dogz had not gone down well. I sat in the battered leather chair in front of his scarred and scratched desk and braced myself. His clear blue eyes were filled with ice cold rage, something I had seen before but never aimed at me.

Deena has been grounded for life with no phone and friends allowed. Knowing the way she was with Doc I had my doubts that it would last. She had him twisted around her little finger.

Maybe this time she had gone too far and he would not fall for her crocodile tears. Doc had turned scarily white and silent when I told him where I had found her and with whom. I did not tell him about the position I had found her in.

Rico and Skinny had been sworn to secrecy.

They agreed because they didn't want to hurt their Prez. And that shit would hurt him, and the hurt would have turned into a blind rage and blood, lots of blood. Dollar's blood and maybe even mine.

Deena was his perfect little girl. His untouched little princess.

Ja right! (As if!)

Unfortunately, I could not control Rick. I hoped and prayed he kept his mouth shut.

Today it was my turn to face Doc's wrath.

"Haven't I taught you to never-fucking-ever approach a target when you're pissed? What the fuck were you thinking?"

I didn't say a word because he wasn't finished, and he wasn't expecting me to answer. This was all about him venting his rage.

"I never wanted a fucking soul, outside of my officers and National, to know what you do for the club. It puts you at risk from assholes like Hawk Walker and his fucking club. He's never going to let this go, you do realise it don't you? His club isn't clean, not as filthy as the ED's, thank fuck, but not clean either. And now my daughter is going to be connected to him. It will put eyes on you. Eyes we fucking do not want to take an interest in you. I don't want the shit surrounding the Dogz spilling over on you or my club."

I froze in my chair.

There was something more going on here. Something I hadn't been made aware of because I wasn't a brother and weren't allowed to attend the club meetings.

"Tell me." My voice was soft and very wary.

Doc shook his head. Ice blue eyes met dark eyes and held.

The ice softened, became warm, and became my dad's eyes in his otherwise expressionless face.

"I can't, baby. I have to take this to the table, see where the brothers stand with letting you in. This is going to pull you so deep into club shit you will never be clear of it. Something I don't want. We've been walking a very fine line with the work you do for us, keeping you outside but secure within the club's protection. I never fucking wanted you in at all. I fucked up."

Sitting forward I shook my head, grinned, and winked at him.

"There was no way you could've kept me out, Dad. I'm too nosy for my own good. I like digging out secrets. It might be harsh but I don't give a shit what you do with what I bring you. Stoney trained me well. He would've had my ass for the shit I pulled at the Dogz clubhouse. That was all on me, not you or the club."

If I hadn't known him so well, I would've missed the instant transition from father to president because it only happened in his eyes.

His cold, hard expression never changed.

"Hawk is going to want more than just information. They've got shit raining down on them that will eventually pull all of us in. I can tell you that much. Let me take this to the brothers and see where they stand on letting you into club business. I'll talk to you before you have to meet him on Friday. I don't trust the fucker, not at all."

I agreed with him.

"He might want more than just information but it doesn't mean I'm going to give it to him. I'm with you on the trust thing. I don't trust him either."

Doc was back to being my dad as he nodded.

The business part of our meeting was over.

I gave a soft sigh of relief as I walked out of his office.

It could have gone so much worse. I might bitch and moan about him, but he was my dad and I loved him, fiercely.

I was still his DC, his Crow. I would not let him down.

Not ever again.

SEVEN

Hawk

It was Wednesday and he was struggling.

He never struggled to concentrate. It was the damned little bird; he could not get her snapping dark eyes out of his head.

Every time he shut his eyes she was right there in front of his eyelids. He was going to have to do something about it.

She was nothing like the women he usually fucked. She was short, chubby, and dark, where all his women had always been tall, and blonde. Even his ex-wife Candy was a tall blonde. He liked them tall and blonde with big tits and juicy asses, now it seemed his taste was changing.

It was time to take a look at where the little bird worked and who she hung out with. Decision made, he grabbed his keys and wallet, and locked his office door behind him.

As he strode into the common room his eyes met those of Kid and Sin who were sitting at the bar, a beer in front of each. All it took was a slight chin lift and they were following him outside.

"Are we going into the office, Prez?" Sin asked as they walked to their bikes.

"Not right now. I want to check on something."

He left the compound with his friends on either side of him and headed for the highway. It would take a good twenty to thirty minutes to get to the tattoo shop in Melville where she worked. Time he could use to change his mind. He knew he wouldn't.

Hawk had to see her, even if only from a distance.

Pulling into the undercover parking garage of the small shopping centre he rolled his bike back and parked. Sitting on his bike he removed his helmet, ready for the questions he knew were coming.

"Have you lost your mind, Hawk? What the fuck are we doing here?" Sin snarled.

His road captain hated shopping centres and malls. Hated them so much he refused to take part in charity runs starting and ending at a mall, several of those used the huge parking lots as a gathering point. He always joined them on the road and left before the run ended. According to him a mall sucked the life out of you with its fake air and light. He wasn't wrong.

"I want to put my eyes on DC, see her in her workplace."

Sin's eyes went big. "She works in a fucking shopping centre?"

He grinned at his brother.

"No brother, her studio is across the road. I parked here so we won't be seen. I don't need the Warriors knowing that I'm checking on her. We'll go upstairs, there's a small restaurant on the second floor with an open deck overlooking the shop. We'll sit where we can see them but they can't see us or know we're watching."

"Why are we doing this, Prez?"

Hawk could see the smile in Kid's eyes.

"I just told you. I want to watch her, get a feel for her."

Both Sin and Kid shook their heads and laughed.

"Yeah, Boss, we know exactly what kind of feel you want," Sin teased.

"Fuck off."

But he didn't put any force behind the words because they were true. He wanted the little bird, badly.

Bad enough to stalk her.

Relaxing in the sun, beer in hand he kept his eyes on the tattoo studio across the road. It was busy, very busy. According to Ziggy's information, DC wasn't the only Warrior woman working there. Tiny's daughter and Shaka's old lady worked there as well. The Warriors had eyes in the shop. A prospect sat in the reception area, back to the wall, eyes to the door and the customers.

Hawk was glad to see the Warriors had taken steps to protect their women.

The rumble of approaching bikes had the three of them moving further back into the shadow of the awing over the open deck. Three Road Warriors pulled up. He recognised Skelly, Raj and Rover as they got off their bikes and disappeared into the shop. The next moment Raj and DC were back in the front of the shop. His mouth almost dropped open when he took in the smoking hot body, she had kept hidden under the big leather coat. He frowned when the bastard took his shirt off, undid his jeans and DC put her hands on him.

What the fuck?

Frowning he looked at the tattoo climbing out of the man's pants and up the side of his torso. He knew by the way she touched him that he was her lover or had been her lover. They were both too comfortable with her hands on him for it to be anything else.

Hawk's gut jerked as he watched the small woman inspecting the tattoo. He stared with narrowed eyes, taking in her perfect little ass covered in faded blue jeans and her perky tits covered in a black t-shirt with the studio's logo across the front.

Jesus, she was hot as hell.

"That's a fucking kickass tattoo. I wonder if she would work on a Dog," Sin mumbled as if talking to himself.

Hawk finished his beer and shoved his chair back.

"Why don't we go down there and find out?"

"You sure, Prez? Those Warriors are not going to like us walking into the shop. It looks like it's under their protection although it's not in their territory,"

Kid said while staring down at the shop.

"We get on our bikes, ride a few blocks, then come back and park out front. It's neutral territory plus they are our allies, so no problems."

He gave them an evil grin.

Fifteen minutes later they pulled up and parked in front of the shop. He smiled when he caught the little bird's narrowed eyes. She was pissed. Good. He liked her pissed-off.

Hawk walked into the shop with a relaxed confident air and crowded right inside DC's personal space.

"Hey, little bird," he said as he smiled down at her.

"Hi, what can I do for you?" she snapped angrily.

"My man Sin over here wants a tattoo. He's been dragging us all over the city looking for the best. According to what we've heard your studio is rated in the top three."

She nodded, still frowning. Stepping away he waved Sin forward. With his arms crossed over his chest he watched as they discussed what Sin wanted.

He saw the minute she became interested.

Sin grinned as they made arrangements to work on the design. Hawk's eyes never left her face while she talked to his brother. Her eyes flashed with life. His blood headed south and he had to shift his legs further apart to accommodate his thickening cock.

He glanced at Skelly when he moved up next to him.

"What the fuck are you doing here?"

He demanded softly.

"Getting my man a tattoo that won't look like he got it in prison."

"You have tattoo shops in your territory with good artists. Why come here?"

"Because she's the best."

Skelly snorted in disbelief and he allowed a grin to tip his lips slightly.

"Thanks, DC. I appreciate you doing this for me." Sin gave her a chin lift with a smile.

DC grinned at his brother. "You'll be my first Dog, so it's all good."

"And he won't be your last," Hawk murmured softly.

Her grin instantly disappeared.

With a wink and a smile, he walked out of the studio.

He felt her eyes on them as they got on their bikes.

Kid and Sin were laughing as they rode away, leaving a pissed off little bird behind.

DC

My eyes almost popped out of my head when the three bikes pulled up. I watched through the window as Hawk got off his bike, pulled off his glasses and helmet and walked into my shop.

What the hell was he doing here?

I held my breath when he walked right up to me, stopping almost on top of me.

My temper stirred.

He smiled and made hidden parts tingle.

My stupid body was happy, so very happy to see and hear him but my brain ruled. Temper to the rescue.

"Hey, little bird."

"Hi, what can I do for you?" I asked angrily.

"My man Sin over here wants a tattoo. He's been dragging us all over the city looking for the best. And according to what we've heard your studio is rated in the top three."

I ignored Hawk and concentrated on Sin. Quizzing him about his idea for a tattoo. Sin wanted a running dog on his abdomen, a dog wearing armour. Plates protecting its head, throat, sides, and chest, but you had to be able to see that it was a flesh and blood dog, not a metal dog. It was an exciting idea. I agreed to send him designs and we would go from there.

I felt his eyes on me throughout the consultation with Sin and my heart raced uncontrollably. I let out a relieved breath when they left. But Hawk's parting remark unnerved met totally. I was in so much shit.

I just had to get through Friday and then it would be done. Doc and Skelly would get me out of the mess I had created.

I hope.

EIGHT

DC

Friday arrived sooner than I wanted.

They were waiting for me as I walked my last client of the day to the front of the studio. Not Rico and Skinny because they were on Doc's shit list.

Skelly and Rover, as big as damned houses, lounged on the leather couches with shit eating grins. I knew they were going to tease me so I ignored them. Strangely they just grinned and waited as I said goodbye to my client then cleaned my station. Like most Fridays, we stayed open late and I had to reschedule appointments to get away early. Killian and the girls would close for me.

Silently following me out the shop they sat on their bikes watching as I climbed into my beast and fired her up, the deep growl of the engine soothing me as I drove home. I wanted a shower and clean clothes before facing Hawk and his club.

During the week Skelly and I had prepared a comprehensive file I would hand over tonight.

BURNING BRIGHT IN THE BLACK

Skelly was my right hand when I met with women who came to the Crow with information they wanted to sell. They loved the way he looked, all tall, dark and menacing, and undeniably gorgeous. He wore his dark hair braided in a short tail down his back, his beard always neatly trimmed and his clothes clean. His kutte showed some age but it looked good. He got his road name because of the Jack Skellington tattoo on his thigh. To his friends he was known as Skel. Skelly was vicious and dangerous, very dangerous, and was the club's Intelligence Officer. He was also the man my dad wanted for me but it was not going to happen. We had no chemistry, none at all. If we had I would've been claimed and wearing his patch and ink a long time ago.

Instead, we were friends, best friends.

Rover was rougher, looked more hardcore, but he was the softer of the two. A hulk of a man with wild dark red hair and a thick red beard. His bright blue eyes twinkled underneath heavy dark auburn brows. His road name was Rover, apparently, he was wild in and out of bed. Before he settled down with one woman he was known to rove far and wide, hence the name. His old lady was always smiling so I'm sure the talk about his prowess in bed was true. He was one of the club's enforcers and had quite the bloody reputation. Rover and Linda, his old lady, were good friends of mine. She was one of my very few female friends.

Following me into my house they made themselves comfortable on the couches while I got them each a beer.

"You ready for the shitstorm we're about to enter, DC?" Skelly asked mock seriously as he lay stretched out on the couch.

"There's no damned shitstorm, Skel. I fucked up and I'm fixing it. He wants information and I'll give him as much as I can without compromising the Warriors."

"That's not how I heard it," Rover declared. "I heard the Hawk has developed a hard on for a certain little bird and was taking steps to get her in hand."

The two assholes laughed as I jerked upright. I hadn't thought they would know about the bastard's plans. Hawk should have realised his stupid plans would get back to me. The Crow dealt in information and I had quite a few of my informants calling to clue me in on Hawk's moves to ensnare Doc's eldest daughter.

I played it as if I didn't know.

"What? Bullshit!" I growled as I handed them the beers. "The asshole has three women to keep his dick happy. No way am I joining his freaking harem. We have business and that's how it will stay, only business."

"If you say so, sweetheart," Skelly murmured with a grin.

"I do say so. I'm going to change before we get something to eat. I'm not doing this shit on an empty stomach."

"We going to the Rib Shack?" Rover asked with a gleam in his eyes. The man could eat a mountain of ribs and it still wouldn't be enough.

"Sure, we can do that," I threw back over my shoulder.

BURNING BRIGHT IN THE BLACK

"We taking your cage, sweetheart?" Skelly shouted as I turned into the bathroom.

"No, I'm riding. Got my lady back today so I'm on her."

My bike had been in the shop after I had to lay her down to avoid being taken out by an asshole in a cage. I just got her back from Anderson Repair & Restoration, good as new. Usually, my bike would have gone to the Warriors Garage but I decided to try out ARR after I saw their work at a recent bike show. To say I was pleased with the end result would be a vast understatement.

Tonight, with Skelly and Rover riding with me I would be safe, protected, and I knew they would not be the only ones riding with us. Doc would not send me out without full protection.

I was pleasantly full and filled with the scent of the cool night air when we turned into the access road to the Iron Dogz compound. We pulled up at the floodlit gates and sat silently on our bikes when the two armed prospects walked up to us.

I flipped up the visor on my black full-face helmet.

"DC Michaels, here to see Hawk, this is my protection, Skelly and Rover."

They nodded and stepped back, one of them gestured at someone hidden in the dark and the heavy gate slowly rumbled open. The four brothers who had accompanied us on the ride turned and parked their bikes just outside the gates as we rode through. They would wait until we finished our business and ride back with us.

The freaking clubhouse was packed.

Lines of bikes sat in front of the building while vehicles were parked to the side in the obviously designated parking area for cages. The music was loud and there were people everywhere. Women wearing the bare minimum hung on guys wearing kuttes and those not wearing kuttes.

Shit. They were having a major club party.

A night open to their other chapters, support clubs, hang-arounds and tons of pussy.

I backed into a space with Skel and Rover on either side of me. I pulled off my helmet, hung it on my handlebars, then pulled off my riding gloves and slipped them into my jacket pockets.

I hated being out of my comfort zone and surrounded by so many strangers. Especially when I was uncertain about who I could trust.

"We stick together, you do not get distracted tonight, Skel. No pussy, this is business."

I immediately felt the pissed off vibe radiating from him when he turned his head and glared at me.

"I'm not here for pussy, DC. I'm here, protecting you. Tonight, I'm yours."

What? Mine?

Who the hell knew what he meant. He spoke in riddles most of the time anyway. Rover grunted wordlessly.

We stood in front of the bikes for a few seconds. I unzipped my jacket before turning towards the wide-open doors.

I gave a heavy sigh.

Dropping my head I straightened my shoulders then raised my head high.

"Let's do this so I can get out of this hellhole,"

I growled as I started towards the doors.

A hush settled over the partying crowd as we walked in, they'd been expecting us. We were very obviously *not* Iron Dogz.

I was dressed all in black; biker boots, faded jeans, tight tank and a fitted hip length leather jacket. A special Road Warriors patch with my name was sown onto the right side of my jacket telling everyone I was protected by my club, my family in fact. It wasn't something clubs generally did, acknowledging unclaimed women, but as Doc had said, I was a special case. On my back was the Road Warriors patch, the top rocker saying Road Warriors MC and the one below Johannesburg. Not a property patch but a claim, nonetheless.

Skelly and Rover's kuttes drew a lot of attention. Fuck.

I hated the staring eyes, the smirks, the knowing grins.

It changed in the blink of an eye when Skelly clasped his big hand around the back of my neck and steered me towards the bar. Except for tensing ever so slightly I let it go, we've used it before and tonight I was grateful for it.

He had publicly claimed me in front of a rival club, marking me as his territory, ensuring none of these assholes would try any shit with me. Once I had a beer in my hand, I put my back against the bar and scanned the large room for Hawk.

BURNING BRIGHT IN THE BLACK

And there he was, reclined on a wide couch, a woman under each arm and another between his legs. The blonde head in his lap belonged to Laney Wills and the blondes on either side of him were Jane Warne and Lizzy Hamilton. He was kissing them and playing with their tits, exposing them to the watching eyes. A lot of the men were staring with hot and wanting eyes.

Yuck!

Hawk Walker had a type, tall, blonde with big tits and juicy asses.

And he was an exhibitionist.

He watched me with a wide shit-eating grin. His eyes stayed on me as he put a hand on top of the blonde's head and pulled her off.

I raised an eyebrow, he hadn't come.

I turned to Skel with a grin and Rover leaned over to hear what I was saying. "She can't be very good at giving head if she fails to make him come."

Skelly and Rover burst out laughing. I relaxed back against the bar and sucked back some more beer. No way was I going over to the couch to be humiliated. He wants to talk to me he can leave his pussy-posse and take this into the office. We were here for business, not fun.

I narrowed my eyes as he leaned over and spoke to his VP who immediately sent one of the men watching the show over to us.

Skelly moved closer, crowding me as we waited.

The asshole stopped in front of me and looked me up and down with barely disguised scorn.

"Hawk wants you over at the couch. Your protection stays at the bar."

"Not happening." Skelly growled. "Where she goes, we go, no exceptions. Run back to your boss and tell him that."

I saw anger in his eyes, he swallowed it down and returned to the couch. I watched as he gave his Prez the message. Irritation flickered over Hawk's face before he grinned and disentangled himself from the women. He stood and leisurely tucked his still hard big, pierced cock back in his pants, zipped up and walked over to us. Arrogant fucking ass.

"DC, nice to see you again. So glad you could join us tonight," he smiled.

I did not give him an answering smile or an inch.

"Cut the bullshit. I'm here to work, nothing else. Let's get this over with, if you're done getting your dick sucked. I have places to be."

He shook his head slowly from side to side.

"Oh no, little bird, you're not going anywhere. For the next six months this is going to be home. You'll move in with my women and work from here."

Skelly growled low and deep, dragging me into his arms.

"Not happening, fucker."

He snarled at a still smirking Hawk. "Take a good look at her patch, she's Warrior family, she's never been nor will she ever be a club whore. She'll work with your club, give you the information we agreed on, and that's all. I will bring her over when she needs to deliver, but she stays in her home on our turf."

The smirk disappeared and was replaced by a heavy frown.

"You have a claim on her?" Hawk asked menacingly.

"Yes, I do." Skelly grated. "She's been mine since the day she was born. Put in my arms by Doc Michaels himself."

"She's not wearing your patch or your ink. Free game as far as I can see."

The bastard pushed at Skelly.

Suddenly Skelly laughed. Long and hard. He leaned towards Hawk and laid it out for him, softly, and in the process shocked the shit out of him.

"DC has never been free game. She might not sit at the table but she's in a position of trust with my club. If she'd been born male, she would've been Doc's heir and our next president, no contest. But she's not, she's female, and unlike the daughters of other club presidents it doesn't detract from her value. On the contrary, it makes her very valuable to our Prez and to me. Very valuable indeed."

I was confused but hid it, and I could see Hawk was confused as well.

No way was I that important or valuable to Doc. I'm a girl.

"What the fuck do you mean?"

Rover and Skelly both gave him evil grins.

"What it means is when the time comes to pass the gavel, and I hope like fuck it's a long, long, long time from now. DC will be standing beside the man who takes over the gavel, as his old lady. As *my* old lady, standing beside me."

I was shocked speechless as I looked up at Skelly. He was still staring intently at Hawk. I turned back to take in his reaction.

Hawk was pissed, very, very pissed.

"My fucking office, now." He barked as he stormed away.

"What the hell, Skel?" I whispered.

"Doc's play, DC. Heard from a source what the bastard was planning, we fucking can't allow it. His plan to put you in the same house as those whores confirms what the source gave us. Just go along with me, baby, okay?"

"Jake Stoddard, if you get me in shit with this damned play I'm cutting your nuts off, real slow." I threatened as we followed Hawk, Ice and Kid to his office.

A glance at his very public fuck-bunny couch confirmed the three women hated my guts. I wasn't worried; I could take all three at once, while blindfolded.

Jane Warne ran the Iron Dogz gym and fancied herself an MMA fighter. She had some good moves but she wasn't as good as she thought she was. Laney Wills was a stripper and great on a pole but that was as far as her fighting skills went. Lizzy Hamilton worked as a secretary at a Real Estate office, soft, not a threat.

I had files on all three of them and knew all their dark dirty secrets. Well as dark and dirty as two of those club sluts could get, but one of them was dark and dirty as hell.

So here I was once again in the office of a very pissed-off Hawk Walker.

"Does Rick know about Doc's plans for you?" He barked at me.

"I doubt it. He might be Doc's son but he isn't a Warrior and he doesn't sit at the table." I snarled back. I saw something flicker in his eyes before I looked at Skelly. "I'm just wondering why I haven't been informed about some of these plans."

"Baby, decisions made at the table stays at the table until Doc tells me to tell you. And I've just done that."

Skelly had his big damned hand on the back of my neck and directed me into one of the chairs, increasing the pressure until I gave in and sat down.

"Jake, sweet baby, if you're playing with me, I will have the pick of your entire vinyl collection, no exceptions. We clear on that?" I threatened.

The bastard just laughed, leaned over, and placed a soft kiss on my lips. "Going to be yours anyway, baby, just like I am, so no worries."

I snorted with laughter. "You're going to be mine? Are you serious? You've never been mine, Skel."

He was suddenly on his knees in front of me, ignoring everyone else in that room.

"I'm thirty-five fucking years old, babe, and you know very well how much pussy I've had since I was fifteen. You, however, will never ever be pussy, not for me, not for any of the brothers and fucking definitely not for him."

With that last statement he pointed an accusing finger right at Hawk who sat fuming in his big chair. He might have been speaking to me but he was laying it out for Hawk.

"He has a major hard on for you and it's not fucking happening. You will not move into that house with his whores and you will not be in his bed. We will share intel with them for the next six months and that's it. Rover and I will bring you to all meets, which will not take place in front of all those assholes out there ever again. That shit has put you on radar and it's not cool. All future meets will take place in neutral territory. The information will be on a USB which will be handed over and we will be out within fifteen minutes. We will not give the ED's another target. His pussy house is getting enough attention as it is. Give him the fucking info so we can get out of here, sweetheart."

Before I could answer him, Hawk lunged forward in his chair.

"What the fuck did you say? Who is the ED's targeting?"

I rolled my stiff neck to release the super tight muscles. Fucking Skelly.

"We're having a long talk once we get home, Skellington," I snarled before turning to Hawk.

"It's all on the USB I have for you. For the last few months, you've had eyes on your women, inside and outside your compound. I told you that you're leaking information. This is the result of those leaks. You have people vulnerable to blackmail in your club, you need to protect them."

I unzipped the inside pocket of my jacket, dug out the USB and slid it towards him. His big hand smacked down on it.

"I'll look this over and contact you with our next meet. Don't think I don't know I'm being played, Skelly. I know what she means to Doc and your club. We'll continue to meet on our property and make sure you are prepared to stay as long as needed. Don't worry, you won't be in the fucking pussy house. You'll be in my house and we'll work through this shit together. We need to make sure we're ready for what's coming. We're all being threatened by this shit."

After a couple of stiff nods, we were out of the office and marching through the partying crowd towards the door.

And fuck me if a pissed off club slut didn't stop us.

"Don't think you can walk in here and take what's mine, you fucking whore!" Jane Warne shouted as she bent over and stuck her long nose in my face.

It was very obvious she was playing to the crowd, thinking she had the upper hand because she was surrounded by the Iron Dogz.

Mistake. Big fucking mistake.

I looked up at Skelly and then at Rover.

"Did she just call me a whore?" I asked in a very conversational tone, very aware of the avidly listening crowd around us.

"Yes, she did. Heard her loud and clear, babe," Rover said with a grin.

"How's that possible? She's the one who's the whore, not me. I'm not getting paid to fuck the boss, she is." I grinned evilly at Rover.

"Don't know DC, no idea how some bitches' heads work."

"You're right about that. You ever paid for pussy, Skel?" I asked with fake interest and grinned as shock rustled through the listening crowd.

"Nope, had them line up and beg me to fuck them a time or two though."

"Oh, I remember. It was at the Black Cave, wasn't it?"

We ignored the stupid bitch and kept on talking as if she weren't there. In my peripheral vision I saw her getting more and more pissed- off. The men and women around us were openly laughing at her.

"I'm talking to you, bitch!" She yelled, and at the same time tried to grab my jacket.

I slid away from her grabby claws. Slowly turning my head I looked into her pinched and suddenly very ugly face and gave her a cold smile.

"Keep your filthy hands off me or I will kill you." My voice was ice cold as I threatened her.

By now dead silence had fallen around us.

Jane Warne made the mistake almost everyone did.

She was taken in by my size.

She swung a fist at me and I ducked underneath it, letting it swing wildly over my head and into Hawk's wide chest as he stepped up to defuse the situation.

"What the fuck, Jane?" He growled angrily.

Before he could say anymore, I took the opportunity her unprovoked attack gave me. I knew she thought I was weak but the bitch had no effing clue who or what I really was. It was a lesson she was going to learn the hard way.

"Next week Sunday, nine o'clock at Underground. Be there."

Shocked whispers started spreading through the crowd.

"What?" She gritted out in confusion.

Ah. An Underground virgin. This was going to be so much fun.

"Whoa! Wait, wait, wait! What the fuck is going on here?"

Hawk tried to get a grip on the situation spiralling out of control right in front of him.

He knew exactly what Underground meant. All the men in the room knew. Sin stepped up to Hawk's back and spoke to him, his voice soft enough not to reach the surrounding crowd. Hawk's eyes snapped to me and I knew Sin had just told him he had seen me fight. I allowed a small smirk before shutting it down.

"Your club slut laid a hand on the daughter of my Prez, Hawk. She challenged family, and we demand satisfaction. Have her at Underground next week Sunday. No excuses," Rover growled as he gently urged me forward.

"You don't turn up, bitch, we'll come find you and take care of you and no one will lift a finger to protect you. You crossed the line putting your filthy hands on club royalty," Skelly threatened as he followed us out.

Kid Warne joined us as we got ready to ride.

His expression was tight and angry.

"I'm sorry my sister's such a fucking bitch. She thinks he's going to give her his ink, make her his old lady. All she's ever been is fucking club pussy. She's been giving it up for the brothers since she was sixteen and hasn't stopped. They're not exclusive because Hawk doesn't do exclusive. He's going to kick her out soon, so watch your back. She's going to blame you for that shit."

I felt sorry for him, he really didn't deserve the things he was going to learn about his sister once they opened that USB.

"We're fully aware of what she's capable of, Kid." Skelly said softly.

"You need to get back in there, brother, and look over what we just gave you. You have some very unpleasant shit and a house cleaning coming up."

Kid looked at Skel with a frown and then it hit him.

I hated seeing the bleakness in his eyes as he walked away to face what we had given them.

He seemed like a nice guy and didn't deserve the shit about to get piled on him.

NINE

Hawk

Hawk didn't want to believe what he was seeing but it played out on the screen in front of him. The person he had thought was one of the most loyal to him and his club was not. Her betrayal bit deep as more and more facts and photos emerged. Tying her to an unknown man, as well as to the Evil Disciples MC and their VP, Big Ed Morrison.

She was their rat; it wasn't one of his brothers.

"I fucking can't believe what she's done,"

Kid bit out through clenched teeth.

"The stupid bitch knows better. But she's always been damned greedy. Greedy for attention, greedy for your property patch, greedy for the power it would give her. I'm sure she believes this will give her power over the club, power over you."

"What are we going to do about this?" Ice asked in a voice as cold as his name.

"Nothing. Not a fucking thing."

Hawk snarled as he watched the video of his now definitely former lover being taken up the ass by Big Ed.

He needed to get himself checked out and hope like fuck she hasn't passed on some fucking disease.

"We let this play out. She has a man on her 24/7. We make sure her access to information is cut off. I'll lay it out for the brothers at church. We have to find out how much she knows and how much she's given our enemies. We need to know which brothers talked about our business while she was fucking them. I know it's not me. I don't discuss club business with the bitches. Not fucking ever."

"I'm so fucking sorry, Hawk. I had no idea she was doing this shit."

"Not your fault, Kid. Yes, she's your family but you're not responsible for her actions, that's all on her. You've been putting up with her bullshit for fucking years. This shit is because she knows I'm never going to make her my old lady and it pissed her off. If she thinks Big Ed is going to give her his patch after she betrayed our club, she's totally fucking deluded. She's forgotten loyalty to your club is everything. It's the code we live by. The ED's maybe our enemies but they live by the same damn code. And the little bastard has an old lady anyway. All Jane will ever be is easy pussy, a club whore. Just like she is now."

His road name might be Big Ed but the man was skinny as a rake and below average height. Despite being skinny and small he was a dangerous man. His temper was legendary.

"Once they are done with her, they will get rid of her. She's disposable."

Ice stated the very obvious.

"She's so far up her own ass she's forgotten exactly who and what she really is. And that's my fault," Hawk growled in disgust.

"I should never have started up with her and should never have moved them into the fucking house. I told her she was never going to be my old lady. She obviously didn't believe me and this is her fucked up plan to get my attention and payback. I have no idea how she thought this fucked up shit would get her my patch. I want those bitches out of the house by next Friday. I'm done with them."

Slamming his laptop closed he sat back in his chair and looked at his two best friends. The three of them had been through a lot over the years. They would get through this as well.

Both men had been there for him when he lost his parents. Stood by him when he and Candy lost their baby. And again, when Candy blamed him for their loss and left him. He still didn't get how he had been responsible for her losing the baby. She never told him; just said he should know because it was his fault. It's been fucking years and he still didn't know. It was ancient history and he had thought best forgotten but now he wasn't so sure. Maybe he needed to have a talk with Candy. Clear that shit up.

Ice gave a sigh of relief. "About time you kicked the bitches out."

Hawk just shrugged; he had enjoyed the women but now he was done with them.

Kid shook his head angrily.

"My mum and dad spoiled her rotten. Anything she wanted she got. I think she never grew up, never learned some things were not to be. Why the fuck can't she see how fucked up this is? She's not only betraying the club but she's betraying our family, betraying my parents, and betraying me."

Kid looked over at him with a look that said he remembered something.

"Do you remember the fight she had with our dads about a week before she turned sixteen? She wanted to start prospecting when she turned seventeen and they laughed at her, told her to find herself an old man because no bitch would ever become a prospect. She started screaming abuse at them and my mum had to step in and drag her out of the room. That's when she changed and became a club slut."

Kid shook his head angrily.

"I overheard my parents talking about how she had thrown her life away. How she could have had her pick of the available brothers and she chose to be a club whore. I don't think my mother has forgiven her."

He sighed heavily.

"For the longest time I've had to live with the fact my sister, my flesh and blood, totally disgusts me. And now I hate her for what she has done to my family, to my club."

"I'm so fucking sorry, Kid. I should never have touched her," Hawk gritted out.

Kid waved his apology away.

"Her choices aren't on you, Hawk. She became a club whore years before you hooked up with her."

Ice reached over and slapped a hand over Kid's shoulder.

"None of this is a reflection on you or your folks, Kid. This is all on her. Everyone knows how much I despise the bitch. None of you had any idea why. It changes right now."

They watched in concern as Ice paced angrily.

"She tried it on with me, several times. This was before Hawk started it up with her. Wanted me to fuck her, I said no. The bitch didn't like it. She cornered Emmie and told her I had been fucking her for years and wouldn't leave her alone. She was so fucking convincing, tears and all, my girl believed her. Emmie dumped me in front of the club and the fucking slut laughed. Her fucking lies cost me my woman. I've been waiting years to get my shot to take her down, now I have it. Believe me Kid; I'm going to make your sister pay for what she did to me and Emmie."

"Why the fuck didn't you say anything?" Hawk asked in confusion.

Ice shrugged.

"You always stood up for her, believed her shit. I knew if I told you there was a possibility it could fuck up our friendship. So, I stayed silent and waited. I knew sooner or later you would get tired of her or she would fuck up and show her true colours. I was so fucked up after losing Emmie I trusted nobody, not even you."

"That's bullshit, Ice. No way would I have put pussy ahead of family." He was stunned. How the fuck could his cousin believe that shit?

Ice just looked at him then sighed and shrugged. "Like I said, I was fucked up."

"When this is over, I'll go see Emmie and explain all this shit to her." Kid's eyes were filled with regret.

"No." Ice shook his head. "It's too late. She's got a man and she's happy. I'm not going to fuck with it."

Seeing the pain in his cousin's eyes Hawk knew he could not let it go.

He would make sure once their troubles were behind them Emmie learned the truth. He'd make her realise how she'd fucked up. Because that was what she'd done. She had fucked up. How could she have ever believed Ice would cheat on her? They had known each other almost all their lives, she had been his since she turned eighteen.

Ice had supported her while she went to university. He'd been on the verge of giving her his patch when she ran off.

Yes, he was definitely going to open her fucking eyes for her.

"Let's put this shit to the side for now and talk about the little bird challenging Jane to a grudge match at Underground."

Ice changed the subject with a smile that didn't reach his eyes.

Hawk knew his VP wanted the attention off him, and so he let it go.

"I've had Ziggy looking into her, he found almost nothing. Most of it we already know. She's a tattoo artist, works at Mainline Ink II, owns her home outright, has three fully paid for vehicles registered in her name, and pays her taxes on time, no debts at all. A couple of investments and substantial savings. It's like she said, she lives clean, and as far as she can, off the grid." Kid shrugged. "I'll get him to look into Underground, make some enquiries and see what we find."

"I want everything he can find on her. Don't care how insignificant, follow it up. I don't think she's as harmless as she looks. Speak to Sin, he told me he saw her fight in Cape Town a few years ago. If she fought back then she most probably still does."

He turned to Ice.

"Go over everything we know about Doc Michaels and the mothers of his children, and I want a complete report on Skelly Stoddard. If he's the one Doc has chosen as his heir, we need to know more about him."

"We're on it." Ice said as he and Kid left the office.

Sinking back into his chair he closed his eyes tiredly. What a fucking clusterfuck. Not only did he have a traitor but he'd let down two of his brothers when they needed him most. His dad had been right when he told him his indiscriminate fucking would get him into trouble someday.

Minutes later his door opened after a soft knock. He watched with narrowed eyes as the three bitches walked seductively towards him. Not even two weeks ago he would have been all over it.

BURNING BRIGHT IN THE BLACK

Now, they needn't have bothered. He was done with them all.

"We've come to make you feel better." Lizzy smiled sexily and was about to walk around his desk when he silently held up a hand. The three stopped, thighs pressed against the front of his desk.

He didn't make them wait or mince his words.

"I'm done. I want you out of the house by next Friday."

Lizzy's mouth dropped open in shock. Jane started grinning as if she wasn't included in the order, he swiftly disabused her of that thought.

"All of you. I had an agreement with each of you when we started and I will honour it. Spider will transfer the agreed amount into your accounts tonight. We had a good time but it's over, I'm done."

"You have got to be shitting me." Laney gasped.

"Are you sure this is what you want? We don't mind sharing if you want to bring someone else into the house, Hawk,"

Lizzy offered softly, tears in her eyes.

"It's that fucking bitch, isn't it?" Jane growled angrily.

"Shut the fuck up, Jane,"

He snarled, done with their shit.

"There is no one else and all of you knew exactly what this was. Like I said, I'm done and moving on. Sort your shit and move out of the house. You need any help moving speak to Sin and he will take care of it."

They stood frozen, staring at him, Laney and Lizzy looking shocked but Jane was totally pissed off. Then Laney and a silently crying Lizzy rushed out of his office. Jane, typical Jane, stood across from him and tried to stare him down.

"Get the fuck out of my office, Jane."

"You're going to regret this, Hawk. I promise you. You're going to fucking regret this. I would've been the best fucking old lady you could have ever wished for."

He was done with her and her bullshit.

"Bitch, listen carefully and take this in, because it is the last fucking time I will lay it out for you. You will never be my old lady. I will never give a bitch who has fucked almost every one of my brothers, and fuck knows how many other men, my patch."

Hawk stared at her coldly until she dropped her eyes, turned and stormed out.

With a sigh he opened his laptop and went back to the information the little bird had given them.

It fucking sucked. Picking up his phone he sent out a club-wide message.

'Church, Monday, 9am. Attendance mandatory, no excuses.'

Tapping his fingers on his desk he growled in frustration, he had so much pent-up anger churning in his gut he needed to somehow release. Before he laid eyes on DC, he would have found a bitch and fucked it out of his system. It was no longer an option.

That left fighting.

Maybe he should give Ice or Kid a chance to get into the ring with him, beat the shit out of each other and get some clarity.

With an evil grin he pushed up out of his chair and went looking for his brothers.

Stripped down to his jeans he bounced on the balls of his bare feet as he watched Ice climb through the ropes. His cousin never pulled his punches, it was going to be a bloody but damned good fight. Boots was acting as referee and gave them the usual spiel, no biting and all that shit. The fight would continue until one of them was knocked on his ass and stayed down or until Boots called the fight. There were no preliminaries they just got right into it.

The punches flew fast and blood started flowing. After what felt like hours of standing toe to toe beating the shit out of each other he realised he would have to do something or he was going to go down. Ice's last punch had nearly put him on the canvas; he was like a damned machine and his fists like rocks.

But he knew his cousin, knew his one weak point, his chin.

Dancing away and swiping the blood running down his face from cuts to his eyebrow and mouth, he feinted to the right, then let go with an enormous left hook taking Ice right on the chin.

He was about to follow it up with a right when his cousin swayed, and went down on his ass.

His eyes dazed and blinking continuously.

Boots was suddenly there, stopping the fight. Stumbling over he sat down and flung his arm around Ice's heaving shoulders.

"Fuck, cuz, we need to do this more often." Hawk laughed, wincing as his split lip protested.

"Not going to be your fucking punching bag, asshole," Ice growled with a bloody grin.

Not long after they were drinking cold beer with ice packs on their faces and ribs watching Kid and Sin beating the shit out of each other. Lifting his arm, he held his battered fist out and they bumped fists with slightly pained smiles.

"Brothers until the end," Ice growled.

"Brothers until the end," Hawk agreed.

On Monday Hawk sat at the head of the heavily scarred table waiting for the chapel doors to be closed and locked. He watched as his men settled in their seats around the table and the chairs against the walls.

His officers sat at the table, Ice as his VP on his right and Kid his SAA on his left with Sin, Beast, Jagger, Kahn, Spider and Ziggy filling the other seats.

His uncle, their Chaplain, was at the meeting as well.

Gabriel "Bulldog" Walker sat at the other end of the table; his face expressionless but his eyes were never still. He had been the club VP when Bounty sat in the President's chair and had stepped down after his death to allow Ice to take his place next to Hawk. Before he became the VP, he had been the club's Enforcer for many years. He was a very dangerous man to piss off.

Today he was pissed off. Very pissed off.

Looking at his men Hawk knew the shit he was about to reveal could cause a rift in his club if he didn't handle it with care.

After a long discussion with Bulldog, Ice and Kid they'd decided not to reveal the evidence against Jane at the start of the meeting. They needed to know who she had fucked for the information she had been passing on to Big Ed, and why the fuck club business had been discussed with the bitch.

This shit was undermining everything he had worked for since he took over from his dad.

It made him look fucking weak, like his club was out of his control.

Fury boiled viciously in his gut and in his veins. He breathed in deep to gain control as he smacked the gleaming hammer down on the thick square of steel.

The sound of steel connecting with steel had all eyes on him.

Silence fell instantly.

He felt the heat of his anger burning through his eyes as he looked around the room. Taking a deep breath, he started laying it out.

"Since the break-in at the shipping yard all of you must be aware that we have a problem. A problem that needs to be discussed and remedied, fucking fast. We were made to look weak and incompetent. I was made to look like an asshole with no control over my men and my club. Because of the fucking break-in there is a good chance we will lose our business with Dom Maingarde. He went into business with us because we deliver, no matter what, we fucking deliver. We can no longer make that claim. A meeting has been set to discuss the loss of his property. Losing his business won't cripple us but we'll feel it in our pockets. Our reputation took a heavy hit because of this. But it's not the worst."

He looked around the room before he continued.

"We were betrayed by one of our own. Someone we trusted and allowed to get close."

There were hisses and rustles as his men looked around as if sizing each other up to find the traitor. He didn't allow that shit to spread.

"One of the club whores has been gathering information and selling it to our enemies. We have solid evidence she betrayed the club."

Rumbles, growls and pissed off mutters erupted. He slapped his hand down on the table with a loud crack.

"What I fucking need to know is how many of you gave her information when she fucked you? Information she sold to our enemies. In this room every single one of us took a vow of silence. We swore that anything we discuss in here stays in here. On fucking pain of death."

They all started to speak at once, all denying and pointing fingers. He once again slapped his hand down on the table.

"Shut-the-fuck-up!" He shouted.

"You will keep your fucking mouths shut until I tell you to speak. Listen carefully to what I'm saying. You need to get that what is going to happen now will never happen again, not as long as I'm fucking alive. Only for today I'm waiving the usual punishment for talking about club business outside of this room."

At a glance he saw the shock on the faces of his men.

Beast snarled as he jerked forward and slammed a fist onto the table.

"No fucking way. You talk about club business to anyone but your brothers and I shut you up, permanently."

Hawk knew he now had their undivided attention. It was time to drop the fucking bomb.

"Not this time, Beast. Stay calm and listen. Those of you who have fucked Jane raise your hands."

Shock rippled through the men as their heads swung towards Kid.

There was horror and uncomfortable knowledge on several faces.

Hands started going up. Beast's hand one of those in the air.

Boots was the first out of his chair against the wall, his hand still in the air. Horror and betrayal written clearly on his face.

"Fuck, Prez. It's me. We drank together and fucked. The fucking bitch spun me a story about how you valued her input. She knew shit she shouldn't have and I fucking believed her bullshit. I didn't think it through. Should have known you would never discuss club business with a club slut. I should have come to you."

Hawk nodded and gestured for him to sit down.

"Anyone else?"

Spider groaned and grimaced.

"Fucking hell. She tried with me, Prez. Brought me a drink that made me feel strange so I didn't finish it. She wanted to know about our finances. I pretended to pass out because the bitch was fucking insistent about wanting to suck my cock. It happened Friday night. I should have come to you, but you had so much going on I thought I would mention it at church today."

Spook raised a hand while snarling angrily.

"She got to me as well, Boss. I got drunk and strangely chatty. I fucked her and I remember her asking about the containers in the yard. I'm not sure, but I might have given it to her. I passed out and didn't remember that shit until right now. She kept asking about guard rotations. I have never talked about our shit before or since. Something isn't right about this."

"What did she want from you, Beast?" Hawk asked.

"Fuck, I don't remember. I fucked her about a year ago, maybe she did pump me for information, I don't know. What the fuck is going on, Prez? She's family. Why would she do this?"

Beast glanced at Kid who looked about ready to explode.

Bulldog spoke up for the first time since they sat down.

"What you should all have realised by now is that she drugged you to get the information. Then she fucked you because it gave her a thrill to know she had a hold over you. Get over it. It's done, move on. Moan over it in your own time, we have bigger problems facing us right now."

Smacking his fist down on the table Hawk shook his head.

"This fuck up is partly my fault because I put her in our club, gave her the opening she needed."

Hawk wanted to kick his own ass.

The men erupted out of their chairs all of them talking at the same time.

"Not your fucking fault, Prez."

"Bitch is fucking crazy, Boss."

"Bullshit, Prez."

Grateful for their support he waved them back into their places and turned to Kahn.

"In the minutes for today's meeting I want you to add the following. As of today anyone, from the president down to the lowliest member, who talks about our business to an outsider, will be put in the ground with extreme prejudice. I have been lax in enforcing some of the harsher laws when I took over from Bounty. I thought I could bring the club forward to an easier time, minimise the bloodshed and maximise our earnings. It seems I was wrong. Therefore, the easy times are done. As of today, the blood law is back and will be enforced by me and my chosen enforcer. Anyone who is affiliated with this club, be they a brother, an old lady, a hangaround or club pussy, will be subject to blood law."

Seeing the confusion on some of the younger and newer brothers' faces he went on to explain.

"For those of you who don't know, blood law means blood will be taken for any transgressions against the club. The severity of the transgression will dictate the severity of the punishment. It might be as easy as a few cuts with a knife, a beat down or as severe as death."

Hawk was done with this shit and wanted to move on so he did.

"I have taken steps to clean up my own shit. The bitches have been given until Friday to get out of the house. They no longer have my protection but they still have club protection. While we're working on cleaning shit up it will be business as usual until I tell you different. We can't let on we know Jane sold us out. You're going to zip your fucking lips. You're going to treat her exactly the same. You want to fuck her, go for it. Just know that today, at this table, everything changed. You run your mouth while fucking her you will be facing blood law." He glared around the room.

"No excuses, no second chances. Be careful who you accept drinks from."

There were nods all around. He was ready to bring the meeting to a close.

"Anything else you bastards want to discuss?"

"What about the grudge match at Underground? Do you really expect us to support the fucking traitorous bitch?" Sin, his Road Captain snarled angrily.

"I fucking hate it as well, Sin, but we can't let her know we're on to her. So, yeah, we will be supporting her as a club. All of you will attend, no exceptions."

He was about to bring the hammer down when one of the new patches, Rider, stepped up.

"Sorry Prez, I can't be there. There's no cell phone reception down there. My girl is pregnant with my baby and there have been some complications. I can't leave her alone right now."

"Why don't we know you have a girl, and a pregnant one at that?" Ice growled.

Rider frowned at Ice but his eyes immediately returned to Hawk, silently begging.

"She's not my old lady but she is carrying my kid. She's been mine since high school. She's good people but wants nothing to do with the club after a run in with fucking Jane while I was prospecting." He shrugged.

"So, I gave her that. I'm not going to abandon her or my child just because she has issues with the club. There's no one else, we don't have any family. I have to be there, Prez. Her pregnancy hasn't been easy and the doctor is worried about her blood pressure. I can't leave her alone right now."

Hawk ran a hand over his chin as he stared at Rider.

Another of his men Jane had fucked with.

"So, she's the reason you are the first out of here, never stick around on party nights and don't bang the club whores. I wondered what was up with that."

Leaning forward in his chair he made sure the man saw how serious he was.

"Next time you have a fucking problem you come to me. The club could've helped you with this. You're excused from attending the fight and your usual duties until she's had the baby. But brother, I want a daily update on your girl and when she goes into labour you call me. Use this time I've given you to make your girl understand she's family and we take care of our family. Do we understand each other, Rider?"

"Yes, Prez. You have my word." Rider stepped back into place; his relief very clear to everyone.

"Anyone got any other business they want to discuss?" He asked.

When all he got was a lot of shaking heads, he smacked the steel square sharply.

"Then we're done. Go out there and be careful. Anything looks scaly, call it in. Keep your eyes open and watch your fucking backs."

He watched as his men silently filed out. They were pissed off but would do what was best for the club. Just as he would.

But first he needed to get tested.

He hoped like fuck the test came back clean.

TEN

DC

Underground was packed, even more so than usual for a Sunday night. A grudge match was always a big draw. The fact that two women were fighting, made for an even bigger draw.

Underground was exactly what its name indicated.

It was an underground fight club and highly illegal.

The club was in the basement of a large warehouse. On paper it was owned by a distribution company, in reality, it belonged to the Road Warriors MC. It made the club a lot of money legally and illegally.

I only fought when I needed more than a sparring match to level me out. I had no interest of ever fighting in an MMA League.

This was what I needed. It was rough, raw, and with very few rules.

I was a popular fighter and known as a good bet. Not that I fought as often as some of the other fighters. I picked my fights very carefully and only fought on nights when it would be mostly female fighters on the fight card, which meant the MC's stayed away.

They only attended when one of their own was fighting.

Tonight, the Road Warriors and Iron Dogz were out in full force and had claimed opposite sides of the cage. The rest of the space was taken up by fight fans who, when hearing the rumours, had come out to watch and spend money betting on their favourite of the night.

There was a fight taking place right now. Alien, the Road Warrior's road captain, was obliterating his opponent. I grunted in relief when his opponent tapped out.

Alien was good, very, very good. It was why I trained with him.

Grizzly was my coach, and has been since I started fighting. He was my lucky charm. I didn't fight if he wasn't outside the cage or in my corner.

We were expecting some dirty tricks and with Grizzly's experience he would spot shit way before the rest of us. He had insisted on setting me up in the VIP dressing room, away from the dressing rooms where the whore and her crew could fuck with me.

Skelly and Rover were in the security room watching the monitors. There were cameras everywhere, outside and inside the building. This was where Skelly was most comfortable. I knew he would watch every move made by the slut and her crew.

He had my back. Like always.

Jane Warne had arrived with a large entourage and was totally unaware that she was on Warrior TV. Stupid, so stupid. She had her

MMA buddies with her in the dressing room and two Iron Dogz patches were stationed outside the room.

As if anyone wanted to get near the stupid slut.

I was warm and sweaty from warming up with my fight buddy, Booker, when a freshly showered Alien walked in and looked me over, nodding as if satisfied.

Grizzly sat me down and started to wrap my hands. No gloves tonight, just basic wrappings.

"You ready for this, shrimp?"

"Yes I am."

Before he could continue wrapping my hands and give me his pre-fight chatter Skelly's voice interrupted.

"Grizz, I think they are trying to hide shit in her wrappings."

Grizzly hated cheaters.

"I'm on my way. Get the Dogz president in the room. Right the fuck now."

He turned to me and put a hand to my chest when I wanted to follow him out.

"You stay put and keep warm, Demon. I want this fucking slut annihilated, I want blood, a lot of fucking blood and maybe a broken bone or two. You get me? Focus." He turned and gave Alien a hard look.

"I'm trusting you with wrapping her hands. Don't fuck it up." He growled as he left.

I was so ready for this fight. So very, damned, ready.

I'd been in heavy training the entire week preparing to kick her ass. As I kept warm, I watched the crowd on the enormous flat screen on the dressing room wall. Excitement ran high out there.

I was ready to fight when a very pissed off Grizzly got back.

He gave me the usual pre-fight talk adding that he wanted lots of blood and broken bones. I just nodded; no words were necessary. Finally, it was time.

Music suddenly blasted out and the crowd roared.

Fucking 'Eye of the Tiger'.

Really?

Stupid fucking bitch.

Booker started laughing, and then we were all laughing, even Grizzly.

"What the fuck? Since when do we have fucking music as if we're fighting in Vegas?" Alien laughed.

"Stop fucking around down there. DC, keep your head in the fight. You don't concentrate she's going to fucking hurt you," Skel's sharp voice interrupted the laughter.

Silence fell. I rolled my head to relieve the sudden tension in my neck. I was ready. Alien held out my black and red satin robe, I slid my arms in and pulled the hood over my head as I kept bouncing to keep warm.

"Do you guys think Skel is going to have music for me?" I asked.

The guys grinned and shook their heads. Nope, I didn't think so either.

I was focused, very focused. I saw no one, acknowledged no one. The fight was everything. The announcer started his spiel and announced Jane Warne by her fight name.

The bitch called herself 'The Executioner', so damned stupid.

I tuned the shit out listening to Grizzly's last minute instructions.

There was a short silence and then music thundered through the fight club. I grinned as I walked out the dressing room and down the short passage.

Disturbed screamed and the Warriors went crazy shouting and whistling and singing along to 'Down With The Sickness'. Alien and Booker strutted down the aisle between the Warriors who were lined up stamping and clapping.

I danced down the aisle, my eyes on the cage.

Nothing else mattered. I shut it all out and concentrated on taking care of the whore waiting for me.

The music faded when I reached the cage. I slipped off my soft shoes and Grizzly pulled the robe off my shoulders, revealing the tight black sports bra and black Lycra shorts with loose fitting black fight shorts over them. The Road Warriors club patch was embroidered on the left leg and my fight name in large red letters along the bottom of the right leg.

Linda, as usual, had braided my hair.

Somehow she had the braid attached to the back of my head, giving me the security that it would be difficult to restrain me by my hair.

The room erupted when the announcer introduced me as 'Demon'.

Yes, it's lame, I know, but that's what Grizzly billed me as.

I was sixteen when I approached him to teach me how to fight. He actually called me little warrior in the beginning but there was no way I would allow that name. I trained for two years before he would allow me to fight. I continued training and fighting while I lived in Cape Town. I've never stopped fighting, but I wasn't a regular on the fight card. We've had offers to go pro but I wasn't interested in packing on muscle or getting beat up regularly. I liked that I had total control over whom I fought and when I fought.

Tonight's fight was a grudge match, and the details had somehow circulated through the underground community.

Courtesy of Skelly of course.

It meant a lot of the hardcore fight fans were putting down a lot of cash. I didn't know what the odds were and I wasn't interested either. In the outside world Jane Warne had a reputation as a dirty but very accomplished fighter with a lot of wins to her name, plus she had a large following in MMA circles. I was an unknown to her fans and most probably to her club as well.

But down here in the Underground I had a reputation as a vicious relentless fighter. The Warriors were going to make a lot of money tonight because there was no way the bitch was walking away without a broken bone or two.

If she was able to walk at all. She shouldn't have tried to cheat.

BURNING BRIGHT IN THE BLACK

The fight would be decided over five rounds, and a tap out would stop it immediately. Because the bitch was taller than me, I would have to get close, real close, but at the same time had to avoid getting pinned down. It didn't worry me, because it was what I had to do in most of my fights. I wasn't scared of getting hit, or getting hurt, it came with the territory.

I met Alien's eyes, gave Grizzly a nod then climbed into the cage. Everything faded. All I could see was my target. She was grinning, her pink mouth guard was like a flashing neon sign that said, 'hit me right here' and I was going to oblige.

A lot.

I stared into her eyes, waiting for the bell, staying on my side of the cage. I was ready for her, so very ready.

At the sound of the bell, she came storming at me. I let her. I needed her close. I let her get in a few hits. Gave her the over-confidence I wanted her to have before I started taking her down. She kept on running her mouth, telling me how she was going to wipe the floor with my fat ass. I said nothing, just got in my hits like I had been trained to do.

The first round would probably go to her but now I knew exactly where her weak points were. I listened to Grizzly and nodded as he gave me pointers on how to hit her where it would hurt the most. I grinned before I slipped my black mouthguard back in and tapped my fist against his.

The second round was hard from the first minute to the last.

I went in and took the fight to her. Opened up a cut on her left eyebrow with a vicious kick that had her on the canvas, she recovered and swiped at the blood streaming down her face. While her corner took care of the cut, I listened to Grizzly urging me to do it again. I took the rest of the round and hammered her kidneys and ribcage with repeated kicks and punches, causing damage that would slow her down over the following rounds. She was starting to pant heavily and sweat was streaming down her face mixing with the thin line of blood running from her nose and eyebrow.

Then came the last round I would allow her to survive.

I took the fight to her and took over completely. I hammered her into the floor. I avoided getting pinned, as she was bigger and heavier than me. If I let it happen, she could get lucky and hold me down for the count.

It was when she started taunting me about my mother that the door in my head slammed open. I tried very hard to never let that animal loose while I fought. But she pushed me that last little inch and I let it happen.

Icy black rage fell over me as I stared at the smirking bitch.

I went in close and hammered her, with knees, fists, elbows and feet. She didn't stand a chance, her defence was virtually non-existent. Both eyebrows were cut and bleeding, so was her nose and mouth. I danced away, taunting her. She took the bait and moved in. I hammered a kick just below her knee and actually heard the bone snap, but I didn't stop. I immediately launched myself high into the air, delivering a solid kick to the side of her head as she was going down. She flew back, hit the canvas and lay motionless.

I knew she was done. I bounced in place and waited for the ref to declare the fight.

The Warriors were screaming and whistling while the Iron Dogz sat in shocked silence. I had broken her leg. She wasn't getting up off the floor by herself, that's for sure. I did a lot of damage to her ribs as well, might have broken one or two. She was done fighting for a few months. With that break, maybe forever.

When the fight was called in my favour I threw my blood splattered hands in the air, strutting around the cage and grinning as the Warriors and the regulars went crazy. Grizzly, Alien and Booker stormed into the cage and crowded around me as my music thundered around us.

Alien and Booker picked me up and threw me into the air. I grabbed onto the side of the cage and ran along it like a monkey until I stopped in front of the Iron Dogz. Looking down at Hawk Walker, I gave him a bloody grin and a wink before I threw myself back and fell into Alien's waiting arms.

The crowd went wild at my antics. I grinned when Alien shook his head with a laugh.

At the far side of the cage Jane's coach and assistants were crouched around her along with the fight doc.

My job here was done.

I brought the blood and bone. I made her pay.

Climbing out of the cage I ignored the crowd and allowed Grizzly, Alien and Booker to lead me back to the dressing room. Grizzly made me sit down while he taped a butterfly bandage over the cut on my cheek. The bitch had a nasty left hand. All I wanted was a hot shower and to go home. I knew the shower would happen but I would not be going home any time soon. Doc would expect me to join them at the clubhouse to celebrate my win. The Road Warriors had made a lot of money tonight and the celebration would most probably carry on until morning.

The party was wild and I hovered on the edges, not allowing myself to be pulled in. I stayed long enough to throw back a shot or two and drink a beer with my guys. Then I found a prospect to give me a ride back to my house.

I was looking forward to sinking into my hot tub.

When I got home, I immediately put on some music then turned up the heat in the tub. I drank a smoothie standing at the counter in my kitchen swaying to the music playing in the background. I hadn't eaten and couldn't stomach anything either. A smoothie was my usual after a fight.

I cleaned up, put some ice and a face cloth in a plastic bowl and settled two ciders on top of the ice. Walking out on to the wide deck I set the bowl down on the wide rim of the tub.

I undressed, stepped in and sank down into the bubbling warm water to soak away the aches and pains that were already creeping in as the last of the adrenalin faded.

BURNING BRIGHT IN THE BLACK

Sighing in relief I relaxed as the music soothed my soul and the water bubbled around me.

Heaven.

Feeling pleasantly buzzed I sipped my cider and ignored the sound of a bike pulling up at the front of the house. It was most probably Skelly coming by to check on me. He knew my post-fight ritual and had joined me in the hot tub before so I stayed right where I was. I lay with my head back and my face covered by the cold face cloth, my neck supported on a small, folded towel.

I was naked in the tub but I wasn't worried about Skelly seeing me like this, he had seen it all before anyway.

No worries.

I listened to his footsteps crunching through the gravel as he approached my back deck. He sounded a bit heavier than usual but I shrugged it off as him being tired.

I had gravel right around the outside of my house, a great early alarm for intruders.

The wooden steps creaked under his weight as he came up onto the deck and walked over to the tub. I felt his eyes staring down at me and smiled under the cloth.

"Hey, Skel. What are you doing here? Already finished with the red head? What's happening with your stamina stud?" I snickered.

He didn't say a word and I shook with silent laughter as I heard him getting out of his clothes.

Typical Skel.

"You behave yourself in my tub, Skel. I hope you washed your junk after you finished with her," I teased as he eased himself in next to me.

And then I almost drowned in my own tub. The voice in my ear wasn't Skel's.

"You slipped away after the fight, little bird. I was waiting for you."

I jerked and almost slipped beneath the bubbling water but his arm curved around my waist and pulled me against his very naked chest. Ripping the face cloth off I stared at him wide-eyed.

What the hell?

"How the hell did you open the gate? And what the hell are you doing in my tub?"

He grinned gently stroking a finger under the cut on my cheek.

"Does this hurt?" He asked softly, totally ignoring my questions.

His hands slipped down and I gasped when he grasped my legs and pulled me astride him, his big hands clasped over my hips. He pushed his huge erection against my core and I shivered.

Shit.

Perched on his lap my boobs were now out of the hot water and with the breeze chilling my warm skin my nipples were rock hard.

That's my excuse and I'm sticking to it.

"I have no idea what you think is going to happen here, Hawk. I'm not available club pussy and I'm not planning on joining those ranks, ever. I made a deal to work with you, that's it."

I laid it out for him.

He just smiled. Rubbing his thumbs in circles over my hip bones he set off tiny little explosions under my skin.

This man was very dangerous.

"You fucking blew me away tonight, little bird. Woke my shit all the way up. Giving you fair warning, baby. You are going to be mine."

His eyes narrowed as he tilted his head to the side.

"No, fuck that, you are mine already."

I laughed and shook my head.

"Sorry, Hawk. I don't share and your pussy house is pretty full. So, sorry to disappoint, but I have to decline your offer."

He shook with laughter and pulled me closer to whisper in my ear. My hard nipples brushed against the fine hair on his chest.

I sucked in a harsh breath as his hands ran up my back, pulling me even closer.

"You can fight me all you want, little bird, but you are mine. And, sweetheart, in case you value Skelly's hide, don't you ever let him see you like this again. This body, all of you, now belongs to me."

The arrogant ass made my blood boil.

"I don't belong to you or to Skelly. Skel has seen me naked, so have a few others, so what?" I snapped then frowned at him in confusion.

"You fuck your bitches in front of whoever is watching, whenever and wherever you want. I was under the impression you liked exhibiting them and your power over them. Why the sudden turnaround?"

A growl, an honest to goodness growl, erupted out of him.

"I'm claiming you, little bird. No one but me will see you naked from now on. I won't be fucking you in front of my brothers or anyone else for that matter. This body and your orgasms are for me alone, no one else."

I sighed. The bastard pushed all my buttons, hard. But there was no way I was going to get into his overfull bed.

"I don't share, Hawk. I never share. When I take a man to my bed, he knows it and if he can't give me that he is gone. You've more bitches than you know what to do with. I won't be joining their ranks."

I was surprised when he nodded in agreement. I actually felt my mouth dropping open before I snapped it closed.

The bastard winked, smiled, and nuzzled my neck before pulling back and sliding his hands up over my sides, skimming them over my breasts and up to cup my face and hold it captive in his big hands. My pussy throbbed right along with my racing heart.

"Giving you notice, sweetheart. I have moved the bitches out of the house, gave them some money to set them up as agreed at the start. I'm done with them. I haven't been with any of them since our last meeting. All I want is you. I know you are going to fight me on this but I don't care, baby. Tonight, you showed me you have the strength to take on my brothers and my club. You are strong enough to handle me and this life we live. I've been looking for you for years and you were right here, in my own fucking back yard. Not fucking walking away from you, baby. You will be mine, only mine. And I will be yours, only yours."

Holy fucking shit.

"You must be high, or just plain crazy. You don't know me, Hawk. You have no idea who I am just like I don't know you either."

That damned smile again.

"Baby, we're not like the civilians who fucking date for months getting to know each other. We live fast, know what we want and take it. I want you, you want me, I claim you, we fuck, and it's done. But you've been hurt, so we're not going to fuck tonight. I'll give you tonight to build up your strength because tomorrow you're going to need it, little bird."

He grinned wickedly as he leaned in, pushing his face into my neck, sucking hard, marking me, making me squirm. As he pulled away his tongue slid along the side of my jaw and then he was facing me again. Leaving me a shuddering, needy heap of want in his lap.

Oh hell.

"Tomorrow, I will be in your bed or you will be in mine. I don't care which, just as long as it's you I slide into and make come before we go to sleep."

He lifted me off his lap, standing me up in the middle of the hot tub. He rose up out of the water and my eyes ran over his wet body.

Sweet baby Jesus.

He was magnificent, with all those hard muscles, some hair on his chest, a glory trail and a v-line that led to a spectacularly hard pierced cock. Totally the best I've ever seen or had. I bit my bottom lip as my eyes took a survey of his body and the throb between my legs screamed for attention.

Boy oh boy, I was in big trouble here.

I dragged my eyes away from his body and looked up into his laughing eyes. I didn't have time to admire those eyes because he bent down and his lips covered mine. I stopped thinking as his tongue slipped inside. My empty pussy clenched immediately, wanting more. Wanting that huge cock inside me. I moaned as his tongue slid along mine, totally obliterating every other kiss I have ever had.

The kiss burned through me, left me weak, hanging onto him when he lifted his head. Hell, the man could kiss. His cock pushed against me, rubbing ever so slow over my mound. His piercing slid over my wet skin. Inciting a fire he was not going to quench.

"I'll see you tomorrow, sweetheart. I have some things to get done in the morning. I'll text you. Be good for me, little bird."

He tapped my nose, got out of the tub, drew his clothes on over his wet body and his totally gorgeous hard as a rock cock. Oh fuck, I rhymed.

He walked away before I could force a single word out of my mouth. I was about to jump out and run after him when I realised, I was naked. And I only had a small towel to cover my nakedness.

Hawk would not like me running around naked where anyone could see.

What! What the hell was wrong with me?

One kiss and I'm acting like a total *skapie*. (sheep)

I stood listening to the sound of his bike starting. I was frozen in the middle of my hot tub as the deep rumble faded away. Then I slowly sank back down into the bubbling warm water.

What the hell had just happened?

ELEVEN

Hawk

Waking up in his room at the clubhouse with a hard cock and no one to take care of it was a very recent and new experience.

But it was one he relished.

If he had his way it wouldn't last long. Soon he would have a little bird in his bed to take care of his needs.

He was getting his test results today and if he was clean, she would be taking his cock soon.

The thought of her in his bed made him even harder.

With a deep groan he fisted his shaft and slowly slid his hand up and down. His breath hissed through his clenched teeth when he tightened his fist, he needed more. Rolling to his side he grabbed the lube on the bedside table and drizzled some in the palm of his hand. His hand now slid up and down easily.

Closing his eyes, he remembered what her pussy had felt like, hot and wet, pressed up against him in the hot tub.

Remembered her stuttering breaths as he sucked on her flesh, marking her neck.

Remembered her beautiful exotic dark eyes, pupils blown wide, staring into his.

Jerking his dick hard and fast he twisted his hand over his piercing. It was enough to send him over the edge.

His back arched as he gritted his teeth and spurted come over his belly and chest. He kept milking, releasing every single drop. With a satisfied sigh he sagged back, slowly sliding his hand up and down his temporarily satisfied shaft.

Temporarily, because just thinking of her made his blood heat.

Looking down at himself he grimaced at the evidence of his loss of control. He couldn't remember when he had last jerked off and come on himself. It usually ended up in the mouth or on the tits of some bitch. Never inside one, he wasn't stupid.

It would never happen again because he was done with the bitches.

His come now belonged to a dark and dangerous little bird. Even when he jerked off it was all about her.

Standing under the shower he washed quickly. He was drying off and pulling clothes out of his cupboard when it hit him.

There was no way he could bring his woman back to this room.

The bed and the bedding had to go, actually everything had to go. He needed the room gutted, cleaned, and refurnished. It was going to cause some raised eyebrows downstairs but he didn't give a fuck. She wasn't ever going to put her luscious ass in a bed where he had fucked other women. Thank fuck he had never taken bitches to his house; it had always been off limits.

If Hawk got his way his home was going to become their home.

With a plan of action firmly in mind he went downstairs.

He had too many beers with his brothers last night and crashed in his room at the club.

The clubhouse had been buzzing with how DC had taken Jane down. All the brothers now knew how dangerous she was. Other than the talk about the fight, Jane's name hadn't been mentioned at all. She hadn't returned to the clubhouse and that was good.

But she did return with her fucked up posse and tried to move back into what DC called his pussy house. The bitch was under the mistaken impression she could stay there while she recuperated.

Ice took a few of the brothers over there and threw her ass out, broken leg, cracked ribs, concussion and all. He didn't know what she had thought would happen.

After being thrown out twice she had to know without a shadow of a doubt that he was done with her.

The smell of bacon frying had his stomach growling as he walked into the kitchen. Kid and Boots sat nursing large mugs of coffee at the kitchen table, both looked seriously hung over. He dragged his chair out with an irritating screeching noise and both clutched at their heads with pained groans. Grinning at their pained expressions he sat down. He looked up at his aunt with a smile when she put a mug of coffee in front of him. She stood with a hand on her cocked hip staring down at him. Ready to do battle.

What the hell had he done now?

"I hear those slutty women have been given their marching orders. Is that true?"

Hawk nodded. "Yes, Aunty Bee, they're gone. Permanently."

Giving a little squeal she threw her arms around him almost taking him to the ground in her enthusiasm. Thank fuck he wasn't holding his coffee.

"Hallelujah! I've been praying for this day. You need a good woman by your side, not a troop of sluts," She declared giving him a smacking kiss on the cheek.

His aunt did not like most of the club whores and kept them at a distance. It didn't mean she let them slack off. If they wanted to hang out at the clubhouse, they had to clean to earn their way. Kitchen duty only went to those she didn't actively dislike. The ones she really disliked were assigned bathroom duty. Most of the time, the bathrooms in the common areas weren't disgusting, but after a party they were like the outer circles of hell. Very few of the ones assigned bathroom duty lasted more than a week and were quickly replaced.

Not that the brothers cared, there were always more bitches looking to walk on the wild side.

Hawk cleared his throat. "I actually have a favour to ask."

Her head swung towards him; her eyebrows raised in question.

He knew that look very well.

Aunt Beryl was his dad's widowed sister. She'd come to live with them when his mum had been diagnosed with cancer. She had taken care of them all. It had been a blessing to have her around when he lost his parents and his baby. She was like a second mother to him.

"Could you arrange to have my room cleared out, please? I want everything gone, the room cleaned and repainted. I'll buy new shit once it's done."

His aunt gave a little scream and hopped up and down excitedly. The table had slowly filled as the smell of food drew more brothers to the kitchen. All of them snorted with suppressed laughter.

"Don't you worry about a thing, sweetie. If you give me a couple of prospects, I'll have it cleared out today and have them start painting tomorrow. Give me your card and I'll go shopping for bedroom furniture and linens. I'll take care of the bathroom too."

"Thanks Aunty Bee, you're the best." He smiled and winked at her.

Satisfied one problem had been taken care of he sat back to enjoy his coffee and breakfast.

He should have known his aunt wasn't finished with him.

"I have been waiting years for this. Thank the Lord I'm alive to see the day." She narrowed her eyes at him. "But I'm warning you, Cole, don't you mess around with that little girl or you'll have me to deal with."

Having delivered her threat his aunt happily went back to cooking. Around him his brothers no longer tried to hide their laughter.

He just shook his head, smiled and concentrated on his breakfast.

What the assholes didn't realise was that his aunt saw them all as her boys. They were her family. Their time would come, a time when they would be caught in her motherly crosshairs.

He was on his second mug of coffee when Jagger came in and took a chair further down the table. By the look on his face Hawk knew he wasn't going to like what he had to say.

"Do you have anything for me, Jagger?"

Jagger nodded as he took a slug of coffee.

"I'll report once I've had some breakfast. In your office, Prez."

It meant he didn't want anyone to overhear his report. Shit.

Nodding he finished his coffee, thanked his aunt and went to his office. While he waited for Jagger, he texted his little bird. He had to keep her on her toes worrying about his next move.

Good Morning my little bird.

Take it easy today.

Missing you.

See you soon.

His phone was silent for longer than he liked and then she answered as snarky as ever.

I'm not yours.

Not missing you.

Mornings suck.

Hawk was grinning when Jagger and Beast walked in and shut the door behind them.

He immediately dropped his phone, focussing on the two men sitting in front of his desk.

"What do you have?"

Jagger pulled a small notebook from his pocket and slid it across the desk.

"The first list is of all the brothers who fucked her. The second list is the brothers who fucked her and gave her information. The third list is the brothers who fucked her but gave her nothing. The fourth list, and the shortest of the four, is the brothers who wanted nothing to do with her or her pussy."

Hawk opened his mouth to talk but Jagger shook his head and he stayed silent as his head of security continued.

"The fourth list is important because those brothers didn't like or trust her. Some of them have been watching her and were about to come to you with their suspicions when you laid it out at church. And brother, those lists are made up of patched members, prospects and hangarounds."

Hawk cursed violently as the extent of Jane's betrayal became clear. She'd had access to his brothers which meant she had access to a lot of information. Information she handed over to the VP of the Evil Disciples MC.

"Do we have any idea what her ultimate goal was or is?" He gritted through tightly clenched teeth.

Guilt ate at him.

This shit was his fuck up.

He'd been too busy fucking random sluts to pay attention to what was going down right under his nose.

"She pumped the newly patched brothers and the prospects for information on their guard duties. The patched members and officers she quizzed for information on our finances and our business contacts, legal and otherwise. The hangarounds she targeted for general information on the club." Beast growled.

"Fucking hell. How long has this been going on and how deep is the shit we're in?"

Jagger met his eyes, drew in a breath then laid it out.

"My investigation shows that she's been fucking for information for about six to eight months. I think it started on the club run to East London. You spent the entire week we were down there with that hot blonde and ignored her. She must have made contact with Big Ed or maybe he contacted her after she threw that fucking embarrassing hissy fit at the bonfire."

Fuck.

He had forgotten the shit that had gone down on that run.

Why had he allowed his sex life to become so out of control?

His fucked-up choices were what had started this shitstorm. The reality was that Jane wasn't the only one who might have a grudge. He'd fucked and walked away from a lot of women.

Closing his hands over the back of his head he pulled at his braid angrily.

"This is my fucking fault," He snarled.

Beast smacked his big hand on the desk, a pissed off frown on his face.

"Stop blaming yourself for this shit. The bitch knew exactly where she stood with you. Hell, everyone knew you weren't serious about the bitches. You fucked them publicly and didn't give a shit when others fucked them. Get the fuck over it."

Beast was right; he had taken great care to let the women know it was fucking, nothing more. He hadn't treated Jane any differently. Or maybe he did without realising because she was Kid's sister.

"Do you think I gave her ideas, treated her differently because she's Kid's sister?"

Jagger and Beast both stared at him with exasperated expressions, and then Beast, as always, gave it to him straight.

"Boss, the bitch is so far up her own ass she saw shit that wasn't there. When it became clear she was living in a dream world she took steps to hurt you and the club in any way she could. This is all on her, not you. Stop trying to take the blame for this clusterfuck."

Jagger grinned as he added his fucking five cents worth.

"You like a lot of pussy, Prez. Everyone knows you like variety, you always have done. This is not on you. She knew she wouldn't be the one to tame that wandering dick of yours. Bitch just didn't want to accept it."

Beast laughed and high-fived Jagger.

But Jagger wasn't done. "I have to say I never imagined it would be a tiny, dark and dangerous firecracker of a woman who would lock your dick down. Always thought the woman would be an ice princess like your little bird's sister. Fucking glad it's not. You need fire, Prez, not ice."

He couldn't stop the grin even if he tried.

"You're right, Jagger. She's the one, now I just have to get her into my bed and keep her there."

Both his men laughed. The fuckers.

But then Jagger became very serious.

"Good luck with that, Boss. I watched the way the Warriors were around her last night. Those men will die for her and not give it a second thought. You need to arrange a sit down with Doc, lay it out for him and get his blessing. The little intelligence we've been able to gather about her relationship with him tells us they are close, very close. Apparently her mother was the love of his life, and losing her the way he did, changed him. Everyone knows not to mess with him or his girl. He's dangerous, very fucking dangerous."

"How did her mother die?"

Going by their expressions he knew it was going to be bad.

"She was abducted a couple of weeks after DC's birth and tortured to death as a lesson to Doc and the Road Warriors. He retaliated by torturing and killing her abductors, then he went after the boss who gave the order and did the same to him. He erased their businesses, leaving their women with nothing but ashes. No one has fucked with Doc Michaels ever since."

"Jesus. Does she know?"

Beast shrugged.

"I'm not sure, Boss. Maybe. She's been trained by the best fighters in Doc's club. They turned her into a dangerous adversary. As we saw in the cage, she's a fucking killer with perfect control. She destroyed Jane without a flicker of humanity in her eyes. No one is ever going to take her as easily as they took her mother."

Rubbing his hands over his head he remembered the way his little bird had been in the cage.

At first, she had been cool, waiting for Jane to make her move. Playing with her and getting her hits in.

But in the third round Jane had taunted her with something and it was like a switch had been flipped. She became an ice cold killing machine in the blink of an eye.

The only reason Jane was carried out alive was his little bird's training. Training that had her stepping back when her target lay unconscious on the floor of the cage.

His little bird was so much more than the face she presented to the world.

And all of her was his.

Hawk needed to convince her he was serious.

Plus, he had to get the blessing of her damn father. Before he faced him, he had club business to take care of.

"Do we have eyes on the ED's and Jane? We have to be on top of this one, Jagger. I have a bad feeling about Big Ed's involvement with Jane."

"We do. I've assigned Boots and Spook to watch her. They'll switch out with each other. I've got Wolf and Dizzy watching the ED's clubhouse and Big Ed's house. They are watching from a distance so there's no chance of being spotted. If they make a move, we'll know about it. Sin, Kahn and I will switch out with them as needed. I'm not putting prospects on this one, it's too important. I want experienced eyes on them."

Crossing his arms over his chest he sat back in his chair, one hand stroking over his beard as he silently went over Jagger's arrangements.

"Okay, I want to know the minute they make their move. We can't take chances with these assholes. They are up to something and some of our people are vulnerable to attack. I want Rider and his girl in the pussy house until this is over."

Beast and Jagger both snorted and he grinned.

"Fuck, now I'm calling it the damn pussy house."

Shaking his head he turned back to business, all of them losing their smiles as he laid it out.

"Getting back to Rider, he's too much of a target out there alone. I don't give a fuck what his baby mamma says, get them here. Order the club bitches to clean the house before they move in. Tell the brothers with old ladies and those with families to keep their eyes open. They have to bring them in if anything seems even a little bit off. No parties for the foreseeable future, our gates stay closed until further notice."

Beast frowned. "What about your ex-bitches? Do you want them here as well? It might cause shit with your little bird when she finds out they are here."

He shook his head with a shrug. "She grew up in a club and will know it's a safety measure and not me wanting them here."

After Jagger and Beast left, he sat staring at his phone. The next step to ensuring the little bird became his was a call to Doc to arrange a sit down. Taking a deep breath, he dialled and after the obligatory insults had been exchanged the meeting was arranged. It would take place later in the day at a pub in neutral territory.

Hawk pushed because he wanted it done quickly so he and his little bird could move forward. He did not tell Doc Michaels why he wanted the meet. It would be made clear when they looked each other in the eye and he laid it out for him.

He hoped like hell he walked out of the meet alive and with Doc's blessing.

Even if he didn't, he was going ahead with making the little bird his.

Right after Jagger and Beast left his office, he got the phone call he had been waiting for.

His tests had come back clean.

Thank fuck.

Now no one and nothing was going to stand in his way.

He would be making her his, today.

TWELVE

DC

The minute I woke post-fight aches made themselves known and had me grimacing in pain. It made the cut on my cheek sting sharply which added to my collection of aches.

I hated the mornings after a fight. They were the worst.

During the night your muscles stiffened and the only way to get over the aches was to move. Something I was loath to do.

Hissing in pain I crawled out of bed, shuffled to the bathroom and did my business. Then I staggered into a hot shower to soothe my aches and warm my muscles. I stood under the hot water until it started to cool. Drying off I took special care not to rub too hard over my bruises. Barefoot and dressed in yoga pants and a tank top I shuffled into the kitchen.

Skelly and Rover sat on stools pulled up to the island, drinking coffee. I ignored them and silently poured coffee into the mug already set out for me. Inhaling the aroma deeply I sipped then sighed as the warm fragrant liquid slid down my throat. Only after I had taken a few healthy sips did I feel ready to face the two men in my kitchen.

Why were they in my kitchen?

"Morning sweetheart, your face looks like shit," Rover teased with a grin.

"Morning babe, I've booked Lydia to come out and give you a massage later this morning. Killian said he's taking care of the shop so no need to go in." Skelly gave me a big grin and a wink.

"Morning." I mumbled.

I watched them as I sipped my coffee.

"Why are you in my kitchen and what's with the stupid grins?" Those knowing grins were starting to piss me off.

"We just wanted to check on you and once again congratulate you on winning the fight. It was fucking spectacular. Particularly those last two kicks; they were a thing of beauty."

Rover leaned over to have a closer look at my cheek.

"Would have liked it better if you had no damage to your pretty face though."

I shrugged. "It was a fight, Rover. People get hit in the face all the time, it's nothing."

"At least it's shallow and won't scar." Skelly growled as he came in closer to look at my cheek.

"We wanted to make sure you stayed home today. Your crew at the studio has everything under control and Rover and I have put off the meetings the Crow had scheduled. Take the day to relax, sit in the hot tub, and let Lydia soothe those aching muscles. Tomorrow you'll be back in ass kicking form again."

"Are you two stirring with me? Since when do I take time off from work after a fight? Or put off the Crow's meetings?" I frowned at them.

"We can't take a chance with the meetings, DC. Too many people know you fought the bitch last night. If the Crow moves around like he's got aches and pains suspicions might arise. We need to keep you safe."

Skelly laid it out for me and I had to agree. I was moving like a snail today.

"Okay, I'll stay in and recover. The bitch got a couple of hard ones in."

"We'll be back later this afternoon. Relax, enjoy a day off, we'll take care of any shit that pops up."

Skelly stood as he finished his coffee.

They both hugged me carefully, kissed me on the forehead and left. I went back to my bed and slept dreamlessly until Lydia arrived.

She shooed me into the hot tub when she saw the way I moved. We chatted and I drank one of her smoothies while my muscles slowly relaxed and softened. Afterwards she had me on her massage bed and worked her magic.

I still had a little bit of pain but now the tension in my muscles was gone and I felt pleasantly warm and relaxed.

When she left, I vegetated on the couch.

Listening to music and reading, something I almost never had time for. I only left the couch to get something to eat.

It was bliss.

A full day of relaxed bliss.

Hawk

Hawk sat across the table from Doc Michaels, looking into his icy blue eyes. Drawing in a deep breath he laid it out for the president of the Road Warriors MC.

"Last night I laid claim to DC. She is mine, and if I have my way, she will be wearing my patch and taking my ink before long."

Doc Michaels froze, the only thing moving was the fire in his blue eyes.

There was no other way but forward now.

"I know laying claim to her means nothing because she won't accept me without your blessing. So, this is me, asking you for your permission to…fuck, I don't even know what the fuck I'm asking permission for. All I know is she's going to be my old lady."

Leaning back, he crossed his arms over his chest and waited.

Doc didn't make him wait long.

"So, you want my permission to take my daughter away from my club, away from me. Why the fuck should I give it to you? I heard you kicked those whores of yours out. But are you ready to fuck only one woman for the rest of your life? Because, let me tell you boy, it's what my girl will demand from you. If you can give her fidelity, devotion and loyalty then, and only then, do you have my permission. If you can't, you had better get out of here before I shoot you down like a fucking rabid dog."

He liked the straight talk Doc was giving him. He gave it right back.

"Yes, she will have it and more. I'm done with fucking around. All I want is DC. I'm starting it with her today. I will be laying my claim before my brothers, but they already know my mind. I haven't hidden my intentions from them, they're aware she means something to me."

Doc sighed deeply, ran his hands down his face and over his beard.

"Fuck, okay, you have my permission, but hear me boy, you hurt my girl and I will make you hurt in ways you have never fucking imagined. You keep her out of your dirty business, my girl stays clean. Do you get me?"

"I get you, Doc. You won't ever have to make good on the threat. For the rest, there is no way in hell I'll ever pull her into our business. She stays clean, you have my word. If I fuck up and hurt my woman, she will sort me out before you ever get to me. My little bird is a vicious little thing."

Doc and his men laughed, so did his.

"Glad you understand your old lady, Hawk. She's going to give you fucking grey hairs worrying about her. There are a few things you need to know to keep her safe. Things we've kept from her because it's club business and she didn't need to know." He shrugged.

"I'll leave it up to you whether you tell her, or not."

He didn't like the sound of that.

"There's a reason for the bad blood between the Warriors and the ED's. It isn't just because of the filth they are involved in. A few years ago, Snake approached my club with a proposal that, according to him, would assure peace between our clubs. His idea was to arrange for our daughters to be claimed by men in either club, his daughter by Skelly and DC by Big Ed. I laughed in his face and walked out. They didn't like my reaction."

Rage burned through Hawk as Doc continued.

"As soon as Snake hears you have claimed DC he's going to be pissed. He might retaliate for the supposed insult to him and his club. It doesn't worry me. What worries me are the problems you are having in your territory and how it might spill over on my girl. I've been made aware of the situation with Jane Warne and Big Ed. I suggest you fix it as soon as you possibly can. Permanently."

Hawk was no longer relaxed.

"The situation is being taken care of, and if any of those bastards come anywhere near my old lady, they will fucking regret it."

Doc grinned.

"Good to hear. I'm having a talk with DC this afternoon. Skel will text you when we leave. We'll set up another meeting as there are some things we need to discuss."

Soon after Doc and his men left.

Hawk took a long slug from the untouched beer in front of him.

The fucking ED's. Every time he turned, he found their dirty fingers touching what they shouldn't. He would not allow those bastards anywhere near his woman. Her security was going to be updated whether she wanted it or not.

At least he had Doc's approval.

He couldn't wait for the next step, when he would claim her body, making her his.

Before he could go to her, he had to get back to the club and handle some business.

His mind scrolled through everything he knew as he rode.

The investigation into the theft at the container yard was on-going and security has been beefed up. Not knowing exactly what Jane had shared with the ED's made it imperative to change all codes, routes and security for their trucks, yards and depots. They had to ensure all their businesses were secure and safe for employees and customers.

It was a huge undertaking.

Knowing what he now knew about the ED's it was even more important to get it done as soon as possible.

Walking into the clubhouse he sent a text calling all the officers into the chapel.

The sooner they got started the sooner they would have their businesses and employees protected.

And he would be closer to claiming his woman.

When his men walked in, he waited until everyone had a seat and the door was closed.

Looking around the room he met each man's eyes briefly. They all sat quietly, waiting for him.

"Jagger, let's start with you. Give us what you have."

His brother gave a short nod.

"After conferring with Kid and Sin I arranged for armed brothers to ride along on all the long hauls. I had to pull brothers in from the other chapters and we have a lot of pissed off men out there. Not because they have to sit in a big fucking cage for hours on end, which will piss anyone off, but the fact that it's necessary to do so. We've had satellite tracking installed on all the trucks and trailers. The security at all our depots, garages and yards have been beefed up. We've changed guard rotations, changed codes and added more cameras."

Taking a quick look around at the frowning men he continued.

"I want us to think about taking our compound and yards off the grid. Change over to solar power and generators, sink boreholes for water, install rainwater tanks and so forth. We could even look into utilising water from the spring here on the property."

He held up a hand to stop questions from being asked.

Glancing around the table he continued.

"I'm not saying do away with municipal water and power completely, but we need to be able to keep the lights on and have water the next time we're attacked. Plus, we look responsible by going green. A plus for all our businesses."

There were grunts of agreement and nods around the table.

"Right now, we need to concentrate on making sure no one pulls another fucking break-in that isn't noticed for hours." Kahn grumbled.

"Going off the grid is something to talk about at the table during an open meeting." Ice said.

"Any questions for Jagger?" Hawk asked.

A lot of no's echoed around the room.

"Are all the loads we're running right now legit?" Kid asked.

Ice nodded and gave them an update.

"We pulled all of our less than legit loads. I've let our customers know there will be a delay on their deliveries and we've had no one pulling their loads as of yet."

Most of the loads run by Iron Dogz Trucking were totally legit but some weren't. It's been years since they got out of transporting drugs and guns. And they were fiercely anti-poaching and anti-human trafficking. Even going as far as anonymously tipping off the authorities a time or two. They had no problem transporting other less than legal products though.

"Spider, what do you have for us?" He moved on to the next brother.

"There have been several attempts to hack into our systems and access our bank accounts. They've failed because Ziggy's firewalls are impenetrable. I changed all system, account codes and passwords as a precaution. Only three people now have those codes. I'm confident our money is safe."

An intense sigh of relief came from everyone.

"Ziggy?"

Ziggy rolled his neck tiredly.

"Our systems are secure, as Spider said. They won't fucking get in, not on my watch. Jagger's got Dollar keeping an eye on Big Ed and Jane through the cameras we installed outside their homes and the ED's clubhouse. Big Ed is a constant visitor at her house but we have no idea what they discuss. We need to get some bugs in there. Right now, we're just waiting and watching for an opportunity. I've not been able to hack into the ED's computers. I'm not giving up. I'll get in; it's just going to take some time."

"Before we move on, one more thing."

Jagger threw in quickly.

"I made some calls to a company specialising in trained guard dogs. I was thinking about hiring them to patrol our premises. I researched them and found they supplied dogs and train their handlers. I think we should look into getting dogs and having a few of the brothers trained."

"That's a fucking good idea. We'll bring it to the table," Hawk agreed before moving on.

"Kid? What do you have for us?"

"I've kept in contact with the detectives investigating the theft. They aren't on payroll so we have to be careful. So far, they have nothing but will keep me updated."

"Ice? You have anything you want to add?"

"I've been talking to Dom Maingarde and he's given us time to figure this shit out. We're fucking lucky it's him and not his bitch of a step-grandmother. He offered his help but I turned him down. We don't want to end up owing them a favour or have some of their dark shit rubbing off on our club."

Meeting his eyes Ice continued.

"I've made it my job to investigate Dom's sister, Pixie. She's your woman's boss. I'm happy to report she's clean. She distanced herself from her family and the Road Warriors chapter in Cape Town keeps an eye on her. She's considered club family."

"Thank fuck." Sin growled. "DC doesn't need their kind of shit in her life. She's got enough going on with that little bitch of a sister of hers."

There were nods of agreement all around.

"Anyone else have anything to report?" Hawk asked glancing around the table.

"I think that's everything,"

Ice rumbled while the others nodded.

"Great. Think about what was said and we'll get together again before church on Friday. Let's get out of here."

He was done and ready to hit the road and get to his woman.

"You going to claim the little bird as your old lady, Boss?" Beast asked with a wide grin.

"Yes. If I ever get a fucking minute to myself." He snarled in frustration.

"We've got things under control, Hawk. Go claim your woman." Kahn grinned and winked when he frowned at him.

"Can't leave yet because Doc might still be there, waiting for a fucking text to give me the all clear." He grumbled.

"Fuck that, Boss. We can leave now if you want." Beast said. "Maybe by the time we get there he's left."

"What do you mean, we?"

There were shaking heads all around.

"Not letting you go alone, Prez. Kid and I will be going with you." Beast said.

He knew arguing wouldn't help, and he wasn't going to. He was the one who'd ordered the brothers not to ride alone until this shit was behind them. He wouldn't go against his own orders.

His phone pinged, his heart jerked in his chest, the coast was clear.

His little bird was alone.

The time had come.

"This meeting is done. Beast, Kid, let's ride."

His brothers were giving him wide grins as they left but he didn't care. Locking the chapel doors, he followed Beast and Kid outside.

Before he got to his bike a heavy arm settled around his shoulders and Bulldog's voice rumbled in his ear.

"Bounty would've been so fucking proud to see the man you've become, son. As am I. Bring your woman over for dinner soon, before your aunt comes looking for your ass."

After a one armed hug his uncle walked back inside.

He stared after him for a few seconds before he joined Beast and Kid.

Throwing his leg over his bike he relaxed into the seat, pulled his bandanna up over his nose and mouth, pulled on and fastened his helmet, then slipped on his dark glasses. He smiled to himself as the big bike rumbled to life beneath him. Riding out the gate with Beast and Kid behind him he laughed softly.

He was so ready for this.

Ready to make her his.

He had a little bird to tame. No, not that, he didn't want to tame her.

He just wanted her to be his.

THIRTEEN

DC

The beeping of the gate alarm disengaging woke me. I heard my dad's bike, but his wasn't the only one pulling up to my front door. I heard at least four others.

I so didn't feel like talking business today, but they were here and there was no way I could avoid them or whatever they were here to discuss.

Pushing myself up from the couch I zombie-walked to the kitchen to turn on the kettle. Not for the men who would soon be taking up the air in my house, but for me. I couldn't do this without a strong cup of coffee. I had already dumped a good amount of ground coffee in the French Press when they trooped in. Doc, Tiny, Grizzly, Skelly, Rover and Shaka.

Shit.

This wasn't good.

I had six of the club's officers standing in my kitchen and none of them were smiling.

"I'm making coffee, anyone want some? There's beer in the fridge if you want." I ignored the unsmiling bastards and played the good host.

Skelly immediately moved to the fridge and started handing out beers.

"Make your coffee then get your ass to the lounge. We have shit to discuss," Doc said as he took the beer Skelly handed him.

Without another word they all walked out, leaving me standing in the kitchen with a million questions flying through my head. Shaking it off I poured a mug of coffee and got my ass to the lounge, as ordered. The men were spread out but they had left one seat open. Right opposite Doc.

Doc started talking as soon as I sat down.

"You grew up in the club. You know bitches are never brought into club business unless it is unavoidable, and then they are only told what they need to know, nothing more. Even as my Crow you don't know everything that goes down at the table and you never will."

I nodded and sipped my coffee. I kept my face blank but inside I was shitting myself. The way he started the conversation wasn't good.

"You gave up your time and dreams for your sister and the club. Don't ever think I don't know or appreciate what you gave up for me and my club. I do, as do every single brother who sits at the table. It was never my intention to turn you dark but because of my decisions that's what happened. But, DC, even if I could turn back the clock and change my decision I wouldn't. My decision made you a strong, self-confident badass who can take care of herself and her family. I know I have never said it but I am so fucking proud of you."

I was stunned and could only nod, but he wasn't done.

"I am proud you had the balls to walk into the Iron Dogz clubhouse and do what you did. Proud you took down the bitch and gave us blood and bone. Proud of who you have become and will always be."

Tiny cleared his throat and I gave him a quick glance before looking back at my dad.

"You are my daughter and a very valuable part of my club. I had expectations of you taking the property patch of one of my brothers. It would have kept you close and safe. At one time I thought it would be Skel but it didn't happen. So, I started looking around to find a brother strong enough to stand beside you. I looked over the men at every single chapter and no one was good enough. And then shit went down and I found a man who might just be strong enough for you."

What the hell? Was he really going to try and give me away as if I was some sort of present?

I opened my mouth to let him have it but he didn't give me a chance.

"I found him but I'm not fucking happy. I'm pissed as hell. I didn't want him for you. I wasn't going to give him a chance until he laid it out for me and my brothers. He wanted to see you with no interference from me or the club and he wanted my assurance we would leave the decision up to you. I very fucking grudgingly gave it to him. The next move is up to you."

I had a tight hold on my temper as I slowly leaned forward. Carefully placing my mug on the Road Warriors MC coaster on my coffee table.

"So, just to be clear. You have been looking for a man for me and now you think you have found him."

He nodded and so did the other men. Fucking assholes. Skelly grinned evilly.

"So, who is this paragon of manhood who has your approval?"

"Hawk Walker."

I had been prepared to shoot down whatever name he was going to give me. Just not this one.

I did not see it coming. Not at all.

He had asked my dad's permission.

Holy shit.

"Dad…"

But Skelly interrupted before I could continue.

"Stop the bullshit, DC. You are sitting there with his mark on your neck and we've all seen the chemistry between the two of you. He's strong enough to take your shit, just as you're strong enough to make him back off when it's needed." He suddenly grinned wide. "And it will be fun watching those clueless Dogz trying to handle you."

The men burst out laughing but I didn't find it funny at all.

"So, if I say yes what happens to the Crow?"

It wasn't my dad who answered but Shaka, the club's security officer. His deep voice rolled through the silence after my question.

"You were born a Road Warrior and will always be a part of our club. We will always have your back, no matter what. Like Doc, I would have preferred a Road Warrior as your old man. But he's right, there aren't any brothers in the Road Warriors MC besides Skel who can give you the position you deserve. No one who can support, take care of, and protect you like Hawk Walker and his club."

His smile flashed white before his face settled back into its usual ebony mask. The word inscrutable had been invented for Shaka.

"If you choose Hawk and become his old lady, I won't lie, there will be repercussions. Before it happens there will be a meeting at National, and they will determine what happens to the Crow."

"National aren't the ones who will decide, Shaka." Grizzly snorted.

"We won't let them take it away from you, not unless it's what you want, squirt." Grizzly said softly. "You have given your youth to this club, to your father and all the brothers. We just celebrated your thirty first birthday, and I'm afraid if you continue down this road you will be forty and still alone. We had hoped you would choose one of the brothers as your man but then you started working as the Crow and it became very important to you. Maybe the dark path of the Crow kept you from settling down, we'll never know. Right now, you are standing at another crossroads, and sweetheart, I want you to take a chance. I want you to take a chance and see where this thing between you and Hawk goes. I love you like you're my very own and I fucking hate to say this, but the man will be good for you and to you. Give him a shot, squirt."

I had not seen this coming, at all. I was hovering between shock and disbelief at the support shown to Hawk Walker by my dad, Grizzly and Skel.

Shaka was an absolute stickler for the rules and his views weren't a surprise at all.

Tiny and Rover were the only ones who hadn't said a word. I sort of knew where Rover stood with the Hawk situation but had no idea as to Tiny's thoughts.

I didn't have long to wait to find out.

"I agree with Grizz, you have done more than enough for the club. It is now our turn to do something for you. For years I have watched as you sank deeper and deeper into the dark. You smile, you laugh, you've taken a few lovers but no one reached your soul. Your eyes have been cold and emotionless for far longer than I've been comfortable with. But not anymore, now there's fire burning behind those beautiful eyes. A fire Hawk Walker put there."

Tiny smiled at me.

"Do this one thing for you and no one else. See where it goes. If it doesn't work out, so what? You will always have us, your family, waiting to pick you up should you fall. No fear, sweetheart. We've got your back."

I was stunned speechless as I looked at the men watching me. Taking a deep breath, I tried to settle the out-of-control thoughts scrolling through my head. I tried to make sense of it for them and for me.

"I didn't expect it or want it. I knew he wanted me, he was pretty damn obvious about it, but I had no idea it was a serious interest. Until he came here last night and explained he was laying claim to me. I've been there before, had men say shit they regretted the next day or week. I shrugged what he said off. Put it aside to think about later."

Skel's laugh pissed me off and I scowled at him before continuing.

"Now you walk into my house and tell me he's serious. I don't think I've ever heard of a president from one club approaching the president of another to ask for permission to claim his daughter. Shit like that just never happens. Relationships between adversaries almost always end in blood."

It was as if the air in the lounge had suddenly been sucked out and into another dimension. That's how suddenly the atmosphere changed.

Doc's body had turned to stone, the same with Grizzly and Tiny.

What the hell?

"What's wrong, Dad?"

There was a long moment of silence before those cold eyes met mine. When he spoke, his voice was cold, hard, and rough, so very rough.

"I never wanted you to know. Maybe I was wrong, maybe you should have been told from the very beginning, I don't know. I wanted to spare you. But it's a part of our history and something you should have been told. What I do know is I can't be the one who tells you. I vowed those names wouldn't cross my lips ever again, not in this lifetime. And it fucking won't. Not fucking ever."

Doc stood and clasped a hand over the back of his neck, staring down at the wooden floor.

Then he looked up and the pain in his eyes nearly gutted me. So much pain, so much suffering it had tears burning in my eyes. He saw my tears and a sad little smile tipped one side of his mouth.

"Take a chance on finding love, sweetheart. Do it for me. Let me know your decision, DC. Soon."

He walked out of my house with Skelly, Rover and Shaka silently following him.

FOURTEEN

DC

What had just happened?

I blinked back the threatening tears and looked at Grizzly and then Tiny. They were both staring at the floor, anger mixed with sorrow on their faces.

"Who the hell hurt my dad? Are they dead? If they aren't I want to know why not. And then I will see to it that they die, slowly, and as painfully as possible."

Grizzly was the one who looked up first and his eyes were no longer filled with sorrow. Rage burned deep inside. I waited as Tiny, with the same look in his eyes started talking. The story he told me broke my heart and at the same time filled me with so much rage and sorrow I didn't know how to deal with it.

Working out or sparring was my usual way of dealing with the things I couldn't talk about. It was how I dealt with feelings when they threatened to overwhelm me.

I couldn't work out or spar. I was still too banged up.

I had to sit there and take it.

I had to allow the tears to leave my eyes and run unchecked down my cheeks while I clenched my teeth trying to keep the sobs from escaping.

It was a lost cause.

Pretty soon my nose was running and I was sniffing and sobbing uncontrollably.

I had no idea why it was hitting me so hard.

Maybe it did because no one had talked about her or said her name my entire life. She was always referred to as 'your mother' if she was mentioned at all.

After one really shitty Mother's Day at nursery school when I was four, Zelda, Stoney's old lady told me my mother had died giving birth to me. She said it made my dad very sad to think about her. This, to my already screwed up young mind, made it my fault. She was never spoken of again by me or anyone else.

I was a very angry little girl and refused to answer to the name my mother had chosen for me.

Jasmine.

I hated it.

The only name I acknowledged was my dad's name for me, Demon Child.

It was around that time I became DC, even at school.

Grizzly left the room and came back with a roll of loo paper, dropping it into my lap. I blew my runny nose, patted my eyes dry and cleared my stuffed-up throat. Picking up my forgotten mug I took a mouthful of cold coffee and swallowed it down, getting rid of the big lump in my throat.

"Have they all been taken care of? There's no one left who could hurt him or our family?" I had to be sure.

"They're all gone, DC. He erased them and their businesses completely. They had no children and the women left behind aren't a threat. You're all that's left of that family. You are the best part of them, the best part of your mother. She loved your dad, loved him so much she defied her family, her religion, and her culture to be with him. She was only 19 when she died, and you were two weeks old."

I looked into the sad eyes of Tiny and Grizzly and knew in my gut there was more.

"Why? Why would they do such a horrible thing to someone they had raised and loved? It just makes no sense. There must have been more to it."

The males in my mother's family had snatched her from the little house where she had been living with my dad. They took her to an open piece of veldt near the Road Warriors compound where they took turns beating her, mutilating her and finally when she was near death her father strangled her. In the name of family honour. What absolute bullshit.

Luckily for me, Liddy, Tiny's old lady, had taken me for a few hours that day to give my mother a chance to rest. It saved my life.

Both Tiny and Grizzly nodded in agreement.

"There was. Your mother's people, the Sharmas, controlled a large part of the drug trade countrywide. They were feared, but not by the Road Warriors. At the time we had our own pipelines in direct competition with theirs. Killing your mother was their first shot in the war to take over our business. After Suleina's body was found your dad, along with a small team of brothers, killed everyone who had a hand in her murder. He killed the head of the Sharma family who gave the initial order. The Road Warriors broke the Sharmas hold on the local drug trade but we didn't move in to take over their territory."

Tiny scrubbed his hands through his short hair, making it stand on end. More than it usually did.

"Your mother wasn't the only one in the club who lost her life. We lost two brothers and four women to those bastards. When it became time to vote on staying or getting out of the drug trade, Lefty, the Prez back then, and his supporters lost. We wanted out, and with the winning vote we took the first steps toward making it a reality. It was the start of Doc's climb up the ranks. Today we live free and clear of that shit thanks to how far your dad was prepared to go for his family and his club."

Tiny sat back and I knew he was done talking. I had so many questions and so much to think about.

"I have a lot of questions but I need some time to work through this. You have my word I won't approach Doc with what you have told me. He has suffered enough. I'll come to you."

I gave them a small smile. And then tried to lighten the atmosphere.

"My dad needs a good woman in his life. Those club whores he screws are nasty, and if we don't watch out we'll end up with another damn Misty on our hands."

They followed my lead in the change of subject.

"Shut your mouth, woman." Tiny growled. "We don't need more shit coming down on our heads."

"Have you heard from her again?" Grizzly asked.

"No, she's gone silent and my informants tell me she left town rather suddenly. I don't know if she's been talking to Deena though. The little shit isn't speaking to me right now."

Tiny shook his head, no sympathy in his face at all.

"You and Doc bought this bullshit. You spoilt her rotten and look how it turned out. She thinks she shits gold and farts moonbeams, and let me tell you, this is only the start. Now she has that dumb fuck of a Dog on the leash along with the two of you. You need to stop covering for her, step back and let Doc get a taste of the shit she has been throwing at you the last year and a half."

"I…what are you talking about?"

Tiny snorted angrily.

"You think I don't keep an eye on the girl, DC? She's been a miserable bitch to you for years and you just take it. You wouldn't take that crap from anyone else, so why do you allow her to treat you the way she does? She threw an almighty fit when you bought your own place, and the only reason you're not still living in Doc's house is Skel. He put his foot down and she backed off. You don't own a dog, cat, canary or even a fucking goldfish because when she's home and Doc takes off, they know you will step up while he does his thing. For years now Doc has dumped his responsibility for the girl in your lap."

He threw out an angry hand when I tried to interrupt.

"Don't say a fucking word. Liddy and I've had enough. This shit ends now. I will be the one to let Doc know your part in raising the little bitch is done. No, no, don't try to argue with me, DC. Liddy and I raised four wild kids, you being one of those kids, so we know how fucking difficult it is. Doc has no fucking clue because everyone did and still does it for him, including you. It's done, sweetheart. No more."

He wasn't talking to me as the VP of the Road Warriors, now he was just my uncle Tiny and surrogate dad.

"You can't tell me what to do, Uncle Tiny. She's my little sister, she needs me."

"Yes, she's your little sister and yes, she needs you to take her back. But sweetheart, you're not her mother or her father, you're her sister. Stop being her mother and be a sister. Just be her sister. Leave the rest to Doc."

I nodded, not really convinced but prepared to give it some thought.

But Tiny wasn't done.

"We've talked about a lot of hard shit today, DC. But I want you to know, no matter what, we will always have your back. I held you in my arms when you were born, watched you grow into an amazing woman. At one time Liddy and I had hopes Skel would give you his patch and you would be our daughter for real. It wasn't to be, but it doesn't mean Liddy and I don't consider you one of our own. You are and will always be ours. Even after the big bastard makes you his."

Tiny's eyes met mine and I had to breathe deeply to keep from crying.

I flung myself at him. Sinking into his big body for the hug I so badly needed.

"Thanks, Uncle Tiny." I whispered.

"Thank you for always taking care of me and for having my back when I wanted to go to Cape Town. For teaching me how to survive in this life. I love you."

"Any time, sweetheart, any time at all," he said softly as he hugged me tight. "Love you too, baby girl."

Grizzly was up and pulled me from Tiny's arms into his.

"We have your back, sweetheart. We'll always have your back,"

He growled against the top of my head.

I was so blessed with the family my dad had given me. Because that's what he had done, he had given me a family.

The Road Warriors family.

FIFTEEN

DC

I sat on my couch long after the sounds of Tiny and Grizzly's bikes had disappeared. My mind was in a whirl but one thought kept on rising however much I pushed it away.

I didn't kill my mother.

However stupid it made me feel, and however much I knew it was bullshit, it's what I have always felt deep down inside. I never talked about it, about how I blamed myself for her death. Now I wished I had someone I could talk to. Someone who would listen to my shit and help me understand why I still felt as if I were to blame.

Even now that I knew the truth.

"Pull yourself together, bitch,"

I admonished myself softly.

"It's club business."

Hearing my own voice had me up off the couch. I wasn't going to sit and wallow about things I couldn't change. And, if I was totally honest with myself, didn't want to change.

Opening the fridge, I took out the big tub of yogurt, found a long-handled spoon and leaning against the granite topped island ate straight from the tub. After about four loaded spoons I realised it didn't taste like anything. So, back in the fridge it went.

I needed music and wine.

I selected my relaxed playlist, pulled a bottle of wine out of the wine rack, and speedily removed the cork. Filling the big balloon shaped glass almost to the rim I grabbed the bottle, walked out onto the deck and sank down in my favourite lounger.

Sipping my wine and listening to some of my favourite bands I watched as the sky slowly changed colour from bright blue to shades of orange and pink as the sun disappeared.

The sound of bikes intruded over the music. I didn't stir. I didn't care who was at the gate. They could come back another day.

The bikes didn't go away. They pulled inside and soon after loud crunching footsteps came towards the deck.

Fuck.

I slowly turned my head and frowned as three men came around the side of my house.

Not who I expected to see at all.

My biggest temptation walked up the steps and onto the deck, and still, I didn't say a word.

I just watched as Hawk followed by Kid and Beast walked over. Kid and Beast gave me chin lifts as greetings along with knowing grins as they sat down.

Hawk, of course, did not take a chair, it would have been too easy. He made himself comfortable at the bottom of my lounger, lifting my feet onto his lap.

"Hey, baby."

He reached over, took my wine out of my hand, and drank.

I sighed and shook my head.

"Hey yourself, and give me back my wine, there's beer in the fridge and a chair right over there."

I pointed to one next to me.

Hawk frowned as he looked at me then did the chin lift thing at Beast who got up and walked into my house.

"What's wrong, little bird?" Those amber-yellow eyes were narrowed on my face.

I wasn't going to unload my damned shit in front of an audience so I just shook my head.

"I'm fine." I gave the age-old cop out of women all over the world.

I'm fine, the world's fine, everything is fine.

Fine, fine, fine.

Not even close.

Hawk tipped his head to the side and gave a little nod as he accepted the beer from Beast. I waited until he had the cap off and had taken his first long swallow before I spoke.

"Why are you here?" I took a huge glug of wine hiding my face in my glass.

That's when he grinned, really, really wide.

"I had a meeting with Doc today."

"Yes, I know, he told me and he left it up to me to decide. I haven't made a decision yet so you might as well leave." I replied snarkily.

He gave me an evil grin. Bastard.

"Baby, there's no decision to be made. We are who we are, and we do what we do, no regrets, and no recriminations. We are perfect for each other. No other man will ever be able to give you what I can."

I sighed; this wasn't going the way I thought it would.

"And what is it you can give me that no other can?"

His teeth flashed through his beard as he grinned.

"I am the only one who can give you the freedom to continue to be the Crow even after I claim you as mine. Believe me, no one else can give it to you, only I can."

My breath stuttered and my hand instinctively clenched around the stem of my glass.

But he wasn't finished.

As he continued, he glued the broken pieces of my soul back together.

One tiny piece at a time.

"I am the only one who understands your needs, the only one who gets turned on by the ruthless bitch living inside you. And, my little bird, I'm the only one who sees the soft and the dark and want to hold on to both. I was made for you just as you were made for me.

We had to go through the shit in our pasts to get here, to be able to understand what it is we have in each other."

He laid it out for me, not giving a shit his men were listening to every word.

Taking my hand, he removed the glass and pulled me up and led me into the house, through the kitchen and down the passage to my bedroom. I didn't say one word to stop him. I allowed him to lead me.

The door closed with a quiet click and he pulled me into his arms.

"There's dark pain in your eyes, baby. What the fuck happened today?" His voice was deep and rough as he sat on the side of my bed and settled me in his lap.

I sighed and relaxed into his hard, wide chest. God, he felt so good, his arms around me so big and strong. I felt safe, protected, and for once taken care of. Maybe this was what I needed, a safe place of my own. Taking a deep breath, I let it all out.

"Today was a good day but it was a bad day as well. My dad told me if he could pick a man for me, it would be you. He wants me safe and he considers you to be the only one besides Skelly who is worthy. He asked me to consider taking you as my old man. That was the good part."

I had to take a deep breath before I could continue.

"The bad part was finding out how my mother really died. As a little girl I was told she died giving birth to me. I always felt guilty about causing her death. About causing the sorrow my dad lives with every single day. After years of lying to me, I was told the truth today. Her family murdered her because she fell in love with their white enemy and had his child. If any of those bastards were alive today, I would have made it my mission to kill them all." My voice trembled.

Hawk's arms tightened around me, pulling me hard against his chest.

"Fuck, baby. I thought you knew. Ziggy brought it to me and we dug around to see if any of those fuckers were still alive because I wanted to end them for you. They're all gone, little bird. There are other branches of the Sharma family still operating, but they distanced themselves from the family when it all went down." He said with his mouth against my hair.

There was a burning in my throat and eyes and then the tears I had held back overflowed and I sobbed against his wide chest.

Feeling safe, feeling protected and as his hands smoothed over my hair and back, I felt like I had at last found my home. I moved, closed my eyes, and wrapped my arms around his waist, holding on.

Holding on to my rock, my protector, and I hoped this was one man who would take special care with my heart.

It was something only time would tell.

Right now, this was enough.

Hawk

His fucking heart was breaking as he held his sobbing little bird in his arms. All he could do was give her the comfort of his arms and big body as she crawled into him. He soothed her by gliding his hands over her hair and down her back. Willing his stupid dick to behave he lay down on the bed and just held her. Listening as her sobs became soft sighs and eventually turned into even breaths as she fell asleep. He held her a little longer, making sure she was sleeping deeply before he moved.

Sliding out from under her he went back to the deck where Kid and Beast were waiting for him.

"She okay?" Kid asked as Hawk walked out the house.

"No, brother, she's not. They never fucking told her how her mother died, she found out today. It wrecked her. I'm not leaving her tonight. I was going to tell her about the shit between Snake and Doc, but now's not the right time."

His brothers nodded and were about to talk but he lifted a hand to silence them. He needed them to be aware of the shit he felt was going to come at them soon. Hawk had a bad feeling, a very fucking bad feeling about Jane and Big Ed and what it meant for his little bird.

"I have a bad feeling, brothers. I don't want her alone, ever. She's going to be a target for Big Ed the minute they hear she's mine. Jane hates her because my woman kicked her ass but also because of my shit. I want her protected twenty-four-seven and it's not because I think she can't protect herself. She's fucking lethal but they won't come at her when she's ready for them, the fuckers will sneak up on her. Her security is tight but I want it even tighter. Her gate is a weak spot, we need to fix it. She's got cameras, perimeter walls with electric fencing on the top and a damn good alarm but it's not enough. I want as much of the electronics as possible off the power grid. I want firewalls that make her shit unhackable and I want the same at her shop. I'm going to talk to her about us getting two guard dogs. Jagger can arrange for us to go through the training. She has to be as safe as I can possibly make her. I can't fucking lose her."

He continued on before his men could interrupt.

"Call two of the brothers to take over from the two of you. Set them up at the front and the back of the house. The only prospects I'll clear for this job is Sam and Terror, they've both proved themselves. I'll arrange shit with Doc tomorrow, get more men on the job and make it clear my woman is to be kept safe at all costs."

"I hope like fuck you're not sending me away because the crazy fucking slut happens to share my blood, Hawk." Kid growled.

Hawk immediately shook his head. "No, brother, that's not the reason. I trust you with my life and now with hers. I need both of you back at the compound and following up with Ziggy. We need to get ahead of this shit and fast."

"We're not leaving until the brothers get here, brother. Don't care what you say. I won't budge on that." Beast threw in.

"I'm cool with it. It makes it easier for me to concentrate on getting my woman through this shit tonight." Hawk agreed.

"You're a fucking lucky bastard. She's exactly the kind of woman you need. Still not sure how you lucked out on this one because she sure as shit did not like you when you first met. Those black eyes of hers were shooting fucking fire when you tried to get her into the pussy house. Not sure if she's forgiven you for it yet," Kid said with a wide grin.

The fucking bastard was enjoying Hawk's discomfort too much.

"My little bird is unlike any other bitch I've ever known. She will never be easy but she will be mine in every way that counts. She is the perfect woman for me and was always meant to be mine."

Hawk left them sitting on the deck and went back to the bedroom. He had to take care of his woman.

His woman.

His and only his.

His to protect. His to love.

It shocked the shit out of him but it was what it was.

He was falling for her, fast.

No, that wasn't right. He was there already.

Fallen. In fucking love.

Hers.

SIXTEEN

Hawk

Standing beside the bed watching his woman sleep, her eyes swollen from crying, Hawk silently swore to never be the cause of her tears. He would rather shoot himself in the junk than make her cry.

He couldn't promise not to piss her off or even disappoint her, he knew himself. He wasn't a fucking angel. He was going to fuck up, it went without saying, but what he could promise was that he would love her like no other could. Along with his love came a promise that he would always be faithful. He knew some of the brothers with old ladies fucked club whores, and it was their business, not his. He wouldn't be doing it.

Not fucking ever.

Having her in his bed would be enough.

Bending over the bed he carefully removed her clothes, leaving her in her panties. Fuck, she was beautiful. Lifting her up he pulled the duvet down and slid her into bed then pulled it up over her shoulder. She slept through him undressing her and moving her around, proof of how hard today had hit her.

Stepping away from the bed he undressed and walked naked into the bathroom for a quick shower. He might have been naked but his firearm went with him. It sat on a very handy shelf right outside the shower. It made him smile and shake his head. Drying off he wrapped the towel around his hips, picked up his weapon and walked back into the bedroom. His little bird was still sleeping and he drew the curtains plunging the room into darkness.

Setting his gun on the bedside table with his wallet and cell phone he lifted the covers and slid in next to her. Lying back against the pillows he pulled his woman into his arms and settled her head on his chest. She gave a little sigh as she settled into him, her hand resting over his heart.

Hawk pressed a kiss to her hair and closed his eyes.

He fell asleep with her scent in his lungs, in his head, and in his blood.

DC

I woke slowly and for a moment I lay there, confused, trying to work out where the hell I was.

Then it all came rushing back.

I slowly lifted my head to look at the man lying on his back in my bed, my chest on top of his, his arms around me and our legs entangled.

His hair was loose and wild around his head, his beard ruffled, he looked peaceful, and way too freaking beautiful.

Staring down at the sleeping giant I suddenly, and jealously, wondered how many women had seen him looking like this. The totally icky thought was enough to have me sliding out of bed pretty damn quick. Picking up his t-shirt I pulled it over my head, breathing in his clean male scent as I made a quick stop in the bathroom before heading to the kitchen.

I needed coffee.

I was standing sipping my coffee and staring out at my back garden when I felt him. His heat hit my back before his arms came around me, pulling me back against his warm, hard chest. I smiled as he moved my hair away from my neck with his bearded chin and nuzzled into me, laying little kisses against my neck. His beard tickled and I shivered deliciously. He made a growly sound along with the little kisses.

I turned my head towards him as he lifted his head. His voice was sleep rough and deep.

"Morning, my little bird. Woke up and found you gone."

Before I could answer he turned me and I slid my hands and my eyes up over his naked skin, stroking his beautiful abs and pecs, drawing my hands up over his shoulders and down to his huge biceps. The man was heavily muscled but not like those steroid swallowing gym rats, his muscles came from the life he lived and from working out with his brothers.

His club tattoo was on the right side of his chest, his arms covered by tattooed sleeves that crept over onto his hands. On his ribs on the left side of his chest were initials and dates and I knew without asking they were in remembrance of his parents and his child.

The skin over his heart was untouched and called to my tattooist heart.

With his partly buttoned jeans hanging low on his hips, it exposed some of the good stuff that made up Hawk Walker. Especially the golden happy trail leading down into his pants.

I looked up into his amazing amber-yellow eyes and smiled at his sleep rumpled hair and beard.

My very, very sexy man.

"Morning. Would you like some coffee?"

"Please, babe."

He bent and ran his lips over my forehead then let me go, obviously so I could get him his coffee. I didn't mind getting it for him, it was my pleasure. It wasn't something I have ever done for the men who came before him.

Strange. But it felt right.

When I handed him his mug he took my hand, leading me out through the slider onto the deck. Sitting down he pulled me into his lap. I relaxed back against him, watching the wind moving through the trees and enjoying the peace of my wild garden. The wild greenery almost completely hid my studio at the far end of the property.

"Your garden is crazy, baby. It looks like you threw some plants out there and let them take over and do as they please. It's fucking beautiful. What is the building being swallowed by all this crazy?"

I gave a pleased grin.

"I know it looks crazy but it's carefully planted to look like this. Zelda did it as a housewarming gift and she still comes out and takes care of it for me. I can sit here and watch the seasons change and there is always something beautiful even in the middle of winter. It's not swallowing the building, just covering it, and it's my studio. It's where I paint when I have the time."

"I like your garden. We'll have her come out to the house and do the garden there as well. Why didn't I know you painted? Why is it a secret?"

"I like that you like my garden and my painting isn't really a secret it's just mine, you know? Something I do for me."

I turned and grinned at him.

"You actually own one of my paintings. The one in your office is one of mine."

His body jerked and he held me away from his body so he could see my face.

"I fucking love that painting, which is why it's in my office. I tried to buy more of DJM's work but found nothing available. Why is that? You're an incredible artist, baby. Why do all this other shit when all you should do is paint?" He asked with a confused look on his face.

I shook my head and smiled. "Life happened, my family, my club. I compromised, became a tattoo artist and I paint when I have free time. I haven't sold any of my work for quite a few years now, which is why you couldn't find any of my paintings."

Pulling me back against his chest he rested his chin on my head as he spoke.

"We'll sort it out as soon as we've got things back to normal around here. I'm going to build you a studio and hang your work all over our house. We need to arrange for Zelda to come out to the house to give us some ideas regarding the garden. We'll just have to train the dogs not to wreck it."

I shifted so I could see his face. He talked about his house as if it were ours, the garden and dogs ours as well. I wasn't going to touch the house or studio thing right now.

"You have dogs? How do you keep them happy when you have to be gone so much?"

He smiled and rubbed his nose over my cheek and my stupid nether regions fluttered.

"No, babe, I don't. It's something I need to talk to you about and now is as good a time as any. I want us to get two trained guard dogs. Dogs trained to listen only to us. And before you say no, baby, we have fuckloads of enemies. I'm very aware you can take care of yourself and that you have good security here and at the shop. I just want to add another layer of protection, an extra layer that would give me peace of mind when I'm not with you. The dogs will be an early warning system plus they will attack any bastard that comes onto our properties."

He stopped talking, eyes narrowed as if he thought I would fight him on it. He had no idea. I have always wanted a dog but with my work schedule I felt bad about leaving a little puppy alone at home.

A fully grown dog though?

Now that was totally doable.

"When can we go get them? How long does training take? Will they live here with me or with you?"

His head tipped back as he laughed and I held my breath at the beauty of the man. He sat on my deck with his faded well-worn jeans half-way buttoned exposing his golden happy trail, his hair a loose wild mess and his beard sleep rough. His laughter chased the harshness from his face and eyes, deepening the lines made by the sun and laughter around his eyes. He was unbelievably beautiful. I was a seriously lucky bitch to be the owner of the beauty.

"I'll talk to Jagger, baby. He's arranging it for the club but we'll get first choice. The dogs are young but fully grown. I'll get him to send us some photos. When we get them, they will be wherever we are."

I bounced excitedly, grinned then planted a smacking kiss on his mouth.

"I've always wanted a dog. I can't wait. Thank you, baby." I whispered against his cheek, smiling as he tightened his arms.

"Before we get to the good stuff, there's something I have to tell you. It's not good but together we can handle it."

BURNING BRIGHT IN THE BLACK

He tilted my head back until he could look me in the eyes and didn't give me time to consider his words before he laid it out.

"Snake and Big Ed approached your dad a few years ago to arrange a marriage between you and the asshole. Doc told them to fuck off. They were not pleased. Now you are mine and they are going to hear about it. It's going to piss them off. There's shit going on between Jane and Big Ed. I want you to be extra careful, little bird. Those fuckers are crazy, and we don't want them getting their filthy hands on you."

As he spoke my face scrunched up in disgust.

"*Sies!* (Yuck!) He's disgusting, Jane's welcome to him. Why didn't my dad tell me? No, wait don't tell me…it was club business. Okay, consider me informed. Now, when are we getting to the good part of the morning?"

With a deep growl Hawk swooped down and dragged his beard over the sensitive skin on my neck. I was suddenly up in the air, clasped against his naked chest as he strode into the house, down the passage and into the bedroom.

He threw me at the bed.

Threw. Me.

I flew, bounced, and was still laughing wildly when he was on me.

My laughter ended when his mouth slammed down on mine. His lips hard, but a good kind of hard. His tongue sliding deep and dominating my mouth, taking me over, sending me spiralling into searing lust. My hands were clasped around those huge biceps, my legs tight around his thighs as he ground his cock against me. He had his hands in my hair, keeping my head where he wanted it as he kissed me.

Sliding my hands up and over his shoulders then down to skim over his abs I headed unerringly for his partly buttoned jeans, undoing those few buttons and setting his magnificent cock free. Shoving his jeans down his legs with my feet I surrounded the bounty with both my hands and slowly slid them up and down his rock-hard erection. He reared back suddenly and my hands lost him as he ripped the t-shirt up and over my head, leaving my boobs bouncing with the violence of the act. He snatched my panties down to my knees, lifting my legs up and to the side, resting them against his shoulder as he pulled them all the way off and tossed them over his shoulder. Opening my legs wide he settled them around his waist and stared down at my totally exposed and very wet pussy.

"Condom, baby."

His voice was so rough it was barely recognisable and his facial muscles were tight, giving him an almost feral look.

All I could do was point at the drawer in the bedside table, and that elicited a whole other growl, a slightly pissed off growl.

It confused me for about a second before I forgot all about it as he lowered himself over me and reached into the drawer. I rubbed myself against him, groaning as his beautiful cock slid through my wet pussy and his piercing bumped against my clit. It was my first pierced cock and it felt absolutely amazing sliding over my clit.

I couldn't wait to find out what it would do to me on the inside.

He reared back and I watched avidly as he rolled the condom on. Thank the Pope I still had condoms.

I licked my kiss-swollen lips, my eyes fixed on his hands around his cock.

His large, pierced cock.

"You're going to have to take it slow with that big cock of yours, babe. I haven't done this in quite a while." I said softly.

He growled at me before telling me exactly how it was going to be.

"Don't want to fucking hear about you with anyone else. As of this minute our pasts no longer exist for either of us. I promise I will take care of you. I'm big, I know, and you are so fucking tiny. Not going to hurt you, ever. Trust me, baby."

He came over me, kissing me, so deep, so consuming it set my mind soaring. Rough fingers were playing with my clit, rubbing, circling, dipping down to gather moisture then up again and rubbing, rubbing, rubbing. I writhed underneath him, lifting my hips, begging him wordlessly to take me but he didn't, he played with me until I felt I was going to burst into flames.

Sliding one finger inside, getting it wet as he slid it in and out. I was panting when he added another, scissoring them, stretching me, still slowly sliding in and out. And then he added a third, it felt so very, very good, I didn't care about the pinch of pain.

I just wanted him in me. Now.

Throughout he kissed me, nipped at my lips, slid his tongue over mine, and breathed me in. Dipping down he licked and sucked on my neck before going lower to take my nipple in his mouth. He sucked hard, going from one to the other.

And all the while his fingers played, stretching me.

Suddenly his fingers were gone and I felt him at my entrance, so big, so intimidatingly big. I tensed, but I needn't have worried. He had prepared me so well I was soaked for him as he slowly started pushing inside. I couldn't take all of him in one thrust.

He groaned against my mouth, it joined with my moan as he carefully slid out and back in, just the head of him inside me.

"My little bird has such a tight little pussy, and it's so wet and ready for me. Hold on to me, baby. You're going to take all of me now."

His eyes held onto mine as he slowly and insistently pushed deeper. I gasped feeling my eyes go wide as he kept on pushing, stretching me, sliding inside. So deep inside it felt as if he had reached a place no one else had ever been before. Groaning deep and long he slid all the way in, his pubic bone flush against my clit.

"You're so big and so deep. Please, please keep still, just for a minute while I get used to this. Having you inside me feels incredible."

I moaned against his lips as he lifted his head.

He looked down at me, his eyes burning amber-yellow and his eyelids half-mast with lust.

"Anything you want, little bird, but I'm struggling here. You feel so fucking good I want to slam into to you over and over until we both explode. But I won't, I won't hurt you. Tell me when you're ready." He growled.

I smiled and lifted my hips, testing, and he groaned.

All I felt was pleasure, so much pleasure.

"Move, baby." I whispered.

It was like setting a wild animal free. He braced his forearms on either side of me. Looking down at me with his hair falling down over his face he gave me a feral grin. His gorgeous lips curved as he grinned, making my heart race and my pussy clamp down around him.

"Brace, little bird." He whispered.

His slowly withdrew then slammed back inside, stretching me, reaching so deep, his piercing touching and sliding over something and sending shock waves through me. Shock waves of the deepest pleasure I had ever felt. My hips lifted to aid him but he was moving so fast I lost the rhythm and gave up trying to match his. I used the strength in my abdominals to raise and lower my hips, and tightened and released the muscles inside my pussy as he slammed into me over and over.

It felt incredible.

Rough and hard, but so very good.

I felt it approaching, gathering in my toes, my fingertips and running through my body to where his cock was laying waste to me.

And then it was on me, arching my back as every muscle in my body clenched and I screamed.

I fucking screamed. I never screamed.

My arms and legs snapped tight around him trying to keep his cock from leaving me but he was too strong. He plunged into my spasming pussy over and over, prolonging my orgasm, making me writhe, moan and scream in pleasure. I felt the muscles in his back ripple under my hands as he slammed his entire length in me, keeping himself deep inside as he climaxed. I watched my beautiful man as his muscles bunched and the tendons in his neck became hard and pronounced. His lips were drawn back, his teeth gritted as a groan of pleasure rumbled deep in his chest. Throughout his climax his intent and narrowed amber-yellow hawk's eyes stayed on me.

He looked as if he was dying, but it was a welcomed death. A pleasurable death. As his muscles and tendons gradually relaxed, he gave me a slow smile.

A knowing smile, a conquerors smile.

He had wrecked me.

He had taken me over.

He destroyed me. Only to remake me.

Then he gave me life.

A new life with us at its centre.

I lay under him and felt him still pulsing deep inside. My poor pussy was full, so very full. He moved slightly and I groaned at the small aftershocks still rippling through me.

His hands moved to either side of my head, holding me still, his head dipping down until our noses touched.

"You are mine now, little bird. This body, this pussy belongs to me."

I frowned at him.

"You can't claim me just because we've had sex."

He didn't even hesitate before laying it out for me.

"That wasn't just sex, baby. This was me claiming you, making you mine and mine alone."

Kissing my nose, he slowly started pulling out. I moaned and flinched at the same time.

He grinned, the damned bastard.

"You feeling a bit tender, baby? I like that. You will feel me all day and know you are mine."

"You are such a caveman," I griped, but deep inside I was smiling.

"Yes, I am, but I'm your caveman, little bird. Always yours."

He slowly pulled out, making me shudder, then moved off me and the bed, sauntering his gorgeous ass into the bathroom to get rid of the condom. I listened as he flushed, washed his hands and started the shower.

Was he going to shower without me?

"Get your beautiful ass in here, DC. We need to shower and get out of here or I'll be tempted to spend the rest of the day in bed fucking you breathless and that's not going to happen."

He sounded pleased.

"You're too sore to take me again right now and I don't want you to hurt more than you already do."

I grinned as I slid out of bed but immediately grimaced as my poor pussy complained bitterly. *Ja* (Yes), I was definitely going to feel him all day.

But it wasn't a bad thing. It was the best thing.

SEVENTEEN

DC

My great sex afterglow was disappearing, fast. And all because of a freaking overprotective, dominant biker. I stared at him; my arms crossed over my boobs as he ranted.

Yes, ranted

My shit-hot biker man ranted.

"You will not ride your fucking bike today or any day until I tell you it's safe to ride. Use your head, DC. You're vulnerable on your bike. You will be in your cage until the shit with the ED's is resolved. You will have either a brother or a prospect in the cage with you."

He kept on angrily laying down the law according to Hawk.

"You do not go off alone. You do not go out unarmed. You do not go anywhere without your phone. You text me throughout the day letting me know where you are. You text if anything seems even a tiny bit off."

He growled when I rolled my eyes at him.

"Stop rolling your eyes at me, baby. I'm fucking serious. I cannot lose you, so I need you to keep yourself safe for me. Promise me. Promise me you'll do as I ask."

I sniffed angrily. "But you're not asking, you're telling."

His face suddenly lost its pissed off look and softened.

"I'm telling and asking, baby. Do this for me and I will fuck you so good tonight you will have to take a day off work to recover." He winked, giving me a sly smile.

My traitor of a pussy quivered, it really and truly quivered. It was acting like damn biker slut.

"Fine. I'll do it, but I don't like being managed."

"Not managing you, DC. I'm just trying to keep you safe."

And that is why I arrived at work with an Iron Dogz prospect sitting next to me. My temper wasn't at its best and it didn't become any better when I saw the security around my shop. There were Road Warriors and Iron Dogz very obviously hanging out, inside and outside the shop.

Doc and Hawk were going freaking overboard. Surely the bitch and the ED's weren't crazy enough to come at me in broad daylight with the obvious protection I had around me. But, then again, they were crazy. So, who knew what they would do.

I worked through my morning appointments without any problems.

It was in the late afternoon that my day turned into a total freaking disaster. And the reason for the disaster was a bitch who, for some unknown reason, had been allowed to storm into my shop. Wrecking my awesome post sex glow and my day.

Lizzy Hamilton.

What the hell?

She stormed right past Trina at the front desk and right up to my station. Thankfully, my last client had left and I was busy cleaning. Clenching my teeth tightly, I silently swore. She was pale and obviously frightened, but she was angry and very determined at the same time.

"What can I do for you, Ms Hamilton?" Staying calm wasn't easy but I succeeded.

"You give him back to me. You have to." She bit out through gross spit covered wet lips.

"I don't understand. Who do I have to give back to you?" I played stupid, wanting to see where the hell this was coming from.

"We were happy. I did everything he wanted me to, even sharing him with those whores when it made my heart ache. I knew if I had a baby he would be mine, he would marry me and be mine. I was trying so very hard to give him one. Then you came and ruined it all. You took him away from me. But I'm going to fix it. I know when he finds out I'm going to be pregnant he will be mine for ever and ever."

"Are you out of your mind?" I snarled. "Since when is trapping a man using an innocent child a good plan? You do realise people no longer get married because of an accidental pregnancy, don't you? He won't marry you; he'll give the kid his name and take care of the two of you but there will be no marriage."

She shook her head wildly while I spoke.

"Stop! Stop saying that! He will marry me. He will!" she screamed angrily.

With my hands fisted on my hips I stared at the wreck of a woman who used to be the cool and calm Lizzy Hamilton. What the hell had happened to her?

"Are you trying to tell me you're pregnant, Lizzy? Is that what this is?"

She started shaking her head violently from side to side.

"No, no I'm not and it's your fault. We had a plan; a good plan and you ruined it. He was supposed to be with me, not you," she whispered. "He was supposed to be mine."

I slanted a quick glance at Sam, an Iron Dogz prospect. He was slowly making his way towards her. I looked back at her. Looking in her eyes. I suddenly realised she was on something. She was as high as a damned kite. And crazy as a freaking loon.

Holy crap.

Hawk Walker had truly shitty taste in the women he chose to fuck.

Excluding me of course.

The thought pushed me over the edge. Suddenly I've had enough. Actually, I've had more than enough of his damned whores stomping roughshod over my life. I had no idea if my words would sink in but I was going to give them to her anyway.

Whether she heard them or not.

"Grow the fuck up, Lizzy. You're no longer in effing high school and at the top of the freaking food chain. You've been used and put aside, accept it, and move on. It's not as if it comes as a huge damned surprise, bitch. Everyone, including you, knew he was only temporarily yours. Knew that he would eventually move on to someone new. Stop acting like a whiny bitch, grow the hell up and get out of my shop before I completely lose it and put a bullet in your stupid head," I snarled angrily.

A deep angry growl came from behind me and I glanced around. A very pissed off Hawk stood in the passage leading from the back of the shop. His pissed off eyes were on me. The bastard was pissed alright, and he was pissed at me.

What the hell?

"Liz, what are you doing here, sweetheart?"

His voice was so damned soft and caring, my back snapped straight when she burst into tears and flung herself at him. I watched as he closed his arms around her, holding her tight against him, soothingly rubbing her back and whispering softly in her ear.

What the hell?

Oh, no. Oh fuck no.

This was not freaking happening.

He did not just take her side in my own damned shop. In my territory. In front of my people. Not taking that shit from anyone, least of all him.

The Crow rose instantly, and I let her out.

"Get your ass out of my shop." I hissed, reaching for the gun I had stashed in my cabinet.

"Every single Dog needs to vacate my premises right the fuck now or I will start taking out the trash."

Hawk raised his head slowly and just looked at me as I pointed my gun at his head.

"Get the hell out and if I see a Dog anywhere near Warrior territory, they will be made an example of. And that's a promise you can take to the bank, asshole."

He said nothing, just moved Lizzy to his side then slowly led her out the front of my shop. I kept my gun up, watching until every single Dog was out, getting on their bikes and pulling out into the road.

There were only two men left in the shop, both Road Warrior prospects and part of my family. It seemed like the Dogz had been trusted to watch over me. The Warriors had only sent two freaking prospects. Luckily, they were like little brothers to me and would follow orders without question.

Crow moved away until she was a slight presence at the back of my mind.

"Gav, check the back and make sure the security doors are locked and no one else can get in." I snarled.

He nodded, anger burning in his eyes as he made his way to the back of the shop and the backdoor.

"Law, close the door, lock it and keep your eyes peeled out the front, we don't need any more surprises right now."

Laying my gun down I picked up my phone and called Skel. He immediately started talking, not waiting for me to say a word.

"What the fuck is going on there, DC? I'm getting conflicting reports."

"One of his bitches, Lizzy Hamilton, came into the shop and started freaking out. I told her some home truths. Told her to get the fuck out before I helped her leave. The bastard came in through the back, took her in his arms and took her side against me. I ordered all the Dogz out of my shop at gunpoint. I need more protection in case they or the damned ED's return."

There was a long silence and then Skel sighed.

"Grizz, Shaka and I are on our way with more brothers, close the shop and sit tight. We'll be there soon."

Setting the phone down I moved to the front of the shop and changed the sign from open to closed while Law watched the street. I quickly checked the appointments and heaved a sigh of relief when I saw we were basically done for the day.

I returned to the back of the shop where Killian, Grace, Nadja, Alex and Trina stood looking shell shocked.

"What just happened, DC?" Grace asked softly.

"What always happens, Grace. What always happens." I answered just as softly.

"I need a fucking drink." Killian snapped.

BURNING BRIGHT IN THE BLACK

Going into the office he came back with the bottle of Patròn one of my very pleased customers had given me as a gift.

"Let's get away from the windows, everyone except Gav and Law, into the office." I ordered.

As I sank into my chair Killian held the opened bottle out towards me. I took it and threw back a healthy slug. Shivering as the top shelf tequila burned its way down my throat and into my belly. We passed the bottle around and pretty soon I had a bit of a buzz going on. Drinking on an almost empty stomach will do that to you.

We kept passing the bottle around until we heard the growl of a lot of bikes coming down the road.

"Skel and the boys are here!" Law shouted. I heard the locks as he unlocked the front door.

Rubbing my hands over my face I pushed up out of my chair and swayed ever so slightly. I had more than a bit of a buzz going on.

Nice.

Skel, Grizz and Shaka walked into my office and everyone sidled out, closing the door behind them. Leaving the almost empty bottle sitting on my desk.

"What the fuck happened here?" Grizz asked.

"Lizzy Hamilton happened. Came into the shop high as a fucking kite telling me to give him back to her. Apparently, they had plans to get pregnant. She went on and on and on and I lost my temper. Told her to stop being a whiny bitch, grow the fuck up and get out of my shop before I put a bullet in her. Hawk came in the back. Took her side and I threw them all out. I might have pointed my gun at his head." I explained with a shrug.

"You sure he took her side?" Shaka asked quietly.

Really?

And just like that my buzz was suddenly gone and I was stone cold sober.

"I'm not a stupid bitch, Shaka. He took her in his arms, held her, walked her out of here, put her on the back of his bike. On the back of his fucking bike. What do you think that means?" I snarled coldly.

"I knew this shit was going to end up in a clusterfuck." Shaka growled as he started pacing around my office. "Doc wants you at the clubhouse. Let's go."

I followed them out of the shop, locked up and passed Gav my beast's keys, then climbed in on the passenger side. I had my gun next to me on the seat, ready for anything.

Nothing happened.

The minute we drove through the tall solid steel gates into the compound and they slid closed behind us I knew I was home and safe. Doc stood waiting on the wide steps leading up to the steel reinforced double doors behind him. The windowless red brick building glowed deep red in the late afternoon sun. As we pulled up next to the steps the Road Warriors MC insignia above the doors welcomed me home. He walked down the steps as I got out and then I was in his arms and he was hugging me tight.

I relaxed into him with a sigh.

"So fucking sorry, baby girl." He whispered against my hair. "Let's go inside and see what we can do about this fucking disaster."

I didn't say anything because there wasn't anything to say. I let him lead me inside and frowned when instead of his office we went towards the chapel where they held church.

I have never been invited inside.

"Phone, babe." Skel said and I pulled it from my back pocket and dropped it in the basket Law was holding before following my dad into the room.

I wasn't a stranger to the room. I had sneaked in here more than once as a little girl and again a time or two as a grown girl. The photos and memorabilia on the walls documented the club's history, my family's history. I sat in a chair against the wall on Doc's right and waited as only the officers of the club filed into the room, most of them not surprised to see me there at all.

When the chapel doors were closed and locked Doc raised the gavel, smacked it down and the buzz ceased, immediately.

"We have a situation which is why DC is here." He said quietly, so very unlike my dad. He was almost always loud. "At the meeting we had this morning I told you the Iron Dogz MC President, Hawk Walker, asked my permission to claim DC. I gave it to him, but I made it very clear, if he fucked with my girl I would in turn fuck with him and his club."

There was an intense silence as he looked around the room. His eyes met mine and they were burning with icy rage.

"Today, a fucking day later, he fucked with my girl. This is not a meeting at which we are going to make a decision on how to respond to the insult, it's a meeting to let everyone know what has gone down. Our girl has now been disrespected by two of his whores and, even though she took care of one of those bitches, we cannot let this insult to her or our club stand. By disrespecting her they are disrespecting my blood and my club. Unfortunately, we can't settle this tonight or even tomorrow, but we will meet again when I get back. When we do I want to hear from you, get your take on this fucking mess."

Doc was about to bring the gavel down when there was a rustle of movement and a single tap of heavy rings on the table. Doc set the gavel aside and nodded at Alien who had tapped.

"I want to hear from DC before we close this meeting." Alien sat forward in his chair, his heavily tattooed forearms on the table. Large hands with big silver rings on almost all his fingers clasped together.

I took a deep breath, nodding in agreement when my dad raised an eyebrow in question.

"Did he claim you as his woman?" Alien asked softly.

Lord, this was so damn humiliating.

"Yes, he did."

There were frowns and nods all around as Alien continued.

"What happened at the shop? What did he say?"

"Lizzy Hamilton, one of his whores, came into my shop. Told me they were planning on getting pregnant. I called her out on it. Called her a whiny bitch and to get out of my shop before I put a bullet in her. He came in, took her in his arms, whispered some shit in her ear and walked her out. Put her on the back of his bike and left. Didn't say one word. You can watch it all once Skel pulls it off the cameras at the shop." My voice was soft but filled with ice.

"Could it be he was doing it to fool those who've been watching you?" Alien kept on pushing.

I shrugged. "Don't know and don't care."

"DC, Alien might have a point here. He could be playing those bastards to keep you off their radar." Skel added his voice to the discussion.

Men, always taking a brother's back.

Stupid. So stupid.

"If it was his play, he should have given me a heads up. I'm not some stupid little bitch with no idea how this life works. I was born into this life, have seen more than my fair share of shit go down. Have seen blood flow, and even spilled some of it. I know how to freaking handle myself." I shook my head. "Plus, it's too late to try and protect me. I'm on their radar and nothing is going to change that. At least not until we kill the bastards."

The men burst out laughing.

Doc shook his head while smiling with obvious pride.

"Okay, we'll pick this up when I get back. Think on it, and when we meet again I'll hear your thoughts. In the meantime, there will be four brothers on DC's protection detail at all times. Grizz, you see to it. We will be making the run to Durban tonight. DC will be riding with us. Grizzly, Alien and Rover, get ready to ride. Grizz, you know who I want on her detail, make sure they're ready." He turned and his eyes caught and held mine. "Call Killian, let him know you'll be away for a few days. Tell him there will be brothers keeping an eye on them and the shop. They will be safe until we get back. I sent Gav and Law to fetch your bike. Everything else you need is in your room upstairs. Have a shower, eat, and drink some coffee. We'll be leaving within the next two hours."

Done talking he smacked the gavel down and ended the meeting.

Why did he want me on a club run? It wasn't something he had ever done before. Was it a way to get me out of the area? Or was there something he needed the Crow to do at the Durban chapter? Usually we slipped quietly into town, this time I would be very visible.

Why?

I knew it was useless to ask. He would fill me in when it was time.

I followed Skel out of the chapel and dug around the basket for my phone. As I turned it on it a gajillion messages came through all at once.

Scrolling through I saw most were from Hawk. I slowly scrolled through all his messages.

They went from asking me to call him to demanding I answer my phone to threats of getting my ass spanked if I ignored any more of his calls.

Not even thinking twice I typed out a message and sent it flying back.

Your choice has been made.

Away on business.

Talk when I get back.

I didn't have a lot of time before we had to leave. I immediately went up to my room on the same floor as Doc's. I was packing my saddlebags when my phone rang. Hawk, again. Growling I let it go to voicemail. I didn't want to talk to him, not when I might lose my shit and start screaming. I shut my phone down and dropped it on my bed. After a quick shower I dressed for the long run down to Durban.

Summer was almost over and according to the weather report we would be riding into a cold front. It was going to be a miserable cold, windy and rainy ride. I pulled on thermals close to my skin then dressed in thick leather pants and a long-sleeved tee. Thick socks and calf length riding boots protected my feet. Picking up my thick leather jacket I slid my phone into an inside pocket along with earphones, my wallet went into another.

An hour and fifteen minutes later we left through a disguised back entrance. At the front of the clubhouse the guys were raising mayhem, music blaring, bikes revving and doing burnouts to disguise the sound of our bikes as we sneaked out the back.

I rode behind Doc and Grizzly with Rover next to me. Rico and Skinny then Gav and Law behind us with Raj and Alien bringing up the rear. We joined the N3 and made good time because the road wasn't too busy. There were a lot of trucks but it was normal. My heart sped up as we passed three trucks belonging to Iron Dogz Trucking. They were very obviously riding in convoy, and with the shit going down around their club I didn't blame them. All three blew their air horns as we passed and we gave low waves as we rode past.

Our first short stop to fill up was at Villiers and then we were back on the road.

When we reached Harrismith, we topped up our tanks, stretched our legs, and had something hot to drink to warm our insides. Doc did not allow us to linger and after a quick visit to the facilities we were back on the road. It was freezing and very windy when we rode down Van Reenen's Pass, ahead of us lightning lit up low lying clouds. We were going to get wet and even colder.

Doc pushed hard to get to our next stop before the rain but we weren't that lucky. Nottingham Road was wet, foggy and miserable. I was jumping around like a crazy person to get my circulation going while we filled up. Any hopes of Doc pulling over to wait out the rain was useless, he pushed on relentlessly. We had a few very hairy moments coming through the Midlands and Pietermaritzburg due to the slippery conditions along with stupid ass motorists and truck drivers. At some stage after Pietermaritzburg the rain changed into a steady fine mist-rain and we had to ride with fog lights because visibility was really crap. We were tired, cold, wet and cranky when we rode into the Road Warriors MC's compound in Durban.

BURNING BRIGHT IN THE BLACK

All I wanted was a room with a shower and a large mug of something hot to drink. I was so cold I didn't give a shit what it was, as long as it was hot. I was quickly shuffled through the silent clubhouse by Doc and Boeta, the Durban chapters' SAA, and set up with a room. It was small but had its own bathroom and was spotlessly clean. It actually smelt like flowers. On the wall behind the door was a wooden rail with several hooks for hanging things and pushed against the far wall was a double bed with a small bedside table and lamp.

"It's small, I know, but it's the only one available right now. I didn't want to put you in one of the crash rooms," Boeta rumbled in his Afrikaans-accented voice. He was a big guy with wild dark brown hair and a moustache that curved over his lip and down the sides of his mouth. He was a prankster of note and no one was safe from his crazy sense of humour. Usually, his hazel eyes would have been twinkling, but not tonight. His eyes had lost its twinkle and were filled with shadows. Maybe his job as SAA for the club was starting to get to him.

At least he didn't try to trick me into a crash room like he had done once before.

There was no way on earth I wanted to sleep in a crash room, they were disgusting. Those beds have seen more action than the swinging doors at a pub.

"This is perfect, thanks, Boeta. I'm going to have a shower before I go to bed. Is it okay if I go down to the kitchen for something hot to drink?" I didn't want to wander around the clubhouse without him knowing about it.

Doc didn't give him a chance to answer. "Law will take you. Stay in your room until he fetches you."

They were gone before I could say a word.

Taking off my wet leathers I spread them over the hooks behind the door. Hopefully, they would dry fairly quickly.

An hour later I was snuggly settled underneath the duvet with a cup of hot chocolate on the bedside table. I knew it was time to read and listen to Hawk's messages. Going by his voice messages he was pissed.

His last message was short and not sweet.

Answer your fucking phone

I was about to send a message when my phone rang. Staring at it I closed my eyes, sighed and answered.

"Hawk."

"Where the fuck are you?" He growled in my ear.

"I'm on a run with Doc. He needs me for something."

There was a heavy silence before he spoke, his voice filled with violent anger.

"You were seen riding down the N3, at fucking night, heading into a fucking storm. What the fuck, DC? Where the fuck are you, little bird?"

The violence had tapered off towards the end into obvious concern.

"I'm in Durban, at the Road Warriors compound. I'm safe."

"But you weren't safe on the road, DC. I have reports from my trucks that the rain is fucking bucketing down and the road is as slick as snot. What the fuck was Doc thinking riding through it? He put you in danger, baby, and for what? What could be more important than keeping you safe?"

Wow, he was seriously pissed at my dad. I couldn't give him any answers because I didn't know anything. And even if I did, I would not be allowed to tell him a single thing. At least not until Doc gave his okay.

But that was not what I wanted to talk about. I wanted to know about the fucked up scene at my shop with Lizzy Hamilton.

"Instead of giving me the third degree about doing what my president asks me to do and I can't discuss with you, why don't you try and explain Lizzy Hamilton to me?"

There was deathly silence, then a heavy sigh.

"I can explain, little bird, but it has to happen face to face, not over the phone."

"Is she at your clubhouse?"

More silence.

"Yes, she is, but the only reason she's here is to keep her safe."

Ja, right.

"I'm tired. I'm going to get some sleep. I'll talk to you when I get back from the run."

I didn't give him a chance to answer.

I turned my phone to silent, dropped it on the bedside table next to my gun, wallet and keys and turned off the light. The room was filled with the pale light of pre-dawn as I snuggled down under the duvet.

I stared blindly at the wall, emptying my brain of all the shit rolling around in it.

Closing my eyes, I slid into sleep.

EIGHTEEN

Hawk

Hawk knew the minute he walked through the back door of Mainline Ink II, and heard the shit Lizzy was sprouting, what he was going to have to do. It burned his gut to disrespect his very new old lady, but if he had to choose between disrespecting her and keeping her alive it was a fucking easy choice.

What he hadn't expected was the dead black eyes and the gun pointed unwaveringly at his head.

Safety off, finger on the trigger. Ready to take him out.

Leading fucking Lizzy out of his woman's shop he met Ice's eyes and saw the shock in his. Hawk knew they had just seen and survived a confrontation with the Crow. It wasn't a good feeling at all. It fucking killed him to put the crazy bitch on the back of his bike but he clenched his teeth and went through with their play.

At the clubhouse he dragged her through the common room and into his office. Kid, Ice and Beast followed and once the door was closed, he sat in his chair and stared at the woman standing defiantly in front of his desk.

"What the fuck were you thinking? Do you have any idea what you have just done?" Hawk snarled at the stupid bitch.

"I'm not sorry." She whispered. "You don't really want her. She's not a good person. Jane told me she's a Road Warriors club whore. You and I, we were happy until she came here, we were going to have a baby and then you threw me out."

As she rambled on and on Hawk felt his rage building but he swallowed it down, letting her carry on.

"We were going to be a family. You were going to keep me and let the others go. I love you, Hawk. How can you not see it? How can you choose her over me? I'll be the best mother for your children, not her. She acts like a man and not a woman and she's so ugly. All muscles and dark. You don't fuck dark; you only fuck light. Jane told me what I had to do and I did it. Now you're all mine and we can go back to how it was before, but this time it will only be the two of us. I won't allow any of the others to fuck you, only me."

Hawk had heard enough.

"The only reason I took you out of the shop today was to save your stupid fucking life. I don't love you, Lizzy, I've never loved you. I don't even fucking like you. I fucked you, that's all it ever was, just a fuck. It's my mistake I let you hang around as long as you did. A mistake I have since rectified. There's some shit going down with the club which is the only reason why you were brought back to the clubhouse. You weren't brought back because I wanted you back. I'm done with you. Forever."

Hawk watched her shrink inside herself but he didn't give a shit. He continued to lay it out for her.

"What you did ripped apart the peace I worked hard to arrange between the Iron Dogz and the Road Warriors. People are going to die because of what you did today. How does it make you feel? Are you still not sorry? Are you okay with men, women and children dying because you didn't fucking get what you wanted?"

Her head was whipping side to side and she moaned softly but Hawk didn't let up. He needed to know where the fuck Jane was and this bitch knew, had been in contact with her. Jane and Big Ed had slipped away and disappeared, and they needed to find them. This bitch was their only lead.

"You fucked up, Lizzy. Why would you believe anything Jane said to you? She fucking hates you."

Her crazy eyes flipped around the room, her mouth open wide and wet with saliva.

"No, you're wrong. Jane said if I went and saw the bitch you would come back to me. She said if I wanted you back, I had to help her. So I did. I want you back, I love you. I don't want people to die because of me. I didn't know. I promise I didn't know. I thought if I could get her to leave, we would be together again. Jane said she'd help me get rid of her. I didn't know she meant to hurt people. I didn't, I promise I didn't." She moaned.

"Where is Jane? Did you see her today before you went to see DC?"

Lizzy nodded. "Yes. She came to my house this morning, with a scary man. She said they were going to take care of it. I don't know how, she didn't say. I thought they would chase her away or something."

But Hawk could see the lie in her eyes, she wanted DC dead.

"Did she say when she would see you again?"

"No, but she did say they had someone on the inside who was helping them. She said this woman would help them get to her, and she won't expect it. I don't know anything more and I didn't ask. I wanted her gone but I didn't want her dead."

"Stop lying to yourself, bitch. What the fuck did you think Jane meant when she said she would take care of it? Are you so fucking clueless you go along with arranging to kill someone? What the fuck, Lizzy?"

Hawk didn't wait for her answer, he turned to Kid.

"Get her out of here and lock her down. No one talks to her. If she needs anything get one of the brothers with an old lady to take care of it, not the women. They might feel sorry enough for the slut to help her escape."

He stayed silent as Kid took Lizzy's arm and forcefully removed her from the office. The bitch didn't want to leave. When the door closed behind them, he turned to his cousin who had been silently watching.

"My woman is going to cut my fucking balls off for this shit. What the fuck do I do now, Ice?"

His cousin gave him a look he couldn't read.

"We go to the Warriors and lay this shit out for Doc and Tiny. We have to let them know they have a rat before Jane makes her play. It's all we can do and you will have to explain to them why you did what you did today. DC is a club kid, she'll understand, eventually."

Ice suddenly gave an evil laugh.

"After she's made you suffer. She is one harsh motherfucker of a bitch."

Picking up his phone Hawk sent his woman a message. Through the course of the afternoon he sent a fucking slew of texts, and no answer. He tried calling. No answer. He left her voice messages, a lot of them. In the last one he threatened an ass spanking if she didn't call him.

"Stop fucking around with your phone. Let's get out of here, Hawk." Kid growled in exasperation. "We have to have a face to face with Doc and get this shit sorted. They took her to the Warriors compound. She'll be there and you can fix your shit while we hunt for their rat."

Following Ice and Kid he frowned heavily at the sudden silence his presence caused in the common room. He paused, looked around the room then focused on the brothers hanging out with the bitches. Sin and Beast stood at the bar and both of them gave him a chin lift. They would keep things tight while he rode out to get his woman.

His phone beeped and the message pissed him off. His woman was going to get a red ass if she carried on with her shit.

He gave a chin lift to his men and walked out while trying to call his woman back.

No luck, it went straight to voicemail.

Jesus, she was so fucking stubborn.

It took time to get to the Warriors compound because of the early evening traffic and they had to take care while splitting lanes because there were some clueless motherfuckers on the road. He didn't need to get taken off his bike right now.

Pulling up to the partly open steel gates at the Road Warriors compound Hawk frowned at the party going on behind the heavy gates. Music blared and bikes roared as they did burnouts in front of the open garages.

He swore viciously when he spotted DC's cage pulled up next to a few other rides.

He tried calling again, and again it went straight to voicemail so he left a message.

"When I get my hands on you, baby, your ass is going to be red. That's a promise."

Hawk cursed long and inventively as Skel walked up to him with a sly grin.

"She's so fucking pissed at you, Hawk. I'm glad I'm not you, our girl's going to make you suffer."

Hawk sighed heavily and shrugged.

"It was the only fucking play I had, brother. I got a call to alert me to the shit going down. I raced over to intercept the bitch but I was too late. So, I played it the only way I could to keep DC safe."

Shaka and Tiny strolled up and Hawk met Tiny's ice-cold eyes, refusing to back down.

"What the fuck happened today?" Tiny demanded. "My girl has shut down and we've had to fucking deal with the Crow in full on pissed off mode. She's going to demand retribution and if she asks, we'll have to have a fucking good reason why we can't give it to her."

Hawk clenched his teeth.

"I had a very good fucking reason. We need to discuss this somewhere there are no ears listening. Apparently, you have acquired a rodent problem. I need to talk to Doc."

Hawk watched as Tiny's entire demeanour changed. He went from slightly pissed to full on enraged in seconds.

"Doc's on a run. Bring your rides inside." He stalked off back to the clubhouse without another word. Shaka following after shooting him a scathing glance.

"Fuck."

Skel motioned for the gates to be opened fully to allow them entrance.

When they walked into the common room of the clubhouse it was filled with Warriors but no women, and definitely no DC. Skel led them through the silently watching men up the steel stairs and down a passage to an open door. The large office was a mess, dust, dying plants, papers and bike parts everywhere. The walls were covered with paintings done by his little bird, some obviously done at the same time as the one he had in his office. But there were some very dark and ominous paintings as well. He would have liked time to study them but now was not the time.

Hawk took the chair at the desk and waited as Kid, Ice, Skelly and Shaka settled in the remaining chairs and on the messy couch. Tiny sank into Doc's chair.

"Let's hear it." Tiny snarled.

Leaning forward to get closer to the desk he started to lay it out.

"Earlier today two of my men went into Jane Warne's house. It was obvious she was long gone. We immediately hit Big Ed's place and his old lady, who happens to be Snake's daughter, was happy to tell us she found some shit on his phone and kicked him out. He told her he was moving in with his girlfriend. So, we know they are together. I called Snake to see if he had anything to say. He wants us to sit down at a neutral table as soon as possible."

Tiny nodded. "It might be a good idea, but you be careful, he is not to be trusted. His name is very appropriate."

Hawk gave a small nod in acknowledgement before he continued.

"We were lucky we got to Big Ed's old lady first because she had his phone. It was because of what we found on his phone that I played it the way I did at DC's shop. We needed to find out more about their plans and Lizzy had the answers. The bitch told us Jane is planning on taking DC from here, from inside your clubhouse. One of your club whores is a rat. Someone no one suspects and she can apparently get close to DC without raising any suspicions. She's going to deliver DC to Jane and Big Ed in exchange for their help in solving a problem she has. And of course, for a large sum of money. Lizzy has no idea what her problem is or who the rat might be. Do you have any ideas?"

Tiny turned in his chair and looked at Skelly. Something went down between the two of them. Tiny sighed before he turned back.

"Yes, we do, but I need to look into it before we make our move. There are others who'll be hurt if we move too quickly," Tiny said quietly.

"Right." Hawk was done talking about this shit. He wanted to speak to his woman. "Where's my old lady? She hasn't answered her phone for the last couple of hours."

Tiny grimaced. "Ja, about that. Doc needed her skills for some club business. They left about an hour ago."

Hawk sighed and rubbed his hands over his tired face. How the hell was he supposed to deal with this? She was his old lady. How could he let this disregard of him and his club pass?

"Hawk, brother, this is part of who she is." Skelly interrupted his thoughts. "Doc knew it was going to piss you off so he left me behind to try and explain."

Hawk was pissed and he showed it.

"So, explain this shit to me, Skelly. Explain how my old lady is not where she's supposed to be. Explain how I was not informed about the need for her to go on an unscheduled run and without my men having her back."

Skelly held his hands up in supplication. "We received some totally fucked up information late this afternoon. If not handled properly it could impact both our clubs, and not in a good way. If it's allowed to play out the way it's been set up to play out, we will all be sitting behind fucking bars very fucking soon. Doc needed his Crow to get to the bottom of it."

"Where the fuck is she?"

"On the road. The informant is in Durban." When he saw the look on Hawk's face Skel immediately set out to assure him of his woman's safety.

"She's safe, Hawk. She has four brothers as her personal security and there are ten of them on the run. Rover and Grizzly will be on her ass, keeping her safe."

"Fuck, I have so much shit going down in my own club I don't have time to deal with this right now." Hawk came up out of his chair. "I've got to get back. Keep me in the loop regarding your rat."

Hawk rode away with rage burning through his gut. How dare Doc give his woman an assignment without speaking to him first? DC belonged to him, not to Doc and not to the Road Warriors MC.

He was in a foul mood when he walked through the doors of his club and everyone saw it. They made sure they stayed out of his way.

He tried to catch up on work to keep his mind off his woman. But after receiving several messages from the brothers who were riding along with the trucks on the way down to Durban he was in an even worse mood. He gave up on work and went up to the guestroom he was using while his room was being decorated.

Hawk lay with his hands behind his head, staring up at the ceiling unable to sleep. He was worried about his little bird. They had not ended the day on a good note at all. She was pissed at him, and he totally understood, but she didn't know why he had done what he did. And not answering her fucking phone did not give him an opportunity to explain.

Rolling over he picked up his phone and sighed as he saw the time. Four in the morning. He would call once more and then it would be up to DC.

It rang twice and suddenly she was there, her voice so fucking tired his temper spiked.

"Hawk."

"Where the fuck are you?" He growled.

"I'm on a run with Doc. He needed me on this one."

He was silent for a few seconds. He didn't try to disguise the anger and violence in his voice when he spoke. But it became concern for her safety and he let her know it as he asked where she was.

When she told him she was safe he wanted to shout bullshit but reigned himself in.

The reports from his brothers had let him know how fucking dangerous the weather conditions were on the N3.

Hawk was so fucking pissed off with Doc and even though he knew DC couldn't tell him what the hell they were doing in Durban he still asked.

She didn't answer him instead she threw the fucked up situation with Lizzy at him. And then it was his turn to evade answering because there was no way he could adequately explain the shit over the phone.

He knew she was going to give him hell for it.

She didn't, she left him listening to dead air as she shut her phone down.

NINETEEN

DC

It felt as if I had been asleep for four minutes when Doc woke me four hours later. My eyes felt scratchy and were puffy as hell, and it felt as a load of sand had taken up residence behind my eyelids. My body ached from the very physical ride down, getting dressed wasn't any fun. Once I was done, I made my way to the kitchen looking for coffee and breakfast.

My dad wasn't in the kitchen. I ate my breakfast surrounded by strangely silent men. The tension in the air kept my mouth shut and I focused on my food, avoiding their eyes. I was enjoying the last of my coffee when Doc came in and with a quick tilt of his head indicated I had to follow him.

What the hell was going on here?

I walked into a windowless office behind him and sat down when he pointed me to a chair pulled into the corner of the room. There were seven of us in the room. Doc, Grizzly, Rover, Alien and me from the Jozi chapter, and Boeta and Fisher from the Durban chapter. Fisher was their club's information officer. Everyone in the room was a club officer except me. I had no idea why the Prez and VP of the Durban chapter wasn't in the room, but I felt sure I was about to find out.

"You called me with some truly fucked up information, Boeta. I hope like fuck you can back up what you told me." Doc's first words were not encouraging.

"*Ek fokken wens ek was verkeerd*, Prez. (I fucking wish I was wrong, Prez.) After I spoke to you, I knew we needed proof of the shit that's been happening. I called in a few of the brothers I trusted and we snatched their cargo. We've got them secured at a safe location."

Boeta's eyes were haunted and he looked like his heart had been stomped on. But deep-down anger burned fiercely. I knew just how upset he was by the way his explanation was peppered by Afrikaans words and phrases.

"*Die klub en my broers is my lewe*, Prez. (The club and my brothers are my life, Prez.) I've bled for my club and my brothers, *maar ek kannie meer nie*. (but I can't anymore.) You know we were the last Warrior chapter to get out of the drug trade. *En jy weet hoe diep ons in daai fokken kak was*. (And you know how deep we were into that fucking shit.) I voted yes to get us out of the shit the club was drowning in. To live free and clear, to stop looking over our shoulders all the time, to stop fucking dying for no good fucking reason. *Speedy was nie happy n*ie. (Speedy wasn't happy.) The shit Speedy and some of my brothers are involved in makes what we used to do look like a fucking kid's game. I won't allow their greed to take down my club or my brothers."

"How many of the brothers are involved?"

It was Fisher who answered.

"Nine that we know of, Prez. And it includes our President, our VP, our Enforcer and our Treasurer."

The news was not good. The men who made the decisions and the one who handled their money along with the one who made sure their orders were enforced had all gone rogue. But why had they gone rogue? They made a damn good living so it certainly wasn't about money…or was it?

The room was silent as everyone waited for Doc to react. His voice was deep and rough when he did. He was pissed and disappointed. Speedy was a friend, a friend who had now gone rogue it seemed.

"I've spoken to Freeze and he's given me the go ahead to investigate. I'll be keeping him in the loop about whatever we uncover." Doc sighed heavily. "Lay it out for us, and brother, don't leave one fucking thing out. I want it all."

Boeta's eyes snapped towards where I sat quietly in the corner of the room.

"In front of her, Prez? This is club business."

Doc gave an evil grin. "We need her for the cargo and to be able to help she needs to know it all. I've cleared it with National, so let's hear it."

I could see Boeta was very uncomfortable with me there as he nodded. When he started laying it out, I felt the tiny hairs at the nape of my neck rise in horror.

Speedy and his men were involved in a trafficking ring. They were the last stop before their products were shipped out of Durban in shipping containers to ports in Asia. It was their so-called products that freaked me the hell out.

They weren't only shipping rhino horn, elephant tusks, and lion pelts and bones to Asia. Every couple of months those containers contained young girls and boys who had been snatched throughout Southern Africa.

Boeta had no idea who the kingpin of the operation was. He was convinced one of the three girls they had taken from the warehouse knew more than she was saying. She was older, in her early twenties, while the other two girls were twelve and thirteen respectively.

Doc twisted in his chair and gave me the look. I nodded.

"I need Rover and Alien with me and Law to do the usual," I said quietly. "The sooner I start the sooner we finish. Take me to them."

Rover and Alien along with Skelly usually accompanied me when I did what I did for the club. Law was the one who made sure I had what I needed and disposed of the evidence once I was done. He was the only person outside of the club's officers who knew I was Doc's Crow.

I followed the men out of the room with my gut in a tight knot. What had we walked into down here?

We rode through Durban Central and deep into an industrial area where we pulled in behind an abandoned factory. I followed the men inside and Boeta led us to the lower level where the girls were being kept. I would be using the empty room next to the one where the girls were kept as a changing room.

After changing my clothes, I stood in the empty room and closed my eyes, going inside myself where the other me lived. When I opened my eyes, she was there, waiting.

I breathed in deep before I walked into the dark windowless room. I had left my humanity in the other room. I looked into the scared eyes of the two little girls and my heart clenched and bled for them. The other set of eyes was different, she was trying really hard to look frightened but she failed. She was weighing her options, trying to come up with a plausible excuse. Some of the men might have fallen for her shit but not me.

"Take the kids into the other room." I whispered through my mask.

Rover immediately scooped them up and left. He returned almost immediately with a kitchen chair which he placed in the middle of the room.

"Put her in the chair." Again, a whispered command.

Rover and Alien picked her up and sat her protesting body in the chair. Rover fastened her ankles to the chair legs with cable ties while Alien pulled her hands behind her back and cable-tied them to the chair back. She wouldn't be going anywhere soon.

Rover went back out and came back with another chair and placed it in front of her. Then he and Alien retreated, leaning against the wall with arms crossed and silently watched.

I sat down, crossed my arms and stared at her silently. She couldn't hold my eyes and started squirming.

"Tell me a story." I hissed coldly.

"I...I...I don't know what you want. I've been kidnapped. Please. I want to go home." She begged pitifully.

"Please let me go home."

Pulling my knife from my boot I played with it. Twirling it through my fingers, over and over. I wore black Nitrile gloves, the very same ones I used in my shop.

Her eyes were riveted on the swirling, twirling blade.

"Tell me."

"I don't know what you want to know. Please. Let me go!" She screeched.

"You can stop screeching. No one can hear you, and there's no one here who will help you. You're alone. You know what I want. Tell me," I hissed and twirled the knife close enough to her face she jerked her head back in fear. "Or don't tell me and I'll get to play. With you."

And right on cue she wet herself. So fucking predictable. I pulled my feet away from the growing puddle. I didn't want my boots to stink.

She started to babble, words tumbling out of her stupid mouth.

"I look after them. I swear that's all I do. Speedy and the men bring them to the warehouse and I look after them until it's time for them to leave. That's it, I know nothing about anything."

Her eyes snapped towards the door before they returned to me. Leaning towards her I gently lifted the edge of her little flippy skirt with the point of my knife then slowly moved it up her thighs. I stopped once I had both thighs and her disgustingly wet black panties exposed. Tears silently ran down her cheeks as she watched with terrified eyes.

I tapped the top of both thighs with the flat of my knife.

"Very pretty." I hissed. "Such a pity. Did you know a straight cut is easiest to repair and usually leaves behind very little scarring? But I don't like straight cuts. That's not what I like to do. I like patterns. Zig zags are my favourite. Very difficult to repair without heavy scarring."

I had no damn idea if it was the truth or not. I just knew with women it always worked. No matter how hardened they were, after the first couple of cuts they talked. No one likes ugly scarring anywhere near their pussies or tits.

I drew the knife up the inside of one thigh across the top of her mound and down the inside of the other thigh hard enough to leave a raised red line, but not hard enough to cut into her skin.

This one was even easier, no cutting needed.

"Please, don't. They are working with someone called May…May… something, a woman. I've never seen her; she never comes here. She calls Speedy with her orders. I swear I don't know anything else. I'm not important. They use me for the kids and when they need to get off. Please don't hurt me, please."

"Where is Speedy?"

She sobbed loudly. "They went on a run to fetch the rest of the kids. They're bringing ten more to the warehouse tomorrow morning. The container is ready and they are being shipped tomorrow night."

"Good. Very good. You answer what I ask and I might not draw pretty patterns on you. So, the kids are loaded into a container and put on a ship. Do you know the name of the ship?"

"Yes! That's what happens. It's Josephine, the ship's called Josephine."

"Two last questions. Do they wear their kuttes while they are doing their business and what is the name on the back?"

She looked confused. "What? What is a cut?"

Fuck, I did not have a good feeling. I pointed with my knife at Rover and Alien.

"Those leather waistcoats with their names on them. That's called a kutte."

"They take them off when they go to the ship but they wear them the rest of the time. Sometimes it says Road Warriors and sometimes Iron Dogz."

I sat back and tapped the knife against my leather covered cheek, my eyes never leaving hers as I went over what she had given me.

There was one thing I didn't know and it was a crucial bit of information.

"Where is this container?"

By the sudden flare in her eyes, it was obvious she had hoped I wouldn't ask that particular question.

"I...I...don..."

I waved the knife back and forth in front of her eyes as I slowly shook my head from side to side.

"No, no, no. No lies now. You know what happens if you lie."

Hope died in her eyes and her whole body slumped.

It poured out in an unending stream, chilling me to the bone.

"Speedy arranges for the special containers to be brought to a pre-arranged rendezvous point. It is always close to the harbour but never the same place. The container is sealed after they load it. He has a contact at a trucking company who arranges the transportation of the containers and fixes the paperwork. Once the product is loaded, they escort it into the harbour and onto the ship where Speedy hands it over to the captain. He pays off a lot of people to look the other way, even the harbour cops."

She gave a loud broken-hearted sob. Unfortunately for her we weren't done yet.

"Which trucking company?"

Her answer shoved a spear of ice into my gut.

"Iron Dogz Trucking."

"How far up does this go? Are the owners involved?"

"No, Speedy hates the Iron Dogz. He is always saying their president, Hawk Walker, is the perfect scapegoat. I know everything I've done to help him is wrong. I know. I know. But if I don't do as he says he will put my little sister in the next container. I'll do anything to keep it from happening. Anything."

I slid my knife back into the hidden sheath, slowly stood, bent over and pulled her skirt back down over her legs. I gave her thighs a tap before I straightened.

"There's someone here who wants to talk to you. Don't make me come back." I whispered.

I stood in the empty room after I had changed clothes with my hands over my eyes and tried hard to keep myself from screaming in rage and despair. Those poor, poor kids. All the ones we couldn't save. A heavy hand settled on my shoulder. I whirled and threw myself into my dad's arms. I held onto him as I battled to get my raging emotions under control. He moved me slightly and closed the door behind us.

"This shit has just escalated. I don't want you back at the clubhouse. I sent Raj to pack your things and bring it here. I've spoken to Hawk and he trusts us to keep you safe until he gets here." I tried to interrupt. "No, baby, no. Boeta can't guarantee there aren't more of their men involved. I don't want you anywhere near when shit goes down. Hawk called me after he spoke to you early this morning. I gave him what I knew. Your old man is fucking stubborn, DC. Wouldn't wait to hear from me before coming down. Now I'm glad he's so fucking stubborn. We're going to need all those we trust in order to handle it without blow back on the clubs."

I rolled my head against his chest and tightened my arms around him.

"I can't imagine doing something like this to an innocent child, Dad. How the hell did Speedy get involved in this shit? How do these people live with themselves? How do they sleep at night? How do they…"

I didn't get any further because the rumbling thunder of a lot of bikes filled the air.

Law stuck his head into the room.

"The Dogz are here, Prez, and there are a few surprises in the pack."

Doc nodded. "I'll be out now."

Doc pressed a soft kiss to my forehead before we walked out of the room and down the long passage to the wide-open back doors of the factory. I frowned when I saw the bikes. There were at least twenty. I groaned when a visibly pissed off Hawk, with Tiny, Skelly and Shaka following him, stalked towards us.

TWENTY

Hawk

Hawk growled with anger and relief when he saw his little bird standing next to Doc in the wide-open factory doors.

Relief disappeared when he got closer.

His woman stood there dressed in black from head to toe. Her hair was in a tight braid down her back, lying against a long sleeved and high-necked black tee. Her face and hands were the only visible skin. It was when he looked down into those icy black eyes that he knew he was close to losing her.

Suddenly he didn't give a flying fuck about the shit that had brought him here. All he cared about was his little bird.

Cupping her face in his palms he tipped her head up, bent down and fitted his lips over her cold mouth.

It took some persuasion before those lips softened and started kissing him back, and when they did, he lost himself in her warm welcoming mouth.

He went in even deeper when her arms slid around his waist under his jacket and his woman moved to fit her small body to his. Sliding a hand away from her face to her waist he pulled her tight against him before he slowly ended the kiss. Lifting his head, he looked down into her warm eyes.

"Never, ever leave without telling me exactly where you're going and who you're with, little bird. That's an unbreakable rule."

He snapped angrily.

His woman didn't wait to snap right back at him.

"Never, ever put another bitch on the back of your bike and expect me to just take that shit. It happens again and there will be blood, most of it yours."

Hawk didn't get a chance to answer.

"Enough," Doc snarled.

"Get inside. We have some shit to talk about."

They were spread out in what at some point in the distant past had been a conference room. The heavily blacked out windows allowed no light in. Solar lanterns placed around the room supplied the light. There wasn't any furniture as such, just scrounged up crates and a couple of battered chairs.

Hawk sat on a crate near Doc with his little bird firmly settled in his lap.

She was not happy. He didn't give a shit; he needed her close.

Ice and Kid sat behind him while the rest of his brothers spread out around the room.

Doc started speaking and as he laid it out for them Hawk felt rage building higher and higher. He had a traitor in his club. Someone in a position of trust was selling them out and leaving evidence behind implicating the club. Evidence that would have them behind bars for fucking life.

Hawk had his woman off his lap and plonked on the crate in the blink of an eye.

He stormed out of the room pulling his phone out. He had Jagger on the line as he walked out of the disused factory and into the overgrown yard.

"Brother, I need you and Ziggy to go over every single employee who has access to trucking schedules and logistics. Check everyone with access to import and export documentation at Head Office and at our yards and offices countrywide. Look into their bank accounts, their properties, fucking anything and everything you can think of. We are being set up as human traffickers, brother. Find the fucker and get Ziggy to start cleaning house. Use Dollar, Sam and Boots to help you. Our containers and our businesses are being used to smuggle kids out of the country. There's a container scheduled to be shipped out of Durban on a vessel by the name of Josephine tomorrow night. Find out where the container is coming from and who will be delivering it. Do a complete sweep of every single office and yard, search every single one. I'll get back to you when I have more. Get on it, brother, and if the bastard is at the office up there keep the fucker on ice until we get back."

As Hawk spoke, he could hear Jagger swearing softly and his boots hitting the hard floor as he ran.

"I'm on it, Prez. Will send updates as we have them," he gritted out as he ran.

Shutting his phone down Hawk stalked back into the building and into the conference room. Meeting Doc's eyes he lifted his woman, sat down and placed her back on his lap. Her irritated growl almost made him smile, almost.

"We need to discover who this May woman is and we have to cover up the shit at the warehouse. I don't want Speedy suspecting Boeta of messing with his business. Any suggestions?" Doc continued with the meeting.

"We burn it down." Skelly suggested, getting nods of agreement from everyone. "We blow the fucker sky high and make it impossible to get anywhere near it. An explosion and hot fire will have the fire department, the fire investigators and the pigs crawling all over it. We fill the warehouse with shit that will burn hot and blow it just as he gets there. If it burns hot and long enough his informants on the force won't be able to tell him if anyone died in the fire. At least not for a while. Plus, we just happen to have our very own little firebug right here."

Tiny gave a furious snarl,

"Your brother is supposed to stay away from that shit, Jake."

DC stiffened and Hawk pulled her against his chest.

Tiny looked about ready to explode.

Using Skelly's real name clued everyone in on how fucking pissed off he was.

Suddenly this was all about blood family and not about the club.

"He's a genius with fire, Dad. We need him on this one. You know very well this won't be the last time he has to do shit like this for the club. I promise I will be with him every step of the way. I won't let it get away from him, you have my word."

"He starts burning shit down once we get home it's on your head and you will handle it," Tiny growled.

Doc's face was expressionless as he handed out their orders.

"Rover, pick two of the brothers and follow Speedy when the warehouse goes up. You stick with them. We need to know where he takes those kids. Skel, pick a team to go with you and Gav. Keep our boy from getting too creative."

Hawk didn't have time to wonder what it meant, as he was next on Doc's agenda.

"Hawk, I want you and your men to keep a low profile until tomorrow night. Raj and some of my brothers are taking DC to spend some time at the beach. It will explain their sudden disappearance from the clubhouse. We need to sort accommodation for the rest of you, preferably not in the city itself."

"That's not a problem, Prez." Boeta grinned. "This place is a safe house I prepared for my family when shit started to go wrong with the club. No one knows about it. There are rooms upstairs where they can crash. There's water and solar power for hot showers and a kitchen I keep stocked. All the windows have been blacked out, and because this is an old industrial area, we don't have to worry about being seen. We pull the bikes into the loading bay and no one will know we're here. *Maklik*." (Easy)

Doc nodded slowly. "That's good. I'd rather we stayed off the roads until it's time. We all know what we've got to do. We'll meet again before we take them down tomorrow night."

Doc ended the meeting but he pointed a finger at Hawk to keep him from leaving.

He waited until only Ice, Kid, Tiny, Skelly and Raj were in the room with them. Doc leaned back in the dilapidated chair glaring at Hawk and DC.

"Now that we've handled our shit, how about you get your heads out of your asses and fix the fucked-up shit between the two of you. I need both of you to have clear heads. We have a lot going down tomorrow and I need to know I can depend on you to pull your weight without coming to blows."

Hawk grinned when DC snarled angrily at her dad. His woman was a total badass, no fear whatsoever.

"My little bird is pissed with me. She has good reason to be pissed, but if she thinks it through, she will see I had no other options. I had to do what I did to ensure her safety. She would have done the same if she were in my shoes."

Those snapping fierce black eyes focused on him and Hawk felt the burn down deep.

"Maybe. Maybe I would have done the same. But I would have taken the time to give you a heads-up. Had I pulled this shit with one of my exes you would have lost your mind. You're lucky I didn't kill both of you. The only thing stopping me was that there were too many witnesses," his little bird said with a smirk.

Skel burst out laughing and Hawk glanced over at him before looking at the man standing next to him. He glared at the grinning bastard. Fucking Raj.

"No way would I walk into the Iron Dogz' place of business and put my hands on you, DC. I like my life too much." The fucker joked. "Plus, he won't give a shit about witnesses."

"Shut up, Raj." His little bird snarled, but her eyes were laughing. Fuck.

Hawk wanted this done, now.

"Can we finish our chat without a fuck load of onlookers?"

Doc grinned, stood and flicked a hand at the others. The room emptied, leaving the three of them.

"Fix this. I have to get back to the clubhouse. Grizz, Rover and Alien will be with me along with the men Boeta trusts, so you can stop giving me the look, DC." Doc ordered before he walked out.

When the door slammed shut Hawk stood and pushed DC down on the crate. Kneeling in front of his little bird he put his hands on her thighs.

"I'm sorry. I fucked up. I should have called to warn you and I didn't. I'm still getting used to sharing my life with you, baby. I can't promise I won't fuck up again, but I can promise I will always be there to fix my fuck ups. Like I am now."

He rubbed his hands over her tightly clenched muscles, coaxing her to soften to him.

"I'm still pissed at you, Hawk. You have no idea what could have happened. I don't react like the bitches you are used to. I don't scream, cry or throw a tantrum. I get even, any way I can. Don't ever do that to me again."

Hawk knew exactly what she meant. It would be the Crow who would get even with him.

"I promise, baby. I realised the minute I looked into your eyes I had made a mistake. But I had to get her out of there and get the information I needed. I can't lose you, DC," Hawk said softly as he pulled her off the crate and into his arms.

He was still kneeling on the floor and closed his eyes as she came to him, settling herself over his thighs, her arms around his neck. He clasped her tight against his chest and shoved his face in her neck, breathing her in. Settling her scent deep in his lungs to calm his shit down.

"So relieved to have you in my arms again, little bird," Hawk murmured against her neck then pulled back to look at her. "But we both know you have to be seen checking into a place at the beach. Where are you going to go?"

"Raj booked us into a beachfront apartment in Umhlanga. Easily verified if they check up on us. And close enough if you need us."

Keeping her in his arms Hawk stood and sat back down on the crate, keeping her straddling his thighs.

"As long as the bastard keeps his distance he'll keep breathing."

Hawk mumbled as he nuzzled her neck. He couldn't get enough of her scent.

Lifting his face from her neck he slammed his mouth down on hers, his lips softening as her lips opened under his. He licked over her full lower lip, catching it between his teeth for a soft nip before sliding his tongue in, playing with hers, and tasting her. His cock jerked as she rubbed herself against him, the heat of her pussy burning through the thick fabric of their jeans.

He wanted her, so fucking badly but they couldn't go there, not here in this place.

Slowly pulling away from her mouth he looked down into her hazy eyes and smiled. She was as gone as he was, drunk on his kisses.

"I love kissing you, baby. I can kiss you for fucking ever but we have to stop because I'm not fucking you here. And believe me I would fuck you anywhere, anytime, just not here."

She laughed and nuzzled his neck.

"Okay, my Viking."

Just the sound of her voice filled with want almost had him forgetting why he didn't want to fuck her where everyone could hear. Her calling him her Viking had his aching cock begging for release. He held her, soothing both of them before he stood and carefully set her on her feet.

"We need to get you out of here, little bird. If you and your boys aren't seen to hit the road to Umhlanga it might raise some suspicions."

Hawk grabbed her hand and dragged her out of the conference room. His little bird was smiling and he grinned as he looked down at her.

Her eyes were no longer dead, they were sparkling.

Those fierce dark eyes of his little bird sparkling up at him filled him with warmth.

He had given up on love a long time ago. Never before had he felt like this, not even with Candy.

What he had with this dangerous woman was real. Very fucking real.

There was no way he was ever going to let her go.

TWENTY ONE

DC

I sat on the wide shady balcony of the fourth-floor beachfront apartment staring down at the people on the beach. Some were playing in the shallows with their kids, while others were lying on beach towels soaking up the late afternoon sun. When I initially sat down, the broad walkway next to the beach hadn't been busy but as the sun started to set more people were out taking walks, running or cycling. I would have loved to go for a run but Raj very quickly vetoed the idea.

That's why I sat up here, sipping on a cider, wishing I were down there.

Where I really wanted to be though, was back in Durban with Hawk and my dad. I had a bad feeling about the shit set to go down in the morning. The last update hadn't been very encouraging. Boeta had talked to the men still at the clubhouse but couldn't say if they would follow Doc's orders. Their loyalties lay with their chapter president and the fact he was a low life slaver might not matter to them at the end of the day. It would come down to loyalty to the club and their conscience.

For them it would be a very tough call to make. For me, not at all.

I trusted Grizzly, Rover and Alien to guard my dad's back but they were surrounded by men who, though loyal to the Road Warriors MC, were loyal to their own president first. The uncertainty sucked.

Not having heard from Hawk since we left was to be expected, they were busy setting up to take down Speedy. The knowledge, however ,did not make me feel any better. I was worried about all of them.

I flinched when Rico suddenly plopped down in the chair next to me. I was so deep in my head I wasn't paying attention to my surroundings.

"Stop worrying about shit we can do fuck all about, DC," he said quietly. "No matter what we do, tomorrow will come and shit will go down. People are going to get hurt, that's a given. All we can do is hope it all comes down in our favour and none of our guys get hurt or dead."

After delivering his speech he fell silent, drinking his beer and staring out to sea.

"I just wish we could have been there to help," I muttered as I scratched at the label on the bottle.

"They've got this, DC. And no, you do not want to be around the shit that's going to go down tonight and tomorrow. It's club business. Freeze arrived an hour ago, what's happening in Durban is not for you to worry about and not your business."

Bloody hell. These men.

I wanted to rip Rico's head off as he coldly laid it out for me. He made it sound as if I didn't know how shit worked in the club and it pissed me off. But I kept my mouth shut. Debating club business with him was a lost cause. I would lose every single time.

The news that Freeze was in Durban made it easier, and again more difficult, not to worry about my dad. With the national president at the clubhouse, it was very unlikely the men would turn against them. One less thing to worry about.

My phone started vibrating across the table and I grabbed it, hoping it was Hawk. It wasn't, it was Pixie, my boss.

"Hey, Pixie. I'm sorry I had to take off so suddenly. I'll make up the lost time as soon as I get back, no worries." I hurried to reassure her.

"Hi, DC, it's not the reason I'm calling. I'm not worried about the studio, Killian's got it under control. What I would like to know is why Freeze, Rooster and a few brothers flew out of here as if their tails were on fire? All Rooster would tell me was shit was going down in Durban. You're in Durban, so what the hell is going on?"

Pixie was pissed but I heard the worry in her voice. Rooster was like a brother to her. His dad, Wild Man, had taken her in when she was lost and alone. They were her family. I understood her worry but I could not give her the answers she wanted. It was club business.

233

Maybe if Rico hadn't been sitting next to me, I would have given her some details, but with him watching and listening I couldn't say one word about what was going down.

"I'm not actually in Durban, Pixie. I'm in Umhlanga. I've got no idea what's going down. I'll try to find out and get back to you. Okay?"

She gave a huge sigh,

"You're not alone, are you?"

Crap. "No, not right now, maybe later."

"Okay. Try and call me when you don't have a watchdog on your ass. Oh, and while I've got you. There's a major convention coming up in the US I want us to attend. I'll send you the information and we can talk about it once this shit is done."

I grinned wide. "It will be awesome. I'll check my e-mails and call you for a chat later."

"Cool, babe. Talk to you later."

I was still grinning as I slid my phone back onto the table.

"What did she say to get you so fired up?" Raj stood with his arms crossed staring down at me.

"Pixie is taking Mainline Ink to a tattoo convention in the US. It is going to be so freaking awesome." I was so damned excited.

Raj was pissed off as he shook his head.

"You won't be going. It's up to Doc and Hawk whether you go or not and I'll advise against it."

What?

"I'm not sure I heard you right. Did you just tell me I can't go until Doc and Hawk gives me permission to go?"

The bastard nodded his stupid head.

Shaking my head in disbelief I laid it out for him and the rest of the guys avidly listening in.

"I'm never going to allow a man to make my decisions for me. It is my career, my decision. As much as club business is none of my business, my career is not the clubs' business. Doc knows this, and if Hawk doesn't, he soon will. And you thinking you have a say in it is absolute bullshit."

Grabbing my phone I shoved past him, stomped into the kitchen, grabbed another cider and stomped into my room. I wanted to slam the door shut but I didn't. It was a waste of energy.

Stupid male posturing.

What had happened out there was one of the reasons I had ended it with Raj. He had very traditional views regarding women. I hoped to heaven Hawk didn't have the same ideas. If he did, we were in big, big trouble.

I sat fuming on my bed and was about to access my e-mails when Hawk called.

One of the bastards out there has obviously been flapping their lips.

"Hi, how's it going?" Start out easy, I warned myself.

"Good. What is this shit I hear about you going to the US with your boss?" His tone of voice was clipped. Even a tiny bit pissed off.

"Do you have a problem with it?"

"I do have a problem with you leaving with her on your own. Not fucking happening."

Cold anger slithered down my back but I reined it in. He had a lot on his mind and to talk about this right now would piss both of us off.

He didn't need to have me on his mind when he needed to concentrate on the shit about to go down.

"I don't want to talk about it now. I don't even know when we'll be going as Pixie only mentioned it a few moments ago. I'll talk to you when she tells me more." There was an angry growl but I ignored it. "Are you ready for tomorrow?"

"You know I can't talk about shit, DC. You tell Pixie she fucking talks to me about you going to the US before she talks to you."

He ended the call.

Staring down at my silent phone I breathed deep to control my anger but it was a wasted effort. Raj had done this, I knew it. I stormed into the lounge where they were all sitting pretending to watch some shit on television. Their heads swivelled as I stormed in.

Raj smirked at me and I exploded.

"You fucking asshole. You couldn't wait to swing your little dick around, could you? Want to know the real reason I ended it with you? It was this type of bullshit and your damned arrogance. You tried to control me and failed so now you're trying to do so through others," I hissed at him.

"I'm so very done with you and your games. Stay the hell away from me and out of my life."

Shocked silence hung in the air as I turned and went back to my room.

Opening the sliding door onto the balcony I stepped out and leaned against the railing, breathing deep and rhythmically to calm the rage boiling inside.

Hawk basically told me I had no say in whether I went to the US with Pixie or not. He would be making the decision. I tried very hard to view his reaction as an overreaction due to the crap swirling around us at the moment.

I freaking tried.

But he was pushing buttons that had me ready to bolt.

I would never be a conventional old lady. I loved my job as a tattoo artist and over the years the work I did as the Crow had come to mean something to me. I might be able to give up being the Crow but I couldn't give up my job. I've sacrificed enough for my family and the club.

There were no more pieces left to sacrifice.

There was only one person who understood.

Skel answered after the second ring.

"Hey, babe, a little busy here. What do you need?"

"Damn. I shouldn't bother you. You're going to have a hard enough time keeping Gav from burning down more than just one little warehouse."

His deep laugh elicited a small smile.

"You are so right about that. The little shit is totally stoked he's allowed to burn shit down. But that's not why you called me, is it?"

"No." I bit my lip before I continued. "Pixie wants me to go to the States with her to attend a tattoo convention. Raj overheard our call, told me I would only be allowed to go if Doc and Hawk clears it. I didn't like it and told him so. He called Hawk. Hawk called me. I've been told I would not be going to the US and he would talk to Pixie about it, not me."

I drew in a deep breath.

"I am ready to go home, right now."

"Fucking Raj. Fuck. Why the fuck can't he leave well enough alone? Always stirring shit." Skel kept swearing but his phone was no longer near his mouth and it seemed as if his voice was coming from a long way off. Then he was back.

"Give me a few to sort shit out here, DC. I'll call you back. Okay?"

Bending over I laid my head on the railing and groaned. I shouldn't have called him.

"Ja, okay. Sorry I dumped all of this on you, Skel. I shouldn't have bothered you with it."

"Hey, that's not true, you and I, we are family and family look out for each other. This is me looking out for you. I'll talk to you soon."

Going back into my room I curled up on the bed and stared out the open door as the setting sun turned the scattered clouds into a kaleidoscope of pinks. I watched as the colours slowly started to fade as the night rolled in.

A soft knock on my door had me lifting my head and looking over my shoulder, but I didn't answer.

"Dees, it's Law, can I come in?"

"Sure, Law." I called softly.

He slowly opened the door and came in, silently closing it behind him. I sat up against the headboard and frowned as he slid the sliding door closed before he sat down next to me.

"Raj is a dick. He's been pissed at you for fucking ever because you ended it with him. He strutted around like he was something so fucking special while you dated him. Gav and I are convinced he started dating you because he had his eyes on the Prez's chair. Tonight, he purposely pissed Hawk off. He made it seem like you and Pixie were arranging the trip to the US behind his back. I think he wants you and Hawk to split up. Maybe he thinks with Hawk out of the picture Doc will back him when he tries to claim you."

"What the hell are you saying, Law?"

Law turned those eyes that were so like his dad's on me, they were very serious. God, I wish Grizzly were here with us now. He dropped his voice and spoke in an almost whisper.

"I'm saying we need to watch our backs. I don't fucking trust him, DC. Neither does Gav. As prospects we see a lot of shit no one else pays any attention to. We've been watching him and something isn't right. He's too fucking slick. And there's something else everyone has forgotten but we need to remember. He used to be in this fucked up club. And it was Speedy who recommended him to Doc. He transferred in three years ago as a brand-new patch and now he's already being put forward for a position at the table. How did he manage that? What's his next step?"

I sat looking at him with narrowed eyes as I ran through everything he had said. Yes, Raj was a dick, but a traitor? I was about to answer when the door was jerked open.

An enraged Raj stood in the open door.

"Prospect, what the fuck are you doing alone in the room with Hawk's old lady with the door closed? Get your fucking ass out of this room, right now."

My temper went totally nuclear. I'd had enough of him being a dick.

"Get the fuck out of my room, Raj. I'm talking to my little brother, to my family. And you are not my family. Get the hell out."

Behind us Rico slid the sliding door open, frowned at Raj then looked down at Law and I.

"What's going on?"

"Raj is insinuating Law and I are fucking in here. He needs to get his ass out of my room or I'm going to lose my shit."

Rico moved to the side as Skinny shoved in next to him.

"Are you fucking crazy, Raj? Law is like a little brother to her. She's been his big sister since the day he was born. What the fuck is wrong with you? First you piss her off, then you rat her out to her old man. I'm not an officer, just a lowly patched member and going against a brother who might be sitting at the table soon could get me dead, but I'm just going to say it and fuck the consequences. I heard what you told him when you called. You fucking lied to him. Straight up fucking lied." Skinny shook his head in confusion. "Why the fuck would you do that?"

The room felt crowded with all of them there. Law slowly got off the bed and stood at the bottom. Rico and Skinny were at the sliding door and Wolf, one of Hawk's men, stood behind Raj in the open door.

Raj's eyes glittered with rage.

It came out of nowhere. He lost control and venom came pouring from him.

"I didn't lie as much as enlighten him. Hawk deserves to know the kind of bitch she is. She will never put him or his club first. It will always be about her and what she wants. Doc is a fucking pussy where she's concerned. Hawk won't be. He'll control her and keep her on her back where she belongs. If he can't there are a few of us who will fuck her until she learns her place. She's pussy, a club slut, nothing more."

Hatred shone out of Raj's dark brown eyes as he spat out how he really felt.

I couldn't believe this was the same man I had known for the last three years. Neither could I believe I had shared my body with the piece of shit, even if it was only for a few months.

Faster than I could blink Wolf had a gun pressed up against the back of Raj's head.

"Keep your hands where we can see them." He ordered as he moved back, stepping out of Raj's reach.

Guns appeared instantly in Skinny and Rico's hands pointing at Raj and Wolf. I did not want to think what Wolf holding a gun to Raj's head meant. When we left the factory Hawk had insisted on replacing Gav with one of his men. Wolf was that man.

"Law, get the cable ties and lock this bastard down." Wolf ordered and Law obeyed. "Rico, Skinny, get your asses up against the wall and stay there. You move and I'll fucking fill you full of lead." He threatened through clenched teeth. "Until I know I can trust you, you stay right there."

"DC, babe, move onto the balcony and wave at the brothers down at the pool. This is fucking happening sooner than we planned but, what the fuck, we'll go with what we have. Law, where are those fucking cable ties?" he shouted over his shoulder.

I slowly got off the bed, moved to the balcony railing and looked down. There were four men with Iron Dogz kuttes sitting around a small table next to the pool. One was looking up at me. I waved. He kept his eyes on me as he spoke to the others. Then they were out of their chairs and walking into the building.

What the hell was going on?

Rico and Skinny looked as confused as I did. Law did not look confused at all.

BURNING BRIGHT IN THE BLACK

The little shit had been in on this from the start.

Whatever this is.

He had some explaining to do.

They all had some explaining to do.

TWENTY TWO

Hawk

Hawk watched as his little bird rode away with fucking Raj. He did not like or trust the fucker. One bright spot was he'd been able to get Wolf on her team. Knowing he had a man he trusted watching out for her had him breathing a little easier.

"She'll be okay. Law will watch over her." A rough voice interrupted his musings.

Turning he nodded at Tiny who had watched the group ride away as well.

"I just don't like that Raj fucker. He's too fucking slick," Hawk snarled.

He turned back to the open factory doors as Tiny threw a heavy arm around him and laughed.

"She's safely out of the way in Umhlanga and my girl knows how to watch her back. Stop worrying and let's get shit done so we can go home. You don't like Raj and I really don't like this fucking city."

Hawk laughed as he followed Tiny back inside. He was right. His woman was strong and knew how to look out for herself. And she had Wolf with her. His brother wouldn't let anything happen to his woman.

It felt strange riding his bike without his kutte. Not just strange, it felt like he was naked. He had been calling on club contacts to collect the shit Gav needed and thank fuck they were almost done. He looked forward to getting back to the factory and pulling his kutte back on.

Hours later Hawk glanced over his shoulder at the cage being driven by the prospect and sighed. The kid had the widest fucking grin on his face. At least one of them was happy he thought as they rode back into the open doors of the loading bay.

After offloading all the shit, he grabbed a cold beer and walked outside. Taking a deep drink of his cold beer he sat on the steps outside the bay doors staring at the weed and kikuyu infested yard as the light slowly faded. He had his phone in his hand contemplating calling his woman when it rang. He didn't know the number.

"Hawk."

There was a beat of silence, then a throat cleared. "Hawk. It's Raj."

"What's wrong?"

"Nothing is wrong, as such. I just thought I should call and give you a heads up. Your woman is making arrangements to leave the country for the US with her boss, Pixie Maingarde. I'm not sure what's going down but I thought you should know. I tried to talk to her but she shut me down."

It hit Hawk right in the chest and he had to take a breath before he answered.

"Thanks for letting me know. I'll take care of it."

He didn't wait, he called her as soon as he finished the call.

And then, once again, he fucking blew it by being a total dick.

He knew the minute he ended the call he had fucked up. But he would not back down. He couldn't. Her safety was all that mattered.

Her boss was a Maingarde, not to be trusted.

He was still sitting there when Skelly stormed outside.

"Why the fuck would you treat DC like she's some airheaded bimbo? No, don't answer because I will tell you why. It's because every single bitch you've ever fucked was a fucking airhead. Your ex-wife included. Between them those bitches don't possess one fucking functioning brain cell. Now you're with a woman with more brains in her fucking pinkie than all of your whores put together and you're treating her the way you treat them,"

Skelly snarled, waving a hand to shut him up when he tried to answer.

"No, I don't want to hear a fucking word from you. You're a stupid fucking prick for believing a word that ass-wipe Raj tells you. He hates you and the shit he just pulled confirmed my suspicions that he hates DC as well. Now I have to find a way to calm my girl down and get her to stay put and at the same time do this fucking job with

Gav. She wants to go home, right the fuck now. Stay off the fucking phone, don't call her, don't text her. Not a fucking thing. I'll take care of this and once we get home it will be you and me, fucker."

He didn't give Hawk a chance to say a bloody word as he stormed back inside shouting for Gav. Hawk rubbed his hands over his face with a heavy sigh. Yip, he had fucked up. Finishing his beer, he chucked the bottle at the bin in the corner and felt a tiny bit better as he listened to the glass shatter as it fell into the bin. He might as well go back inside and help.

They had all the shit Gav required laid out in neat lines on the loading bay floor when he got a call that turned his insides ice cold.

"Prez, we've got them. One of the traitors is the Logistics Manager up here. The other one is the Manager of the shipping and imports office in Pinetown. The bad thing is they're both bitches. We've got the one up here in lock up. I asked Hotdog to collect the bitch down there and bring her to you. We've checked into everyone. Our brothers are clean. You've got the Crow down there. Get her to open the bitch up and extract what we need. We'll work on the one up here. We've found more and Ziggy will send it to your phone."

Hawk grinned evilly.

"Good work, Jagger. DC has been sent to Umhlanga because Doc didn't want her around this shit. He sent Raj and three of his guys with her. I put Wolf on her, so I know she's okay."

"Fuck!" The sound of breaking glass rang through the phone.

"Jagger! What the fuck?"

"Sorry, Prez. I threw my beer at the wall."

There was a beat of silence and then he was back,

"Boss, call in our brothers, you need to find Skelly and Tiny and put me on speaker. I have some fucked up shit to share."

"I'll call you back."

Ending the call Hawk beckoned a still pissed off Skelly to follow him.

They were gathered around the small table in the conference room with his phone lying in the centre of the table. Jagger was on speaker.

"We're all here, Jagger. Go ahead."

"You asked us to check into everyone and Ziggy got a bee in his fucking bonnet and started searching really, really fucking wide and deep. What he found goes back years. He checked on every single person around DC and they all came back clean. All except one. We couldn't find dick on him and it freaked Ziggy out. So, he gave Dollar what he had to hit up his Home Affairs contact and he got back to us about fifteen minutes ago."

The room was so silent you could have heard a pin drop, if any of them had a fucking pin. Hawk's heart was beating too fast and his gut was churning.

"Give it to me, brother. Don't drag this shit out."

Then Jagger gave them news they did not want to hear.

"Colin "Raj" Chetty does not exist. Oh, there are surface documents making it look like he does but he really doesn't. He was born Dinesh Sharma Maharaj, illegitimate son of Ravi Maharaj and his mistress Veda Chetty. Ravi Maharaj is the cousin of Vinesh Sharma, one of the Sharma's Doc exterminated, and Vinesh was DC's grandfather."

It felt like a stone had settled in Hawk's gut. He stayed quiet as Jagger continued.

"Dinesh Maharaj was raised in the Sharma gang and quickly rose through the ranks before he suddenly disappeared. The photos we found are very grainy, but even with the fancy suits, sunglasses, short beard and short hair he's our man. He reappeared as a supposed transfer at the Durban chapter of the Road Warriors MC going by the name Colin "Raj" Chetty. Speedy very quickly transferred him out to the Johannesburg chapter which stopped the questions being asked by his men. Any normal background check would have found he was legit."

"What the fuck?" Tiny was frowning heavily. "How did this shit get past you, Skel?"

But Jagger jumped in before Skelly could answer.

"He would have done the usual background check, Tiny. It would have looked totally legit. It fooled us when we checked him out. It was only when Ziggy started digging, we found this shit. It was buried really deep and without Dollar's connections it would have stayed buried."

Rage burned in his gut and Hawk had to reign in the desire to pick up his phone and hurl it at the wall. It wouldn't help his woman who was in the hands of one of her family and club's biggest enemies.

He could now clearly see the bastard's original play. Claim the club princess, make her his old lady, and then use her to slowly destroy her father, his club and in the end her.

It was a masterful plan, but they had failed. Failed because whoever had planned it had not foreseen the strong independent woman DC was.

At the end of the day his little bird's damned independence had saved her and her club. Turning to Skelly he took control.

"Right. He's with her right now and pissing her off, a lot. I have Wolf on her and I trust him implicitly. Are the rest of the team trustworthy?"

Skelly nodded. "Yes, they can be trusted."

"Law is like her little brother and Rico and Skinny would die for her. Raj is on his own but we don't know if he has help out there." Shaka spoke for the first time.

Tiny was texting furiously and Hawk knew he was talking to Doc. He left them to it, picked up his phone, quickly ended the call with Jagger and called his man.

Wolf picked up almost immediately.

"Boss, glad you called. This Raj fucker is a dick. Can I fuck him up?"

"He's the fucking enemy, Wolf. I'm sending Beast with three brothers to take your back. Keep your eyes open, brother. Beast will text when they get there. You keep her safe and bring her back to me."

"Haven't let the fucker out of my sight, Prez. Got eyes on him right now. He fucking lied, brother. No way was your woman planning on leaving the country. She was talking about attending a tattoo convention with her boss. Just thought I'd put it out there."

Hawk nodded even though he knew Wolf couldn't see it.

"Thanks, brother. We got shit to do this side; I'll call as soon as I can."

"No problems, Prez. I've got her, no worries." Wolf assured him.

Hawk turned and pointed to Beast. "Take Sin, Dizzy and Spook, ride to Umhlanga. Wolf will hold him until you get there. Kev will follow in the cage. Load the fucker and his shit then bring him back here."

Outwardly Hawk was calm. But internally he was a boiling vat of rage that he kept under tight control. Once he had the piece of shit in his hands, then, and only then, would he let his rage free. Time passed too damned slowly while he waited to hear from Beast. Doc had arrived earlier and just one look at the man made everyone back off. He was beyond angry, his eyes like burning blue ice in his stony face.

Hawk looked down as his phone vibrated with an incoming message.

Got him. Woman safe.

Relief shot through him.

"What do we know?" Doc had ice sliding through his voice.

Tiny nodded towards Hawk, leaving it to him to answer.

"DC is safe. Beast has Raj, they are bringing him in."

"Who's riding with my girl?"

"She's got Wolf, Law, Rico, Skinny, Beast, Sin, Spook and Dizzy. Kev is driving the cage bringing the bastard in. My woman insisted on escorting them in."

"My demon child is going to have me in a fucking early grave." Doc growled as he sat down. "Skelly, give me the short version of what we have. Is there anything else I need to know?"

Skel started explaining and Hawk tuned them out, he had gone over this more than once. Everything pointed towards Speedy teaming up with the Sharma gang. Together they had set up the trafficking ring operating out of Durban harbour.

Why they had targeted the Iron Dogz MC was still a mystery but they would soon be extracting the information from Raj or rather Dinesh Sharma Maharaj.

Apparently one of the big men in the Sharma organisation.

It was going to be a very interesting night.

And not just for him.

DC

I rode in the middle of the pack as we hit the N2 South and sped towards Durban. Law, Rico, Skinny and Dizzy were riding sweep behind the cage. I rode with Beast, Sin, Wolf and Spook at the front.

Law and Kev had made short work of loading and tying down Raj's bike. Beast and Sin hadn't said one word when the two wrapped him in duct tape like a damned mummy and threw him in next to his bike.

Not one fist had been laid on him.

That was a concern. It meant they had orders to hold off.

Hawk's orders.

We stayed with the cage through the traffic, causing motorists to get out of our way the minute they saw us. The guys weren't wearing their kuttes but they were still darkly intimidating.

As we pulled into the yard at the back of the factory I breathed in sharply. My dad stood waiting with his arms crossed over his chest next to Hawk, who held the exact same stance. Behind them stood Tiny, Skelly, Ice and Kid, all of them with arms crossed. Behind them, in a rough semi-circle, waited the rest of the brothers, arms crossed. Every single one wearing their kuttes. And the ranks of the Iron Dogz had grown, which meant brothers from the Durban chapter had joined them.

Beast led us to one side of the yard and we parked as Kev turned the cage and reversed until he brought it to a stop right in front of Hawk and Doc.

Beast immediately pulled his kutte from his saddlebags and pulled it on, the others followed his example. We silently joined the waiting group.

Kev unlocked the back of the cage and when he opened the doors and Raj in his duct taped mummy form was revealed laughter rang through the still air.

"Getting that shit off is going to fucking hurt," someone remarked happily.

Doc turned to his men. "Rover, take him and don't get him too comfortable."

Then it was my turn.

"DC, conference room, now."

He walked through the men back into the factory and I followed. He sounded pissed, hopefully not at me.

I sat on a crate and watched as the room filled with officers from both clubs. Hawk was the last to walk in. He took a chair on the opposite side of the room.

Good. I was so not into him right now.

Doc cleared his throat and I gave him what he wanted, my attention.

"We've brought in another prisoner. We need you to do what you do. She's part of the trafficking ring. She's the Shipping Manager at the Iron Dogz Trucking offices in Pinetown. The bitch personally prepared the shipping documents."

I nodded. I knew what he wanted from me.

"Don't go easy. Break her, any way you have to. I want results tonight. Have a look at her and let me know who you need."

Fuck. I nodded again.

"The bitch worked for the Dogz, I want one of my men observing," Hawk growled at Doc.

Doc nodded his agreement then turned to me. "Get on it, now."

I was dismissed. Not saying a word, I left the room and found Law waiting for me.

"I've got your saddlebags and found you a room. You're lucky, no one has crashed in it, yet."

Wrinkling my nose at him we both grinned as he led me upstairs and down a long corridor to a room at the end. It was a tiny room, only big enough for a single bed and a tiny bedside table. Now I knew why no one had claimed the room, the bed was too damn small. Lucky for me.

"There's a bathroom two doors down, just lock the door when you use it."

Damn, sharing a bathroom with a bunch of guys wasn't good. It would be filthy.

"I've had it cleaned for you, if you jump in now, it will still be okay."

"Thanks, little brother. I have to look in on the woman they brought in. Do you know where she's being kept?"

"Yes, she's not where you talked to the other one. Get your scary shit together. I will be back to take you to the bitch."

He backed out of the room and closed the door.

Dumping my saddlebags on the bed I drew out black jeans and the same black long-sleeved tee I had worn when I had questioned the young woman earlier this morning. I couldn't believe it was only this morning I had been here. It felt as if days had passed with everything that was happening.

BURNING BRIGHT IN THE BLACK

I was dressed and had my knife in the sheath in my boot with my gun in a holster at my back when there was a knock at my door. Taking a deep breath, I prepared to become someone else. I opened the door in my head and Crow walked out to join me. Law was waiting outside my door. I handed him my mask and gloves.

On the way down I used the bathroom and slid the black contact lenses in, blinking to situate them comfortably. I wore them for no other reason but that they masked my feelings. Meeting my dead black stare in the mirror I smiled.

Play time.

That's how fucked up I was inside. I was looking forward to making her talk.

The building seemed strangely empty as we made our way down the stairs, we kept going past the ground floor down worn cement stairs into a dank basement. It smelt wet and mouldy. Bare light bulbs hanging from electrical wire led down a wide corridor and off into the depths of the basement. The lights were weak pools of light and outside of those pools, darkness lay like a smelly blanket. We passed several doors but kept going.

Law stopped in front of a thick steel door. It had a big lock on the outside along with a heavy slider. No one was getting out of the room without outside help.

I slipped my braid into the back of my tee and quickly pulled on the black leather mask with the fine gauze insert over my mouth, leaving only my eyes visible, and pulled on the black Nitrile gloves.

"Shit, I didn't bring my jacket." I muttered.

A big hand holding a black hoodie appeared next to me, I looked over my shoulder. Hawk stood silent; the black hoodie still held out to me. Not saying a word, I took it, slid it on and pulled the hood up over my head and was instantly engulfed by Hawk's scent.

Shit.

It was almost enough to pull me out of my Crow persona. I forced my humanity to take a back seat and breathed in slowly. Swallowing it down I nodded to Law.

The door silently opened and a room covered in thick black plastic was revealed. Even the ceiling was covered. It was like being inside a plastic cube. In the centre of the room, cable tied to a steel chair bolted to the floor was the woman.

She wasn't what I was expecting.

A well put together, slightly heavy, middle-aged woman sat in the chair and stared back at me with curious eyes. Greying blonde hair was cut in a no-nonsense bob. Her white blouse was silk and the red knee-length pencil skirt was obviously part of the power suit she must've been wearing. Her feet were bare, black cable ties were tied around her ankles and just below her knees.

"So, you are Doc's infamous Crow." Her cultured voice filled the silence. "Must be the lack of height and a fully functioning penis that brought you to this work. What a sad little man you are, hiding behind a mask to torture women who would never otherwise let you touch them."

Looking behind me she smiled. "Oh, and look. The high and mighty Hawk Walker got off his latest whore long enough to come and talk to me."

Then she looked back at me and carried on being what she was, a scared and talkative bitch.

"I have nothing to say at this time. Try again the day after tomorrow, maybe I'll have something to say then." She smiled, nasty and cold.

Deep behind her eyes something flickered and disappeared. It was exactly what I had been waiting to see. Now she was mine.

I turned, walked out, and heard Law closing the door but he didn't lock it because he knew what was coming next. I pulled the mask up as I spoke to Law.

"I need Alien and Shaka, wearing their kuttes and some men's cologne, two bottles should do it and a bottle of tequila. The usual."

Reaching into his back pockets Law pulled out two bottles of cheap cologne with high alcohol content and handed them to me. I slid them into my back pockets with a grin.

Law ran down the corridor and up the stairs to bring Alien and Shaka to me. And the tequila, I could not do a dark job like the one waiting for me without drinking to get through the heavy parts.

Hawk had followed us out and stared at me blankly. He needed to leave, if he did not, he was going to see a side of me he would never be able to forget or live with.

Crow wasn't me, but she also was me.

Not everyone who saw me work were able to accept and understand that part of me.

"You might want to let one of your brothers sit in on this and take a step back." I didn't look at him as I spoke.

"No. She works for me. I'll be in there while you ask your questions, and Ice will be with me."

He was in for a rude awakening.

I didn't really ask a lot of questions.

My subjects talked; they told me what I wanted to know. They kept on talking until I had all I needed to know.

Then they either went back to their lives or disappeared.

This bitch would most probably disappear.

And I would most probably be the one to make it happen.

TWENTY THREE

DC

Alien, Shaka and Ice came striding down the badly lit corridor. Even in the bad light I could see the darkness in their eyes. Alien pulled me into his arms, hugging me tight and whispered in my ear.

"Do not let the shit get to you, babe. I've got your back."

Hugging him I nodded against his shoulder and stepped back.

Only to have Shaka enfold me in his heavy arms.

"We are your way back out of the dark, Crow. Use us, do not go there alone."

Again, all I did was nod then stepped back and nodded towards the door.

"You go in, stay against the walls. I want one behind her, two on either side, and one at the door."

Meeting Hawk's eyes I coldly laid it out for him.

"Do not, and listen carefully to me here, do not, fucking interfere. This is what I do, no matter what happens you stay out of it. You do not talk. You are here to observe and take note of what she says. Nothing more. Leave your phones with Law."

I pulled the mask back over my face, settling it over the top of my tee. Giving a nod to Law he opened the door.

I stood to the side watching as they walked through the door, leaving it open for me. I waited until they were where I wanted them, took the bottle of tequila from Law, picked up the chair standing against the wall outside the door, walked in and placed it in front of the woman. The bottle of tequila I set on the floor next to my chair. Behind me the door closed with a heavy thunk.

Hawk stood with arms crossed against the wall behind her. Right in my line of sight. I ignored him and concentrated on the woman in front of me. I could not let him and Ice being in the room change the course of what was going to happen. What had to happen if we were to stand a chance of finding out what Speedy had planned.

Sitting down in front of her I studied her and she studied me in turn. The only sound in the room was a faint crinkle of sound as a foot moved over the plastic.

Leaning forward I spoke in a soft hiss.

"Tell me a story."

"You are a pathetic excuse for a man. You're a puny loser and this is the only way you can get off."

Behind my mask I grinned.

Such a stupid old bitch.

"Tell me a story." I hissed once again.

"Why don't you bend over and let one of them do you up the ass? It might be more entertaining than listening to your voice," she tried again.

I bent down and slid my knife free from my boot. And the bitch laughed.

"Oh look. You've got a big knife to compensate for your little dick."

Staring at her laughing face it suddenly hit me. She had been coached by someone I had questioned at some stage. Someone who had made it through without a single cut. Someone who had talked when she or he shouldn't have. A pity they hadn't found one of the others to coach her. But it would prove to be rather difficult, none of those would talk to anyone, ever.

Oops, sorry for you old bitch.

Getting up I slowly walked around her. Picking at her shirt sleeve with the point of my knife I took it between two fingers lifted and slid the knife in and down. Splitting the sleeve from shoulder to wrist. I didn't say a word, just moved to the other side and did the same. Very carefully I slid the knife around the armholes of both sleeves and let the fabric drop down over her cable tied wrists.

Her breath hitched as I cut and when I slid my icy cold gloved fingers into the fabric at the top of her shoulders her breathing became choppy. I said nothing as I cut her expensive blouse from her body, leaving her sitting in her pretty white bra with the remnants of her fancy blouse hanging around her waist. I carefully unbuttoned what was left of the blouse and as expected she snapped her head forward, hoping to hit me in the face. She misjudged the distance and as she pulled back, I hit her hard on her forehead with the hilt of the knife. She moaned in pain. Ignoring her pain, I pulled the remnants of her blouse out of her skirt and threw it into a corner. The sleeves soon followed.

I slid back onto my chair and hissed. "Tell me a story."

She decided to lie.

"I don't know what you want me to tell you. I don't know anything."

I cut her. Lightning fast. From shoulder to elbow. Not shallow but not too deep either.

Her shocked scream had Hawk going solid. But he didn't move.

"Tell me a story." I hissed.

"You are crazy! I don't know anything. I'm nobody. I do my job, that's all I do. I don't know what you want."

The next cut was slow, not fast. I slowly cut the other arm from shoulder to elbow.

"No! Stop! I don't know what you want! Tell me what you want!"

I again started to circle her and she tried desperately to keep me in view. Sliding a bottle of the cologne from my pocket I slowly unscrewed it and standing behind her dribbled a few drops into the cut on her right arm.

Her scream of pain didn't do anything to me.

I felt nothing.

Walking back to my chair I sat down, leaning against the backrest I stared at her.

"Tell me a story." My whisper cut through her pain filled gasps.

"I'm telling you, I don't know anything. I just do my job, like Hawk Walker tells me to."

And there it was. The first step.

"He tells you what to do?"

She hesitated for a few seconds and then it seemingly poured out. She was good, but not that good. The lies she had been coached to give us fell like lead from her lips.

"He always calls with special instructions for certain documents. I make sure they are in order and then send out the truck with the special container. Like he ordered me to do."

"On your cell phone or the office phone?"

Her eyes flipped around like mad marbles in her head as she looked from side to side.

"Mostly on the office phone, sometimes my cell phone."

"Hmm. So, there will be a record of those calls on the telephone system at the office and on your cell phone. Good."

I nodded at Shaka and he left the room. I watched her eyes and almost laughed. She thought she had nailed Hawk as the bad guy and we were swallowing her story.

Not giving her any warning, I leaned forward and poured cologne over both of the cuts. Then sliced two more lines on each arm. Screaming she jerked at the cable ties holding her prisoner.

"I told you what you wanted to know! Why are you doing this? I'm innocent, I didn't do anything. I just followed orders."

"I only have your word for it. Hawk says you're lying." I hissed. "You have lied to me so I choose to believe him for now."

I brought the knife towards her face and her eyes stayed on it until it was too close to watch. Her eyes shot up to mine, fear now very evident. I slid the tip of the knife down her nose and over her lips and chin, letting it drag over the soft skin. Leaving behind a red line. Keeping my eyes on hers I put the tip of the knife just inside the strap of her bra at her collarbone and cut a shallow line down to the top of her breast. Ignoring her screams I did the same on the other side. Blood ran down and into her pretty white bra, turning the top of the cups red. Tapping the flat of the knife against her sternum I leaned in close and hissed out the next step.

"Do you like patterns? I love patterns. Just love decorating my girlies, leaving my mark behind on pristine skin. You're a bit old, but your skin is still good. I'm going to enjoy decorating your breasts. Big breasts are so much better than small ones. More space to play. So many pretty patterns to give you."

I made a few shallow cuts across her abdomen. Not saying a word. By now she was shuddering and crying. I ignored her as I slowly poured cologne over the wounds. The smell was cloying but the alcohol did its job.

I sat back and twirled my knife then suddenly dropped it to the hem of her skirt and started slitting it up the middle.

"What are you doing? This is not supposed to happen! This is not supposed to happen!"

I ignored her and kept on sliding my knife up between her legs, over her belly up to the waistband on her skirt. Once I sliced through it, I pulled the two sides away from her body and let it fall. Sitting back, I crossed my arms over my chest and let my eyes run over her body as blood ran down over her white high cut panties, turning them red.

"Not bad for an old bitch." I hissed.

"What are you doing? This isn't supposed to happen! He said it would be easy. He said the Crow wouldn't hurt a woman. Why? Why?"

Tears and snot mingled on her face as she cried.

Reaching down I picked up the bottle of tequila, cracked the top and tipped it up to my covered lips, filled my mouth and swallowed. It burned all the way down and I suppressed the shudder but I welcomed the heat spreading outward.

"He lied." I hissed. "I hurt women all the time, sometimes I even kill them."

Her eyes were wide with shock and fear.

The door opened and Shaka walked back in.

"No calls from Hawk's cell to the bitch or the office. No internal calls from his office phone to the bitch. We did find calls from the landline at the Warriors clubhouse here in Durban and a few from two unknown numbers. Most of the calls originated near a cell tower here in Durban. It just so happens to be near the Road Warriors compound. The rest of the calls originated near a cell tower in Cape Town. Verified Hawk's whereabouts, he was in Johannesburg at the time of the calls. Impossible for him to be in two places at the same time. She lied."

Shaka's face was impassive as he gave his report then took up his position against the wall again.

I tipped the bottle back and took a long drink then set it back down.

"Glad you lied. So very glad because those lies now make you mine. I like patterns." I slowly shook my head.

"No, I lie, I love patterns, love drawing them on the skins of my girlies."

Leaning towards her I slowly started slicing a grid into her left thigh. Her screams echoed around the room but I didn't pay any attention to her. I kept cutting into her jerking flesh until I had what I wanted.

A noughts and crosses grid filled the top of her left thigh.

"I'll be crosses you can be noughts. If you win you might just leave here alive." I hissed as I carefully put a cross right in the centre.

Tapping the empty spaces with the knife point I looked up. "Where shall I put the nought? Here? Here? Or here, no, maybe here."

"No! No, please stop. Please. Anything you want, I'll give you anything."

I slowly drew a nought with the point of the knife, not cutting too deep and splashed it with cologne.

I continued taunting her as I played on her skin until I had three crosses in a row.

"I win." I hissed gleefully. "We have to play again or maybe we play until you win. We have a lot of skin to cover with my patterns."

I cut a deep line through the centre of the grid and tipped more cologne over the cuts. By now the bottle was empty and I threw it towards the remnants of her clothes. I saw relief shine in her eyes but it disappeared as I pulled the other bottle from my back pocket and set it down next to the bottle of tequila.

She started to crack.

"It wasn't Hawk! It wasn't Hawk! I swear it wasn't him. I was told what to say. I was told to tell you he was guilty."

"Too late. I already know," I murmured as I cut her bra from her body and threw it towards the corner.

Tilting my head, I stared at her breasts then slowly sliced an easy curve from the side of her right breast to the centre of her chest. I did the same to the left and poured cologne over the shallow wounds. Blood dripped from her heavy breasts and ran down joining the blood from the cuts I had made on her belly and soaking into her high cut white panties.

She broke. Wide open. Started spilling her secrets, like I knew she would.

Like they always did.

"My…my…my orders, they came from…Speedy and from…a woman. I only spoke to her a few times. She…she threatened my family if I didn't do as she said. Please you have to believe me, please."

"I need more. Who is she?" I hissed as I played with my knife. Her eyes never left it.

"I don't know. I swear I don't know. She kept her voice low but I heard a slight English accent and her voice…it was so cold. Emotionless. They are going to take my granddaughters if I don't do as they tell me. You have to save them. Please. You…you have to keep them safe. They'll know I'm gone, they'll take my granddaughters, put them with the others. Please, please, save them."

I shook my head. The bitch disgusted me.

"I don't have to do anything. Did you even once think about the children you sentenced to hell? About their parents and grandparents? Your offshore accounts are full of blood money. Innocent children's blood is on your hands and it has stained your money red. Why should I do anything for you? Why should I stop making lovely patterns on your skin?"

I dragged the tip of the knife down over her left nipple and her body shook with fear.

Her head dropped to her chest as she sobbed and when she looked up again, I knew there was going to be more.

And there was.

"I recorded everything. For insurance." She whispered.

"All the calls, every single one. I have…I have it on a USB hidden in my garden. No one would expect me to hide it there. It's in a small, sealed plastic container with the cell phone they gave me. It's buried under the Japanese warrior in my front garden. All of the calls are on there. Every single message. Please, you can have it, just save my granddaughters, please. I know I'm going to die. I don't care what happens to me as long as they are safe. Speedy is bringing in the product, they call them the product, tomorrow morning and they will leave tomorrow night. I send out the order for the truck and container and prepare the shipping documents implicating Hawk Walker and the Iron Dogz when he calls. All I do is handle the paperwork. The driver is one of them, but he works for Iron Dogz Trucking. His name is Charlie. That's everything, I don't know anything more. I swear on my son and granddaughters lives it's all I know."

Nodding at Alien I waited until he was out of the room. Hawk shifted uneasily making the plastic rustle.

Taking another deep drink of the tequila I sat forward and held the bottle to her lips. She took a drink and coughed as it burned down her throat.

"Why?" She asked. "Why did they lie about you?"

Giving a soft snort I shook my head and hissed.

"They didn't lie, they just didn't know everything. Have a drink it will get you through what comes next." I pushed her head back and held the bottle against her lips.

Forcing her to take two long gulps.

I drank as well, taking down about three shots worth. My belly was pleasantly warm even if my heart was ice cold. The next step was never easy.

"How the fuck did you get caught up in this shit?"

Hawk suddenly burst out. I was amazed he had kept his mouth shut this long.

"It was my husband; he was a gambler and he owed the wrong people a lot of money. They broke into our home while my daughter-in-law was there. They…they killed them both right in front of me, threatened to kill my son and take his little girls if I didn't do as directed. They knew I worked at Iron Dogz Trucking, knew exactly what my position in the company was. I couldn't let my son and his little girls pay for my husband's mistakes. I…I agreed to do anything they wanted me to. They…they beat me up, shot me and left. The SAPS never really investigated the murders. I think they might have been paid off. I've been working for these people for almost eight months now. At first the containers contained poached animal products. But it changed when the woman got involved. She promised Speedy a lot of easy money and that's how it started with the children."

She gave him everything. The longer she spoke the more I saw compassion glowing in his eyes.

This was not going to end well.

Alien walked back in and I waited as he took his place.

"Sent some men to retrieve the items. They should be back in an hour or so."

Rising up out of my chair I looked down at the woman as I tapped the knife against my thigh. "While we wait, I'm going to take a little break. I'll see you again soon. Don't go anywhere."

Picking up the tequila I looked into Ice's carefully blank and narrowed eyes as he opened the door for me. I needed to breathe fresh air. I needed to cleanse my soul of the dark shit I had boiling in my blood. Stripping off Hawk's hoody I dropped it on the floor as I walked away. The mask, gloves, contact lenses and tee shirt I handed to Law to dispose of. He held out a clean tee and I pulled it on and nodded my thanks. He was my little brother and I trusted him implicitly. Those items would disappear and never surface ever again.

Sitting on the outside steps sipping on the tequila I stayed silent when Rooster sank down next to me.

"Need to ride, baby?" He asked softly.

"Yeah."

"Let's go."

He lifted me off the step, passed the bottle to Law who had been watching over me and drew me to my bike. Law knew I would need to ride and had already pulled it to the front. My helmet, gloves and jacket lay on top of the seat, waiting for me. Alien and Rover's bikes stood ready next to Rooster's loaner. I breathed easier knowing they would join me on my ride.

The weight inside my chest slowly started to release as we rode.

BURNING BRIGHT IN THE BLACK

I let Alien and Rover lead me wherever they wanted to. I wasn't even aware we were on the South Coast road until we hit the tollgates.

We rode hard and fast, letting the night slip past in a blur. It was late when we rolled into Margate and parked above the beach. Everything was closed except the nightclub that was doing a brisk trade.

I pulled my helmet off and walked down the paved walkway onto the deserted beach. The waves were lit up by the security lights and streetlights all along the beach.

Standing just out of reach of the breaking waves I breathed in deep. Holding it before letting it out, and letting the last of the black coating my soul float off into the night sky.

"We're not riding back tonight, baby. Got us an apartment at the Margate Sands for the night. I'll take you up while Alien and Rover find us some food. Okay?" Rooster spoke in a low voice.

All I could do was nod and follow as we rode our bikes up into the parking garage and checked in at reception. The poor receptionist tried hard not to be freaked out by the bikers standing in front of her. She only succeeded once Alien started flirting with her.

Not too much later we sat on the balcony eating burgers and drinking beer and watching the dark waves rolling onto the beach. No one spoke, we didn't have to.

The four of us have been friends for a very long time and the silence wasn't uncomfortable.

"I put your saddlebags on your bed. Hop into the shower before you fall asleep in your chair." Rooster poked my shoulder as I started nodding off.

After a long hot shower, I pulled on clean panties and a tee and crawled into bed. I fell asleep almost immediately. I slept deeply, so deeply I didn't hear my phone vibrating madly on the bedside table.

Alien's hand on my shoulder in the early hours had me up and out of bed. There were things to do today and we had to get back.

The sun was rising as we rode into Durban and made our way to the safe house.

I wasn't looking forward to seeing Hawk.

He had seen too much.

Way too much.

He now knew what the Crow really did for the club and as with some of the brothers would never be able to get past it.

But I had to try and explain. I had to at least try and save what we had because he was it for me.

The one who made everything worthwhile.

Even the Crow liked him, and that was a damned first.

TWENTY FOUR

Hawk

The small dark person torturing the old bitch in the chair was fucking scary. And very obviously didn't feel a thing while doing it.

Fuck.

It wasn't some small dark person.

It was DC, his little bird.

Right now, though, she wasn't his little bird and she wasn't DC either. She had slipped into this other persona. One who didn't hesitate to cut into the bitch tied to the chair. The person with the hissing voice liked it, liked torturing the bitch.

She was the Crow. Doc's dark hand. Feared by all who knew about him.

Now he knew why the Crow was so feared. He was fucking insane.

How the fuck could a father have his daughter do this shit? What happened to bring this frightening personality to the forefront?

As the old bitch cried, he knew he had to step up, step up before his little bird had to escalate the interrogation and scar her soul even more. He knew his little bird, knew this wasn't fucking easy for her. This shit hurt her, down deep where no one could see.

It was from that deep dark place the paintings he had seen in Doc's office originated.

They listened as it all poured out.

The fucked up reason why the bitch betrayed him and his club. About the children that had been lost. To some extent he felt sorry for her, most people would have. But she should have asked for help. She could have approached him and he would have stepped up, protected her and her family.

She didn't. She chose to take the money and doomed innocent children.

When Alien came back into the room and let them know they would soon have the evidence she had hidden the tension suddenly leaked out of the room.

The Crow left after hissing his promise that he would be back. Hawk knew he could not allow it to happen. His woman drank to get through this shit and now it was fucking done. He was up next. His little bird would not take more damage to her soul.

Cutting the old bitch loose he scooped her up and carried her out with Ice at his back.

Boeta stood at the head of the stairs.

"Do you have a room where you treat injuries?"

Boeta gave a chin lift and Hawk followed him up the stairs. Opening the first door at the top of the stairs Boeta stepped back and Hawk walked in. A gurney stood in the centre of the room while around the room in and on wooden glass fronted cupboards there was an array of medical machinery, instruments and medications. Through an open door to the side, he could see another small room with a made-up hospital bed.

Setting the woman down on the gurney he held her down gently as she squirmed. Ice started looking through the cupboards for what they would need to patch her up.

"We need to have a look at these cuts, lie still."

Boeta and Shaka watched silently.

He hadn't been aware that Shaka had followed them up. Alien must have gone to report to Doc.

Shaka broke the silence.

"Don't fuck around with those cuts, you'll just make it worse. The club medic is on his way." Shaka smiled without any humour. "He has experience with this shit."

Ice and Hawk ignored him and kept on putting gauze strips over the bleeding wounds.

The woman looked up at him beseechingly.

"Please, find my son and granddaughters. Bring them in and keep them safe. Please."

Boeta snorted in anger and stormed out. Shaka stood like an ebony statue, filling the doorway.

"Did you ever think about those other parents and grandparents out there? Those people have lost their children because of you. Those children are living in a hell you could not fucking imagine." Shaka snapped.

"I had no choice, no choice," she whispered.

"We always have a fucking choice. You just took the easy way out. I wonder how your son is going to feel about this. How he's going to get past the fact his mother is part of a human trafficking ring. That his children's grandmother had sent innocent children into the hell of being drugged and raped day after day after day until they die in fucking agony."

Shaka turned on his heel and left, slamming the door shut behind him.

Ice froze with his hands holding gauze against the cuts over her chest. Lifting his hands, he slowly stepped back and dropped them to his sides. Looking up at Hawk he shook his head, his eyes tormented.

"Sorry, Boss, I can't do this."

He silently closed the door behind him, leaving Hawk alone with their traitor.

Taking the sheet from the bottom of the gurney he covered her then looked for a chair.

Drawing the one chair in the room up next to the gurney Hawk sat down and looked at the woman lying there.

"You've worked for my company for the last ten years. You know me and my brothers. You know we would never have left you out there to suffer. You could have come to me; you could have gone to Hotdog. You had options, but you didn't use them."

"I...I didn't know who to trust."

"Stop. Stop lying. You knew exactly who you could trust but you were unable to resist the bribe, the money they paid you. Even after losing your husband and daughter-in-law to these people."

Rubbing his hands over his face he ran his fingers through his beard and shook his head.

"My club isn't the only club you disrespected and drew into this mess. The Road Warriors are going to demand justice for those children. I can't protect you from them, what I can do is promise to keep your family safe."

A sob came from her.

"Thank you. You are right, I was greedy. When I'm gone can you make sure the money is used to fight against human trafficking. I don't want my family to be tainted any further by what I did."

All Hawk could do was nod and sit next to her in silence.

He stayed silent as the club doctor came in and set about cleaning and stitching her wounds. He gave her a shot of antibiotics then stepped back from the gurney with a strange little smile.

"You will have scars but they won't be so bad. The worst will be the one on your thigh. The Crow must have been really fucking pissed at you. He only draws grids on those he wants to hurt, really, really badly. I'll be back later to check on you."

He looked over his shoulder at Hawk as he walked out the door,

"You're wanted downstairs."

Hawk left the woman sleeping on the gurney. The doc must have put something in the shot to knock her out.

The conference room was filled with everyone not on guard duty. Both clubs were now represented. Hawk took the chair next to Doc and scanned the room for DC. She wasn't there, neither were Alien, Rover, Rico, Skinny or Rooster.

Where the fuck was his woman?

Crossing his arms over his chest he waited.

He didn't have to wait long. Freeze started the meeting.

"We got information about the shit going down here in Durban. As you all know by now, we have found a human trafficking ring being operated by men we can no longer call our brothers. The Durban chapter of the Road Warriors will be undergoing a change of leadership but we aren't going to address that issue now."

Feet shifted nervously and Hawk saw Doc's eyes swiftly sweep through the men. Glancing at Tiny and Boeta he saw them doing the same. Hawk knew instinctively what they were doing. They were moving fast to secure Boeta in the vacant President's seat in Durban. He couldn't fault them on it but he wished they would get on with it. He wanted to get out of here and find his woman.

His little bird had to be thinking he had been disgusted by what she had done to get to the truth. Nothing could be further from it.

Shocked. Yes, he was that.

Disgusted? Definitely not.

What he did know was his woman was being mentally violated by the fucked up shit her club asked her to do. If it was the fucking last thing he did on this earth he was going to make it stop. He would find a way to give her the peace she deserved.

The meeting went on around him as Skel selected the team that would accompany him and Gav on their mission in the morning. After a short discussion on what would happen later Freeze ended the meeting. He asked the officers of both clubs to stay behind. All the officers present, that is. Thank fuck he had asked Hotdog and Growler to stay because it gave him a few men of his own in a room filled with fucking Road Warriors.

What the fuck now?

Doc didn't leave him to wonder very long at all.

"We have a tough time ahead of us. None of us want it to go wrong and lose those kids. Freeze, Hawk and I will each lead a team tomorrow night. We have to shut this down and shut it down hard. Freeze's team will be at the harbour, keeping an eye on the ship in case we miss the container. Hawk and I will lead the teams to take out Speedy and secure the container and the children. We will clean up the scene and get the kids to safety."

He took a deep breath and glanced at Hawk as if in apology before he continued.

"The best we could come up with if they give us the slip is to alert the coast guard and port authorities, but we all know they've been paid off. Freeze came up with an alternative plan of action. The information on the trafficking ring will be leaked to the taskforce investigating human traffickers. The bitch upstairs will be dropped in their laps. Our hands stay clean but it means the Iron Dogz are going to take a serious amount of heat. Hawk in particular, but it can't be helped. We all have to do what we have to do to bring an end to this shit."

Doc could not meet his eyes, neither could Tiny or Skel. Grizzly was seriously pissed off and standing to the side, his arms crossed tightly and he was the only one who met Hawk's eyes before he gave him a tiny chin lift. Ignoring his presidents. Those bastards had pissed him off as well.

Then Hawk knew, he knew. The fucking bastards.

They were going to throw him at the taskforce to save their own asses. They were fucking with his business. Fucking with his club's business. They were fucking with the lives of his brothers and fucking with his life and in the process, they would take his little bird from him. He had suspected Freeze hated the idea of DC being his old lady and this was him making his play to get rid of him. To use what they had to implicate Hawk and have him spend the rest of his fucking life behind bars.

Not going to fucking happen.

Thank fuck for Ziggy. Thank fuck for Jagger and his club brothers who had his back.

By now every single piece of incriminating evidence would've been scrubbed out of the system. All paperwork would've been fixed.

The truck and trailer reported as stolen. He and his club would be clean and the old bitch upstairs, the bitch at his club and those who helped her would be the only ones left in the line of fire.

Suddenly he knew why his little bird wasn't here. Doc and Freeze had shuffled her off somewhere so she wouldn't interfere with their plans.

They had a huge fucking surprise coming. He had claimed his woman and no one and nothing was going to stand in his way.

Glancing at Ice and Kid he saw they were onto Freeze's play as well. Sin, Beast, Hotdog and Growler stood frozen; their arms crossed tightly over their chests. Their expressionless faces hiding their reactions to the Road Warriors MC stabbing their president, and their club, in the back.

Tonight, would not be forgotten nor would it be forgiven.

"What is happening to Raj?" He needed to know before he got out of this fucking room.

"It's Warrior business and has nothing to do with you." Freeze snarled.

"The bastard went after my old lady, and that makes everything about him my business."

Freeze laughed. The fucker laughed and Doc was stone cold but his eyes were burning.

Hawk had a bad feeling, a really bad fucking feeling.

"Doc, where is my woman?" Hawk gritted his teeth so hard he swore it felt as if they were cracking.

Doc wasn't the one who answered. Freeze condescendingly gave him the answer.

"I sent Rooster to take her on a run to clear her head. They will be back in the morning and I expect by then she will be well fucked and his, not yours."

Hawk laughed.

Partly to calm the rage burning in his gut, but for the most part it was at Freeze.

The man had no idea the shit they were going to be in when DC found out about the future they had planned for her. She was going to explode when she realised they were throwing him and his club to the wolves.

His little bird was a loyal little thing but what she treasured above all was honesty.

The truth would get out, no matter how hard Freeze, and Doc, would try hiding it behind their fucked up lies.

Pushing up out of his chair Hawk looked at Doc, then at Tiny and Skel and shook his head.

"I have no fucking idea what you are trying to achieve with this shit, but you have to know it's going to backfire and fucking badly. My old lady is a force to be reckoned with and you obviously have your heads up your asses where she's concerned. Keep your eyes open so you take it all in when the shit hits the fan. The Iron Dogz will clean some of this shit up; but be warned. I will be taking this fucked up so-called alliance of ours to the table and end it. And here's a friendly warning, having the daughter of the president of the Road Warriors as my old lady isn't going to make a fuck of a difference as to the outcome of the meeting. We will be enemies, no longer allies once I'm done."

He walked out and his men followed him, leaving the Road Warriors in the conference room.

"Get the men in the parking lot, now." Hawk gave Ice the order.

They stood in the far corner of the lot and Hawk looked around the ring of his brothers and felt their loyalty and support. He was surprised when Grizzly and Law joined their circle.

"I don't have a lot of time before they notice I'm missing," Grizzly held his hand out to Hawk. "I love my club and I've always done what was best for all of us. This shit is going to break us apart. Freeze has fucking lost the plot. He ordered Rooster to take DC to Margate, keep her there and claim her. Rooster came to me asking for my help. I arranged for Alien and Rover to ride along as protection for both of them. She's safe tonight and they'll have her back here at sunrise. Don't stay here. Stay at your Durban compound where you have your men to protect you. Be back before sunrise. She will be here, and Hawk, fucking promise me you'll take her away from this shit. Doc's been trying to stop this Crow bullshit for years but Freeze vetoes him every fucking time he brings it to the table. It's fucking killing him just like it's killing her. Until the fucker is voted out or put in the ground, she will never be able to live a normal life. You take my little girl and keep her safe, son."

After dropping the bomb Grizzly and Law walked away and stood at the other side of the parking lot as if they were out there to have a smoke and keep an eye on the Iron Dogz.

Ice took over. "You heard the man. Let's get our shit and get out of here before they try to lock us up in their fucked up basement. Beast, pack up Hawk's shit and bring it down. He's not going back inside."

Hawk sat on his bike at the head of his men. All of them wearing their kuttes. Fuck the Road Warriors and their orders. He revved his bike, let out the clutch and rolled away from the factory. Doc hadn't reappeared but Tiny, Skelly and Shaka watched as they pulled out and rode away.

Hawk had no idea how this was going to affect the fragile alliance between the two clubs but he couldn't worry about it now. He had too much to see to once they were safe behind the walls of the Durban chapter's compound.

Tomorrow he would be fetching his little bird.

He would be keeping her safe.

He should have gone after her and left the old bitch to Ice but it was too late for regrets. He had to deal with the here and now, not with what couldn't be undone.

Not right now anyway.

TWENTY FIVE

DC

Riding into the yard of the safe house I was shocked to see the Iron Dogz sitting on their rumbling bikes in a large semi-circle facing the steps. Doc and Freeze stood on the steps, arms crossed and looking seriously pissed off. What the hell had happened while we were on our run? I glanced at Alien who rode next to me and he shrugged. He didn't know what was going on either.

Backing my bike into a spot between Alien and Rover I looked up and met Hawk's eyes. He immediately got off his bike, left his helmet on the seat and stalked towards me. I flipped open my visor and pulled off my sunglasses then sat frozen as he approached.

His face was like stone but his eyes were alive with something.

Something a little bit crazy.

His hands were on my helmet, loosening the straps and gently lifting it off and setting it down between my legs. All the while his eyes never left mine. The kiss, when it came, was surprisingly soft and short. Pulling his head back a few centimetres the corner of his lips quirked up in the beginning of a smile, but it didn't go any further.

"You got most of your shit in your saddlebags, little bird?"

"Yes, I think so. Why?"

"Think carefully before you answer, baby. Are you my old lady?"

His eyes were almost completely yellow and he looked as if he was holding his breath.

I didn't hesitate.

"Yes, yes I am."

A huge smile broke over his face as his arms swept around me and his lips crashed down onto mine. The world disappeared as he kissed me senseless. Leaving me panting and buzzing with want. From far away I heard the howls from his men as he pulled away and settled a soft kiss on either eyelid.

I opened my eyes and smiled at my beautiful man.

"Helmet back on, baby. We're leaving. You ride next to me."

He lifted my helmet and held it out to me. Frowning I took it and slid it on, fastened it, slipped on my sunglasses but didn't close the visor. Alien got off his bike, looking down at his phone he leaned slightly towards me and spoke in a whisper.

"Stay with your man, DC. There's club shit going down and Doc needs you safe with him."

Drawing in a deep breath I nodded, flipped my visor closed then started my bike and slowly rolled to where Hawk was waiting.

BURNING BRIGHT IN THE BLACK

We rode out of the yard and the Iron Dogz peeled out behind us, forming a line of bikers riding two abreast.

I had no idea what the hell was going on but riding next to Hawk made the last of the bad stuff disappear. He had come for me was the only thought that played through my head.

He had come for me.

When we rode through the gates into the Iron Dogz compound in Pinetown I started to get nervous. There were men waiting outside the front door and I saw some club women off to the side watching as we parked.

I immediately spotted the tall blondes in the group and knew those bitches had most probably fucked my old man at some time in the past. They were going to be freaking difficult to ignore, but I had to or else I would go crazy with jealousy.

Hawk slung his arm around my shoulders as we walked over to the men waiting in front of the clubhouse.

"Hotdog, Growler, this is my old lady, DC." He introduced us before looking down at me.

"Baby, Hotdog is the president of the Durban chapter and Growler is his VP. You have any problems and you can't find me you go to them. Okay?"

I nodded, because what else was I going to do? Say no?

The guys were shocked at Hawk's revelation but they hid it behind welcoming grins. It sucked being the short one in a group of alpha dogs.

"Welcome to my house, DC. Congratulations on snagging the old hound dog." Hotdog teased as he drew me away from Hawk and into a hug.

Growler drew me from his president and hugged me hard making me squeak as his arms squished my ribs. Of course, it had them all laughing.

"Welcome, DC. I'm happy to see my brother found what he was looking for."

I instantly knew why his name was Growler; his voice was very low and growly.

"Thank you." I smiled as Hawk possessively pulled me back into his side.

I tuned the men out as we walked inside. The common room of their clubhouse was large and laid out very much like the common room at Hawk's clubhouse. The bar at the back, the pool tables to the side and deep couches and easy chairs scattered around battered coffee tables. A big-ass TV hung against one wall while on another there was a huge Iron Dogz MC banner stretched from one end to the other. The other walls were covered with framed photographs and shelves that held memorabilia relevant only to the club and its members.

Being here and not knowing anyone except Hawk and to a lesser extent Ice and Kid was an unsettling feeling. It wasn't a setting I was used to at all. Doc kept me away from visiting clubs as much as possible so I was sort of new to all of this. We were standing at the bar being served large mugs of black coffee when my phone started ringing. I thought nothing of it and answered when I saw it was Pixie.

"Morning, Boss."

She sounded frantic.

"What the fuck is going on? Rooster called Wild Man earlier and now he's having conniption fits and not telling me why. What did Freeze do this time?"

Shaking my head, I stood frowning down at my feet. "I have no idea. I left Rooster with the brothers and I'm with Hawk, we're at…" I didn't get to finish; my phone was rudely pulled out of my hand and Hawk took over the conversation.

"Pixie, my woman can't talk now. She'll call you back."

He didn't give Pixie a chance to say a single word. He ended the call and slipped my phone into the inside pocket of his kutte. Anger started bubbling and boiling looking for an exit. Which it found when I opened my mouth.

"You did not just do that. You did not take my phone and ended a call I was on. And you definitely did not put my phone in your pocket." I hissed angrily, not realising the Crow was starting to peak her head out.

"Baby, calm down. Pull it back. I'll explain but not now," Hawk bent his head and whispered in my ear.

I knew I had to hold back because to go at him in front of his men would be an unforgivable insult. They didn't know me well enough yet and I didn't know them. Actually, I didn't know Hawk either just as he didn't know me. We were too damn new and with everything going down around the clubs it made it so much more difficult to find the time to get to know each other.

So, I let it go. For now.

I was standing against the bar drinking my coffee. Hawk stood to the side talking to Hotdog and Growler with Ice and Kid listening. Then it happened.

Something I could not, would not let go.

She'd been watching from the far-end of the room, dressed in barely-there shorts and a tiny excuse for a tank top, waiting for an opportunity. After our short difference of opinion she made her move. She strolled over to where Hawk stood surrounded by the men.

Her hips rolled in an exaggerated sway her barely covered large tits bobbed with every step. Almost all eyes were on her. but some were on me, watching for my reaction.

I grew up in a MC. I knew I had to make my point. Make it viciously enough that no other bitch would dare cross the line, ever again

I waited. Waited until she plastered herself to Hawk's front, lifted up and kissed his jaw. He grinned, gave her a hug, and pushed her back. Not far enough. Her bottom-half still touched his thigh, rubbing against him slowly, deliberately. They started a whispered conversation.

Hotdog was frowning so were Ice and Kid.

Sin appeared next to me at the bar, leaning over to whisper in my ear right when Hawk looked over at me and frowned.

"That's Kathy, the local club whore. When we're down here she's the one he usually fucked. She's pissed because he blew her off last night. Why don't you fuck her up a little? The way you did Jane. We could all do with a little bit of a distraction."

He pulled away. I laughed up at him and handed him my mug. He looked down at me, took a sip and winked.

I moved fast.

Before anyone realised what was happening I was across the room.

I grabbed her by her teased-to-shit hair and pulled her off Hawk.

I hit her hard, fast.

Five times in quick succession.

I made sure I blackened her eyes, broke her nose, split her lips, and cracked her cheekbone. The sixth blow on her chin knocked her out. I let go of her hair as she fell to the floor. Then I kicked her in the ribs, hard.

I knew when I looked up the vicious fighter I am was right there, visible in my eyes.

"Anyone else?" I snarled and flicked my fingers, inviting them to bring it on. "Come on bitches, now's your chance, step up or stay the fuck out of my way."

Deathly silence hung over the room. Then Sin's voice rang out in the tense silence.

"That was fucking quick, Demon. I was hoping it would last a little bit longer but this bitch isn't as tough as Jane Warne. And that bitch didn't even last three rounds."

He laughed while toasting me with my own mug of coffee.

I gave the bitch one last kick and walked away to lean against the bar next to Sin. He patted me on the shoulder. Hawk watched with narrowed eyes but said nothing. He knew. I knew he had done it on purpose.

To see what I would do. Testing me.

Mistake.

Big fucking mistake.

Turning to the bartender, a girl with brown hair and shocked hazel eyes, I asked for a bottle of water and some serviettes. I had the whore's blood all over my knuckles. I wanted it gone. It didn't feel like the tough skin covering my knuckles had broken but I wanted to be sure. The bitch most probably fucked anything that moved. I didn't want to pick up some disease from her.

My hand was clean and the bloody serviettes piled into an empty ashtray when Hawk appeared next to me.

He took my hand and started lifting it to his lips. I snatched it out of his.

"You put your lips on my knuckles and I'll hit you so hard your damned ears will ring. My hand hasn't been disinfected, we don't know if she's clean or not."

I looked at Sin and grimaced.

"And now I want to dip him in disinfectant knowing he fucked the slut."

The men including Hawk laughed as if I was making a joke.

I wasn't.

"Babe. Give me your hand I need to see if you hurt yourself."

It was my turn to laugh. I shook my head in disbelief and tapped my chest.

"Cage fighter, baby. My hands are my weapons. I pulled back, didn't hit her that hard."

Hawk laughed and so did those around us as he drew me into his chest with one long arm. I looked up to see him looking around the room until he found who he was looking for.

"Kev, you take my old lady's saddlebags up to my room?"

"Yes, Boss. Left them on your bed," the prospect, who had driven the cage with Raj and his bike, replied.

"Taking my woman upstairs. We'll see you later." Hawk growled as he literally dragged me out the room and up the stairs.

Knowing laughter followed us as we left the room.

Bloody assholes.

A long corridor led away from the landing with closed doors on either side. Hawk unlocked the last door on the left and drew me into an average sized room with a big king-sized bed standing front and centre. Through an open door I saw a small bathroom, another closed door was most probably a cupboard.

He let go of me to close the door then shrugged out of his kutte.

Folding it carefully he laid it over the back of a very small couch set beneath the windows.

I stayed right where he had left me.

"How many bitches, excluding the one whose face I rearranged, have you had in this bed?"

The question flew out of my mouth before I could even blink.

I did not expect the laughter it evoked.

"Exactly…uhm…let me think. This might be difficult. I think it was…none" He teased.

"How sure are you of that?"

"Damn sure, little bird, seeing as it's a brand-new fucking bed."

"Really?"

"Yes, baby. I had the beds in all my rooms replaced."

"How many rooms do you have? I thought there were only two."

Hawk grinned. "I have a room at all the chapters, baby. As a prospect and a patched member, I hated sleeping in crash rooms. I'd fuck bitches in there but I never slept in them. Took my sleeping bag with me wherever I went and crashed out on the floor somewhere."

He's so weird.

"That's just crazy. You had no problem putting your dick in bitches most of your brothers had fucked but you would not sleep in the beds they had those bitches in. Makes absolutely no sense whatsoever."

I shook my head while he laughed and sat down to take off his boots.

"What are you doing?"

"What does it look like I'm doing?" His grin was knowing and dirty.

"It looks like you are getting undressed and though I would be happy to do what it is you want to do; I'm starving. We didn't stop to eat this morning and I've been on the road for hours with no food. I don't think I can perform on an empty stomach."

By now Hawk had his boots and socks off and was pulling his tee over his head.

"No problem, little bird. I can fix that." He pulled his phone from his pocket and started texting then looked up. "Baby, get out of those clothes. Kev will bring up some food."

With a sigh I shrugged out of my jacket and hung it over the back of the couch, sat down and started to take off my boots. I did it slowly, dragging it out. I did not want to be naked when our food arrived.

"You do know we have some shit to discuss, right?" I watched him through my eyelashes as I undid my boots.

"After we've eaten and I've fucked my little bird in my bed, then we can talk about any fucking thing you want."

He laid his phone, gun and wallet on the bedside table closest to the door before he turned. My eyes snagged on the golden trail revealed by his unzipped jeans hanging low on his hips.

"Can I just ask one thing before it happens?"

Frowning at me he nodded.

"Gav is doing what he does, too damned well, this morning. Are any of your brothers going to follow Speedy when he runs with those kids?"

"Yes. We've got brothers ready to follow him after it goes down. Bikes and cages so he doesn't notice he has a tail. We have brothers who will be following the truck with the container when it leaves the yard. Skel and I worked it out together, so no problems."

He wasn't happy about something and I knew he would stubbornly keep it to himself until he felt it was time to reveal it to me.

A knock came right as I opened my mouth. Hawk shouted, 'it's open' and the strangest thing I have ever seen in a biker clubhouse happened.

The door opened and a woman pushed a trolley into the room. On the trolley were two covered plates, a rack of toast and a small dish with tiny, wrapped blocks of butter. Knives and forks wrapped in real serviettes were set to the side. On the bottom shelf was a large pot of coffee, a small milk jug, a sugar bowl and two big coffee mugs.

My eyes must have been wide and my mouth hanging open because the woman laughed as she settled the trolley in front of the small couch.

"Good morning. I'm Molly, Hotdog's old lady. It is my pleasure to welcome our president's old lady to our home. We're so happy he has found a woman who won't take any shit."

She grinned slyly at me.

"You have the gratitude of all the old ladies for taking care of our slutty little problem downstairs. We'd like you to join us for a drink later so you can get to know us, and we you. There aren't many old ladies in the club but we've formed our own network to support each other and our men. I hope you will join us."

I liked the way her eyes twinkled and I grinned at her.

"I'm DC and I'd love to join you, thank you. The slutty little problem downstairs might be gone but believe me it's *not* forgotten. Thank you for breakfast, it looks delicious." I glanced at where Hawk was lifting the covers from the steaming plates.

Molly nodded and grinned.

"My pleasure, DC. You're a lucky man, Hawk. She's gorgeous and good with her fists, a total winner," she teased as she backed out of the room and shut the door.

We could hear her laughing as she walked away.

Shaking his head Hawk grinned as he sat down on the couch and patted the seat next to him.

"Come and eat, little bird. I don't want your grumbling tummy interrupting when I have you underneath me."

"Such a caveman," I grumbled as I sat down next to him.

The food was delicious and I had barely finished when Hawk pushed the trolley out into the corridor and locked the door. He leaned with his back against the door and watched me through heavy lids. My breathing sped up when he pushed away from the door and stalked towards me.

"Get naked, baby. I need you so fucking much."

His growl and burning eyes pinned me next to the bed. I slowly pulled off my tee and bra. Teasing him. Until he lost it, took over, tipping me onto the bed and dragging my jeans and panties down.

Naked and already panting I lay on the bed and smiled up at my Viking.

I was ready to give him this but we would be talking about the shit he'd pulled downstairs.

After I got what I needed.

TWENTY SIX

Hawk

Hawk looked at his woman lying naked on his bed, smiling up at him. His eyes stroked over the defined muscles playing under her golden caramel skin every time she moved. She was in peak physical condition and he knew she must work hard to maintain it. But she had not worked out once, that he knew of, since he met her.

He ran a finger over her biceps softly, up over her shoulder blade and down the centre of her body. Her stomach muscles clenched and went hard under her silky skin.

"I love your muscles. I love that you can take care of yourself. And I love how you claim me as yours."

By the way her eyes narrowed he knew he was not going to like what came next.

"You may like my muscles but you have a very definite thing for tall blondes with big tits and soft asses. Before you try to deny it remember what happened downstairs. I did not appreciate being forced to beat up one of your whores in front of your club to assert my position as your old lady."

Between one blink and the next she rolled over to the other side of the bed and stood looking at him out of cold dead eyes. The fucking Crow stood in front of him and he knew he had to be careful what he said and did next.

"If you think what happened to the old bitch was bad, I can assure you it was *not*. It was nothing. She was nothing. You push me, and every single one of your bitches will appear outside the gates of your club. They will be covered in my patterns and they'll be dead, very, very dead. Do. Not. Push. Me."

It was said in an icy hiss he now knew belonged to the Crow.

His little bird's eyes closed and she shook her head violently, when she opened them again, she was back.

But she also wasn't back.

He had fucked up badly, testing her in front of his club. For a minute down there, he had forgotten who she really was. Had forgotten she had grown up in a MC and knew the whores would always be there, ready to fuck him. She knew some brothers banged club whores even though they had an old lady.

His actions had made it clear to everyone, however untrue, that he was one of those. A brother who fucked whores while he had an old lady.

He should have pushed Kathy off him, should never have allowed her to touch him, to put her lips on him. But his gut had been burning after she had gone on the run with Rooster and he had let it rule his actions.

"I no longer feel like this." She waved her hand between them. "I'm going to have a shower and when I'm done, I want my phone. I have shit to do today and I have to call Killian and Pixie. You don't own me. You do not decide to whom I can and cannot speak." Her voice was dead and filled with ice.

She shut him out so completely he felt it like a punch to the gut. He had to fix this. Tell her his fucked up reasons for being a damned fool.

"Little bird, I'm such a fucking asshole. I was jealous. It ate at me that you spent the night with Rooster. I called and fucking messaged and you didn't answer or call me back. I couldn't sleep last night and nearly lost my motherfucking mind thinking I had lost you."

His explanation earned him a cold look and an icy reply.

"You really don't trust me, do you? No don't answer, the question was rhetorical. Rooster is a friend who became a lover and after it was done our friendship didn't end. He will always be my friend. Unlike your whores he has integrity and respected your claim. His only motivation for taking me on the run was to help dispel the shit that was clogging my head."

Cold black eyes met his and Hawk felt anger start to coil in his gut but he pushed it down as he tried to explain.

"Freeze fucked with my head. Told me Rooster was going to fuck you and claim you. I didn't know what to expect when I saw you this morning. Didn't know if you were still mine when you rode into the yard."

DC rubbed her hands over her eyes and sighed heavily, and to him it seemed as if she was sad.

"Like I said, you obviously don't trust me. I had my own room, Hawk. Have your guy check out the Margate Sands. It's where we stayed over. In a three-bedroom apartment on the fifth floor."

Fuck.

"I do trust you, baby. One of the things I love about you is that you don't lie. Not about what's important to you."

She stood on the other side of the bed, totally naked, but oddly it wasn't sexual, not anymore.

"I am thirty-one years old, Hawk. I've had lovers. Raj and Rooster aren't the only men I've been with. Some of them are still my friends, while some aren't. Unlike your whores hardly any of my exes are a constant in my life. And both of us know there's a good chance we'll never see Raj again. That leaves Rooster, and he lives in Cape Town, hundreds of kilometres away from Jozi. Regardless of the distance he will always be a constant in my life. Deal with it, like I have to deal with your sluts."

Hawk's dick was no longer hard, hadn't been for a while now. Somehow, he had to turn this around, convince his woman of his commitment to her and only her. Losing her wasn't only unthinkable it was unacceptable. It wasn't going to happen, not if he had anything to say about it.

"It is good we are having this talk now. I've been in one relationship my entire life and it was with my ex-wife. It did not end well. Every single bitch that came after her got nothing from me. The only thing I gave them was my cock. I never wanted an old lady until I met you. You changed everything. Changed what I wanted in my life and forced me to acknowledge the inevitable. I now know why I never settled down with one of those bitches, it's because I've been waiting for you. What happened down there will never happen again. You have my word. You and I, we are inevitable. We are meant to be. Soul mates. I love you, little bird."

Her eyes never left his as he laid it out for her.

As he gave her what he hadn't given to another woman, ever.

He watched as his little bird's rigidly held body softened.

"I can't help but wish your cock hadn't been so fucking busy while waiting for me. I can deal with it, though. But I don't need the evidence shoved down my throat. Like earlier. I never wanted to be someone's old lady because I knew only too well what an old lady had to put up with. I had a job I enjoyed, family who loved me and I could take a lover whenever I felt like it. Life was good. I didn't need an old man to make it better. And then you happened. You changed everything I thought I wanted. You turned my world upside down from the very first minute I saw you. I love you too, my Viking."

Relief flooded through him when her declaration registered. Wordlessly he held his arms open wide. He laughed as she jumped on the bed ran across and flung herself into his arms with a wild yell. He wrapped her in his arms keeping her tight against him, shoving his face into her neck, breathing her in.

His woman was wild and complicated.

When he first met her, he only wanted to fuck her then put her behind him. Her fight with Jane had opened his eyes when he saw the real woman behind the façade she showed the world. A woman he had fallen in love with so deeply he could not imagine his life without her.

"Arms and legs around me, little bird,"

He whispered as he slid his hands down to her firm ass cheeks and lifted.

"Wrap around me tight, my little love."

Her face immediately went into his neck and he felt her breath against the sensitive skin as she whispered.

"Never let me go, my Viking. Promise you will never let me go."

"You are mine, little bird. You will always be mine and I'm never ever letting you go, I promise."

Her arms and legs tightened around him and his little bird, his old lady, the love of his life sighed with contentment.

Moving carefully, he crawled onto the bed and laid her down in the centre while staying connected to her. Giving her his weight, he lifted his head and grinned when she groaned. Pushing up on his forearms he dropped his head and kissed her, slow, invading her mouth with his tongue. She kissed him back, nipping at his bottom lip and sliding her little tongue over the slight sting.

Her legs were clamped high around his waist, holding him against her.

Balancing on one forearm he reached down, unbuttoned and kicked his jeans off. The jeans slid away and his rock-hard cock pushed up against the wet heat of her pussy.

Hawk groaned. There was no way he could stop from slowly thrusting against her, sliding his cock through the wet, slick heat. His slow slide bumped the head of his cock against her swollen clit. They both groaned.

"Whose pussy is this, baby?"

He ran his tongue over her top lip and pulled it into his mouth for a short sucking kiss as he slowly rocked against and through her wet heat.

His woman moaned as his cock teased her clit.

"Yours."

"Tell me again, baby. *Who* does this pussy belong to?"

Her moans were coming almost continuously now.

"You, my Viking. It belongs to you."

"That's right, little bird. You are mine. Your pussy, your body, your heart, it all belongs to me now."

Her small hand slid down and grabbed his cock, squeezing it tightly.

"This cock belongs to me. You belong to me and no one gets to touch but me."

Hawk groaned as she squeezed again.

"My cock is yours, little bird. It only wants your touch, no other. Your hand feels so fucking good but I have to get inside you, right fucking now." Pulling away from her hand was torture. He endured it because what was to come would be so much better.

Pushing insistently against her tight little pussy he slid in and thrust hard, seating himself so deep inside her he felt as if he had become a part of her. He slowly thrust in and out, relishing the feel of taking her bare, shuddering as her slippery walls tightened around him.

"Love feeling you on my cock."

"And I love feeling your cock." She hissed as he thrust harder. "But we need a condom."

"You're taking me bare, little bird. I don't want anything between us. I'm marking you as mine, inside and out."

Hawk didn't give her a chance to answer because he could no longer hold back the wildness boiling in his blood. Dropping his head, he found her mouth and slid his tongue in deep as he started fucking her hard. Their deep moans joined the sounds of flesh slapping on flesh. The walls of her pussy started convulsing around his cock as he slammed into her repeatedly.

Her body arched under him as she climaxed and gave a short sharp scream as she shuddered underneath him. Hawk slammed deep inside her convulsing pussy; his climax hit as her silky walls clamped down on his cock. Spurting deep inside her, he marked her with his seed.

Coming inside her was unlike anything he had ever felt in his life. Her spasming pussy drained him dry and he pulled her tight against his hips, keeping them connected as he rolled to his side. He wasn't ready to sever their connection.

"Are you okay, baby?"

"Hmmm."

Hawk chuckled. "Does that mean it was good for you too?"

"Hmm, it was so good I can't feel my toes."

Kissing her nose and pressing little kisses over each eyelid Hawk grinned.

"That's good but we have to shower. I have to get on top of the shit going down this morning. Don't want to talk about business while I have you on my cock and in our bed." Hawk slowly pulled his still semi-hard cock from the wet warmth surrounding it.

He chuckled when his old lady shuddered and moaned.

Scooping her up he walked into the shower where he washed her. Very thoroughly, it led to him fucking her again. He couldn't get enough of her, knew it would never be enough.

Hawk didn't want to leave their room but eventually they had to.

He wanted the memory of their time together to carry him through the shitty day facing his club. And to some extent it did.

Sitting at the table surrounded by his brothers he knew by the look on their faces this day was as fucked up for them as it was for him. As the national president of the Iron Dogz MC he was at the head of the table in the chair usually occupied by Hotdog. He now sat on Hawk's left while Ice sat on his right. Looking around the table and the room he tapped the gavel on the square of iron in front of him.

The only phone in the room lay on the table in front of him. Jagger and Ziggy were on the other end of the call.

"Have you got anything else for us, Ziggy?"

Hawk couldn't keep his fingers still and they drummed on the arm of his chair.

"Still looking into the cell phone calls originating in Cape Town, Prez. The phone hasn't been RICA'ed so no ID or address to follow up on. All I can tell you it's an unregistered pre-paid last used at the Waterfront in Cape Town."

The sound of fast typing and mumbling came through the speaker.

"Got you now you fucker."

More typing and mumbling and then Jagger spoke.

"The bastard in Durban just used the phone. Zig is doing his magic and trying to pinpoint the location. Okay, we've got him. It's near the cell tower in Hillcrest right now. Looks like he might be on the N3 moving towards Durban. If he is he'll have to go through the Marianhill Toll Plaza, or MTP, and Zig's hooked into the cameras. Dollar's keeping his eye on the smaller trucks coming through. Don't think they'll need anything bigger than an eight tonner." Jagger grunted in annoyance. "We'll try for facial recognition but it's a long shot."

"Good work, brothers. Ziggy, can you hook up with Mad Dog? I want to be able to follow the shit from this side as it goes down."

An irritated snort sounded and Hawk's eyebrows rose. Ziggy wasn't in a good mood; it wasn't usual for his information officer.

"Sure, Boss. If Mad Dog can log in now, I can hook us up."

"Good."

Nodding at Mad Dog he watched as the man left to get to work.

"If no one has anything to add I think we're done. I'll talk to you once I'm in the communications room, Ziggy."

Hawk ended the call abruptly and sat back.

"We all know what we have to do today and tonight. We stay focused until the threat to our club has been eliminated and we have freed those children."

Several 'hell yesses' sounded around the room and Hawk tapped the gavel to end the meeting. He had to get to the communications room, check on Ziggy and then he wanted to find his old lady.

Fuck it felt good to be able to think and say those words.

His old lady.

Hawk sat watching Mad Dog as his fingers flew over the keyboard. The man sat in front of an array of monitors on which several scenes were playing out. They had the MTP on one screen, and on a second screen the warehouse that was set to blow. Another screen showed several outside views of the clubhouse and, another one inside views of the clubhouse. One screen covered the streets around the clubhouse. But the screen right in front of Mad Dog was the one they were watching intently. It gave them several different views of the N3 into Durban. Every single truck with a closed bed was scrutinised. The faces of the drivers compared to the photos they had of Speedy and his band of rogues.

It was an irritatingly slow job.

Sitting back while still staring at the screen Hawk started to run through the information the old bitch had given them. Suddenly it hit him. They were looking at the wrong trucks.

"Ziggy, how many trucks do we have coming into Durban today?"

Ziggy immediately got it, so did Jagger.

"Fuck, fuck, fuck. Give me a second, one second."

Silence and then a long gust of breath.

"Four trucks. I've got them on satellite tracker. Three are running together as ordered and they've already passed through the MTP. The fourth is behind them, running alone and against orders. It's about to come down Marianhill. We'll be able to see the truck as soon as it hits the cameras around the tollbooth."

Furious clicking from both Ziggy and Mad Dog filled the room.

"Aaaaannnd there he is. The fucking bastard. Do you have him, Mad Dog?"

"Yeah, brother, got the fucker front and centre." Mad Dog thumped a fist next to the keyboard. "Got you, you slimy bastard. Going to fucking gut you later, bitch."

Hawk had to grin. Mad Dog was highly pissed off. They watched the Iron Dogz truck start its descent towards the tollgates and roll through the e-tag gate, not stopping. The faces of the driver and the two men next to him where very clear. Hawk had no idea who they were. He had made an effort to get to know all their truck drivers and their assistants.

"Jagger, those aren't our drivers. I don't recognise the fuckers." Hawk had a very bad feeling in his gut.

"No, Boss. Dave and Petey are supposed to be in that truck. Just pulled up a report, they got food poisoning had to pull into the PMB depot. Two depot drivers were supposed to take over and bring the truck in on schedule. Those fuckers sitting in *our* truck are not on the list of employees at the depot. Zig just pulled up the personnel files and we got nothing on those guys. There shouldn't be a third man in the fucking truck."

"We need to know if the depo has been compromised. Find out if Dave and Petey are safe, Jagger."

"Already on it, Boss."

The reason behind the elaborate setup of the Iron Dogz MC had been banging at the door in his brain. He had to talk to DC, find out if the young woman she'd questioned had said anything significant. If he was right, he had no one but himself to blame for this clusterfuck.

Leaving the room abruptly he went looking for his woman. He found her with Molly and two other women.

"DC, I need you for a minute."

He beckoned her out of the room where the four women were hanging out.

Hawk drew her into the empty meeting room, their chapel, and pulled her down in a chair next to his. His eyes met her confused and worried ones.

"This is important, baby. When you interrogated the young woman, did she identify anyone other than Speedy?"

DC sat quietly and he could see her going over it in her head.

"She said it wasn't just Speedy. There was a woman involved. She thought her name was May but she didn't know her surname. That was all, except she thought the woman was the one in charge. It would make what the old bitch said the truth. A woman with an English accent, a cold voice and her name is May. Not much to go on."

Hawk knew better. It was everything he needed. He knew exactly who was in charge of this operation and he knew why she was coming after the Iron Dogz. He had shot down her overtures to draw his club deeper into their dark business. This was her making her move to get him out of the president's chair and out of her way.

"You know who it is, don't you?" DC's soft voice intruded.

All Hawk could do was nod.

"Can she be eliminated?" So cold, his little bird.

"No, baby. She's very, very well connected and protected. But I do know how to get around her." Kissing his woman, he stood and pulled her up. "Have to get on this right away, DC. I have shit to do to save my club. To save all of us. I'll come get you when it's done."

"You be careful, Hawk. Don't take unnecessary risks."

Hawk shook his head, grinning as he walked her back to the other women. After another short kiss, he left to go do what he had to do.

Dominic Maingarde had some fucking explaining to do.

TWENTY SEVEN

DC

I watched as he walked away and went over the questions, he'd asked me. I needed Skel and his computer but he was with Gav, getting ready to blow the warehouse sky high. I didn't want to approach my dad or Tiny because they would have to tell Freeze. There was one other I could ask and I knew if I explained he would keep my questions to himself.

Alien.

I sat pretending interest in the conversations going on around me, while in my head I quietly weighed all my options. Over and over. The only answer I came up with was I had to do everything in my power to save my new family.

When I made my excuses Molly held my hand for a few seconds, without saying a word. She understood and didn't ask any questions. I ran up to our room, locking the door behind me. I was so paranoid about being overheard I went into the bathroom, locked the door, turned on the shower and only then made the call.

Drawing in a deep breath I waited as it rang. On about the eighth ring he answered, sounding pissed off and surrounded by other voices.

"A, it's me. Can you talk?"

And then he covered like I knew he would.

"Hey baby, let me take this outside where these fuckers can't listen to me talking dirty to you."

I heard fading laughter as he walked away.

"Okay, I'm outside in the yard. What do you need?"

"I need to put together what the two bitches gave us. I need to find out who the woman is they were both talking about. Do you remember?"

Alien laughed. Of course he did, the man had a brain like a damned computer. He remembered everything, could see patterns where no one else could. That's why his road name was Alien.

"This is fucking club business and you know how deep the shit would be if anyone found out I talked to you. So keep it in mind, please. I know what you're looking for. I've been looking into it on this side. It just made no fucking sense that a man like Speedy would let some bitch tell him what to do. Unless she was someone to be feared. There is only one who fit the little bit of information we have. She has the high-class English accent, the cold voice, but her name isn't May. The girl only heard part of the conversation and got it wrong. Your man is in deep shit, babe. Somewhere along the line he crossed this woman and she's making moves to destroy him. The way

I'm reading it she's set to take out the Iron Dogz officers and take over the club. Or so she fucking thinks. Don't know who fed her the bullshit about Hawk Walker being a pussy that would be easy to eliminate, because nothing could be further from the truth. The man is fucking lethal, everyone knows it. I have a suspicion the trail might lead back to Jane Warne and Big Ed Morrison, but it's only a suspicion. I've got no evidence they're involved but I have this burning in my gut telling me they are."

I didn't need to see any evidence because I had the same burning in my gut telling me they were definitely part of the plot to get rid of my old man. I was so sure of it I would bet my shiny new Doc Martens on it, and I loved those boots.

Jane and Ed would have to wait, I would get to them soon enough. What I needed right now was the name of the woman at the top of this pile of shit.

"Who is she?"

Alien was silent all I could hear was him breathing. And then he drew in a breath as if he'd made a decision.

"You need to brace for this, DC. She's close to a very good friend of yours."

"Just spit it out, A. Who is she?"

"Pixie's step-grandmother, Winifred Harrison Maingarde. Along with her brothers she heads up one of the biggest crime families in Europe and Southern Africa."

I was stunned.

Pixie? My boss, Pixie, who wouldn't harm a fly? And her bitch of a step-ogre being a crime boss implicated her?

Never.

"Not Pixie. She wouldn't, she's not like that."

"You're right. She's not involved, but Dominick is."

Oh fuck. Fuckity, fuckity, fuck.

I leaned against the vanity and breathed, I just breathed. Alien's revelation explained so much about my boss. She was the sweetest person I knew with a heart as big as the African continent. She loved her big brother even though he hardly acknowledged her. Could it be he was keeping her safe by keeping away from her?

Maybe?

Most probably.

"You can't say anything to her, DC. It would put her life in danger. The old bitch is fucking dangerous. The same goes for you, keep your mouth shut. I'm not sure how far the rot has spread through both our clubs. She has to have her puppets ready to take over once Hawk and his officers are gone."

I found it almost impossible to believe any of the men in Hawk's club would be involved in something as vile as human trafficking.

"I'll be careful. The only one I'll talk to will be Hawk. I have to tell him, A."

"Yes, you do. He has to cover his ass and the asses of the men in his club, babe. Skel and I are working on it on the down low. As far as we know it's all set to go down over the next few days. Skel picked up some chatter on the dark web about a take down, but no one is saying who is being taken down or how. He will follow it up once this morning's shit is done. Tell Hawk to get Ziggy on it. Skel left him some crumbs to follow on the dark web. I've got to get back inside before someone comes looking for me. You take care of yourself, babe. Watch your fucking back, okay?"

"I will and the same goes for you. Be careful A. I don't want to go looking for a new trainer when we get back home."

Alien laughed, I heard another voice in the background. And my mouth hung open as I listened to the shit he sprouted to cover his ass.

"Okay babe, glad I could help you take care of your wet little pussy. I'll be back soon and then I'm going to fuck your ass so fucking hard you won't be able to fucking breathe or sit for days."

Holy shit. I stabbed my finger at the face of my phone ending the call.

"*Siiiieeess!* (Yuck) That was way more than I wanted to know about your freaking sex life A." I muttered. "Need to go wash out my ears with bleach now."

Turning the water off I unlocked the bathroom and rushed into our room. A room heavy with a strange emotion. Hawk sat on the bed watching the bathroom, his face like stone. I knew he'd heard me talking but he said nothing just looked at me and waited. I walked to him clasped his face in my hands and brought my own close enough our noses almost touched. Then I whispered.

"Is this room secure? Has it been checked for bugs or cameras or shit like that?"

His frown and nod had me sagging against him with relief.

"Okay. I just talked to Alien and we compared notes on the two interrogations. We worked it out. We know who she is. Do you?"

Shadows flitted through his beautiful eyes. My man breathed in deep before he nodded.

Shit.

"I know it's club business and I shouldn't ask but I have to. Do you, the Iron Dogz I mean, do business with her?"

Hawk stood, set me away from him and walked to the window, silently staring out. Turning back, he sat on the window ledge and just looked at me.

My heart clenched in fear.

And then he started to let me in.

"What I'm about to tell you stays here, between the two of us. Between Hawk and DC. You can't talk about it to anyone because to talk means one or both of us will die. And that's fucking unacceptable."

I nodded my agreement because my voice was frozen in my throat. This did not sound good. I had a really bad feeling in my gut.

"I can't give you everything but I'll give you what I can. I think you know some of it already. You know we're not as clean as the Road Warriors. We haven't run drugs and guns for the Maingarde Organisation for quite some time. And we won't ever again. But, sometimes, not very often, we will do a favour for one of our old friends. We definitely don't work with poachers or human traffickers, never have, never will. Knowing our businesses have been used to smuggle kidnapped children out of the country is something we won't forgive or forget."

Hawk took in a deep breath. I could see he had made a decision. I wasn't surprised when he gave me the name, it was as I had suspected but had hoped wasn't true.

"We've been doing business with Dominick Maingarde for a long time. We've an agreement outlining exactly what we will and won't transport for him. Now our agreement has been broken. Dom and I will have to sit down and talk. I don't know when but what I do know is when it goes down, I want you somewhere safe. Somewhere his organisation can't reach you. I'm not taking any chances with your life."

My heart leapt in my chest. My man and his club were in deep shit. Very, very deep shit.

"Do you trust him?"

"I did. Now, I don't know. We'll have to wait and see what happens next."

"Alien said Skel found something about an imminent take down on the dark web. He said Ziggy must check it out and that he left him some crumbs. Whatever the hell that means. The thought of you getting hurt or worse scares me, Hawk. I can't lose you when I've just found you."

It actually more than scared me and I could no longer stay away from him. He opened his legs, held his arms out and I went to him. Pulling me between his legs, he held me against his chest, the side of his face against mine.

"I'll get Ziggy on it as soon as we're done here. Let's get through the shit waiting for us today, little bird, before we tackle the rest of it. We're going to work with the Road Warriors today but I'm not entirely comfortable with it. I do not trust Freeze, something about him is off."

It was time to explain about Freeze. It wasn't a club secret but it wasn't general knowledge either. After taking in a deep breath, I explained.

"His name should be enough to clue you in on how he handles everything. He's frozen inside, has been since his old lady was gunned down in a drive-by years ago. There were rumours, and they still persist today, that a woman Freeze had been banging on the side ordered the hit. He shut those rumours down ruthlessly. He used to be a nice man, always laughing and joking. But he also stepped out on his old lady, regularly. Everyone knew, including his old lady. You know the 'what happens at the club stays at the club' kind of bullshit. It stopped after she died. No more club whores, no more whores on runs, no more random women. But it was too little too late. His wife's parents went to court and petitioned for full custody of their granddaughter. During the hearing it was revealed that Freeze's wife had started divorce proceedings. His infidelity and being a mostly absentee parent were cited as reasons for the divorce. There were rumours a woman with a bad reputation was named in those papers. He lost his daughter. Both losses were his own fault."

I stayed silent for a beat before I gave him the rest of my hastily put together theory. Because suddenly it seemed to make sense.

"It would explain a lot if the woman he'd been banging was named in those divorce papers, and she ordered the drive-by to shut it down it. I am almost certain he's been waiting years to get even. To avenge the death of his old lady and the loss of his daughter. What if the woman is the Maingarde bitch? She's about the right age, and she was, and still is, beautiful enough to seduce most men. Even back then she had the manpower. It would've been easy to set it all up."

Hawk looked at me then shook his head from side to side.

"Baby, if Freeze stuck his cock in the old bitch's snatch, I know why he's called Freeze; it's because she fucking froze his dick. Fuck, we never learn, do we? Always sticking our dicks where they don't belong. You know what? Let Freeze sort out his own mess. All I'm interested in is saving my club. Freeze and his shit can wait for the next time the sky falls."

"You're right. We have enough to worry about today without adding Freeze to the pile."

Straddling Hawk's thighs I slid my arms around his neck and rubbed my cheek against his, loving the soft scratchiness of his beard. As we kissed, I brushed my fingers over the shaved hair above his ears, then over his tight braid. We kissed long and slow, heat slowly spreading through my chest and down, way down, tingles started between my legs. I felt him harden against me and smiled against his mouth as I rubbed against his rigid cock.

"Stop, DC. Not fucking you now," he groaned as he ended the kiss and I straightened.

"Just wanted to give you something *hard* to carry with you, you know. Like a hard cock to show those bitches downstairs what they can no longer touch."

Hawk laughed as he dragged me out of the room, locked the door and led me back downstairs. At least the worry in his eyes wasn't as heavy anymore. I had made him laugh.

But I wasn't laughing. I knew Freeze. He wouldn't hesitate to destroy anyone who got in his way. There was a reason he was the national president of the Road Warriors MC. Not only was he damned scary but he would do anything for his club, no matter what.

But the loss of his family…where would it lead him?

I wondered if his club was still his first priority. Or did his involvement with the Maingardes go deeper than any of us knew?

And my dad?

Where did he fit into this mess?

And who were the puppets the bitch had lined up to take over Hawk's club? Were they Hawk's men or were they men she would slot into the club once she eliminated Hawk?

So many questions with no answers.

I needed to find the answers.

BURNING BRIGHT IN THE BLACK

I needed to help my old man any way I could.

I needed to lighten the load on his shoulders.

TWENTY EIGHT

Hawk

Walking into the crowded communications room Hawk's mind was filled with the information his old lady had just given him. But it disappeared as he looked at the screens.

"It's about to go down, Hawk."

Hotdog flicked a hand at one of the men and a chair appeared next to Ice.

Hawk sat down with a nod of thanks.

"What did I miss?"

"Not a thing," Ice murmured. "Fireworks are about to start. Our fucking truck is approaching right now."

They all flinched instinctively as the warehouse went up in an enormous fireball. Hawk leaned closer to the monitor, his eyes on the truck sliding to a stop a block away from the furiously burning building.

"Where are Kid and Sin's teams?"

"They're staying out of sight. Our people are the only ones who know you're not leading the attack. We didn't want the fuckers to suspect we're onto them."

Hotdog started swearing and Hawk glared at the screen. Bikes came pouring out of the basement parking of a building two blocks from their target. They surrounded the truck, one of them gesturing at the driver, the truck reversed then turned into a side road leading away from the burning warehouse.

Mad Dog tracked them on the traffic cams while Ziggy tracked the truck on the satellite tracking device hidden in the truck's engine compartment. Mad Dog lost them when they turned onto a little used road with no traffic cams. Ziggy still had them and directed those following the truck. Mad Dog reacquired them when they approached the abandoned Durban Airport and drove unhindered through heavily guarded gates and disappeared behind the buildings.

What the fucking hell?

"Fuck."

"Ziggy, what do you have?"

"The truck is still moving. I'm pulling up schematics for the Airport but I'm not sure how it's going to help us." There was a short silence with humming and swearing. "Okay, I've got thermal imaging, and don't fucking ask me where or how I got it. We have three in the truck cab, six around the truck and there are ten small signatures in the container."

Before Hawk could ask the screen filled with the thermal images.

"Where are they heading, Ziggy?"

"Looks like they're heading towards the old cargo terminal. And here's the bad news. Look at the thermal images at the fucking building. We're so fucked."

Hawk stared at the screens with narrowed eyes dread knotting his gut. Where the fuck was the fucking Road Warriors? Why hadn't they followed the truck?

"Are there any cameras you can get into? I need to know who the fuck we're up against before we make our next move."

"Not that I can see. But give me a minute, I have an idea."

Mad Dog had been typing furiously while Hawk spoke to Ziggy. His head jerked up and he glared at the screens, swearing softly.

"Come on, come on, come on,"

He whispered over and over as he typed, his screen filled with shit that meant absolutely nothing to Hawk.

"Boot up you piece of shit. Come on, come on,"

Mad Dog slapped a hand on the desk next to him in frustration then started typing again.

"Yes." He hissed with satisfaction.

"Ziggy, I hacked into the system running the perimeter and access security. We have to somehow turn on the cameras. I'm going to need your help with that."

"I'm with you. Let's do this."

Silence reigned in the room as Mad Dog and Ziggy worked. When he hunched over and growled everyone tensed.

"We've got some of the cameras back up. Not all of them though. It seems some of them have been removed or damaged. We've got nothing inside the building but we don't need them. According to the thermal images we have a group of people waiting for the truck just inside the open doors of the cargo terminal. We've got cameras on the light poles outside and a few of them are trained on those doors."

With a single keystroke the outside of the building appeared on the screens. Four big black SUV's were parked outside the building, a driver in each one. Mad Dog zoomed in on the group waiting in the open doors and Hawk's hands fisted on his knees.

Fucking Winifred Maingarde and her top enforcers stood in the open doors. Another close up appeared and he swore viciously. Speedy and his fucking rogues were wearing Iron Dogz kuttes and they had been caught on traffic cams wearing those fucking kuttes. It was the bitch's fucking plan from the start. His truck, his container and supposedly his men.

He had to move fast if he was to get ahead of this.

"Mad Dog, I want close ups of every single one those fuckers on the bikes, as many as possible. The same for the driver and those other two in the cab with him. Ziggy, get Jagger up to speed. Go back and track the fucking container and the truck. I want to know where and when they loaded those children. It did not happen in our yard. Find out where. Do we have updates on exactly what happened to Dave and Petey? How the fuck did they get food poisoning? Get Dollar on it and let me know what you find."

Turning in his chair he looked around the room.

"Ice, call back every single man we have out there. I need Kid and Sin back here and away from the fucking Road Warriors. I don't want any of the Iron Dogz near the fucking airport. I have a nasty feeling in my gut."

"Fuck, Hawk, got something here, brother." Ziggy's voice was tight.

"Go ahead, give it to me."

"I got a ping from our bank accounts. We suddenly have a new offshore account. Filled with fucking hundreds of thousands of dollars. And brother, according to the online information it is your account with your signature on the paperwork. Deposits in several different currencies were made to the account over the last year."

This was it, Hawk thought, as he made instant decisions that would safeguard everyone in his club and especially his little bird.

"Find out when and where the account was opened and then kill it. I don't care how you do it, Zig. Fucking *kill* it. They are setting me up to be convicted as a human trafficker. I'm not going to let the fuckers do this to me or my club."

"Brother, even if I kill the online account, they are going to have papers implicating you."

"I know, Zig." A thought occurred and he gave it to Ziggy. "Banks have security inside and outside their branches and videos are most probably backed up on security servers. I haven't been out of the country or inside a fucking bank in fucking years. They won't find me on their tapes opening the fucking account. Unless the fucking Maingardes found someone who looks like me. You better work fucking quick, brother. Find the fucking footage and back it up in more than one place before it disappears. I'm going to need it."

Spider's pissed off face suddenly filled one of the screens.

"I've got this, brother. I'm the fucking Treasurer of the club and these fuckers are fucking with my job. This is one of those online accounts, no need to visit a bank to set it up. So, no fucking worries about footage and shit. It has Jane's fucking dirty claws all over it. Give me a few and I'll fix it. I'm going to fix her and fucking Big Ed. Going to turn this back on them. I'll talk to you soon, cuz. I've got your back, Prez."

As suddenly as he had appeared he was gone.

"Okay, so Spider gave me some orders and I'm following them." Ziggy mumbled. "Hands off the bank account until he tells me what he wants done. Sorry, Boss, we are following Spider's orders on this one. He says we need to stay away from the bank because it's a trap. I'm following up on the truck and container as you ordered."

"Send Gerhard Van Wyk a file with everything we know."

Ziggy's subdued okay pissed him off, badly.

This should not be happening.

Rubbing his hands over his suddenly very fucking tired eyes Hawk sat back in his chair. Around him silence hung heavy in the air. The door swinging open violently had them all turning in their chairs, all except Mad Dog who kept on working.

Kid stormed through the door; his eyes wild.

"Why the fuck did you pull us off those fuckers? We could have had those kids safe by now."

Hawk silently stood and faced his best friend.

"No, brother, it was a set up."

Kid frowned and looked around the crowded room.

"What?"

"We're being set up, brother. Actually, I'm being set up and with me the entire club. The Maingardes with the help of the Road Warriors have set us up to take the fall for their human trafficking ring. They manufactured evidence that makes a damning statement of our involvement in human trafficking. Ziggy is working on it but proving it false is not going to be easy."

Kid looked devastated as he whispered. "Jane, this is fucking Jane. She helped them do this. How the fuck could she do this to her family? What the fuck am I going to tell my mum when she asks about this shit?"

Hawk got out of his chair and clapped a hand on his best friend's shoulder. There was nothing else he could do to ease the pain Kid felt at the betrayal.

He had to get out of the room.

Slipping his phone from the pocket of his kutte he found the number he needed. He'd called Rick after the shit went down with Doc and Freeze and he started suspecting he was being set up. He had put it off as long as he could but he was going to need help to save his club. He dialled as he walked into the common room and found a corner where he would not be overheard.

"Yes."

"Rick, as you predicted they've made their move and shit is about to go down. I need you to keep DC safe."

A short silence hung between them before Rick answered.

"She's safe, Hawk. We're on top of this, brother. As we anticipated, you and your men are being set up to take the fall. But not all the players in this shit show have shown themselves yet. It means we'll have to hang back a little longer. Cover your ass, call your lawyer and have them throw a tonne of paperwork at the SAPS. Stall them as long as you can. If they arrest you, we'll keep you out of jail and in the holding cells where you'll be safer. That's the best I can do for now. Sorry man."

"I haven't told my club I've called you and your team in on this. Don't let me regret it. Keep my woman and my people safe. If I go down you fucking finish this."

"You have my word. Don't worry, brother, it's almost done. And you won't fucking go down on my watch, believe me."

Fucking Rick. Fucking secret agent shit. When he finished the call Hawk immediately dialled the club's lawyer.

"Van Wyk."

"Gerhard. Hawk. There's a good possibility I'm going to be arrested for human trafficking later today. I'm being set up. Ziggy is sending you everything we have. I'm at the Iron Dogz compound in

Durban. Can you send one of your associates to take care of this until you get here?"

A long silence had Hawk's gut clenching.

"Sorry, Hawk, I was just reading Ziggy's e-mail. I'll be there as soon as I can. After a quick look through what you've sent me it's very obviously a set up. I'll study the file on the plane. One of the lawyers from our Durban office will take care of this until I get there. Her name is Saskia Gordon. She can be at the clubhouse within minutes if you need her. Keep your mouth shut, my friend, you say nothing, let Saskia do the talking for you."

He was silent for a few seconds before he spoke again.

"Okay, good news, I'm on a chartered flight out of Lanseria to Virginia in an hour. Listen to Saskia, she's good at what she does. See you soon, Hawk."

He was gone before Hawk could say anything more. Next, he had to let his little bird know what was going to happen in the following hours, he wasn't looking forward to it. Taking a deep breath, he made his way to the room where he had left her with the other old ladies.

She was laughing and looking so relaxed Hawk hated to interrupt. But he had to. He had to warn her about what was coming.

"Baby, can I have a minute?"

Her smile was wide until she looked into his eyes. It dropped and became a frown.

Holding her hand, he led her up to their room, locking the door behind them. Drawing her to their bed he sat down and pulled her into his lap, holding her tight against him, his face in her neck. He breathed her in, using her scent to steady his racing heart.

Not hesitating he laid it out for her.

"We were set up, little bird. They knew we were at the warehouse and played us. The Road Warriors never showed. Speedy and his men wore Iron Dogz kuttes and made sure they were caught on fucking traffic cams as they escorted the truck to the cargo terminal at the old Durban Airport. Winifred Maingarde and her men were waiting but left without the kids. I don't know how but I'm sure she has some asshole that's going to point the finger at me as the kingpin. I suspect I, and all my officers, will be arrested sometime today or late tonight by the human trafficking task force. I don't want you to worry. My lawyers and brothers have their orders. They will protect you no matter what happens. Wolf will take over as acting president. Please listen to him and let him keep you safe for me. Do not leave the compound, baby. If the fucking Maingardes get their hands on you they will use you to destroy my club, my brothers and me."

Her eyes were narrowed and he saw ice creep into those dark eyes.

"They will pay for their treachery, Hawk. No one goes after my man or his family and lives to talk about it. You won't be safe if they arrest you. There will be a hit out on you the minute you step inside a cell. It will most probably be one of your guards. They can't have you talking, you know too much."

They sat quietly for a few seconds.

Suddenly his woman jerked and grabbed his face.

"I suspect the reason we never saw Raj again is because he's part of this elaborate freaking farce. Freeze played you and by playing you he played me. I bet you anything they let the bastard go once he played his part."

In front of his eyes his little bird morphed into the Crow.

"They will regret their actions," her cold voice whispered into the room.

"Yes, they will, little bird. They most certainly will." Hawk agreed.

He hugged her tight then loosened his arms.

"Pack your shit just in case we need to get you out of here fast. I have some things I need to sort out with my brothers."

He stood and set DC on her feet.

"I'm on it," she said. "I think we should get all the old ladies and girlfriends out of here. They are a liability if they stay. It would be too easy to grab one of them and blackmail her man to help them get to us."

His little bird stood with her mouth clamped down in a tight line. He could virtually see that amazing brain of hers working through what they knew.

She spoke as if to herself.

"We know they want Iron Dogz Trucking. They're going to come with demands and if you don't give them what they want they'll threaten to give their so-called evidence to the human trafficking taskforce." She tapped her fingers to her lips. "The cops will hold on to you for months before your lawyers will be able to get you out. By that time, you will be dead and the Iron Dogz will belong to the Maingardes."

She stood in front of him, her fingers tapping against her lips, her eyes narrowed as her cunning brain worked on their problem. He watched as a sly smile curved around her beautiful mouth and darkness settled in her black eyes.

The fucking Crow.

His beautiful fucking Crow.

"We need to find Jane. She likes talking. She will like it even more if she can lay it all out for me."

Hawk looked down into those icy black eyes and agreed. But finding Jane would not be easy…unless.

Unless he called her.

Smiling at his cunning little bird Hawk pulled out his phone. Jane didn't answer.

It was time to start fighting back. Fighting back dirty.

Jane, call me. We need to talk. I made a big fucking mistake.

"This should get her attention." Hawk grinned as he showed his woman the text he had just sent.

The sly smile returned and her black eyes shone as she nodded.

The game was on.

TWENTY NINE

DC

Packing our bags didn't take long. While I packed my mind raced through every single option we had. We didn't have many but I could work with the few we had. If I could get my hands on Jane, I would make her talk. All we needed was her pointing fingers at the Maingarde Organisation.

How bloody irritating is it to have to say 'Maingarde Organisation' every time? From now on they are MORG to me, and if I had my way, they would all end up in the morgue damned soon.

How my dad and Freeze fitted into this mess I still didn't know, but I would. Very soon.

I crawled to the middle of the bed, plumped the cushions against the headboard and sat back. I needed to solve the puzzle.

Where did it start and who was involved?

Breathing deeply, I focussed on what I knew and started drawing it together.

According to the information I had it all started with Jane Warne.

She had made it all about me.

About me and Hawk, but it wasn't.

Not at all.

It had been about the club all along.

Her double-dealing started long before I came into the picture. She gathered information by sleeping with as many of the members as she could and pumping (ha-ha) them for said information. She was the one who supplied the information enabling Big Ed to break into and rob the Iron Dogz Trucking container yard.

Whose container did they rob?

The way Hawk reacted it had to have been Dominick Maingarde's.

What did they steal? And why did they steal it?

Or even better yet.

Why did the step-ogre order Big Ed to steal whatever was in the container?

Or was it done to test the Iron Dogz defences?

Or the loyalty of Dominick Maingarde?

What was Freeze's involvement? And my dad?

Was the Road Warriors working for the MORG?

And if they were, where did it leave my dad and me?

Was I his daughter or an asset being used to bring Hawk to his knees?

I could not let it happen. I would never let it happen.

There were markers I could pull in from people who owed me, and there were many who did.

But first I needed to talk to Alien or Skel. I hoped like hell they were still on my side.

Alien picked up after the first ring.

"Babe, you need to get your ass to a secure location, right now. Tell your old man there will be a raid on the clubhouse late tonight. The fuckers Freeze brought in are talking about using fucking grenades and shit. They don't fucking care if women and children get hurt or die as long as they get their hands on you and Hawk."

I was shocked silent as my friend kept talking.

"Freeze has fucking lost it and Doc isn't doing anything to stop him. I have no fucking idea what's going on. Shit is dark on this side. The brothers were fucking pissed-off we double crossed the Iron Dogz. Skel has locked himself in his room. Gav threw his prospect kutte at Tiny and walked out, disrespecting his VP and president. He threw it, DC! Even if this shit gets sorted, he'll never be allowed back in, fucking never. He left. I hope like fuck he comes to you, where he'll be safe. Tiny was gutted when Gav called him a traitor as he walked out. Freeze wanted Boeta to take care of him and Tiny lost his shit. He swore if anything happened to Gav he wouldn't rest until he put Freeze's daughter in the ground, and if they took him out before he could do it someone else would finish the job for him." He sounded both furious and shocked.

"Jesus, DC, we are fucking falling apart over here, while fucking Raj is strutting around like he's the fucking king. I just can't see what the play is here."

I took in a big breath and then I gave him what I knew. He was silent as I spoke, only his increased breathing letting me know he was still there.

"So that's what I think might be going down, A. I don't think any of us are safe. We're all being used in some freaking major play against the clubs. They made sure we are enemies so none of us get to see the full picture. Raj being related to the Sharma's and making a play for me is keeping Doc's head out of the game. Seeing Raj strutting around keeps Doc stuck in his head. This is exactly what they want."

"Shit, DC, you might be right." He muttered.

"I think I am. The MORG is at the bottom of this. Oh, and MORG stands for Maingarde Organisation, easier to say. They want Iron Dogz Trucking and the properties the Dogz own around the country and are moving to take it over. They could move whatever the hell they want if they had ownership. I'm not sure why they want the Road Warriors. Maybe Freeze and the step-ogre have plans to take over drug and gun running in Southern Africa, I don't know."

Even to my ears it didn't sound right, but it was all I had.

"I need to take this to Skel, Rover and Grizz. I trust them. Right now, they are the only ones I trust. This shit is going to kill my club, babe." Alien sounded totally despondent and wrecked.

I was so very afraid he was right. This was betrayal on a massive scale. For Tiny to threaten Freeze's daughter in order to keep Gav safe was unbelievable. But it had happened.

And then it hit me. Like a tonne of bricks falling from the sky.

The damn sky was falling.

"Shit, shit, shit. I know what's happening with the Road Warriors. Fuck, A, they got to Freeze. It's his daughter. They've either got her stashed somewhere or they have eyes on her. It's the reason why Freeze is acting so damned weird. He's trying to save his fucking daughter and destroying his club and the Iron Dogz in the process."

Alien's shocked gasp echoed over the line.

"Fuck. If you're right then why the fuck didn't he ask for help? Fucking hell, that's why he sent Rooster back to Cape Town. It wasn't because he was pissed off about him not claiming you. He needed someone there besides Wild Man when shit goes bad. What are we going to do?" He growled angrily.

"You talk to Skel, get him up to speed. We'll get hold of Rooster and give him all the help we can to move Freeze's daughter to a safe location. The minute we can assure Freeze she's safe the game changes."

"I'm going to Skel right now. What do you want me to do about Tiny and Doc? Do we bring them in on this?"

It was a very difficult question to answer but after only a few seconds of doubt I went with my gut. I loved those two men and couldn't believe they would turn against me.

"Yes. But A, be careful, we don't know who else is on the MORG payroll. Call me when you've spoken to them. Watch your back, please. I don't want to lose you."

Staring at my phone I shook my head. I needed to speak to Hawk to assure save passage for Gav if he came to us. I hoped and prayed he came to us. He wouldn't be safe anywhere else. Freeze could not let the insult go however much he might want to. He couldn't if he wanted to keep his position as national president and president of the Cape Town chapter.

It was going to be difficult enough to retain his presidency once his brothers found out how far over the line he'd stepped for his daughter.

It suddenly hit me, right between the eyes.

Freeze, you fucking asshole. That's why he threatened Gav. He knew Tiny, knew exactly how he would react to any threats against his sons. Tiny would do whatever he could to get even. He would turn on the families of those who threatened his boys. And who was Freeze's family?

His daughter.

He knew Tiny would threaten her and in doing so, he knew someone would go looking for her. I was amazed my dad hadn't clicked yet.

Or maybe he knew and was playing his own game.

It would not surprise me at all.

I needed to find Hawk but first I had to ensure Gav knew he had a safe place waiting for him.

I sent a quick text telling him to get to the Iron Dogz clubhouse. Promising him safe passage. I hoped he listened.

Hopping off the bed I left the room to find my old man and give him the latest.

I found him deep in conversation with Ice and Kid at the bar. There was no one else around so I deemed it safe to talk. Even so I kept my voice low.

"I just spoke to Alien. The Warriors are falling apart. Gav threw his kutte at Tiny, called him a traitor and stormed out. Freeze wanted him taken care of and Tiny threatened to put Freeze's daughter in the ground if they touched his son. Skel has locked himself in his room and is refusing to talk to anyone."

"Jesus. What the fuck is going on?"

Ice shook his head in confusion.

"Some of the brothers feel betrayed and are considering leaving the club. Raj is walking around like he's the king, Alien's words. And Doc is losing his mind. Alien asked me to keep Gav safe if he comes to me. I sent him a text and told him to come here. If you could send Dollar to pick up Deena just in case she's being targeted that would be good."

Hawk nodded and I saw Kid texting.

One thing down a few more to go.

"There are men who aren't part of the club around Freeze. Alien couldn't tell me who they were because he doesn't know. They plan to raid the compound tonight and they will be using grenades and heavy arms. They want Hawk and me. No one else matters."

I shrugged.

"I don't think we have to worry about the cops storming in here to arrest you just yet."

"Could he give you a time?"

Hawk now had his phone out as well and was furiously texting.

"No, only that it will be tonight. But I have more to tell you and it's going to sound crazy but I swear if you listen to the end, you'll see it makes sense."

I laid my theory out about Freeze being blackmailed. They watched me with hard eyes as I explained, no one said a word after I finished.

I held my breath as I waited. My man did not disappoint.

"Okay, so here's what we're going to do. Step one. Secure the compound against the coming attack. Increase the perimeter patrols and have eyes on the cameras at all times. I want everyone armed and vigilant. The minute those bastards attack we'll have SAPS on our asses, so prepare for it." Ice and Kid nodded their agreement.

"Step two. We need to secure Freeze's daughter. Rooster and Wild Man can run the search in Cape Town. They might have to find a safe location because neither of our clubhouses will be safe. Maybe stash her with Pixie, no one will think to look there. Once we have her safe, we'll get a message to Freeze."

He pulled on his beard as he contemplated his next step. Then he looked at me and smiled.

"Step three. I'm going to have to piss Doc off to get him out of his head." He grinned.

"It will be easy enough because he's already pissed off. We need him back in the game and taking care of Raj"

There were nods all around.

"Step four flows out of step three. We need to find Jane and Big Ed and neutralise them or keep them on ice for later use."

I totally agreed with the last one but I was worried about him pissing Doc off, which might not go well.

"Step five is already in the works. Our lawyers are working on proving the club's non-involvement in the trafficking ring. I'm working on arranging a sit down with Dominick Maingarde. But we'll discuss our options at the table before I meet with him."

Hawk's face was cold and hard as he laid out the final step and it actually made a chill race up my spine. My man was a total badass and exactly what I have always wanted in a man.

"Step six is taking care of the traitors. In our club as well as in the Road Warriors. Speedy and his rogues wore Iron Dogz kuttes, they disrespected our club, our colours, and our code. They brought the Iron Dogz to the attention of the authorities which we don't fucking need. They will be handed over to us. I won't accept anything else."

He looked over at Ice.

"Did I cover everything? I don't want to have anything biting us in the ass at a later date."

"If there's anything you left out, we will take care of it, don't worry. We've got your back, Prez," Ice said.

Kid nodded in agreement.

"See to it that Gav has safe passage into the compound. He'll be riding without a kutte but he's still a potential brother. I think I might poach him from the Road Warriors, he would be a good man to have at our backs."

The men laughed, I didn't. Gav was a hothead and after the shit died down the Road Warriors would most probably offer him his prospect kutte back. But only after they made him pay in blood for disrespecting his VP, his prez, his kutte and his club.

Most probably. Maybe.

If the worst happened and they didn't, he would find a home with the Iron Dogz. It would break Tiny's heart and devastate Skel. But they would just have to deal with it.

Hawk's heavy arm came around me and drew me into his side as Ice and Kid went off to set his orders in motion.

"What has you so deep in thought, little bird?"

"Gav. I'm worried about him."

"He made his decision, baby, there's nothing you can do about it. He's welcome here and after this is done, we'll see what Doc and Tiny has to say. I have a feeling Freeze will not be the one making the decisions for the Road Warriors once this shit has died down."

I sighed heavily because I knew what it would mean for my dad. He was already at the national table as Freeze's VP and travelled a lot. With Freeze gone he would have to step up and it meant he would be gone more than he was at the moment.

It would dump Deena right back in my lap.

Shit.

Ignoring those thoughts, I concentrated on the now.

"Did Hotdog make a decision about the women?"

"Yes, little bird. Every single one of my chapters has an underground escape route. There's a secret tunnel leading to the property next door. The previous owner was a conspiracy theorist who built an elaborate bomb shelter underneath it. After his death, the property went up for auction and the club bought it using a shell company. We discovered the bomb shelter, realised it was the perfect hidden safe house and built the connecting tunnel. The women have been moved and they have prospects guarding the access points."

That was definitely a sneaky move.

"I want you to join them, baby. I won't be able to concentrate on what's coming for us with you in the clubhouse. I need to know you're safe. And I think Hotdog wants you to watch over his old lady and the other women. None of them have ever held a gun or received any self-defence training. They'll be sitting ducks if the fuckers make it past us and discover the tunnel."

The ass, using the one thing that would sway me to leave him at the clubhouse.

Helpless women.

But the young man walking through the doors made me forget all about it. For all intents and purposes he was my little brother and I loved him. The rage and heartbreak in his eyes had my eyes burning with unshed tears.

I could not let him see it when he was struggling so hard to control his own, so I swallowed my tears and smiled.

Ignoring the silently watching men I walked over and wrapped him in my arms, just holding him, not saying a word.

He hugged me tight, breathing hard.

Hawk gently removed me from Gav's arms and set me to the side.

I held my breath.

"Gav, you're welcome in my club."

There was a beat of silence before he continued and my heart jerked in my chest at the coldness in his voice.

"You acted like a spoilt child and disrespected your president, your VP and your club colours." He held up a hand when Gav's mouth opened. "I understand you were under immense strain that's why I will let it pass without consequences. There are reasons for what is happening right now, and as a prospect you would not have been in the loop. Once we've sorted the shit between our clubs I will put in a good word for you if you want to return to the Road Warriors. Tonight, I need you to stand with us against a mutual enemy. I need your skills, Gav. What do you say?"

My little brother didn't disappoint.

He tightened his shoulders and nodded.

"I know what I did and I'm aware of the consequences. I'll deal with it when the time comes."

His mouth was a thin hard line, his eyes still filled with rage.

The sadness had been replaced by hard resolve.

BURNING BRIGHT IN THE BLACK

In front of my eyes my irresponsible and fun-loving little brother became a man his brothers could rely on.

"I'm in. Whatever you need, Prez."

THIRTY

Hawk

Music pumped through the outdoor speakers as the brothers who weren't on watch stood around on the large paved area outside the back door of the clubhouse. They sipped beers or whatever they were drinking. At the enormous *braai* (barbecue) built out of breeze blocks two prospects were cooking steaks and *boerewors* (sausage) on a grid set over glowing coals.

Large cooler boxes sat under a semi-circle of tables. Ostensibly the boxes were filled with ice and beer. They were not.

They were filled with extra guns and ammunition.

The tables were heavily reinforced, and would be tipped over to become a defensive wall the minute the attackers gained entry to the compound.

Everyone knew the pigs would descend on them the minute gunshots were reported coming from the compound. They had to be seen as the innocent party by those bastards. That was why they were having a braai. But it was a braai with a difference. Only brothers were invited, no bitches. The women were staying out of sight.

After the bullets stopped flying, a prospect and two patched brothers were tasked with the job of collecting every single illegal firearm used by the Dogz. The bags of weapons would then be dropped in the steel storage bin cleverly hidden beneath the row of black wheelie rubbish bins. The two prospects currently busy with the meat would fill up the empty coolers with ice and water and waiting cases of beer. This would cover up the fact there'd been guns and ammo in the cases.

An easy clean-up. If everything went to plan.

Hawk knew it wouldn't be that easy. The Iron Dogz would be in trouble the same as their attackers, once the fucking bullets stopped flying. The pigs had been looking for an excuse to get inside one of their compounds for a long time. The fuckers are going to think Christmas came early; It was a given they would snuffle, like the pigs they are, through the compound looking for anything that would get them warrants to raid all Iron Dogz chapters across the country. As a precaution the entire compound had been scrubbed clean of anything even remotely linked to illegal activity.

Hawk had grinned at the amount of weed that was taken away to be stored at a safe location.

The clean-up meant moving quite a few of Mad Dogs toys to a safe location, the bunker next door. He accompanied his toys and would continue tracking their enemies from down there. The communications room had been cleaned; it now looked like they only monitored the outside and inside of the compound.

Nothing was left to chance.

The women helped to clean the club. Afterwards the hangaround bitches, who were only allowed to clean the common areas and bathrooms, were sent home. The old ladies and club girls were escorted through the tunnel into the bunker. Hawk sent DC with the women with strict instructions to Spanner, the brother who would be watching over them, to make sure she stayed put.

Hawk knew his little bird, and he knew she would be chomping at the bit to join the fight. He could not allow that to happen. She was too important to him. He would not be able to concentrate on the job at hand if he had to worry about her safety. The last time he'd checked on his woman she was with Mad Dog in his new operations room utterly focused and typing furiously on a laptop. Mad Dog just rolled his eyes when he raised his eyebrows. He'd silently backed out of the room and gone back to the clubhouse without disturbing her.

There were two entrances to the compound:- the heavily fortified front entrance with guard posts and the smaller back entrance which was fortified and protected but not as heavily as the front. It was through the back entrance they were expecting the attackers to launch their main force. And it was here Gav had set up their main defensive line. Shallow foundation trenches had already been dug on either side of the entrance for the guardhouse they were in the process of building. Gav was using those trenches. He was setting small charges he could control from a central point that would force the attackers into a narrow corridor where they would have no cover at all.

Along with the small charges he had a lot of fireworks set to go off with the explosions around the back gates. Hopefully, the fireworks would cover some of the noise. Plus it would completely disorient the attackers and light up the sky, making it easier to see them. They were all expecting that the bastards were going to mess with the electricity supply. Gav had taken great care to ensure the inevitable investigation would not implicate the Iron Dogz. It would all land on the shoulders of the attackers.

The attack came just after midnight at the back entrance as expected.

The bastards blew the heavy steel gates to smithereens, shredded pieces of steel flew like angry bees across the back lawn. Had they not been expecting the attack the Iron Dogz would've been decimated by the lethal projectiles . Fortunately for the Dogz they were one step ahead in the game; the reinforced tables were tipped on their sides shielding the men crouching behind them.

They were ready for the attackers when they came streaming through the wrecked entrance. Hawk waited until most of the bastards were through the gate before he gave Gav the nod. Fireworks and explosions went off simultaneously. Disoriented and dazed the attackers dived for cover.

But there was none to be found.

Then they were firing at each other. Hawk could hear the thud of bullets striking his table almost constantly. It seemed he was the focus of the attack.

How the fuck did they know which table shielded him?

Around him his men returned fire. The attackers went down, they had nowhere to hide.

In the distance they could hear sirens fast approaching. The clean-up started immediately despite some of the attackers still firing. It was a fast and very efficient scrubbing. By the time the pigs arrived the scene was set.

Headlights and flashing blue lights pierced the dark as the pigs crowded around the destroyed back gate. Screaming orders they rushed through. The attackers were on the ground hands behind their heads before they approached the Iron Dogz. Hawk and his men rose slowly with their hands in the air, guns on the ground as the pigs surrounded them.

Hawk knew brothers had been injured. He needed to see to them. Towards the end of the firefight Hotdog had sprinted to the front gates and opened them to let in emergency vehicles and the rest of the damned pigs who were now streaming through both gates. Pigs were shouting orders and pushing and shoving his men to the ground.

Thank fuck they had all dropped their guns where they'd been crouching behind the tables. So no one was accidentally-on-purpose shot by the assholes tearing through their property.

He hadn't had time to call Mad Dog and he hoped like hell his side of the operation had gone down without any problems. He was tasked with leading the women back into the clubhouse once he was sure it was safe so they could further confuse the pigs.

Hotdog came walking back towards him, a cop on either side of him pushing him along, his hands cuffed behind his back.

Hawk had had enough.

"What the fuck is going on here? We were attacked and you are cuffing my men and leaving those bastards free to fucking run off. Our women…"

The sound of women screaming in fear suddenly ripped through the air. Hawk and the others swung around. Molly came stumbling out of the back door, her face bloody. Hotdog howled with rage as he tried to get to her.

Hawk ran, he flat out ran, ignoring the shouts behind him as he raced into the clubhouse. Pandemonium reigned. Mad Dog lay in a pool of blood on the floor. Next to him lay two of the club girls.

His eyes raced over the women crouched on the floor next to his fallen brother, searching for her. He didn't find her. His little bird wasn't in the room.

What. The. Fuck.

"Brother…they…took…" Mad Dog struggled to talk as blood gurgled in his throat.

Hawk fell to his knees, ripped his kutte and shirt off and stuffed the shirt against the knife wounds in Mad Dog's chest and side.

"Who took her, brother?"

"Ffffour…fuck…ing…pigs. Came…in…stabbed me…and girls, beat Molly. Don't…trust…pigs. En…e…mee…" His eyes closed on his last words.

"You fucking stay with us, Mad. Don't give up brother, we've got you," Hawk ground through tight lips.

He moved and pulled his kutte on when the EMT's arrived and started to work on Mad Dog and the fallen girls.

Turning slowly he looked at the watching fucking pigs and growled. They all had their guns pointed at him. Glaring at them he slowly slid his phone out of his front pocket, slid his thumb across the face and called Gerhard Van Wyk.

Thank fuck he was in Durban. His orders were short and easy to follow.

"Don't say a word. Help is on the way. I will be there soon."

Hawk seethed as he stood phone in hand glaring at the pigs. They were wasting time, every minute wasted meant the fuckers got further and further away with his little bird.

They had expected the fucking pigs to be nervous and that they would be holding them while they cleared up the situation but something wasn't right.

His men were being cuffed and dragged outside. But he didn't see one of the attackers being dragged to the front of the clubhouse where most of the vans were congregated. His woman had been abducted during the attack.

All these fuckers were interested in was arresting the men and women associated with his club.

His phone pinged and he saw it was a text from Wolf.

Following. Running silent. Not pigs. Need backup.

The fear and rage in his gut calmed a little, but only a little. His brother would stay on her and if he could, he would get her back, but he needed help. He deleted the text and forwarded Gerhard's details to Wolf before he deleted that too.

Then he sent a two-word text. *Jag Skel*

Wolf would know what to do. Even with all the shit going down between the Dogz and the Warriors, Hawk knew Skelly would lose his shit if anything happened to DC. He would send Wolf the backup he needed.

Slipping his phone back in his pocket he watched as Mad Dog was stabilised, placed on a gurney, and rushed from the room. The same with the two club girls.

As the EMT's left with the wounded a short, cocky little fuck strutted into the room. He smirked as he came to a halt in front of him, his hands clasped pretentiously behind his back. Hawk looked down at the piece of shit and waited.

He didn't have to wait long.

"Arresting one of the most notorious motorcycle gang leaders in the country is going to look very, very good on my record. Can't believe you lot are so feared. You are nothing but a bunch of pussies. We took you down without firing a single shot."

Hawk said nothing.

"I am making my career with this arrest. I've got you on drug distribution, gun running, human trafficking, murder and whatever else I feel like adding to the docket."

Hawk smiled.

"What is your name, officer?"

He puffed out his meagre little chest and said ever so importantly. "Captain Warren Samuels."

Nodding Hawk just looked at the little shmuck, not saying another word.

They were cuffed, pushed out the door and roughly shoved to the ground. Hawk lifted his head slightly and slowly turned to look at Hotdog lying next to him, the man was beside himself with rage. Molly lay not too far from him, hands tightly bound behind her back, her bloody face shoved into the gravel of the drive where one of the bastards had dropped her unceremoniously. She had passed out from the pain; the fuckers had refused her medical attention.

The fucking bastards thought they could do whatever they wanted; he heard them smashing everything in the communications room. Little did the assholes know. The cameras were still running, the feed going directly to Mad Dog's new communications room in the bunker. *We have you on camera assholes*, Hawk thought to himself.

As soon as this fuck up is over, the Dogz were going on a hunt; Every one of the corrupt fucking pigs who hurt his brothers, and endangered his woman were going to die.

They were going to feel the pain of IDMC vengeance.

He wasn't worried about what was happening here. Gerhard was going to take the SAPS to the cleaners for their treatment of his brothers and the women. Especially the women.

But that was not what he was worried about now.

He worried, agonised over his little bird. His woman. One of the girls had whispered that her abductors had beaten her badly with a baton before taking her. All because she defended Molly and the other women.

This shit had Winifred Maingarde written all over it.

The bitch had his woman. He knew he had to get his little bird out of the bitch's clutches as soon as possible. If he didn't, DC would never be the same again. The Maingardes' cold-as-fuck torturer would play with her soul, snap her wings, and destroy her spirit. That's what he did to those who knew too much. And his little bird knew way too much about many, many things.

A loud disturbance at the gate had the laughing boasting pigs turning. The next minute a man in black tactical gear, badge on a thin chain around his neck, strode towards them. His short dark blonde hair and moustache was flecked with grey. One look at his face told everyone he was pissed.

"Who's in charge of this clusterfuck?" He clipped out.

"I am." The little shmuck answered. "Who are you and what are you doing at my crime scene?"

"Name." The newcomer snapped.

"Captain Warren Samuels, and who are you?" the little pencil dick answered.

New guy ignored his question. "Are you working with a team on this arrest?"

"Yes, these men here are on my team."

"Good. Did you respond to the 10111 call? *Or* were you already here watching the premises?"

That was an interesting question. Infinitely more interesting were the men in black tactical gear surrounding them now. They carried automatic weapons with only their eyes visible through their black masks.

"I received a tipoff and led my team here. We arrived soon after the fighting started. We entered through the front gate after one of the suspects opened it and arrested everyone here."

New guy nodded. "Where are the men who initiated the attack?"

This was something Hawk wanted to know as well.

"I left them at the back of the property where they gained entrance with some of my other officers. Arresting the Iron Dogz was my top priority."

"What are the charges, Samuels?"

The little shit smirked.

"Distribution of illegal substances, gun running, human trafficking and murder is what I have so far. I'm sure I'll be adding more to the docket as the night progresses."

Again, the nod.

"Show me the evidence."

And then the little fucker started hedging.

"I've got a file at my office. We will be checking all the firearms found on the premises tonight. So far, we haven't found any other guns or drugs but I know it's here, it has to be. If I have to dig up this entire compound I'll find it."

"Do you have probable cause to search the premises, Samuels? Or did you take the law into your own hands and did a dirty search? Where's your warrant?"

"I don't have a warrant, not yet. We were invited in so I don't need one to arrest them. But I will get one for a further search. There's enough here to hold them until I have it. One of the men they shot will surely give us the necessary evidence to take this nest of criminals down."

The man in the black tactical gear nodded.

"So, to clarify, you walked in here, on a tip that will be investigated. You arrested the men and women who were attacked. But you didn't arrest their attackers. You left *them* out of sight at the back of the property, watched over by four officers. Officers, who could have been easily overpowered and those suspects would've been in the wind, never to be seen again."

Hawk watched as the little bastard stuttered and spluttered through an explanation.

"Luckily for you, Samuels, I had men stationed at the back of the property. We took the suspects into custody before any harm could befall your officers. Your gross violation of the bounds of your jurisdiction will be reported to your superiors as will the unlawful arrest of these men and women."

Hawk had had enough of their fucking back and forth and time wasting.

"Could you fucking get these fucking ties off me. Four of his men entered our clubhouse, attacked, and stabbed one of my men. They beat up the woman lying over there and stabbed two others then abducted my old lady. Check with the hospital if you need fucking proof. I need to get out of here to look for my woman before those fuckers hurt her even more."

One of the black-masked men had gone rigid as Hawk laid it out for them. Before he even finished speaking the ties around his wrists were cut and he was helped to his feet.

"How do you know this is what happened?"

Hawk knew that voice.

Knew it very fucking well.

Rick fucking Townsend.

"Mad Dog was still conscious when I got to him. Between him and the other women I got a report of what went down. That's how I fucking know. DC tried to protect the women and helped Molly to get away before they could kill her. The four bastards who abducted DC beat her with batons until she collapsed." Hawk snarled. "Now get me the fuck out of here so I can find my woman."

The man in charge turned back to the smirking little fuck.

"Samuels, you, and the men in your team are under arrest. You will be held under suspicion of corruption, aiding, and abetting a criminal, conspiracy to commit murder, assault with intent… and those are just a few of the charges I can think of right now," he said sarcastically. "Arrest the fucking bastards and take them away. I'll get to them later."

Samuels and his little band of fucks disappeared into the back of a big black van, protesting bitterly. Good riddance. Hawk didn't watch as the van left the compound. All he wanted to do was find DC.

He called Wolf. No answer. He tried Skel. Same thing. No one answered their fucking phones. What the fuck was happening out there?

He had to find her. Fast.

"Do we have a prisoner?" Hawk gritted through clenched teeth.

"Fuck, yes." Hotdog snarled. "We got three."

Hawk gave a short nod. He would get the information even if he had to cut strips of flesh from each of the fuckers.

They were going to talk.

The guy in charge of the 'men in black' was back, holding his hand out.

"Mr Walker, I'm Inspector Marnus van Blerk, head of the trafficking taskforce. I'm sorry you and your club had to go through all this. I know for a fact your club is fairly clean and have been for a very long time. Let us take it from here. I promise we will find Ms Michaels and return her to you."

Hawk snarled at him as he shook his head.

"Don't trust you or any of those fucking SAPS fucks. I will find my woman and the sooner all of you get off our premises the better."

"Don't fucking do this, Hawk." Rick snapped through the stupid black mask.

Hawk shook his head with an angry growl.

"The longer you fuck with me the further away those bastards get with her. You fucking know who's behind this shit and you're wasting my time. Let me do what I do. We'll share what we find… but there is no way in hell I'll sit and wait for you fucks to bring her home."

Marnus van Blerk nodded.

"Okay, as long as you include us in the search."

Hawk nodded in agreement. He couldn't exclude Rick, by his voice Hawk knew Rick was as scared, pissed-off, and worried as he was.

He stalked back into the clubhouse. He had an interrogation waiting for him.

THIRTY ONE

Hawk

Standing with his hands behind his back Hawk stared at the three men suspended by their wrists in front of him. They wore dark combat uniforms without a single identifying mark anywhere. He knew they had to be private operators or mercenaries. They had obviously taken some damage before he stepped into the room. He took grim satisfaction from that.

None of them said a word.

Hawk walked around them slowly until he stood facing them again.

"I need you to answer some questions and the sooner you do the sooner this shit will be over. Answer my questions and death will be easy, don't, and I guarantee it won't."

He stared, holding their eyes.

"Who are you working for?"

The one in the middle answered. "Don't give a shit what you do. You and your fucking gang are filthy human traffickers. We saw the evidence of your crimes. You abduct little kids as young as 8 and sell them on the black market to the highest bidder. To sick disgusting fucks. Can't let that fucking shit happen."

The brothers watching the interrogation groaned. Hawk hissed to shut them up. Silence fell and stretched.

"So," Hawk rasped after what felt like hours. "you're telling me you are the *good* guys who came to take down the filthy fucking biker gang selling kiddies to dirty fuckers. Who hired you?"

There was a long silence before the talkative one spoke again.

"I got no names, just aliases so it won't help you. They're going to take you down, every single one of you dirty fucking bastards. Don't care if you kill us, we got the cops' eyes on you now. We're good with whatever happens next. You won't get away with it."

Shaking his head Hawk motioned for Gav to let the bastards down. He waited as chains rattled and slackened until the three had their feet on the ground.

"Get them some chairs."

Angry grumbles erupted but three chairs were shoved behind them. Gav released more chain and their asses hit the chairs.

Hawk dragged a chair forward, sat down and crossed his arms over his chest.

"I'm going to lay it out for you so you get how deep the shit is you are in. The Iron Dogz MC has never, nor will we ever, kidnap and sell any human regardless of age. You're the ones working for a human trafficking ring and after you've told me what I need, we will hand you over to the taskforce who'll most probably lock you up and throw away the key."

There was a moment of stunned silence and then the one on the end laughed.

"Good try. We saw your trucks; we saw your men surrounding the truck. We saw the kids when they put them into the fucking container. Stop all this talking bullshit and get it over with. We're not talking, not now, not ever."

Hawk nodded slowly then turned.

"Gav, get a laptop in here."

While they waited for Gav Hawk laid it out for them.

"I know you are supposedly working with Freeze Wentzel of the Road Warriors MC in Cape Town. We were warned you were coming, so we were prepared. What you don't know, is that Freeze was forced into it, this dark shit. The organisation *actually* kidnapping and selling kids threatened to harm his daughter if he didn't co-operate. Sadly, he didn't go to his club and let his brothers know he was being coerced. Instead, he started working for the traffickers. He not only betrayed his club but ours as well. Rogue elements in the Durban chapter kidnapped those children and made it look like it was Iron Dogz MC who did it." Hawk shook his head. "You think we work for Winifred Maingarde, but wake the fuck up, you are the ones working for her. She's the one fucking paying you."

The door slammed as Gav ran in, a laptop clutched in his hand. Hawk got up and paced waiting for Gav to boot up the laptop.

The stares of the speechless bastards irritated him beyond reason. His little bird's time was running out because of their stupidity. He unlocked the password-protected files and searched for what he wanted. The interrogations done by Crow.

"What you're about to see is the interrogation of two of the traffickers, both women. You should find it enlightening." He pressed the play button.

The Crow's eerie hissing voice slithered through the silence of the underground room. Pitiful feminine sobs and moans bounced off the walls.

Hawk knew by the sharp shocked breaths that watching and hearing the Crow in action rattled them more than anything else would've. He slapped the laptop lid down as the video ended.

"What the fuck was that?"

Before Hawk could answer Gav was there, right in their faces.

"That was the fucking Crow and if you don't start fucking talking and giving my boss what he wants that's what's coming for you. Stop wasting fucking time. Tell him who took his fucking old lady…my sister."

The three men were shocked, stunned by what they had just seen. One glanced at Hawk then looked at his fellow assholes. They nodded in agreement and, then he started talking.

"She's safe. We were hired to provide a distraction so she could be rescued by a special SAPS team. I promise you she's safe."

Hawk wanted to howl in frustration.

He jerked the laptop open and played the video of the attack in the clubhouse and the vicious beating handed down to DC.

"If she's so fucking safe," he said in a deadly voice, "why the fuck did they brutalize her and try to kill my man and the other women in the room?"

This was taking too fucking long. Hawk was about to explode. He needed the fucker to give him what he needed.

"Jesus Christ. This is a fucking clusterfuck." The asshole snarled. "I need to contact my men on the other end of this. They're in fucking danger."

"Names, right the fuck now." Hawk growled.

"Hendricks, Roodt and Lang. We're part of a specialised hostage extraction team. My men outside, did I lose any of them?"

Hawk shrugged because he just didn't care.

"There were injuries, some serious, some critical they've all been taken care of, hospitalised. The rest were taken into custody. Some of those assholes weren't dressed like you and your men. Who are they?"

The bastard shook his head.

"The men in uniform are mine and I need them out of lock up ASAP. I have no idea who those other fuckers are. They were foisted on me at the last minute. If I had to guess I'd say they work for the person who hired us. Now that I've seen those videos, I'm sure they were here to take us out once the job was done."

Hawk was done talking.

"I can arrange to get them out. Now tell me where the fuck is my old lady?"

Hendricks was obviously the man in charge, giving Hawk the information he needed.

"We were hired to extract DC Michaels. We were told she'd been kidnapped by the Iron Dogz MC. Just as we were about to breach the compound our orders changed. Instead, we were to provide a distraction and allow the SAPS team to extract her. They would then take her to the secure location and hand her over to Freeze Wentzel and her fiancée Raj Chetty who are waiting to transport her to safety."

He blew out a breath before he continued.

"My team and I were shown evidence that you and her father are part of the ring trafficking kids. We were assured Doc and his accomplices would be taken into custody by a special task team once DC was safe. Six of my men are at the handover location for her protection. It's obvious those bastards who took her aren't SAPS, I'll bet my last fucking cent on it. I'm going to lose my men if I don't warn them. Please man, allow me to call and warn them. We don't have much time; they might already be dead but I have to try. We need their help to save your woman."

Hawk waved a hand. Hotdog stepped up and unlocked the shackles around their wrists.

"Where are they taking her?"

"The old Durban International Airport."

Hendricks rolled and flexed his wrists.

"They have a helicopter standing by to get them to Virginia Airport. A jet is waiting to fly them to Cape Town. I need my phone. If I call from any other phone they won't answer."

Fuck. The fucking old airport. Again.

Hendricks frowned as he spoke to his men. "Bad news," he said as he ended the call. "We're outnumbered. Speedy, Jane and some men have arrived and with the four bringing DC in they are in control of the location. One of my men overheard plans to get rid of Freeze and Raj the minute they arrive at Virginia airport."

Hawk smiled grimly. "I'm not surprised. They've served their purpose.

They had a quick tactical discussion and decided that Hendricks' men at the location would volunteer to guard the perimeter.

"Get them cleaned and patched up. When it's done, we ride".

Growler and Hotdog gave him chin lifts.

He called Ziggy, Skel, and Rick.

He needed Rick's contacts to get Hendricks' men out of lock up and to close-down Virginia Airport in case they failed to free DC. His heart ached at the mere thought.

Ziggy and Skel had to work their magic to access the cameras at the terminal and get them in undetected.

Skel loved DC. He would get the Warriors up to speed and lock down Freeze and Raj with Alien's help.

If they were still at the safe house.

Jesus, he did not have much time to save his little bird. So very little time.

He left the dungeon room with Ice, Kid and Gav following. Turning to Kid he drew him into a tight hug, slapping his back before he pulled away.

"I'm so fucking sorry, brother."

"Not your fault, Hawk. Jane bought every single fucked up thing that's going to happen to her. She betrayed her family, her blood, her club. She's dead to me." Kid bit out coldly.

Hawk looked at him for a long time, nodded, and moved off into the night.

Walking across the yard to the clubhouse he drew the cool night air deep into his lungs, trying to dispel the smells of the dungeon. He stopped halfway and drew his phone out of his kutte pocket.

He dialled, his eyes on the brightly lit up front gate.

"Doc, can you talk?"

"Yes."

"Did Skel bring you up to date?"

"Yes."

"Then you know Speedy and the Maingarde bitch has their sights set on taking over both clubs, nationally. You need to cover your asses. I'm going after DC, with or without the Road Warriors."

An angry grunt filled the short silence.

"The Road Warriors will be with you." Doc gritted out.

"We've taken out the rubbish this side, so it's all clear."

For the first time in hours something lightened the load resting on Hawk's shoulders.

"Permanently?"

Doc laughed without any humour.

"No, we're waiting for the rubbish truck to do a pick-up."

Hawk gave a short mirthless bark of a laugh.

"Hold on to those bags, we might have some rubbish to add before the truck arrives."

A soft evil laugh came over the line. "Done. Now, how are we doing this?"

And immediately they were back to business.

"I'm sure Skel informed you of the specialised help we've acquired tonight. They will be assisting when we go in to get my old lady. I'm worried about the Warne bitch at the location, she hates DC and will hurt her. My woman is already hurt. I have no idea how badly but it did not look good. Add the Warne bitch to the mix and it could be deadly."

That very soft evil laugh came again.

"Don't worry about my little demon, Hawk. She's been trained to withstand fuckloads of pain. The Crow will take over and keep her safe, take whatever they do to her and turn it back on them the minute she's free. We are ready to ride. Skel has men close to the airport, watching. No kuttes, no bikes. We have a way in that's not the front door. Are you ready to ride?"

Hawk nodded even though he knew Doc couldn't see him.

"We'll see you soon."

Sliding his phone back into his pocket he gave his orders.

"Get the men ready to ride, tell Sin and Claw I want to see them. I want us ready to ride in twenty minutes at the latest. My old lady's time is running out."

Kid turned and raced off to make the arrangements to get them on the road.

"We'll get to her in time, brother." Ice clasped a hand over Hawk's shoulder before he followed Kid.

"They're going to hurt her before they kill her." Gav said softly. "I feel it in my gut. We need to get there, now."

"Yes, they're going to hurt her, and there's nothing we can do about it from here. But we will be fucking doing something about it when we get there. We have help, Gav. She's strong, she'll hold out until we get to her."

He clasped a hand behind his neck and squeezed.

"I need you to be cool, we're going to blow some shit up, disable a helicopter, take out gates and fences and you're our man. Get what you need and load up, little brother. We're riding the minute you're ready."

Gav stared in his eyes for a few seconds, nodded then darted into the clubhouse.

Hawk looked up at the stars. He frowned as two shooting stars streaked across the night sky.

That's us, he thought, both of us burning bright in the black.

BURNING BRIGHT IN THE BLACK

We will survive.

We will always fucking survive.

He smiled at the thought because it was the truth.

THIRTY TWO

DC

It might have been the voices that woke me from my forced little nap, but it was more than likely the shock of my body making contact with the cold cement floor that did it. I almost groaned out loud in pain. I gritted my teeth and swallowed the sound back down. I lay motionless, kept my eyes closed and listened.

You could learn so much about your surroundings if you stayed perfectly still.

I was somewhere that was large, cold and echoing. There were people with me. I was *not* thrilled to hear Jane fucking Warne's bitchy whine. Why can't the bitch just disappear? She's like that bloody bad penny that keeps on turning up when you least fucking need it around.

I furtively tested my body to gauge the extent of my injuries. My face throbbed, it meant there was some damage. The worst injuries were to my ribs and left arm; the arm was definitely broken, and a few ribs might be cracked or even broken. My breathing, though painful, was okay, no blood froth in my mouth, so no puncture wounds to my lungs. My legs were fine and I still had the use of my right arm.

I may be down but I'm far from broken. Some weapons in my little arsenal were still operational. I knew fighting with my ribs giving me hell would fucking suck, but I could do it. I would do whatever it takes to get out of this shit show.

The bitch's grating nasal whine assaulted my ears again.

"But you promised, you promised we could play once we had her. I want to play with her. I want to do it now. You promised, Speedy."

The sounds of a stinging slap and a pained gasp echoed through the space.

Almost made me smile. Almost.

"Shut the fuck up. Get it through your fucking little sample of a brain bitch. She's not here for our entertainment. She belongs to the boss; we do what the boss orders us to do. When I tell you we're not playing with her, it means we're not fucking playing with her. Now shut the fuck up, go fuck someone out there to relieve the tension."

I heard Jane snort and then giggle.

"Can I fuck one of those commando types we have out there? They look so yummy in their uniforms."

"Jesus, leave them the fuck alone. I need them to keep watch, not get distracted by your snatch."

There was a pissy sniff, then a click-drag uneven sound as she hobbled across the floor.

It was followed by the thump of heavy boots, the screech of a heavy door opening and closing, and then silence.

"I know you're awake."

I snorted in disgust.

"Ja, but no way was I going to talk to the whore. Already broke her leg not sure what I'll break next if I was forced to socialise with her."

A rusty sounding laugh rang out. Then I was turned onto my back slowly, carefully. An involuntary groan escaped past my lips.

"Jesus, girl, they did a fucking job on you. Why didn't you just go with them when they told you to? Why did you fight them?"

I laughed, but damn it hurt.

"They didn't ask and…there was no way I was going to stand by and let them kill…those women without doing something about it."

Breathing and talking was starting to hurt, a lot.

The man crouching beside me rubbed his hands over his face and sighed heavily.

I didn't know him and I was sure I had never seen him before.

"Jesus Christ. This is turning into a fucking nightmare of epic proportions. They weren't supposed to hurt anyone, least of all you. Who did they kill?"

I closed my eyes to shut him out as I replayed the nightmare in my mind. Those bastards dressed like pigs storming into the clubhouse and attacking us. The looks on the women's faces as they fell to the floor, blood blooming across their tee shirts. I will never forget that.

"I think…they killed Mad Dog and two of…the women and Molly, Hotdog's…old lady was hurt very badly. Not sure…if any of them survived."

A rough hand smoothed the hair away from my face and cold brown eyes stared down at me.

Who the hell was this guy?

"Who…are…you?"

He shook his head with a small smile.

"Don't worry about it. I'm going to get the first aid kit and fix you up a bit. Get you some water and pain killers."

My eyes closed and when I opened them, he was gone. I didn't hear him leave or the door open and close. I lay there breathing through the pain and slowly took stock of my surroundings. I was in an empty hangar, a bloody hangar. I was at an airport, somewhere. Not good. Not good at all.

The door opened and the man with the cold brown eyes walked in carrying an enormous first-aid kit. Another man followed close behind him. I noticed with a jolt that both of them were dressed like commandos, not bikers. Who the fuck were they? A scrawny dirty looking biker sidled in after them. His kutte told me he was a Road Warrior from the Durban chapter. The patch on his chest said his name was Meerkat.

The biker came over and leered down at me. His tiny evil eyes glittering with lust. He grinned through his ratty beard, baring nasty-looking yellowed teeth.

"You fix her up good so we can have some fun. Don't care what Speedy says, going to fuck this bitch until she bleeds. Doc fucks with me I will fuck with his blood."

"You won't be touching her, no one will," the new man said as he reached out and snapped Meerkat's neck almost perfunctorily.

"Dispose of the body then get back here, going to need your help wrapping her up," the man with the cold brown eyes said placidly.

I lay staring at the two of them.

What the hell was going on here?

Who were these guys and what the hell was their business with Speedy and his bunch of losers?

Kneeling beside me Mr Commando started straightening my legs slowly. I groaned as the movement jarred my aching ribs. Then he took a space blanket out of the enormous first-aid kit he had dropped next to me and spread it on the floor. Shit, I knew what was going to happen next and I wasn't looking forward to it.

"Okay babe, once my man gets back, we're going to move you onto the blanket. Then I'm going to wrap those ribs and splint your arm." He lifted my head and held two capsules to my lips. "This will help for the pain but won't take you down. Open up."

I opened up like a baby bird. He held a bottle of water to my mouth and I downed the capsules gratefully. By the time we were done the other commando materialised out of the dark recesses of the hangar like a ghost. These guys were pros, no doubt about it. They moved me onto the blanket carefully.

It freaking hurt like a son of a bitch. But soon the drugs started kicking in. The pain receded. Not all the way gone but bearable

They were coldly efficient but careful not to cause me extra pain. Between them my t-shirt came-off without too much fuss. Mr Commando checked my ribs and pronounced them cracked not broken. Once they had them wrapped, it was my well and truly broken left forearm's turn. It pissed me off because cracked ribs and a broken arm meant two weaknesses to compensate for in the coming fight. I had no doubt there would be a fight. I wasn't going down without one. But even with cracked ribs, a broken arm and possible concussion I was more than able to kick ass. I just had to find out who these guys were and if they were friendlies.

I didn't get a chance to find out. Speedy was back. And as usual he was freaking creepy. He's the same age as my dad but looked decades older. He had let himself go, flabby with a belly spilling over a too-tight belt. His hair was long and greasy and hung in thin hanks around his face and onto his shoulders. And he fucking reeked. The stink of unwashed body, beer and weed hung around him in a cloud. So gross I almost gagged.

"Will you look at that?" he said leering at my breasts.

"Leave the t-shirt off, I wanna see those tits and her pretty skin. Doc always kept her away from us but we saw her, oh yes, we all saw her. Doc always acting like she's too fucking good to be my old lady. And what does the bastard do? He fucking gives her to the Iron Dogz. How the fuck is that fair? She's a Warrior, club property, ours to fuck anytime we want. It's my turn now. Screw the boss's orders, she'll never know."

The commandos ignored him like he wasn't there and helped me into a large black t-shirt.

"I said leave the fucking t-shirt off her." Speedy snapped through clenched teeth.

My protectors slowly rose from their crouched positions on either side of me and faced the asshole calmly.

"Not happening. Don't give a fuck what you want or what Doc didn't give you. It's none of my business. My business is keeping her comfortable and alive until we transport her to the airport."

He didn't flinch or budge when Speedy shoved into his face.

"You and all your little boys playing soldier out there are dead once this is done. That's a promise." Speedy hissed. He gave me one last creepy look and slammed out the door.

The two commandos looked at each other, communicating silently for a beat.

"We need to get her out of here. My gut says we can't hand her over to these fucks." Commando number two whispered.

"We're short on firepower. There are six of us and fuck knows how many of them. I heard bikes pulling in earlier. We need a plan, a good plan or we die for nothing and they still take her."

Men, always forgetting the little woman at their feet.

"You forgot to count me. There's seven of us." I interrupted their planning. "All we need is an easily defensible position from which to hold them off until my man gets here. And he will get here, I promise you."

Mr Commando shook his head.

"A large force attacked the clubhouse. Your man was the main target. It's quite possible he went down. We can't count on him coming for you."

I threw him an evil grin and winked when he frowned.

"We knew you were coming we were prepared. Before they took me, I saw a lot of men down, not ours, yours. My man will be coming for me and he will be coming in hard."

A phone started ringing. The two men exchanged a quick look before Mr Commando slipped a phone from his pocket.

"Yes."

That's all he said, then he listened intently, a heavy frown marring his smooth forehead.

"Yes, sir. I understand, we'll proceed with caution."

The phone went back into his pocket as he looked down at me.

"You were right. Things have changed. My people are now aligned with your man and they're coming in hot and hard. But it's going to take them thirty to forty-five minutes to get here. We need to get you out of this fucking hangar and somewhere with real walls around us. I'm Tin Man and he's Leo, by the way."

He turned to Leo.

"Did you see another way out of here when you disposed of the asshole? There has to be more than one exit."

Leo shook his head.

"I dropped the body behind the crates back there, didn't look around. I'll have a look while you pack up. Watch your backs. I don't trust the old fuck or the whiny bitch."

He was so right not to trust them, they were evil. If Jane was here where was Big Ed? Was he out there with her? I so did not want to come face to face with him, especially not when I was weak.

Tin Man started furiously repacking the first aid kit. He had just zipped it up and tightened the last buckle when the damned door screeched open again.

We were too late.

A guy holding an AK47 dressed in dark jeans and a dark blue shirt stood in the open door.

"The boss is on the line. Wants to talk to you. Come with me, now."

Tin Man gave me a knowing look. I knew what it meant. We both knew I was going to be in deep shit the minute he walked out the door. Closing my eyes for a few seconds I gave him a nod. I would fight, no matter what. And he would be back. I saw the promise in those cold brown eyes.

"Help me up. Not lying on the freaking floor for what's coming." I whispered. He helped me to stand and didn't close the door when he left.

I leaned against the cold corrugated iron wall and waited. I knew they were coming; how many of them didn't matter. I breathed in and out, reaching for that part of me I needed desperately to survive. Crow. Closing my eyes, I listened intently and heard the almost silent squeak of a door opening and closing. Not the door across from me, another one.

Leo had found another exit.

I heard them before I saw them. The click-drag of her uneven walk, the thump of their boots.

Jane, Big Ed and Speedy came through the open door, closing it behind them.

I didn't say a word, just watched. They crowded around me.

Jane poked at the wounds on my face. I didn't flinch. I gave her nothing. I no longer felt anything.

The Crow was in charge.

"I'm not fucking her on the floor, drag that crate over here. We'll lay her over it so we can go at her from both ends," Big Ed said with a wide lecherous grin.

"I'm going to shove my pussy in her face while you fuck her," Jane said. "Going to fuck her face while you fuck her ass."

Instead of scaring me the sick slut just grossed me out.

The Crow laughed. A low hissing laugh.

"Fair warning. Don't stick your dirty snatch in my face. You do and I will go Hannibal Lecter on your fucking clit."

Big Ed laughed uproariously.

"I fucking like her. Small but so full of fire." He smirked. "She would have been the perfect fucking old lady for me. Doc should have given me what I wanted. Now I'm just going to take what should have been mine."

I snorted contemptuously looking into his disgusting and glittering eyes.

"Doc was only too glad Hawk claimed me as his old lady. He was getting pissed off with me always turning his suggestions down."

Big Ed's eyes narrowed. "He let you have that much freedom? The man is stupider than I thought."

Asshole.

Behind him Speedy huffed and puffed as he dragged a big crate over to the centre of the hangar.

And then my time was up and hell came calling.

I resisted as they dragged me over to the crate. I fought back. Pain from my cracked ribs and broken arm was nearly unbearable. It spiked through me, making me hiss. I fought them, as much as I could. There were three of them and one of me. I wasn't at my best. They pinned me on top of the crate, head hanging off one side, legs dangling off the other.

I kicked out when they tried to take my boots. Inflicted quite a bit of damage until Speedy grabbed my broken arm and squeezed. I screamed in pain but kept right on kicking. I saw the butt of a gun coming towards me then a flash of pain and everything went dark. I came back from the dark in agony.

OhGodohGodohGodohGod.

The words ran in a continuous loop through my brain.

Did they? Did they? I feared the worst.

Sounds of fighting came from my right. I froze. I was having trouble focusing. Blinking furiously I tried to clear my vision.

And then I saw him, he was back.

Tin Man.

He had taken a beating but he was here, right next to me. Undisguised horror in his eyes as he covered my naked body with the space blanket.

"So fucking sorry, sweetheart. So very fucking sorry." His breathing was ragged. "It was a trap, got jumped. It took some time to take them down. Thank fuck I got here in time. They didn't rape you but they did hurt you. Got to get you cleaned up and out of here. Have to get you to a hospital. It's going to be embarrassing and hurt like a son of a bitch but it has to be done. Hold on for me, okay?"

Drawing in a ragged breath that felt like fire burning through my chest I croaked out my question.

"What did they do to me?"

A warm hand wrapped around the fingers of my unhurt hand, and I jerked.

"Shhh, it's me, Leo. Hold on to me and let Tin Man help you. We've got you now and your man is going to be here soon. Then those fuckers are going to pay. Got them all nicely packaged for him."

"What did they do? It hurts like hell, just tell me."

Tin Man's gloved hand wrapped around my chin.

I forced my eyes to meet his.

"You've been beaten and the fucked up bitch was cutting into your lower abdomen, you're bleeding heavily. I'm going to clean up the blood and disinfect the area as best I can. Pack it with gauze, get you dressed and out of here. Leo has a ride waiting for us at the back door."

His hands were gentle as he cleaned me, Leo never let go of my hand. There were four new commandos in the room, Tin Man and Leo's teammates, I suppose. I caught a glimpse of Speedy and Big Ed on the floor guns against their heads. Where the hell was Jane? The four commandos turned their backs pointedly as Tin Man worked on my belly.

He dressed me in soft sweatpants and a t-shirt, tied my boots and lifted me off the crate. I moaned when I put my weight on my feet. Pain spiked through my body.

Speedy and Big Ed were gagged, on their stomachs on the cement floor. Arms pulled behind them, legs up against their asses. They'd been hogtied; so tight they were groaning in pain through their gags.

Gunfire erupted outside the hangar.

Tin Man pushed me down behind the crate quickly. "Take cover," he muttered. The gunfire stopped as suddenly as it had started. "We've got to move now, we don't know what happened out there," he said. He inclined his head in a silent command. His men moved in and formed a human barricade around me, automatic weapons trained on the door.

BURNING BRIGHT IN THE BLACK

Tin Man, Leo and I retreated slowly towards the open back door where our transportation waited.

The door opened with a loud screech and banged against the wall.

And then he was there.

My man. My beautiful Viking.

He stormed in with his brothers and men I didn't recognise. I ignored them, my eyes fixed firmly on my man. Nothing else mattered.

"At ease." One of the men with Hawk said in a commanding voice. My human barricade lowered their weapons slowly.

Tin Man let out a harsh breath "thank fuck, the cavalry" he said with relief.

Hawk stalked across the hangar like a Viking marauder, gaze firmly pinned on me. He stopped dead when he saw the blood covered crate and rage started burning in those beautiful eyes. He looked from the crate to me, his eyes sweeping my body from head to toe.

He closed the final distance between us swiftly His eyes never left mine. He clasped a hand around my throat very gently, tenderly.

"What did they do to you, my little bird?" His voice rasped with barely banked emotion.

Stupid freaking tears started to burn my eyes. I shook my head. I couldn't stop the damned tears from brimming over and streaming down my cheeks.

What the hell? What was wrong with me?

Hawk was losing it and I was a blubbering mess.

How am I going to calm him down? Tin Man stepped up as if reading my thoughts.

"They didn't have time to do their worst but she's seriously injured. Not sure she can walk. We have to get her out of here, right the fuck now. I've done what I can but it's not enough, she needs a hospital."

Strong, hard arms slipped around me, lifted me so very carefully and cradled me against his broad, warm chest. I relaxed into him, sighing as the heat of his body seeped into my icy limbs.

My man, my Viking.

He had come for me. Like I knew he would.

I was safe.

THIRTY THREE

DC

The ride to the hospital took every bit of my training to keep from screaming in pain. I controlled it, kept the screams locked behind my teeth. Hawk held me, trying to be gentle, but it wasn't possible because I felt every bump, every turn, every gear change.

The rest was a blur, the arrival at the hospital, the scans, x-rays all of it was lost in a haze. My last memory was of Hawk bending over me, his yellow eyes glowing with too many emotions to pinpoint.

He was sitting beside my bed, holding my hand, when I opened my eyes. Our eyes met and held.

"I made it." I whispered, trying to smile.

He didn't, smile, that is.

"Never again, little bird, we're not doing this fucking shit ever again." He growled, leaning over to press a soft kiss to my forehead.

I opened my mouth to agree when the surgeon walked in, and Hawk instantly turned into a demanding ass.

He refused to leave when the doctor asked him to. Stayed as the dressings were removed.

"Fucking hell."

Fury transformed his handsome face as he inspected my bruised abdomen and the incisions. He reached out a hand but pulled it back before touching me.

"I know this is going to scar what I want to know is how badly. And will it cause problems during pregnancy?"

What?

I certainly wasn't planning on getting pregnant anytime soon.

Was Hawk thinking about it? He had to be. With him asking the question.

I refused to even think about it much less discuss it with him. Not that he tried; afterwards he acted like he'd never asked the pregnancy question.

That was a good thing.

Wasn't it?

My stay in the private hospital was short, very short.

"You can't stay here baby; their security is shit and we can't bring in brothers to guard you."

The only reason I was allowed to leave was my promise to follow the strict instructions from my surgeon. No strenuous activities until my injuries were healed, completely.

Doctor speak for no sex.

They needn't have given us the warning.

Hawk wasn't touching me, at freaking all. Not that I blamed him.

I looked hideous.

Although no longer swollen, my face was a mess of black, blue, green and yellow fading bruises. The large cut on my forehead and the smaller one on my cheek, were expertly stitched by the plastic surgeon and would leave me with minimal scarring. The rest of my injuries were healing as well. But I was stuck in bed with strict orders from Hawk not to put a toe on the floor. The inactivity was driving me crazy. Thankfully I had Molly and the other old ladies fussing about and keeping me company.

Mad Dog was recovering well and would be home soon. Miraculously none of the club brothers had been seriously injured during the attack. Everyone was doing well and already back at work.

Unfortunately, the club girls who were hurt during the attack were not as lucky. One died from her injuries. The one who survived was so traumatised she was not coming back to the clubhouse. She had gone home with her parents to recover.

On the face of it, everything was back to normal or as close normal for a motorcycle club under threat.

No one said a word about Speedy and Big Ed no matter how many times I asked. My gut told me they were locked up tight in a dungeon somewhere. In the confusion during the fight at the hangar Jane Warne had disappeared.

Poof.

Just gone as if she'd never been there.

I knew she would be back. She hadn't accomplished what she had set out to do and she was definitely not finished with us.

My dad and his brothers came to visit me often. I loved seeing my family. But it pissed off some of the Iron Dogz to see Road Warriors walking through their clubhouse. It in turn pissed me off and I made it my mission to end the hostility between the two clubs. They might make their money in very different ways but at their cores they were all outlaws and always would be.

They were brothers in blood and bone.

The fate of the kidnapped children continued to hang over all of us like a dark cloud.

They had not been found.

The taskforce found no evidence that the container had ever reached the docks. A search of the Josephine came up clean. Shortly after the search Hawk told me the taskforce had left to follow a lead on the head of the human trafficking ring.

They weren't actively searching for the children

Them giving up on those poor kids pissed me off.

I was convinced they were locked up somewhere on the outskirts of Durban. They were worth too much money to let them die. I was sure the traffickers would make a last effort to ship them out. Someone knew where they were.

Someone was looking after them. My instincts told me it was a woman.

Someone just like the woman Crow and I had interrogated.

BURNING BRIGHT IN THE BLACK

The Iron Dogz and the Road Warriors were out every single day searching every single container yard for the children. It was like looking for a needle in a haystack. Durban is one of South Africa's main ports. Containers moved in and out of the country every day by sea and by road. It was an impossible search.

Some of the brothers were convinced the children had been shipped out under our noses. My gut said no the children were still in Durban. And they were turning into a heavy liability for the traffickers. If we didn't find them soon, the traffickers were going to cut their losses, kill them, or leave them to die.

There was one bastard who knew where they were. Speedy.

But he wasn't talking. No matter what they did to him, he gave the brothers nothing.

Very different to Big Ed, he swore on his children's lives he knew nothing about kidnapping and selling children. He insisted all he knew was that Speedy was taking out the Dogz and the Warriors and that it would benefit his club. Which was why he got involved. Jane Warne had played him, and pulled him into her sick world. After a very short phone call to Snake, Big Ed was handed over to his club. He was now their problem. Good riddance.

There was one who could make Speedy talk.

The Crow. I just had to convince Hawk to let me do it.

He refused point blank to talk about it. If I broached the subject, he got up and walked out of the room, and didn't return until hours later smelling of cigarettes and whiskey.

After a week, a whole week, of lounging in bed like a cabbage while the world went on without me, I snapped. Enough already.

I tested my strength every day. I was getting stronger. Slowly but surely. My abdomen felt tight and ached when I moved too abruptly but otherwise I was fine. My ribs were no longer unbearably sore.

And of course my arm was still broken.

I was ready to do my bit for the club but mostly for those poor children. I was extremely worried they would die before we got any closer to finding them.

There was no other way. The Crow had to extract their location from Speedy.

I was about to do the unthinkable. Act without the president's permission.

Most of the men were out searching for the kids or taking care of the day-to-day business. There were brothers watching over me but with Molly's help I was going to give them the slip for an hour or so.

It hadn't been hard to convince Molly to help me. We had taken one of the other old ladies into our confidence. Ina was a mother with two little boys who needed no convincing to get involved. They were going to help me get into the dungeon where Speedy was being kept.

Our plan was simple.

Molly and Ina would take me to the old ladies sitting room for tea and a chat. It was a good plan because the men avoided the room like the plague.

My guards would hang out in the common room while I visited with the women.

There was a door from the old ladies sitting room into the passage that backed the common room. The passage gave access to the club president's office and apartment on the far left. The kitchen, dining area and crash rooms were on the right before the passage came to an abrupt dead end at a tall bookcase.

This was our target. The bookcase that hid the entrance to what lay underneath the clubhouse.

Molly and Ina helped me to change into black cargo pants, a long-sleeved black t-shirt and my boots.

We plastic-wrapped my cast before I pulled on my gloves, forcing the black Nitrile glove over my slightly swollen fingers and part of the cast.

Sneaking down the passage was nerve-racking.

I only started breathing easier when we walked down the stairs hidden by the bookcase.

The stairs ended in passage lined by doors. Behind them were rooms that were innocent enough, used for storage.

The passage ended in a heavy wooden door. I knew this was it.

Pulling the heavy wooden door open I turned to Molly and Ina.

"This is as far as you go. Wait here do not under any circumstances step through this door. Okay?"

Both nodded and stepped away from the door.

Where I was going, they could not, should not, go.

I found the room by the stench leaking from it. When I opened the door, it became so much worse. The stench of fear, suffering, despair, and death enveloped me.

I knew there was no way I was leaving him alive once I got what I wanted.

Speedy was naked. His body was suspended from chains in the middle of the icy room and stretched into a star shape. He wasn't looking good. Not good at all. His body had been battered almost beyond recognition, covered in dried blood. It was clear he would not last another night. He was close to the end.

I took the meter wide roll of plastic sheeting from under my arm and rolled it out on the floor, creating a walkway from the door to where Speedy hung. I was protecting my boots and making sure I carried no evidence out of the room when I left.

I approached slowly stopping when I stood right in front of him. His eyes were closed, his breathing heavy and laboured.

"Hello, Speedy." I said softly.

He slowly forced his swollen eyes open. They widened as much as they could in shock and horror.

"Wha…what…are you…doing here? Get out. Leave. Not…place for…you."

His eyes were tiny slits in his swollen face but even in the state he was in he kept them on me.

"I can't leave until you tell me what I need to know, Speedy. Please tell me so I don't have to hurt you."

I continued in that same soft voice as I looked at his abused junk and the dried blood on the back of his thighs. He had been subjected to pretty much everything the little kids he'd sold would be going through.

It was inhuman, horrible and frightening what the man I loved and his men had done to him. But the Crow didn't care. She was here for one purpose and one purpose only. To find the kids.

"Why? Why…would he…send…you? You…shouldn't be…allowed in…this filthy…room." He battled to get the words out.

I sighed and shook my head as if disappointed. I continued in a whisper.

"Unfortunately I'm more comfortable in rooms like this than Hawk or any his men. I can tell you my secret because we both know you aren't long for this world. I'm the finder of secrets, the breaker of lies, the collector of spies, the bringer of pain and for some, the final destination."

He slowly shook his head from side-to-side muttering no, no, no, no through his broken lips.

"Yes, Speedy yes. I am the Crow." I said in a soft whispered hiss.

He jerked in his restraints and his head jerked even wilder until I placed my glove covered cold hand on his chest.

"Stop. Tell me what I need and I will let you go. No more humiliation, no more pain, no more Iron Dogz. Think about it, Speedy. No more pain and free from these chains. All you have to do is tell me."

I drew in a shallow breath trying to ignore the stench in the room as I waited.

I didn't have to wait long.

"Promise me…promise…you'll set…me free. Get…me…out."

I smiled sweetly.

"Of course, Speedy. I promise to set you free. All you have to do is tell me."

It came pouring out. The container's location. The person taking care of the children. And finally, the contingency plans for shipping the kids out once the heat died down.

I drew the long thin-bladed knife from the back of my pants and stepped up to him. I felt nothing as I slipped the knife up beneath his ribs and into his heart. His eyes widened with shock and then he was gone.

I slipped my knife from his body. Cleaned it with a surgical bacterial and bleach wipe from my pocket and returned it to its sheath. I retreated down the plastic walkway I had created to the door. I couldn't take it with me so I left it behind.

I breathed easier as soon as I walked through the door and pulled it shut behind me. Shutting the horror inside with Speedy's lifeless body.

I got what we needed. The location of the kids, and the trafficker's contingency plans.

I re-joined Molly and Ina, dragged the heavy door closed and we silently left.

We made it back to the old ladies sitting room without a problem. I had to move quickly and get back to our room. I knew what was coming. I took off my gloves and removed the plastic wrap, shoving it into a side pocket of my cargo pants. I didn't linger with them, not even to change back into my sweatpants and big t-shirt. I left Molly and Ina and with my silent escort went back to my room.

I hid my knife under the cushions and removed my boots. That's as far as I got. My body ached and I was so very, very nauseous. The smell of that damned room seemed to cling to me no matter how many times I washed my hands and face.

I sank down in the chair and waited.

A furious Hawk stormed in an hour later

"What the fuck did I say?" His voice was cold as ice and his eyes were shooting fire as he shoved his face into mine.

I ignored his rage.

"I know where the kids are. I know who's been watching over them."

A heavy silence fell between us. Not a good silence at all.

"Tell me."

I gave it all to him. Everything Speedy had said. I watched him closely throughout. He shut me out. When I finished he called Gav into the room. Gav looked me over and shook his head angrily.

"Help her to get out of that shit, and then burn all of it. All. Of. It."

Not my boots. Hell, I've just worn them in.

"Not my boots. They're clean. I didn't get anything on them."

He didn't even look at me.

"Everything Prospect, you fucking burn everything. If you don't you'll be answering to me. Do you understand?"

"Yes, Prez. I got you. Burn everything." Gav said with a nod.

Hawk left without giving me a second glance. Gav helped me out of my clothes bundled it up, picked up my boots and left without saying a word either.

As soon as Gav left I cleaned my blade properly and slid it back into its hiding place – the thin sheath at the top of my saddlebag with a stopper fastened onto the sharp end. It looked like a decoration, not a weapon. Hidden in plain sight.

I dressed while I waited for the inevitable. I had gone against the orders of my old man. Disrespected him. Drew two of the club's old ladies into my machinations. Made two of the brothers look incompetent. Entered a part of the clubhouse forbidden to anyone who wasn't a patched member of the club.

And lastly, I had killed a prisoner without permission from the National President of the Iron Dogz MC.

I was in very deep shit.

Deadly deep shit.

I didn't care.

I did what I had to do.

I would do it again if I had to. Those children had a chance at life because of what I, what Crow, had done.

BURNING BRIGHT IN THE BLACK

If I, if Crow hadn't stepped up Speedy would have died without saying a word.

THIRTY FOUR

Hawk

Rage unlike anything he had ever felt before coursed through Hawk as he stormed out and thundered down the stairs. She had fucking ignored his orders. She had gone ahead with her fucked up plan to interrogate Speedy.

And then she had gone ahead and fucking killed him.

Fuck. Fuck. Fuck.

He would have kept what his old lady had done to the officers only but she had involved the old lady of a patched member and the little bastard wasn't happy. He'd been flapping his mouth all over the club, stirring up shit against DC. He wanted her punished for ignoring their bylaws and endangering his woman.

It was a total crock of shit. He'd looked over the videos himself and at no time had either of those women been in any danger. DC hadn't allowed them entrance to the dungeon itself. And judging by the grins on their faces the bitches had loved sneaking around behind everyone's backs.

It was the punishment the bastard was agitating for that made Hawk's blood boil.

He wanted DC to receive a beat down. There was no way it was happening. She had another five weeks in the cast and equally as long with the wounds to her abdomen.

If the fucker thought he would let anyone touch her he was smoking his fucking socks.

When Hawk told them he expected the same punishment meted out to the fucker's old lady there had been a deathly silence. You could've heard fucking crickets it was so fucking silent.

Now they were here and nothing had been resolved.

These fuckers had better not think he was going to let this go. He was their fucking president and she was his old lady. Their fucking president's old lady.

Hawk knew every single brother in the club now looked at her with different eyes. Some of his brothers even saw her as a possible threat. A threat because she was born a Road Warrior and had killed without showing any remorse.

Hawk knew better. She had set Speedy free from his pain and suffering. To his little bird it had been a mercy killing after he had given her what she wanted.

How the fuck was he going to protect her when she wilfully ignored his orders?

He stormed into the chapel and threw himself in the chair at the head of the table and waited for the room to settle.

"We have the location of the kids and the person who's been caring for them. We will discuss how to get them out as soon as I've conferred with my officers."

Hawk looked around the room, met and held the eyes of the smirking little fucker leaning against the wall.

"Now hear me and listen real fucking good. The first fucker who lays a finger on my woman will be eating lead. There will be no fucking punishment handed out by the club. It will be done by me, and it will not happen in front of the club."

Hawk stared coldly at the fucker who was no longer smirking or leaning against the wall.

"You want to humiliate your woman by beating her up in front of your brothers, that's on you. But you need to know one thing. You do this shit and you, and whoever watches and does nothing, are out. We do not, under any circumstances, beat up our women or our children. Not in front of the club and not behind closed doors either."

The rustling in the room became a growing rumble.

Hawk cut it off with a hard slap on the table.

"There will be no fucking discussions. If you're not happy with my ruling throw your kuttes on the table right now and get the fuck out. I will give you a week to black out your club ink, if you don't' I'll be doing it for you. With a blow torch."

Shocked silence hung in the room. No one moved, not even the little bastard who had started it all.

"No one? Are you sure? Not even you, you little fuck? If you walk out of this fucking room with my club's kutte on your back and start whining about my decision I will kill you. Do you fucking understand? Are we all on the same fucking page now?"

The bastards all nodded and gave him what he wanted.

"Good. Now that's fucking handled let's get on to the business of the kids. We know their location and we have to decide how to proceed from here. Any…"

Hammering on the door interrupted him and it pissed him off. Pushing him even further over the line. He nodded, the door was unlocked and opened. Gav stood there sporting a busted lip.

"What the fuck, Gav?"

"Sorry, Prez, they refused to wait or take no for an answer."

The tension in the room went into the stratosphere when Doc shoved Gav unceremoniously to the side and strode into their fucking chapel as if he owned it, closely followed by Tiny, Grizzly, Alien, Rover, and Skelly.

Hawk waited until they were inside and the door closed before he spoke.

"What the fuck is the meaning of this, Doc?"

"I heard you have the location of the kids. If you're planning to free them using guns and force it would be a mistake. A big fucking mistake."

Doc Michaels stood with his legs slightly apart, arms crossed over his chest as he glanced around the room.

"If you and your men go anywhere near the fucking location, what do you think will happen? Think about it, Hawk. Take a minute and really think about it. Do you really think the ice-cold bitch hasn't considered Speedy spilling his guts? She has, I can fucking guarantee you she has. She's playing a long game here."

Doc was silent for a few seconds before he continued.

"What happens if we storm in there, armed to the teeth, and try to rescue those children?" He paused.

"Let me tell you how it will go down. While we're inside looking for the kids the pigs will suddenly arrive, finding only us. We all know the pigs hate us and are looking for any fucking excuse to lock us up. They won't give a shit we were there to rescue the kids. We'll be locked up and charged with human trafficking. And while we're all locked up with fuck loads of lawyers trying to prove our innocence what's left of our clubs will be destroyed and taken over by the bitch and her allies."

Doc's gaze swept around the very silent room slowly before coming back to the top of the table. Hawk gave a nod.

The damn bastard was making sense.

Listening to him laying it out he knew why the man had risen so quickly through the ranks of the Road Warriors MC. It was why he was going to be their next National President.

Hawk's voice was soft when he spoke.

"We have to be as cold and calculating as the old bitch that started this war with our clubs. And make no mistake brothers, this is a war.

Going by what we've found she has been planning the takeover of our clubs for years. Her people slowly infiltrated our clubs, gaining our trust, and worked to take us down from the inside while she attacked from the outside. Luckily for us, she misjudged the loyalty of our brothers and our women. Plus she totally misjudged our intelligence gathering capabilities. She won't make the same mistake again."

"What do you suggest we do, Doc? There's no way we'll leave those children out there to suffer through the hell they have planned for them." Hotdog snarled angrily.

Doc frowned. "And we won't, Hotdog. We tip off the taskforce. We give them the location and let them rescue the kids. As much as I want us to be there we can't, we need to take a step back and sort out the problems in our clubs."

After a long silence Hawk knocked his rings on the table and looked at his brothers.

"I agree. We tip off the taskforce and start taking care of business inside our clubs. What do you say, brothers? Show of hands for yes."

Hands were raised all around him.

"Good, consider it done." Tapping the gavel to the iron block he ended the meeting.

"Hotdog, Growler and my officers stay behind."

He waited until the room had emptied and the doors were closed. Waited until Doc and his men took seats around the table before he began.

"Both our clubs have been compromised by people we trusted. They had access to the members in the inner circles of both clubs and used it to further their agenda. If DC hadn't walked into my club when she did we wouldn't be sitting here today. Making her my old lady forced them to speed up their plans and they made mistakes. Mistakes we will use to our advantage. Right now, we have a tiny window of opportunity to find and eliminate any other rats in our organisations."

Hawk turned to Hotdog.

"I suggest you look into the little fucker. He doesn't feel right."

"I agree, and I'm on it, Prez." Hotdog said.

Hawk smoothed his fingers over the block of iron in front of him before he continued. He was about to suggest something that would change the way the two clubs interacted with each other.

If it worked it would tighten the ties between them.

"We are under threat so I suggest we pool our information resources. Let Ziggy, Mad Dog and Skel dig deep into the background of every single patch, prospect, old lady, club whore and hangaround in both clubs. I know there are some of us with shit in our backgrounds we would rather not have revealed. I swear on my patch whatever we find will stay between me, our intelligence officers and the brother affected. I swear it will not affect a brother's patch or a woman's membership, as long as no traitorous intent is uncovered. It might affect whether I allow a hangaround to become a prospect, but it will be up for discussion when his name is put forward."

"You sure about this, Prez?"

Hotdog was the first to speak.

"Yes, I think if we work together we have a better chance of finding all the rats and cutting off the bitch's reach into our clubs."

"I agree." Doc said.

Doc sat forward, resting his forearms on the table. "Together we are stronger than we would be if we tried to go it alone. We'll keep in touch through Skel. There's another matter I think is only fair to let you in on."

Nothing showed in his hard emotionless face as he continued.

"Freeze has been relieved of his position as president of the Cape Town chapter of the Road Warriors MC as well as his position as national president. He is out bad. Wild Man has taken over as president in Cape Town. After a closed vote by the currently serving presidents of all the chapters I have been elected as the national president. My first act as president was to disband the ruling table. There will no longer be a ruling table. Mine will be the final word in all matters concerning the Road Warriors MC."

Holy shit. That was a huge change to their bylaws.

"It is all I wanted to say. Now I'd like to see my daughter."

He didn't wait for Hawk or Hotdog to acknowledge the bomb he had dropped. He and his men rose and left. Hawk looked at Ice who shrugged.

"We're getting into business with the Road Warriors, is that what just happened?"

Growler didn't sound pleased.

Hawk didn't hesitate to clarify.

"No, what we're doing is banding together to eliminate a common threat. Once that's done we'll all go back to business as usual."

Hotdog gave a short stunned laugh.

"If I hadn't been sitting in this fucking chair, I wouldn't have believed this shit. Most of the bastards who belong to the Durban chapter of the Warriors are pieces of shit. Doc has one hell of a job ahead of him. Fuckers are going to be disappearing from view, permanently."

"Won't surprise me at all. Doc is one ice-cold motherfucker. We're done here for today. One more thing. Has Speedy been seen to?"

Beast grinned. "Yes, Prez. He's gone."

"Good."

He was pushing up out of his chair when a thought occurred to him.

"Oh, and if after what I said here there are still brothers insisting on my woman being thrown in a ring with one of your fighters they'd better read the bylaws. As president I'm allowed to nominate a fighter to take her place if she's too injured to fight. Which she is."

He glared at the men before he continued.

"Let it be known that Alien of the Road Warriors MC will be fighting for her. Let's see how long the fuckers survive in a cage with that maniac."

Laughter followed Hawk as he walked out of their chapel and turned up the stairs, taking them two at a time. He wanted to see his woman and sort out the shit between them before it festered.

He knew what she had done came from a good place but she had to understand that she was no longer a part of the Road Warriors MC. A club where she could pretty much do as she pleased with very few consequences. She was now part of the Iron Dogz and she could no longer take matters into her own hands whenever she felt she could get better results as the Crow.

And if he had any say in it, she would no longer be the fucking Crow.

DC would have to earn her place in his club the same as everyone else and this wasn't going to make it any easier for her.

Gav was standing outside their room, his arms crossed over his chest listening to the conversation in the room with a heavy frown. His slight chin lift let Hawk know he should slow down and listen. He did. And it was enlightening.

"I did not raise you to disrespect your club and your old man. But you still did. We're fucking grateful you got the information out of him, but, and it's a huge fucking but, you did so by going against the specific orders of your old man and club president. Your actions make him look like a pussy with no control over his woman. The man has hundreds of men under his command, men whose respect he needs to be able to do his job to keep them and his club safe."

His little bird tried to argue.

"But Dad, I asked and asked and asked. He was too damned stubborn. I had to do what I…"

"No. You didn't have to do anything. All you had to do was listen to your old man. If he said no then that's that. No arguments. If you had pulled this stunt in my house, you would be facing Alien in the cage, you know this. He would beat you bloody but he wouldn't kill you. The Iron Dogz have different rules. According to the rumours we've picked up the fucker they want you to face is a bastard I had banned from all our venues. He's well known for killing his opponents in the cage which is why he's been banned. Not sure if your old man is aware of his reputation but it's not my problem. My problem is keeping my daughter alive, no matter what. Which is why, if they insist on going down this road, Alien will be taking your place in the ring."

"Dad, this is not how…"

"I know, DC, I know. You wanted to save those kids. It's done, let's move past it. I'm heading home soon and Law is here to load your bike. He will be driving the cage back at the end of the week and you will be in it with him. Not taking a chance on exacerbating your injuries by putting you on the back of a bike. Now give your old dad a hug. I have shit I need to get done before I can go home."

Gav just shook his head as if he couldn't believe what he'd heard as Hawk walked past him and into the room.

Only Doc and Tiny were in the room saying goodbye to DC.

He didn't give them a chance to say a word.

"I will be making the arrangements to get my old lady back to Jozi, don't you worry about it. And rest assured I will never fucking allow her to fight. If these fuckers insist on a fight Alien has my permission to kill his fucking ass. I don't care one way or another."

Doc and Tiny laughed but his little bird sat in the middle of the bed, her arms crossed over her chest with a stubborn look on her face. It was going to get her ass spanked.

"We'll talk soon." Doc said as he walked through the door.

But they didn't leave right away, instead they were looking at Gav. Doc's voice was back to cold and harsh when he spoke.

"Gavin, you have two weeks then I want your ass at the Friday meeting. Do we understand each other?"

Gav didn't say a word, he just looked at his president and then he nodded.

"Yes, Prez. I'll be there."

Fuck. He hoped the kid knew what was going to happen to him when he attended the meeting. He saw no fear in Gav's eyes as he watched Doc and Tiny walk away from him. The kid had heart, there was no doubt about that. He hoped like fuck he had heart enough to survive what the Warriors were going to throw at him.

Hawk sighed as he closed the door, shutting the shit out for just a moment.

A war was coming and he had to get each and every Iron Dogz compound across the country secured. Some of their clubs were small, no more than ten members and they were going to be vulnerable. It was time to call in the support clubs and their allies for a formal sit down.

They all had to prepare for what was coming.

The one light in the darkness was his little bird. He again thanked the fates his old lady had been raised in a club and would understand what he had to do next.

He fucking hoped like hell she did.

He would be calling for a lockdown which meant his old lady was going to be faced with Lizzy and Lacey back inside the clubhouse. Knowing those bitches he knew they were going to get into DC's face and it would not end well. If they pushed her too far there would most probably be blood and broken bones to deal with.

Their broken bones and blood.

And his brothers' reactions to his woman beating up their pussy will definitely not be good.

What if he had to rule for the club and against her? What would she do?

Fuck. All he wanted was time with his little bird.

Enough time to love her the way she deserved.

"You caused a lot of shit, little bird. You know there has to be consequences for your actions. What the fuck those are going to be I don't know. I will have to come up with something that will show the brothers you were punished for violating our bylaws."

His woman sat in the middle of the bed with her arms crossed over her chest.

"If you had just given me a chance to talk to you, and let me explain my plan none of this would have happened." She snarled. "But you wouldn't listen to me. Treated me like I was some helpless little bitch."

Hawk sighed.

"Baby, you were almost fucking raped and killed. How the fuck could I let you go into the interrogation after that shit? I fucking hate the shit you have to do as the Crow. I hate what she does."

He watched as her head snapped up and her eyes narrowed.

"The Crow is a necessary part of me. If you're not comfortable with her it would be better if we ended this right now because she's not going anywhere. She is me and I am her."

Fuck. This wasn't going well.

"I didn't say I hate that part of you, DC. I said I hate what she has to do. There's a vast difference."

He knew he had to apologise because he should've listened to her.

"You're right. I should have talked to you. I should've listened to what you had to say. But you need to know, no matter what you said, I would not have allowed you down there. I would have used your suggestions but that's all."

She just looked at him, not saying anything.

Hawk sighed and sat down at the bottom of the bed and laid a hand on her knee.

"What you did will enable the taskforce to rescue those kids. We are done with it. As soon as I have things wrapped up here we will be heading home. And by home, I mean the Iron Dogz compound, DC. The threat is still out there and I want you safe."

Those cold black eyes just looked at him, then she gave a tiny nod.

"I'm tired and sore. I'm going to have a sleep now," she said in a very soft voice.

Completely ignoring him she painfully turned her back on him, lay down on her side, reached back and with a grimace pulled the duvet over herself.

Hawk moved up next to her, lay down and carefully moved close to her back.

"Sleep, little bird. I'm here with you. You're safe, baby." He whispered against her hair as she sighed and slowly relaxed.

They still had so much to learn about each other and all the shit happening around them was fucking it up for both of them.

Hawk swore to himself he would try harder to help his little bird find her feet in his club. Hopefully she wouldn't gut him when he had to punish her for the shit she pulled today.

Closing his eyes he relaxed against her, breathing her in before he had to return downstairs.

THIRTY FIVE

DC

We left Durban within a few days of my dad's visit. I have asked but I still didn't know what my punishment was going to be. Not that I allowed myself to think about it too much. If I did, I'd drive myself crazy imagining what could happen.

No use worrying anyway.

What would be would be.

Hawk bundled me into the front seat of the cage that was carrying mine and Gav's bikes back home. Thank heavens Gav was my driving buddy and not one of the others. We had the same taste in music and neither one of us liked making conversation just to make conversation. It made for a very enjoyable trip.

I wanted to go home, to my house. I found out, to my horror that Hawk had called for a semi-lockdown.

I was stuck in their clubhouse with all his fucking sluts.

He had dropped me right into hell.

Did the bastard take the time to tell me the whores were going to be there, in my face all the time?

No, he did not. I found out the hard way.

I walked into the kitchen for breakfast and there they were, all over my man supposedly serving him breakfast. He sat there, taking it, not saying a word. I turned around without a word, walked right out of the clubhouse and went to work.

For several weeks now everything has been quiet. Not a single strike against the club.

On a personal front my ribs no longer ached, my cast was long gone. I was back in the gym training with Grizzly and Alien whenever I could.

Besides going to the gym and Mainline Ink II I was stuck inside the hell that was the Iron Dogz clubhouse.

The only family members I had been introduced to were Ice and Hawk's aunt Beryl. I knew he had an uncle, aunt and cousins but I never met them. Aunt Beryl was the only friendly female face, the rest of the bitches hated me.

The brothers weren't much better. They ignored me or treated me like I was Hawk's new fuck toy.

The hatred and disrespect had me avoiding all of them as much as possible.

I stretched out my time away from the clubhouse as much as I could. But at the end of each day I was forced to return to the freaking hell hole. I didn't even eat there. I ate at a little restaurant two doors down from my shop and if I missed dinner because of work I bought take aways I ate alone in Hawk's room.

And why was I alone in his room?

Because my man was busy with club business virtually 24/7. Leaving on long runs which left me at the mercy of the bitches in his club. I trusted nobody and never went unarmed, no matter what.

Hawk's aunt was the only one I ever spoke to or who spoke to me.

Even Ice, his VP, never said a word to me. It was as if I was invisible.

I was totally alone and so freaking unhappy, all I wanted was to go home.

Then came the day that busted the festering boil that was my life at the club wide open.

Very early that morning Hawk, Kid, Sin and Beast with some of the brothers had left on a run that would have them away from the club for four days. Ice and Jagger were left behind to watch over the clubhouse. The bitches made their move when the two of them were away taking care of business outside of the clubhouse.

Lizzy and Lacey along with their posse of whores jumped me as I walked into the common room on my way to work. I fought back, hard.

When it was done there were whores all over the floor, bleeding. I had scratches on my face and neck, two fairly deep slashes to my left arm (again my poor left arm) an aching head where a chair had connected with the back of my head and three shallow stab wounds to my back.

I didn't wait around to find out if I'd killed any of the whores. I got out of there as fast as I could. Racing through the early morning traffic to the Road Warriors compound where I knew I would be safe. There were bikes on my ass but I lost them once we left the highway. I was safe behind the locked gates when they finally arrived and were refused entrance.

My dad and his club would keep me safe and protected.

The call came as Marco, the club medic, was busy working on my arm with Skel and Alien angrily watching.

I didn't answer.

In fact, I didn't answer any of the calls. I handed my phone over to Skel and left it up to him and my dad to handle. My head ached like a son of a bitch. I swallowed the pills Marco handed me and went to bed.

In the safety of my own room, guarded by men I trusted and loved.

When I woke hours later I felt a little better physically, but mentally I was a complete mess.

I knew I was supposed to suck it up and handle the bitches at my man's club. I did. Unfortunately I didn't get the support due to an old lady from any of the men at his club. I totally lost it when the whores attacked me. Thinking back, I knew I had hurt them, badly.

But I had to fight for my life. They had been trying to kill me.

The Dogz were not going to be pleased. Like all bikers they liked constant access to easy pussy. Now those sluts were hurt and most probably unable to put out.

Did I care? Nope, not at all.

I lay there with my hands over my face and just breathed. Then I pulled on my big girl panties got my once again aching body out of bed, dressed and went to face the music with my Dad.

Rumbling voices came through Doc's office door. I knocked and waited.

"Come in." I could hear he was pissed by the tone of his voice.

Taking a deep breath, I opened the door and stepped inside. Doc and Tiny were on one side of the desk. Hawk and Ice on the other and Skel and Jagger against the wall. All the Dogz looked at me with cold eyes. Without even thinking about it I tipped my head to the side in an attempt to loosen the tight tendons in my neck. I usually did it to set Crow free, it wasn't my intention to do so now.

The dark entity that was Crow grabbed the opportunity, rushed in and took over, completely. It was as if I was a bystander in my own life as she faced off against the men.

Doc was the first to speak. "Tell me exactly what happened."

The Crow tilted her head and looked at him out of dead eyes. By his frown I knew my dad saw the Crow was in charge right now.

"We were going to work. Walked into the common room and they attacked. I made them stop." Crow hissed.

"You fucking killed two of their bitches." Dad growled.

"Good riddance, the whores ambushed us, and were trying to kill us, me."

I battled to get back into control but the Crow held me back as she turned her head to stare coldly at Hawk when he let out an angry bellow.

"Jesus fucking Christ, DC. Do you have any idea what you've done?" Hawk raged at her.

Crow saw his eyes widening when he looked into her eyes.

Oh yes, he knew who was in the room with them now.

"Yes. Unlike you I protected DC from your whores. I brought her home where she will be safe with her family."

The Crow hissed at him coldly.

"She was never in any fucking danger. She attacked them without any provocation." Hawk spit out.

Crow hissed at him with icy rage.

"How would you know? You're never there. She's alone now that Gav has come home. Your whores have been making her life unbearable while you come back only to fuck her and leave again. As if she's one of your whores. What was she supposed to do? Lie down and let them fucking kill her? Why would you value her life so little?"

Hawk glared at her coldly but it bounced off the dark ice that surrounded her.

"I checked the footage of the fight, Crow. I'm not convinced you didn't start the fight." He sat forward in his chair as he snapped at Crow. "You need to step back and let me speak to DC. Now."

Crow did not like him, not at all.

In fact, she was starting to hate him.

"I now know Ziggy was in on the attack and altered the footage. He is now my enemy and on the list. It's becoming very long. But the Crow is patient. She will wait. She will have her revenge. She will have their blood. All of your blood."

The Crow tipped her head to the side as she stared unblinkingly at Hawk Walker.

"You hurt my other half. My DC. The Crow hates those who hurt DC. The Crow eliminates those who hurt DC. The Crow has a long list of those who will die. Soon. Very, very soon."

Her voice came out in an icy whisper.

Hawk hissed angrily.

"No one is going to die, Crow. You are going to step back and let DC come back. She needs to talk to me herself. I know you're protecting her but she is mine. As you are mine. I have now spoken to you. I need to speak to DC. Step back, now."

Deathly silence fell in the room.

Crow shook her head from side to side.

"The Crow protects her. Keeps her from harm. They mean her harm. They need to die."

Her cold black eyes didn't blink.

"No one is dying" Hawk snapped.

"No one in this room will ever harm her, as you very well know. I swear on my life I will keep her safe from harm. But you need to calm down and step back. She needs to handle this on her own. And you need to start listening to me."

Hawk laid down the law harshly.

All I heard was Crow coldly declaring her intention to kill the men in the room and Hawk disagreeing.

I had to control my other half. Because that's who the Crow was. She was the other side of me, part of me. She was me.

I shuddered as I forced the Crow to back down. She didn't want to leave. She wanted to protect me against these men but I didn't need her protection. I was safe in this room.

Reluctantly, the dark side of me faded into the background, but she was still there, watchful and very, very angry. But then so was I.

I was furious with the men in front of me.

By the look in Hawk's eyes, I could see he knew the Crow had retreated but not very far.

"I did not attack your sluts. You need to recheck the footage. Or better yet, you need to send the footage to Skel so he can find out where and by whom it has been altered. Do whatever the fuck you need to do with your club. I'm not going back to that hellhole. I'm safe here and when I feel better, I'll be going to my home."

Hawk immediately shook his head, denying me.

"No, you're not." He growled.

"The danger isn't past, DC. As my old lady you will stay at the clubhouse where I can be assured of your safety."

This time I shook my head and denied him.

I laughed mirthlessly.

"Don't make me laugh. Have you claimed me in front of your club as your old lady? No. Have you given me a Property kutte? No. Have you arranged to put your ink on me? No. Do I have any power in your club? No. Your brothers disrespect me and treat me as if I'm your latest fuck toy, nothing more"

I shook my head.

"How safe was I when I came out of your room to go to work yesterday? Oh yes, I'm so fucking safe in your club that when I'm attacked no one lifts a hand to help me. They just fucking watched. Your club is filled with my enemies. I won't be going back there. I don't trust you or anyone in your club. I'm no longer yours."

Hawk was stunned. It was in his eyes as he just sat there and stared at me.

"Yesterday was my fault." Ice rumbled. "I didn't think Jagger and I would be away long. I didn't leave instructions for your safety."

I snorted derisively. My dad and Skelly swore softly. I opened my mouth to answer but Alien got there first jumping feet first into the discussion or argument, whatever the hell this was.

"And right there is your problem. Why the hell do you need to leave instructions to guard your president's old lady inside your own fucking clubhouse? It's supposed to be the place where she is safest. She's right. She's not safe anywhere near any of you fuckers. She stays right the fuck here."

I agreed with Alien. All I knew was I wasn't going to go back.

I didn't trust any of them to have my back. Sadly, right now not even the man I loved.

I didn't have to wait long for his angry retaliation.

"Fucking hell, DC. You know why those bitches were in the clubhouse, it was to keep them safe. You were there when I told my brothers you were mine, my old lady. Everyone knows you belong to me. I admit, I haven't done what I should have and called a full meeting to let them know without any uncertainty you are mine. And I haven't given you a Property kutte yet. But, baby, you know with all the shit that went down there hasn't been any time to do it."

I shook my head and sighed angrily.

"Excuses, excuses, excuses. Always with the excuses. Go back to your clubhouse and your sluts. I'm no longer interested. Are we done here? I've lost an entire day of work because of this shit. I have a headache and I ache everywhere like a son of a bitch. I need to find Marco and get more painkillers."

For some strange reason Hawk was suddenly smiling. What the hell? Is the man bipolar or something?

"Stop pushing me away, little bird. You are mine. You will always be mine and if you don't watch that mouth I'll be turning your ass red."

My back shot straight at his threat.

I snarled at him, I genuinely snarled at him.

What the hell?

He grinned and continued to lay it out.

"I'm sorry I accused you. I don't need to recheck the footage, I believe you. I will find whoever altered it. I will be making it clear to everyone in my club and outside my club you are my old lady. You belong to me and anyone who lifts a hand to harm you will be losing their hand. You will be coming home with me and the bitches who attacked you, the ones who survived, they will find out how very pissed off I am. They won't come after you again."

My dad didn't say a word, he just watched. Very carefully.

Okay, fine. He gave me what I needed but I still wasn't happy about those sluts staying. I opened my mouth to answer but that's as far as it got.

He was up and out of his chair, picked me up and carefully threw me over his shoulder. I groaned as pain streaked through my back. And the traitor Skel opened the door for him.

"Excuse us, my woman needs a quick reminder of who she belongs to." Hawk explained to the grinning bastards in the fucking room.

He stalked out of the office and up to my room with me hanging over his shoulder. I didn't beat his back or dare raise my voice because I didn't want the brothers to see me like this. They would laugh their asses off and never let me forget it.

I bounced as he threw me on my bed and fell down on top of me.

"*Eina!* Ow, ow, ow! That freaking hurts."

I moaned as the cuts in my back stung and my headache throbbed behind my eyes.

Hawk immediately lifted his weight off me.

"Ah, fuck, I'm sorry, baby. So, fucking sorry I let this happen to you, little bird. I promise those bitches will be told in no uncertain terms what will happen to them if they try any shit with you ever again."

He stroked his fingers over the scratches on my face and on my neck and I could see the anger in his eyes.

But it still wasn't enough to soothe the pain and rage I felt.

I knew those sluts were never going to give up. They'll just find a subtler way to get at me.

"That's just it, Hawk. All you do is talk and nothing happens to them. I should be the one shutting them down. As the president's old lady, I'm supposed to have power over those bitches and I don't. If I give an order in your clubhouse, I will be laughed out the door by those sluts and by your brothers. It's as if any respect the brothers had for me suddenly vanished the minute you took me into your clubhouse. They treat me as if I'm just another one of your sluts."

He was on his knees over me and sat back on his calves. Regret in his eyes.

"You're right, I failed you, DC, but it's done. As of today things are going to change, I'm going to make them change. I'm sorry I wasn't there to take your back when you needed it, baby. I grew up in a club where my dad's word was law and my mum stayed home and out of club business. The same as my Aunt Beryl. It's only recently she started coming in to cook and take care of us. I think I tried to shove you into the same box. You will have to be patient with me. I'm trying, baby, honestly, I'm trying."

I sighed. I had no defence against this freaking man.

"Then you will have to be just as patient with me. I'm used to taking care of business and being on the inside and asked for my opinion. I'm used to receiving the respect due to me when I give my opinion. I will never be like your mum, Hawk. I refuse."

He dipped his head and ran his lips softly over mine. "I'm fucking glad you're not, little bird. I need a woman strong enough to take on the shit that's raining down on us. You are that woman. My woman. My old lady. But right now I need to show my old lady how much I need her."

I wanted him to show me.

I was such a pushover for the man.

Pushing away from me Hawk stood at the side of my bed and started to undress. The kutte went first, neatly folded and draped over the small couch. The rest quickly followed. As each piece of clothing came off more of his beautiful body was revealed. And my breathing picked up.

"You are so damned pretty, my Viking." I mumbled as I fumbled with my clothes.

I had them off and kicked out of the way when I looked up.

He was right next to the bed. His hand wrapped around his heavy cock, stroking slowly. Up and down. Up and down. I could not keep my eyes off his hand or his cock.

Hawk bent down and lifted me as he sat down with me lying over his naked lap. Oh shit.

"Told you I was going to turn your ass red because of that mouth of yours. Didn't I, DC?"

A little shiver zipped through me. "Uhm, yes, yes you did. But I only…"

I didn't get any further. The first tap burned but it warmed as he spread those taps out. Never hitting the same place twice. As he laid his marks over my ass with one hand the other played with me. He had me hovering on the edge as he tapped and played.

I burned, from the outside in, I burned and I wanted him. So damned badly I was begging for his cock.

"Please, Hawk, give it to me. Give me your big cock. Please."

He laughed softly as he stroked his hand over my hot ass, soothing away the burn.

"My little bird likes her punishment. She likes the way I play with her ass. When we get home we'll see how creative I can get and how much my woman can take."

I hummed in agreement as his fingers swiped through my folds and gave my clit a hard tap.

I shuddered in his lap.

"But not right now. Not going to play with my little bird's pussy right now. Going to fuck it hard and rough and you're going to take it, baby. You're going to take it all, everything I want to give to you, and you're going to take it."

Lifting my ass to get his fingers back I moaned. I didn't, what I did get was so much better.

Hawk flipped me over, lifted me and lay me on the bed, my legs hanging off the side. He dragged me to the edge of the bed and my back and red ass burned as the duvet scraped over the sore and sensitive skin.

My moan had scarcely left my mouth when he was on his knees between my wide-spread legs. Throwing my legs over his shoulders he dived between my thighs, sucking hard. I gave a soft shriek as my over stimulated clit sent streaks of pleasure through me. He did not let up. His lips, tongue, teeth and beard tortured me. Sucked at me. Licked at me. Bit my folds and clit. Rubbed over my sensitive skin. Driving me insane with want.

I needed to come, so very badly. But he tortured me. Refused to let me come. I was getting desperate. Moaning, pleading. To no avail.

I was a shuddering mess when he rose, my legs slid off his shoulders to flop down like they were made out of jelly. There was no resistance as he moved me to the centre of the bed, flipped me over and pushed two of the pillows beneath my trembling stomach. He pushed my thighs together, stroking his hands over the outside of my legs and up over my hips, sliding them down and over my breasts. Big fingers rolled, pulled and pinched my nipples making me gasp for breath.

Oh, shit. I knew what was coming and I trembled with anticipation.

"Keep your legs together for me, baby. Don't move until I tell you. Going to fuck you, little bird. Going to take you hard and not wearing a fucking condom either. Never wearing that shit ever again. We don't have to worry about diseases, baby. I've been tested, I'm clean. I would never put my dick in this beautiful little pussy if there was a chance of giving you something."

His fingers played with my breasts. I moaned, lifting my hips to get more of him. My hands were clenched into fists beside my head which was turned so I could watch him over my shoulder. My Viking was so damned beautiful as he rose up behind me, kissing a line down my spine and placing soft kisses over my stab wounds. I shuddered as the hair on his thighs rubbed against my hot cheeks. I held my breath in anticipation, I didn't have to wait long.

Sliding his hot, hard cock over my pussy through my tightly clenched thighs he coated himself in my juices. Juices that were running out of me and slicking my inner thighs. He was no longer leaning over me but watching where his cock moved over my needy pussy. That damned piercing of his bumped against my clit at the end of every slide. Setting off visible tremors in my body.

"Prepare yourself, little bird." He suddenly growled.

I didn't have time to prepare. His cock was sliding over me and then it was slamming through my sensitive flesh and the orgasm that had been hovering broke over me. I screamed as my flesh convulsed around his driving cock. He didn't stop fucking me though. That big cock of his kept hammering at me.

Driving me up again to crash in a shower of pleasure.

My orgasm was still hurtling through me when he flipped me and his cock slammed back into my spasming pussy. Forcing its way inside past the contracting muscles. I wrapped my legs around his hips as he kept fucking me hard. His cock felt bigger, harder, and wider.

With his eyes on mine he laced our fingers together and pushed our hands into the bed above my head. Dipping down he ran his tongue over my open lips, licking and sucking at them.

Kissing me deeply before lifting back up to look in my eyes before glancing down to watch his cock shuttling in and out of me, so very hard.

I felt another orgasm building and tightened my fingers around his, holding on for what I knew was going to be a life altering experience. By the look in his eyes I knew it was the same for him.

It came at us like a tsunami, taking us up and over. Slamming us into the ground and lifting us up. Over and over and over.

He growled low and long in my neck and I moaned against his chest as it moved through us. I lay under him, washed to shore, drained and shuddering. Inside me I felt his cock jerk as the tiny aftershocks moved through both of us. His face lay in my neck, his teeth clamped down on my shoulder. I had no idea when that had happened but as the endorphins receded, I started feeling it.

Started feeling all my aches.

There were quite a few.

I liked rough sex, had it before. But what we had just done was more, more than just rough sex.

It was a primitive claiming. He had claimed me, left his mark on me, inside and out.

Pulling his face from my neck Hawk looked down at me, his eyes searched mine. As if looking for something.

"Are you okay, baby? Was I too rough? I fucking bit you there at the end. No idea why the fuck I did that. Have never done it before."

Swallowing hard I licked my lips as I found my voice. "That was freaking unbelievably good. Love you, my Viking."

"Love you, my little bird, more than I have ever loved anyone or anything in my life."

I lay in my man's arms and revelled in the afterglow of really great rough sex.

If I were a psychic and could see into the future I would have seen there would be a next time, and a next time, and a next.

I would be pushing his buttons in the future because rough sex with my old man was out of this world good. So very, very good.

The sluts at his clubhouse had better watch themselves. I would not be taking any shit from anyone anymore. And that included every single patched member.

Hawk wanted me to be his old lady.

Fine, I will be his old lady and I will take control.

I was raised in an MC. I knew exactly how far I could push.

I smiled against my man's chest.

The Iron Dogz and their bitches had better watch out.

There was a new bitch in charge.

Hawk

Hawk lifted onto his forearms, not letting go of his little bird's hands and glanced down their bodies to where his cock and hips were slamming into her. He was taking her so fucking hard and all she did was moan and throw her hips up to meet his. Her legs clamped tightly around him.

His climax hit and threw him up so high he threw his head back and roared then dropped down and clamped his teeth down around her shoulder muscle. Marking her as his. Her pussy convulsed around him, drawing him deeper and deeper into his climax. It hurt it was so fucking good. He held on as his cock jerked inside her, coating her insides with his come, marking her in every way he could.

His hand on her ass. His teeth in her shoulder. His come inside her. Soon he would have his ink on her body. Telling the world she belonged to him. And if his little bird wanted it he would put a ring on her finger, making them legal in the eyes of the fucking law.

Anything for her.

Whatever she wanted he would give her.

Settling her in his arms and on his chest he kissed her forehead. He could relax now that he'd had her and sorted through some of their problems. He'd had to cut short what he was busy doing to race back and take care of his woman.

Sadly he would have to leave her again to take care of club business soon.

And when he left, his woman would have more than enough power to take care of business at the clubhouse. No one would ever fucking disrespect her again. He would see to it.

Right now though, they had to get home. He was going to move her into his house where she would be more comfortable and won't have the sluts in her face all the time.

His little bird deserved more from life than what she'd had up to now. He wanted to give her more. And he would give her more. It would be his honour and pleasure.

Together they would face the coming shitstorm and they would get through it.

His smile was predatory.

The little bird in his arms was a force to be reckoned with and she was all his. Would always be his and only his.

Why the fuck had he thought he could tame this little demon child?

You can't tame a wild child like his little bird.

And you definitely can't tame the Crow. She would always be unpredictable, wild, and dangerous.

Now wasn't the time to worry about what tomorrow might bring.

Now was for them.

As the late afternoon sun painted her body golden, he held his little bird in his arms laying tiny kisses against her hair.

BURNING BRIGHT IN THE BLACK

He knew without any doubt she was his and would always be his. The fucking love of his life.

EPILOGUE

DC

It's never easy when you fall in love with a hard-headed biker and give up some of your freedoms to live in his world.

And when your biker has his ex-sluts hanging around his clubhouse for their own so-called safety, life is not a peach. In fact, it's a bitch.

I gave in and returned to the clubhouse with him because I loved him. I still love him, even though he's an ass and hasn't made any real effort to punish the bitches who tried to kill me.

According to them they didn't, that it was my aggressiveness that pushed them to protect themselves.

Bullshit.

Oh, they got shouted at and there were threats of throwing them out, it never happened. Hawk was so busy focusing on the club's troubles he never finalised their punishment.

Instead I'm the one who has to swallow my anger and lust for vengeance every single day as they strut around the clubhouse and taunt me. They make sure it never happens near any of the brothers who've made an effort to get to know me. It happens around those who think I'm a fuck toy, and those who distrust me because my father is the National President of the Road Warriors MC.

And my man?

He is so busy running around the country trying to prepare his club for the war looming on the horizon he hardly has time for me. I understand the necessity of preparation but it still pisses me off that I'm on my own so much.

If I had friends in his club, it would've been easier but I have no one. His aunt was sweet when she was around but we had nothing in common and I still didn't know the rest of his family. Not really.

Handling the club while he's away fell on the shoulders of his VP, Ice Walker.

Ice is a good man, but he's a man who is lost in his head. There's some shit going down with him I'm not quite sure about and I won't be asking about it either. It's none of my business.

With his head not quite in the game he's missed a lot of the goings on at the club. I can't depend on him to have my back.

All I can do is watch my own back and stay at Hawk's house whenever he leaves on a run.

And work.

I've been working and hanging out with the crew at the tattoo studio a lot.

I stayed away from the clubhouse as much as possible.

Thankfully when I left for training in the mornings it was too early for anyone to be up and around.

I've gone back to training with Grizz and Alien every day. Since the attack we've focused on preparing me to fight more than one opponent at a time. The training has helped to keep the Crow on an even keel as she's still seething with rage. I knew she wouldn't settle down until the sluts had been taken care of.

Therefore I avoided the sluts wherever possible.

My favourite time at the clubhouse was when Hawk was home. We would hang out at the bar and I watched him around his brothers. I could see how much they meant to him.

Crow didn't care.

She was patiently waiting for her time. She knows it will come.

I knew the shit with the sluts wasn't done. Wouldn't be done until steps were taken to take care of them.

Maybe even permanently.

But it wasn't my call.

The decision rested on the shoulders of the President of the Iron Dogz MC.

Was I pissy that he hasn't taken care of it?

Absolutely.

Did I understand his failure to do so?

To some extent, yes.

Was I ready to forgive and forget?

Not even in your wildest dreams.

BURNING BRIGHT IN THE BLACK

I didn't trust the sluts. They were up to something.

The Crow and I were watching.

PLAYLIST

Alter Bridge - Blackbird
The Hu - The Wolf Totem
Jorn - Stormcrow
Disturbed - Down With The Sickness
Audioslave - Doesn't Remind Me
Bjork ft Skunk Anansie - Army of Me
Brother Dege - Too Old To Die Young
Constancia - Lies Within Lies
Dorothy - Raise Hell
In This Moment - Roots
Chris Isaak - Baby Did A Bad Bad Thing
Five Finger Death Punch - Bad Company (Bad Company cover)
Jonathan Davies - What It Is
Fokofpolisiekar - Antibiotika
Seether - Let You Down
Muse - Feeling Good
Muse - Dig Down
Arno Carstens - Highway To Hell (AC/DC cover)

GLOSSARY

I put together a glossary of terms and words used in the book and added a few in daily use around South Africa. We're a multi-cultural, multi-lingual society with 11 official languages and we borrow unashamedly from one another. Most of us speak at least two languages. And yes, our English is somewhat different from the Queen's, sorry the King's.

- Ag Shame: Oh dear; Oh shame; Poor you (can be used in a sarcastic way)
- Bundu: The back of beyond; remote sparsely populated bush regions; the bush
- Bundu bashing: off roading in the back of beyond / the bush
- Braai: A Barbeque, refers to both the appliance and the get-together
- Braaivleis: Barbequed meat
- Boet/Boeta/Broers: Brother / brothers
- Berg: A Mountain; Mountain range as in the Drakensberg, mostly referred to as 'the Berg'
- Durbs: Slang for Durban, South Africa's major port
- Dankie: Thank you
- Eina: Ouch, ow
- Ek: I
- Foeitog: Poor you; shame; same meaning as "Ag shame", can be sarcastic
- Fok: Fuck
- My fok: Fuck me

- Fokken: A favourite South African adjective e.g. "Fokken mooi" which translates to Fucking beautiful
- Ja right: As if
- Ja: Yes
- Joburg: Jozi; Egoli: Slang for Johannesburg
- Just now: as in "I'll do it just now" which could mean anything from a minute to days
- Kosmos: Cosmos flowers and the name of a village at Hartebeespoort dam
- Klub: Club
- Kak: Shit
- Lewe: Life
- Loadshedding: Scheduled power outages
- Maklik: Easy
- Meerkat: Meercat; Suricate, South African Mongoose
- Nee: No
- No worries: No problem
- Skapie: little lamb used as an endearment, can be used sarcastically
- Sies: Yuck; Yuk; Yukky; Yucky
- Siestog: What a pity; Shame; Poor you, can be sarcastic
- Spook: Ghost
- Thank the Pope: Thank goodness
- Veldt: South African elevated open grasslands

ACKNOWLEDGEMENTS

My beautiful three. You are the best of everything. Your support means the world. Now I'm going to be sappy so brace yourselves. You are the bright stars in my night sky. Love you to the outer universe and back.

Dani, I can't thank you enough for the work you did with the logo and covers. Your patience with me is legendary. Thank you for everything you do for me. Love you, babes.

Thank you to my Mum and sibs for their love and support. It means a lot. Big love.

Marianna Couper, my editor. Thank you for taking time out of your busy schedule for me. So much appreciated. Big love and hugs.

Cousin Pieter, thank you for your advice, encouragement and support. Love and hugs.

Nic "Il Padrino", thank you for answering my endless questions and guiding me through the biker world. For suggesting books to read to help me on my journey of discovery and for being a good friend. Live to Ride. Ride to Live. Shiny side up, brother.

Jayne and Mari my beta reading gurus. Ladies you are the absolute best. Thank you for the advice, encouragement and for loving my bikers. Here's looking forward to many more books together.

A massive thank you goes out to Jayne, Mari and Renee for their help in finding slippery mistakes.

My arc team - Wow! You are the best of the bestest. I can't do this without you. Your support and reviews are awesome. Thank you so much.

And finally, to you, the readers who decided to take a chance on a new author. Thank you for giving the brothers of the Iron Dogz MC a chance. Thank you for your support, your messages and loving the brothers of the Iron Dogz MC.

ABOUT THE AUTHOR

René Van Dalen grew up in a small town in the Transkei region of the Eastern Cape Province in South Africa close to the ocean and the mountains. After high school she moved to the city to go to College. She never left and misses the ocean every single day.

Her parents gave her the love of books and music. Haunting the library when she should have been studying helped to satisfy her craving to read more and more books.

Doing what the majority of people do is not for her, she loves who she finally turned out to be.

René likes her music loud and heavy, her coffee with a touch of milk and slightly sweet, and chocolate in all its shapes and forms. She's a voracious reader and a huge fan of J R Ward's Black Dagger Brotherhood. Her three adult children are the loves of her life.

Music is her muse. Her house is never silent. Whether she's writing or reading or just chilling there is always music playing.

CONNECT WITH RENÉ VAN DALEN

Facebook:
facebook.com/renevandalenauthor
Iron Rosez Reader Group:
facebook.com/groups/2202698126475020/
Goodreads:
goodreads.com/author/show/14116196.Rene_Van_Dalen
BookBub:
bookbub.com/authors/rene-van-dalen
Instagram:
Rene Van Dalen Author @renevandalenauthor

Printed in Great Britain
by Amazon